THE STEAMPUNK MURDER

Ian McFadyen

The Book Guild Ltd

First published in Great Britain in 2018 by
The Book Guild Ltd
9 Priory Business Park
Wistow Road, Kibworth
Leicestershire, LE8 0RX
Freephone: 0800 999 2982
www.bookguild.co.uk
Email: info@bookguild.co.uk
Twitter: @bookguild

Typeset in Baskerville

Printed and bound in Great Britain by CPI Group (UK) Ltd, Croydon, CR0 4YY

ISBN 978 1912362 561

British Library Cataloguing in Publication Data.
A catalogue record for this book is available from the British Library.

To Jamie and Tasha, who opened my eyes to the unique world of Steampunk; and to Chris for her unwavering support and encouragement.

Chapter 1

Saturday 13th August

Kendal Michelson stared out of the large bay window at the expanse of smooth yellow sand, which stretched as far as the eye could see. He was aware the Irish Sea was out there somewhere, but in all the times he'd stayed at the Fairfax Hotel he'd never managed to spot it.

Using some considerable effort, he managed to release the stiff latch and pulled down the sash window half way, which, in an instant, allowed a fresh, cool evening breeze to enter the stuffy, tired-looking bedroom.

He remained stationary for the next thirty minutes, watching the sun as it started to slowly descend in the west and surveying the endless stream of cars as they departed the quiet seaside town, ferrying exhausted children and their even wearier parents back home after a day spent in the hot summer sunshine.

He would have lingered even longer had it not been for the loud chimes of the large grandfather clock at the bottom of the hotel stairwell, reminding the young man it was eight o'clock and time to get ready.

After pulling the weighty curtains shut, Kendal Michelson turned on the bedside light; an ancient-looking heavy brass object that would have not looked out of place at home, he thought.

With the room now adequately illuminated, he carefully removed his crimson tunic, with its shiny silver buttons, and his crisply-ironed white collarless shirt from their black suit holder, resting both items gently next to his black riding breeches and the gleaming sword already laid out neatly on the large double bed.

After allowing himself a few seconds to smugly appreciate his uniform, Kendal Michelson then walked the few paces to his suitcase, where he extracted the last four items that would make his outfit complete: a pair of brown-leather, knee-length riding boots; a monocle, complete with a lengthy cord to secure around his neck; a gleaming silver helmet, with its ear-trumpet attachment; and a large gold pocket watch, complete with its long gold chain.

Chapter 2

Sunday 14th August

It had been months since the five Carmichaels had attended church together as a family. And, with Jemma away on holiday with her friends and Robbie working for the summer at Hayley's Chicken farm, the Carmichaels' eldest children had again managed to avoid the weekly chore they detested so much. Only Natalie remained at home and, although she, too, was now at an age where she found the Sunday excursion to the church on Ambient Hill tiresome, she knew it would be foolish to even try and argue a case for missing this weekly pilgrimage. She'd witnessed many heated discussions between her siblings and their father, and was smart enough to know that any attempt at putting a case to be excused would prove futile.

As usual, the unconventional and trendy Rev Green did all he could to liven up the proceedings. And certainly, in Natalie and her mother's eyes, the young cleric had a definite gift for making a ninety-minute service pass by reasonably quickly. However, not even the thought of his talent on the guitar and his charisma could completely eradicate the monotony of the dreaded Sunday morning ritual.

"So, what are you up to today?" Carmichael asked his youngest daughter as they strolled back down the narrow path towards the car park, the Grandshire Doubles ringing-out loudly from the church steeple behind them.

Natalie shrugged her shoulders. "Not sure really," she replied, rather unenthusiastically. "I may go around to Hannah's later."

Penny's eyes opened wide. "Not before you tidy up that mess you made in the lounge," she remarked sternly, referring to the large collection of computer games, magazines, chocolate bar wrappers and empty drinks bottles that her daughter and some of her friends had left behind them after spending the previous afternoon cocooned in the family's biggest room.

Natalie raised her eyes skyward and marched on without bothering to provide a reply to her mother.

"What happened to that lovely obedient little girl?" Penny muttered to her husband.

Carmichael shook his head slowly then smiled. "Who knows?" he replied.

"I'm a bit concerned about Robbie," Penny said, once Natalie was out of earshot.

"Concerned about what?" Carmichael asked.

"Well, not concerned really," continued Penny. "It's just that, for the last few mornings, Ben and Jason have both been coming around before eight and the three of them spend about half an hour together before they head off and Robbie goes off to the farm."

Carmichael shrugged his shoulders. "So, what's so strange about that? Ben and Jason are his best friends."

"Well," replied Penny, "up until now, I've almost had to drag Robbie out of bed for him to get to Mr Hayley's on time in the morning, but he's now up and ready when the boys call, and I know for a fact that neither Ben nor Jason have summer jobs. So, what is it that's motivating three teenage boys to get up so early and meet for just half an hour?"

4

Carmichael, whose routine meant that he would almost always be up and out of the house well before Robbie's friends arrived, continued to look bemused. "Have you asked him?" he enquired.

Penny was just about to answer when Carmichael's mobile rang, and his attention was diverted elsewhere.

Within a few seconds of her husband taking the call, Penny knew it was either someone at the station or one of her husband's team. And the look on Carmichael's face as he listened to the caller merely confirmed that yet another quiet family Sunday was just about to be ruined.

"I'll have to drop the family off at home," Carmichael remarked to the caller in his authoritative Inspector's voice, "then I'll head straight over. I'll be with you in about forty minutes."

"What's happened?" Penny enquired as soon as the call had ended.

"They've found a body this morning on Southport beach," Carmichael replied. "It looks like a murder."

Chapter 3

When Carmichael arrived at the car park to the north of Southport's pier, a large group of spectators had already gathered behind the concrete wall, looking out over the great expanse of flat golden sand towards the billowing, small blue tent that shrouded the victim's body. Despite their numbers, the assembled onlookers were orderly and appeared to be respectfully observing the instructions of the two uniformed officers, posted earlier with the task of keeping the public off the beach.

Carmichael nodded to one of the PCs, who deferentially returned the gesture with an accompanying "Morning sir" before lifting the flimsy plastic cordon to allow the Inspector to descend the few short steps that led down to the shoreline.

Once on the beach, the temperature seemed to fall markedly, which prompted Carmichael to quicken his step in the direction of the crime scene, some fifty paces away.

Just as he arrived, Watson emerged from the tent.

"What have we here, Marc?" Carmichael enquired.

"It's a weird one," replied his perplexed-looking sergeant.

Intrigued by what he'd heard, Carmichael pushed past Watson and entered the tent.

The vision that confronted him was, indeed, as Watson had suggested. A dark-haired, young man in his late-twenties or early-thirties, with distinctive downy sideburns, who was dressed in a bright-red tunic and wearing breeches and boots, was lying face-up on the sand with a glistening ornate sword embedded firmly in his chest.

Dr Stock, dressed head-to-toe in his white forensic outfit, was standing on the other side of the body.

"I hope you're not going to ask me for cause of death?" Stock remarked, facetiously.

Carmichael's gaze shifted up from the body and into Stock's eyes.

"Good morning Stock," he replied. "I'm glad to see you've not lost any of your customary wit."

Stock's expression remained one of solemnity, in keeping with his usual demeanour.

"I assume he's been to a fancy-dress party somewhere," Carmichael continued, his eyes moving from the body to Stock and then over to Watson.

"I'd suggest, more likely the Steampunk convention that's on in town this weekend," replied Watson.

"Asylum," Stock announced, cutting short the sergeant in mid-flow. "They call the event an asylum."

Carmichael looked confused. "What are you talking about?" he asked, his voice emphasising his bewilderment.

Stock shook his head. "There's been posters up for weeks about it," he remarked in a tone that suggested Carmichael's ignorance was inconceivable. "Other than the gathering in Lincoln every year, the event this weekend in Southport is the largest Steampunk gathering in the country."

"Asylum," Watson remarked mischievously, much to Stock's obvious annoyance.

"Come to think of it, I have seen the poster," admitted Carmichael. "But to be honest, I didn't take much notice. What on earth is Steampunk?"

As he spoke, the tent flap was pulled aside and DC Rachel Dalton appeared.

"Morning," she announced before taking a position at Watson's side and staring down at the lifeless body no more than a metre away.

"I'm no expert," remarked Stock, "but, from what I read in the local paper, it's a group of people who enjoy dressing up in, essentially, what looks like Victorian costumes, but with an industrial twist."

Carmichael's mystified expression signified he was still none the wiser.

"It's a big thing," interjected Rachel, the confidence in her voice suggesting she had some knowledge on the subject.

Carmichael turned his head and stared in Rachel's direction. "Well, I've never come across it before," he remarked.

"Until a few weeks ago, me neither," added Watson. "I suppose this is the latest weird fad of the younger generation?"

Rachel smirked and shook her head. "No," she replied curtly. "I'm no expert either, but I know for certain it appeals to all ages."

"You sound pretty well informed to me," Carmichael observed.

Rachel didn't reply, but the uncomfortable, restrained look Carmichael observed on her face suggested to him she may have more to say on the subject. He focused his gaze in the young DC's direction and opened his eyes wide to indicate he wanted her to be more forthcoming.

"It's not really for me to say," Rachel muttered uncomfortably, "I'm not sure he really wants people to know."

"Who are you talking about?" Carmichael barked, his furrowed brow indicating his patience was being sorely tested.

"It's Cooper," replied Rachel rather sheepishly. "He and Julia are both into Steampunk. He told me last week that he's been doing it for years."

"You're joking," exclaimed Watson with a huge grin on

his face. "Are you telling us Cooper gets dressed up like this for kicks?"

Rachel was already regretting opening her mouth. "That's why he's off this weekend, so he can attend the convention," she advised.

"Asylum," Watson interjected, with a smug, sarcastic look directed towards Dr Stock. "We've already established the event is called an asylum."

Carmichael folded his arms and shrugged his shoulders. "Well, Cooper's interest in this movement may prove to be useful," he remarked with a faint nod of his head. "Anyway, let's get our focus back on the victim here. What do we know about him?"

"According to the driving licence and his credit cards, his name is Kendal Michelson," Stock announced before picking up a large plastic bag and handing it to Carmichael. "This is what we found in his pockets."

Carmichael took the clear bag from Stock and looked carefully at the contents, which included a small brown wallet; a gold pocket-watch on a chain; an eyeglass; a few coins; and a white plastic card, which looked like an entry key to a hotel. "Was there a mobile phone on or around the body?" he enquired.

"Not that we've been able to find yet," replied Stock.

"Ok, why don't you see what else his possessions can tell us about him." Carmichael remarked before passing the bag to Rachel. "And, while you're doing that, I'd like to get an initial view from you, Stock, on the time Mr Michelson died."

The sound of Stock sucking in air through his teeth and the pensive expression on his face indicted that the well-renowned forensic expert was still unclear about some of the facts.

"I'll of course have to do a lot more work," Stock replied, his standard precursor to all his crime scene remarks.

"However, I'd say our victim was certainly killed here," he said. "The amount of blood around him, and soaked into the sand below the body, looks to be in keeping with the death occurring in situ."

"But what about the time of death?" Carmichael enquired for a second time.

Stock took another large breath. "I'd suggest between eight and twelve hours ago," he replied.

Carmichael looked at his watch. "So, that would make it between eleven thirty last night and three thirty this morning."

Stock nodded. "I'll have a much better idea once we've done more tests back in the lab, but from what I can see, that's about right."

Carmichael turned to face Rachel Dalton. "What have you found out about Kendal Michelson?"

"Not a huge amount from the contents of his wallet," replied Rachel. "However, there is an address and the entry key has the Fairfax Hotel printed on it, which is the big hotel, almost directly opposite here, on the sea front."

"So, where's he from?" Carmichael asked.

"His address is number eight, Fillary Hill in Barton Bridge," Rachel replied.

"But Barton Bridge is no more than fifteen miles away and on a direct train line," Watson remarked. "Why would he book into a hotel if he lived so close?"

"A very good question Marc," replied Carmichael. "Maybe, like Cooper, he preferred to keep his interest in Steampunk a closely guarded secret."

Chapter 4

Paul and Julia Cooper had located themselves at the end of the row. Being large in frame, Carmichael's dependable sergeant always tried to ensure he had plenty of leg room when he found himself at this type of function.

"He's running late," Cooper observed as he removed his gleaming gold pocket watch from his black waistcoat. He should have been on ten minutes ago."

His wife smiled gently, but continued reading the pamphlet resting on her lap. "I suspect it's quite normal for these artist types to make a late entrance," she commented with an air of authority.

From behind the thick, red curtain, which stretched the full width of the stage, Carly Wolf took off her brown top hat and peeped through to see how large a gathering the event had managed to attract. Turning back to face her co-organiser, she shook her head.

"Where the hell is he, Martin?" she asked angrily. "There must be at least a hundred people out there. I do hope Kendal's not going to do one of his famous disappearing tricks again."

Martin Swift, who was wearing a jet-black flying helmet and his customary full-length trench coat with the union flag emblazoned from top to toe, shrugged his shoulders. "I thought he'd be coming here with you," he remarked. "Had I known he was staying alone at the Fairfax last night, I'd have picked him up on my way in this morning."

Carly, her hands theatrically placed on either side of her tightly-bound leather corset, shook her head. A look of consternation was engraved across her elfin face. "Martin!" she exclaimed, as if she was addressing a naughty child, "Kendal and I are not together anymore. It's over and has been for months. I don't know why you think we'll get back together. That shit had enough chances with me. It's some other poor cow's turn to be taken in by his lies, and to be his therapist and surrogate mother. I've done my stint."

Martin Swift pulled up his flying glasses, puffed out his cheeks and shrugged his shoulders again. "Let's give him ten more minutes and, if he doesn't show, I guess it'll have to be plan B."

On finishing his sentence, Swift wandered slowly away, leaving Carly alone, agitated and exasperated.

* * * *

"What's next, sir?" enquired Watson, as the three police officers made their way back across the windswept beach towards the road.

"I'm going to talk to the staff at the hotel and take a look at his room," he replied. "Why don't you two get over to his house in Barton Bridge and see what you can find out about him."

Watson nodded. "And what about Cooper?" he asked. "Do you want me to call him?"

Carmichael shook his head. "No," he replied. "Leave Cooper while he's off-duty. If we find our murder's related to this Steampunk craze then I'll call him, but we've no evidence of Michelson's murder being connected to their strange, shared pastime."

"Right you are, sir," replied Watson, who was itching to see Cooper again, if only to rib him mercilessly about his guilty secret of a hobby.

Chapter 5

In its day, the Fairfax Hotel must have been an impressive building, commanding the road that skirted the beach. Built of the finest local sandstone, the five-storey structure was located smack-bang in the middle of the coastal road, overlooking the neatly-clipped grass lawns that lay between the road and the beach, with their geometrically-shaped flower beds stuffed with a mass of yellow and marmalade marigolds. However, that heyday had long since passed and, whilst it was still an impressive-looking edifice, the Fairfax looked tired after decades where little had been spent on maintenance, save the occasional quick paint job to the flaking windows and crumbling window sills. And no longer did this once magnificent building dominate the skyline, as it had done when it was constructed, having been usurped twenty years ago by a series of seven-storey retirement flats constructed to house the growing community of Southport's wealthy pensioners.

Carmichael bounded up the four worn steps that led to the imposing entrance and strode out across the heavily-scratched, but immaculately-polished, mahogany, parquet floor.

"Good morning, sir," announced the young woman who greeted him, her faint South African accent and genuinely warm, broad smile immediately inspiring Carmichael to reciprocate.

"My name's Inspector Carmichael," he replied, while simultaneously holding out his identity card. "I'd like to talk with the manager, if I may."

The receptionist maintained her poise, but from the expression on her face, she was clearly a little flummoxed by the request.

"That's my uncle," replied the young woman. "It's his day off today. Is there anything I can do for you?"

Carmichael smiled once more. "I understand you have a guest staying with you at the moment, a Mr Kendal Michelson," he announced. "I'd like to ask you some questions about him, if I may, and take a look at his room."

The receptionist's previously cheery face changed dramatically. "Is that who's been found on the beach?" she enquired.

Carmichael stared back into the young woman's dark-brown eyes. "I'm afraid I'm not able to say more, but my questions relate to an incident on the beach this morning."

"What is it you want to know?" she asked, her voice trembling as she spoke.

* * * *

"I can't believe it," Watson announced gleefully as he and Rachel Dalton headed off in the direction of Barton Bridge. "Fancy Cooper being a fancy-dress weirdo!"

Rachel shook her head disapprovingly. "I wish I hadn't said anything," she remarked. "And, anyway, as far as I'm aware, it's a harmless pastime."

As Watson's car turned left and drove down Lord Street, with its wide pavements and Victorian shop fronts, the first Steampunk enthusiasts became noticeable, as if on cue to provide ammunition for Watson to ridicule the activity even further.

"Harmless it may be," replied Watson, "but it's certainly peculiar. What enjoyment can you get from flouncing around dressed like something out of a Charles Dickens novel?"

Although in her heart Rachel shared her colleague's bemusement, there was no way she was going to allow him to believe she was going to join him in the inevitable ribbing Cooper was going to get when he next was on duty, especially as it had been her he'd confided in.

"I think it looks really impressive," she replied, trying hard to appear to be unfazed by the derision being expressed by Watson. "They clearly spend a lot of time and effort to look the part. And look... there are even families getting involved."

As she spoke, Rachel pointed out the window to a family group, including two small girls all dressed from head to toe in period costume. The girls, the eldest no more than eight or nine, had matching outfits; ankle-length, emerald-green coats, with matching green hats and authentic black boots laced up tightly. To complete their ensemble, each of them carried a tiny emerald-green parasol to shade themselves from the bright rays of the midday sun.

"It's sad," replied Watson heartlessly. "Can you imagine the mickey taking those kids must get at school," he continued. "Now what sort of parent would set their kids up for that sort of intimidation? It's bordering on child abuse in my view."

Rachel shook her head in disbelief. "Your talents are wasted in the force, sergeant," she remarked sarcastically. "Have you ever considered helping out on the Samaritans phone line?"

Watson glanced sideways at his young female colleague with a smirk that suggested he found her comment highly amusing. "Do you know, you're not the first person that's ever said that to me," he remarked. "In fact, Susan mentions it quite frequently."

Rachel sighed deeply before turning her head to look out of the passenger window. "I bet she does," she said quietly under her breath.

Chapter 6

"Well that was a massive let down," remarked a despondent Julia Cooper as she exited the hall in her royal-blue dress, matching bonnet, and frilly parasol, held in her free hand whilst the other was totally enveloped by her husband's huge fingers. "That Martin Swift guy clearly knows his stuff when it comes to the works of Jules Verne, but I was looking forward to listening to Kendal Michelson's talk. I wonder what happened to him?"

Cooper was relieved to get out into the fresh air. His immaculately-pressed costume, whilst precise in its construction to the mid-Victorian era, was nevertheless incredibly tight fitting and unbelievably uncomfortable, especially on such a hot day. "I've no idea," he replied, with a faint shake of his head, "but you're right, his stand-in, was a poor substitute."

* * * *

"I thought that went rather well," Martin Swift remarked, his face beaming as he marvelled in his triumph.

Carly Wolf frowned, the puzzled lines deep in her brow, and her thick, brown eyebrows angled to confirm her bewilderment. "It was passable, I suppose," she replied, with unmasked derision, given just how utterly boring she'd found it. "Having been left well and truly in it by that mate of yours, it could have been a lot worse. At least we managed to put on something for the paying public."

"Yes, I wonder where Kendal is?" remarked Martin Swift, seemingly oblivious to Carly Wolf's blatant indifference. "He's not answered any of my text messages so I think I'll pop over to the Fairfax and see if he's okay. Do you want to join me?"

Carly's frown, and its accompanying angled eyebrows, returned.

"To be honest, Martin," she announced, calmly. "As far as I'm concerned, he can go to hell. He's someone else's problem now, thank god!"

After delivering that message, Carly sauntered away down the aisle of the hall. As she made her way out of the building, a small group of middle-aged men, who'd remained inside following Martin's presentation, stopped talking and quietly enjoyed the sight of the attractive young woman gliding past them in knee-length, brown boots, matching corset and hat, and a short white cotton skirt, which left little to their leery imaginations.

* * * *

With the receptionist now having departed, Carmichael stood alone in the dead man's hotel room. He remained motionless for a few seconds, inwardly digesting the scene around him. His first observation was that Michelson appeared to be a neat and tidy man, with his discarded clothes neatly folded on the bed next to a zipped-shut black suit holder. Other than those items, the only other obvious possessions visible in the room were Michelson's expensive-looking black suitcase, which had been left resting on the foldaway case-stand and, through the crack in the open door, Carmichael could see Michelson's toiletry bag sitting on the narrow glass shelf above the sink; its toothbrush already extracted and placed in the plastic tumbler at its side.

* * * *

It had taken Watson and Rachel Dalton no time at all to get to Barton Bridge.

"He was clearly not short of a bob or two," remarked Watson as his car pulled up outside 8 Fillary Hill.

Rachel nodded. "Yes, I wouldn't mind living round here," she replied as she looked across at the lavish modern houses set back from the quiet road.

"Maybe you should put it on your Christmas list for daddy," quipped Watson acidly, a reference to the fact that Rachel Dalton's father was one of the wealthiest people in the district.

"Maybe I will," replied Rachel calmly, with a look designed to demonstrate to her colleague that she felt unscathed by his barbed comment. "I wonder whether there's anyone else living here," Rachel continued as she turned her head once more to look at Michelson's house.

"There's only one way to find out," replied Watson, who, as he spoke, was already opening the car door, and clambering out.

* * * *

Carmichael spent no more than ten minutes in Michelson's hotel room. Having found nothing of any great interest, Carmichael closed the door behind him and wandered the few paces down the threadbare carpet that took him to the wide staircase that led back down to reception.

As he descended the stairs, he could hear the familiar accent of the South African receptionist holding a conversation with a stridently spoken man who, as he finally made it to the bottom of the stairs, Carmichael caught sight of at the reception desk.

"Why are you being so vague?" enquired the stridently-spoken man in a flying-helmet and an expensive-looking, ankle-length coat, cut from union flag material. "Why can't you tell me which room Kendal's in?"

"Can I ask you who you are?" Carmichael enquired.

Martin Swift turned around and stared in bewilderment at the person who'd interrupted him so rudely. "I could ask you the same question," he retorted irately.

Carmichael smiled calmly and produced his warrant card. "My name's Inspector Carmichael," he replied. "Can you now tell me who you are, please, and what relationship you have with Kendal Michelson?"

Chapter 7

Watson arrived at the front door a few strides ahead of Rachel and, without bothering to wait for his colleague, rang the doorbell. Within seconds, the door was opened by a petite young woman who, by the look of her, he guessed was from the Mediterranean.

"Can I help you?" she enquired in a soft Spanish accent.

Watson smiled and held up his identity card. "Is this the residence of Kendal Michelson?" he asked.

The young woman returned the smile. "Yes," she confirmed, "but he's not at home."

"Can we ask who you are?" Rachel interjected.

"I'm here to do some cleaning," replied the young woman. "I come here three days a week."

"Is there anyone else at home?" Rachel asked.

The young woman shook her head. "No," she replied. "Mr Michelson lives here alone, but he's out this weekend."

"May we come in?" Watson enquired.

On hearing the question, the young cleaner's expression changed and she moved the door slightly so there was less of a gap between it and the doorframe. "I'm not sure I can let you in without Mr Michelson saying it's ok," she replied.

Watson and Rachel Dalton exchanged a quick look.

"I'm afraid there's been an incident involving Mr

Michelson," Rachel announced. "It's really important we are allowed into the house."

"Is Mr Michelson in trouble?" the cleaner enquired, her expression showing clear signs of concern.

"No, he's not in trouble," replied Rachel, "but it would help us a great deal if you could let us in."

Reluctantly, the young woman slowly opened the door wide enough for the two officers to enter Kendal Michelson's house.

* * * *

"I can't believe it," muttered Martin Swift as he sat facing Carmichael in the lounge of the Fairfax Hotel. "I saw him only last night. Are you sure it's him?"

Carmichael nodded gently. "We've still to locate his next of kin and do a formal identification," he confessed, "but we're almost certain the body we found on the beach this morning is that of your friend, Kendal Michelson."

Swift, his face pale, and his eyes staring blankly into space, bore all the hallmarks of a man in shock.

After waiting for a few seconds to allow Martin Swift to gather his thoughts, Carmichael cleared his throat. "Do you know who's Kendal's next of kin?"

"His dad, Gavin," replied Swift, his voice trembling as he spoke. "He'll be devastated."

Carmichael paused again before continuing his questioning. "When was it you last saw Kendal?" he asked.

Martin Swift considered the question. "It would have been at about eleven thirty," he replied. "We'd had a meal together at a small Chinese restaurant with a few friends. We all left the restaurant together."

"Are you sure about the time?" Carmichael enquired.

"It may have been a touch later, but not by much, as I

drove home, which takes only about twenty-five minutes from Southport," replied Swift, who appeared to be trying desperately to recall his movements from the night before through a fog of stunned bewilderment. "I was in bed by twelve thirty, so I'd say the last time I saw him was between eleven thirty and eleven forty-five."

"So, tell me," continued Carmichael, "Who else did you go out with last night?"

When Swift didn't respond, Carmichael repeated the question. "Who were the other people that were with you last night?" he enquired.

"They were two ladies," replied Swift. "Carly Wolf and Gabby Johns."

"Are these ladies your partners?" Carmichael asked.

Swift shook his head. "No," he replied with a wry smile. "They were both previous partners of Kendal, but not anymore."

Carmichael was intrigued to learn more about Michelson's two previous partners, but could see that Swift was still traumatised by the news and had more pressing questions he wanted to ask. "And, after the meal, where did Kendal, Carly and Gabby go?" he gently probed.

"Like me," Swift replied, "Gabby drove home. Kendal and Carly walked together back here."

"So, was Carly Wolf booked in here, too, last night?" Carmichael enquired.

Swift looked a little uncomfortable at Carmichael's question, it clearly having dawned on him that he may be implicating their friend Carly in his murder. "As far as I'm aware, she was," he replied rather vaguely. "But she'd have had nothing to do with Kendal's death, she and he were once very close."

"But not now," remarked Carmichael.

"No, not now," confirmed Swift.

Carmichael eased himself back into his chair. "Do you have the addresses of Carly Wolf and Gabby Johns?" he asked.

"I know Carly's address," replied Swift, "but I've never been to Gabby's. I have her address at home, but I couldn't tell you it off the top of my head."

"Are they both local?" continued Carmichael.

"Carly lives here in Southport; near the football ground in Haig Avenue," replied Swift, "Gabby lives in Linbold."

"What about Gabby's mobile number?" Carmichael asked.

Swift nodded. "Yes, I have that stored in my phone."

"Good," replied Carmichael. "I'll need to talk with both ladies urgently so that will be helpful."

Martin Swift raised his eyes and looked directly at Carmichael's. "Well, we're all planning to meet at Harri's Bar at two thirty," he remarked. "If you want to talk to both of them, I suggest you meet us there."

"Harri's Bar?" enquired Carmichael. "Where exactly is that?"

"It's on Lord Street," replied Swift, in a tone that suggested everyone should have heard of Harri's Bar. "It's the most popular place in town. It's part-owned by Gavin, Kendal's dad, and it's a great favourite with the Steampunk fraternity when they come to Southport."

"Talking of Kendal's father," added Carmichael, "do you know where he lives?"

Swift nodded. "That's easy," he replied. "Gavin lives two doors away from Kendal in Barton Bridge, it's 12 Fillary Hill."

Chapter 8

Despite allowing the two police officers into Kendal Michelson's house, Carmen Martinez, Kendal's cleaner, ensured she remained a matter of a few feet from Watson and Dalton, as they proceeded to wander around the decidedly eccentrically-decorated house.

"Have you ever seen anything like this?" Watson remarked as the two officers entered the third room on the ground floor, which, like the other rooms they'd been in, was decorated as if the house had been caught in a nineteenth century time warp.

Rachel Dalton shook her head. "It's unbelievable," she replied, her eyes wide open as they slowly scoured the furniture, carpets, paintings, and ornaments that festooned the room.

"It's like a museum," Watson remarked.

"Or a house of someone famous from Victorian times, lovingly restored by the National Trust," Rachel replied in awe. "It's absolutely astounding."

"Bloody creepy, if you ask me," Watson remarked in a whisper, so that their chaperone could not hear him. "What sort of nutter would live in a gloomy old dump like this?"

Rachel turned her head to face her colleague, her expression indicating she disagreed. "I'm no expert, but I suspect the paintings in here alone would be worth tens of thousands of pounds, maybe more," she remarked. "This is no dump, Marc. It's a treasure trove."

Watson appeared unmoved by his colleague's pronouncements. "It still gives me the creeps."

As he finished his sentence, Watson's mobile started to ring and, as he removed it from his pocket, he saw the name Carmichael emblazoned across the small screen.

"It's the boss," he told Rachel, before pressing the receive button and placing the phone to his ear.

"Hi Marc, how are you and Rachel getting on at Michelson's place?" Carmichael enquired.

Before answering, Watson took a few paces away from the cleaner and turned his back on her and Rachel to avoid being heard.

"It's like a Victorian time capsule," he replied in a hushed voice. "Everything here is old; it's weird."

Carmichael allowed himself a wry smile. "Have you discovered anything that you think could help us understand why he was killed?"

"Not yet," Watson replied. "To be honest, we've only just started. Michelson's cleaner let us in and she's been suspiciously following us around since we arrived."

"That's unusual," remarked Carmichael. "There can't be many cleaners who work on Sundays."

This had never crossed Watson's mind, but he didn't want to let his boss know that. "I was going to talk to her about that later," Watson lied. "I wanted to make sure we had a good look around here, though, first."

Carmichael suspected his sergeant was being less than honest, but didn't want to make anything of it. "So, tell me, what's his cleaner like?"

"She's actually quite a pretty young thing," replied Watson. "She can't be older than about twenty-five, Spanish or maybe Portuguese; and if she'd smile a bit more she'd be quite a looker."

Carmichael shook his head in despair. "And does she have a name?"

Watson nervously cleared his throat. "As I say, Rachel and I are focused on getting as much information as we can from the house at the moment. My plan is to have a good chat with her once we've finished looking around."

"Well, I want you both to stop what you're doing there for the moment and get yourselves over to the house next-door-but-one. Number twelve," Carmichael instructed. "It's where Kendal Michelson's father lives. His name's Gavin Michelson and, if he's in, I need you and Rachel to break the news to him and bring him down to the mortuary." As he spoke, Carmichael looked at his watch, which read 12.40pm. "I'll meet you down there in forty minutes."

"Right you are, sir," replied Watson.

"But, before you go," continued Carmichael, "take the cleaner's details, as we may need to talk with her again."

"Will do," confirmed Watson, before Carmichael abruptly ended the call.

Chapter 9

It was 1:15pm when Carmichael entered the mortuary. As he'd expected, Dr Stock had already completed his autopsy by the time he arrived and, true to form, the outline of his findings was clear and comprehensive.

"He died at between midnight and two o'clock this morning," Stock announced in a confident tone. "He'd consumed a considerable amount of Chinese food a few hours earlier and a few glasses of red wine. Merlot I suspect. He was killed where we found him, by a single stab wound delivered by the sword that was still impaled in his chest when we arrived at the scene. There were no signs of any struggle and, given the sword went straight through his heart, I'd expect he died within seconds of receiving the fatal blow."

Carmichael nodded gently as if to acknowledge the pathologist's thorough synopsis. "Was he drugged or bound before he died?" he enquired.

Stock shook his head. "He certainly wasn't drugged," he replied confidently. "And if he was restrained, it was with minimal force as there are no marks or lesions on his body to support such a hypothesis."

Carmichael's forehead wrinkled and his closed lips turned down at the ends to suggest he was confused.

"If he was killed where he was found, with his own sword, he probably knew his attacker," Carmichael suggested. "He must have allowed the person who killed him to take his sword and then, when his guard was down, that person must have delivered the fatal blow."

Dr Stock nodded. "That would make sense, I suppose," he replied, "but, as always, I'll leave the detective work to you, Carmichael. All I'm prepared to commit to is when and how he was killed, and to confirm to you that he put up no struggle whatsoever."

As Carmichael tried to imagine any other possible scenario, he noticed the unmistakeable sight of Watson's car entering the small carpark outside the window.

"Here's Marc and Rachel with Michelson's father," he remarked. "Is the body in a fit state for him to make the identification?"

Stock returned a glare, which indicated that the very suggestion that the body would not be ready was an affront to his professional integrity. "Of course it's ready," he replied caustically. "We're not amateurs here, Inspector."

* * * *

It hadn't been Cooper's idea to get involved in the Steampunk movement. Until his wife had mentioned it, five years earlier, Cooper had never heard of Steampunk. However, as so often in their relationship, when Julia suggested doing something, it was rare for Cooper not to follow through on her wishes. It hadn't always been that way. Before they discovered that they were unable to have children, Cooper would often kick back. However, since that traumatic day, almost seven years earlier, he'd decided to allow his wife whatever pleasure she desired, a decision he'd never regretted and one he'd almost completely adhered too, regardless of what she'd proposed.

"Are there any more events you'd like to attend?" he

enquired of Julia as they strolled arm in arm down Lord Street.

"Not really," his wife replied with a faint smile. "It was Kendal Michelson's talk on Steampunk bloggers and authors that I really wanted to see. And I can see that outfit's a little uncomfortable for you, so we can head off home, if you'd like."

Cooper squeezed his wife's tiny hand. "I'm ok," he replied, his voice trying hard to sound genuine. "I'm happy to go to another event if there's one you'd like to attend."

Julia looked up into her husband's kindly face, which, due to the significant difference in their heights, was over a foot away from hers. "Why don't we stop off somewhere and get some lunch, then we can head-off back home."

"Great idea," remarked Cooper, who was starving. "I know just the place. It's only a few hundred yards down the road."

It was now Julia's turn to squeeze the hand of the man whom she loved so dearly.

* * * *

Carmichael was surprised when he first set eyes on Kendal Michelson's father, as he climbed out of Watson's car. Gavin Michelson looked far too young to be the father of someone in their early thirties. His expression, however, was that same look that Carmichael had seen countless times before, the worried face of a relative on the knife-edge of hope and devastation.

Carmichael had no doubt that the body in the morgue awaiting Gavin Michelson was his son, which made the faint hope that, no doubt, still existed in his father's heart, seem so needlessly cruel.

"Oh, it's just dawned on me," remarked Stock who

had also watched the scene outside the window. "He's the chocolatier."

Carmichael half-turned and gazed at the portly pathologist. "What's that?" he enquired.

"Michelson," responded Stock. "I knew that name was familiar. That's Gavin Michelson, he's the owner of The World of Chocolate, that fancy online chocolate company. Mrs Stock has a sweet tooth, so I always make sure she gets a box on her birthday and at Christmas time. His salted caramel truffles are to die for."

Carmichael stared back at Stock in amazement. "An unfortunate turn of phrase in the circumstance, I'd say," he remarked.

Chapter 10

Carmichael decided to delay introducing himself to Gavin Michelson until after the formal identification had been completed. Given the devastating news the poor man had just received, Carmichael figured his involvement at this stage would add no value. And, at any rate, during the short journey from Barton Bridge to Kirkwood, Carmichael was confident that Watson and Dalton, in establishing a bond with the murdered man's father, would have gleaned as much information as was possible at this stage.

The formal identification took little more than ten minutes and, with the outcome as they'd all expected, Gavin Michelson had already been offered a comfortable seat in the reception area and a cup of hot tea before Carmichael made himself known.

"I'm Inspector Carmichael," he announced in a hushed, compassionate, but authoritative voice. "I'm leading the investigation into your son's murder. First of all, I'd just like to say how sorry I am for your loss."

Gavin Michelson looked up from where he was sitting and nodded gently.

"I can't understand who would do this to Kendal," he remarked, his voice trembling slightly as he spoke. "Kendal wouldn't hurt a fly. He had no enemies in the world, so why would anyone want to kill him?"

Carmichael sat down opposite Michelson senior. "We are keeping an open mind on the motive for your son's murder, but one line of enquiry we're following is that whoever killed Kendal was known to him."

On hearing Carmichael's pronouncement, Watson and Dalton exchanged a hasty glance. This being news to both of them.

Gavin Michelson shrugged his shoulders. "Kendal had no enemies to my knowledge, Inspector," he remarked. "And I cannot believe that anyone he called a friend would have killed him."

Carmichael decided not to push Michelson any further, as it was clear the dead man's father was unlikely to help him with that particular line of enquiry.

"When did you last speak with your son?" he enquired.

Michelson thought for a few seconds before responding.

"Erm, it was yesterday morning," he replied. "Kendal called me at about eleven. He wanted to know whether I fancied going to watch Lancashire with him next weekend. They are playing Glamorgan at Old Trafford, and he reckoned he could get a couple of tickets."

"Did you go to watch cricket regularly with your son?" Carmichael enquired.

"Not really," Michelson replied. "When he was younger, we would go all the time, but since he went to university, we'd probably been no more than half a dozen times."

"And did you agree to go?" Carmichael asked.

Gavin Michelson shook his head. "No, sadly I had to blow him out. I have to be in Belgium next weekend. There's a big European confectionary exhibition the following week and I'm flying over there on Saturday to attend some meetings with our major retailers, so I had to say no."

"That's a shame," replied Carmichael, who could see that

the recollection of this rebuttal appeared to have touched a nerve with Gavin Michelson.

"We'll arrange for an officer to give you a lift home," Carmichael continued. "We'll make sure you're kept informed when we make progress in finding the person or persons who killed your son, Mr Michelson."

Carmichael offered his right hand, which Michelson shook firmly, his dejected eyes fixed in the Inspector's direction.

"Make sure you find the animal that killed my boy," he said.

Carmichael, with Michelson's hand still in his, nodded gently before releasing his grip and walking slowly towards the exit.

* * * *

When Cooper and his wife entered Harri's Bar, he was surprised at how busy it was; and even more startled to see that most of the customers appeared to be fellow Steampunk enthusiasts.

"There's a free table over there," he said, extending the index finger of his right hand towards a small round table to the side of the long, polished, oak bar. "Why don't you grab it quickly before someone takes it? I'll find a couple of menus."

Julia Cooper didn't need to be asked a second time. Having spied the table in question, she made a dash to claim it.

* * * *

Carmichael, Watson and Rachel Dalton watched through the window as PC Dyer and a young WPC accompanied Gavin Michelson to the waiting police vehicle. The car had departed from the small tarmacked area and was out onto the main road before any of them spoke.

"This is the part of the job I hate," DC Dalton confessed. "He seems utterly winded by his son's death."

Carmichael nodded sagely at the apt way his young colleague had described Gavin Michelson's demeanour. "I think people do learn to live with tragedies like his, but I suspect they're never the same."

After pausing for a few seconds, Carmichael continued. "Did he say much about his son when you were at his house or on the journey over here?"

Watson shook his head. "Not really."

"And did he mention what he was doing on Saturday evening and in the early hours of this morning?" Carmichael asked.

"He maintained he'd been at home with a lady friend on Saturday evening, a woman called Harriett Hall," replied Rachel. "They apparently have a joint business venture in Southport; they had dinner to talk about some ideas she had about expanding their business."

"That will be Harri's Bar," remarked Carmichael. "I met with one of Kendal's friends at the Fairfax Hotel. He mentioned the bar to me during our discussions. Did he say what time Harriett Hall left last night?"

"He said it was at around twelve, but he was very vague," replied Rachel. "To be honest, I didn't want to press him too much, given the circumstances."

Carmichael nodded once more. "We'll have to get a statement from him about his movements last night, but you were right to take it easy on him Rachel, now's probably not the time."

"So how did your morning go at the Fairfax Hotel?" Watson asked.

"There was nothing of any particular interest in Michelson's room," replied Carmichael, "but my meeting with his friend, Martin Swift, at the reception desk was very helpful. He's another of these Steampunk followers, and he maintains that he was with Kendal and two ladies last night until about eleven thirty or eleven forty-five. According to Swift, they'd all been out having a meal together at a Chinese restaurant. When they left, he and one of the ladies drove home separately, leaving Kendal to make the twenty-minute walk to his hotel with the other lady; a woman called Carly Wolf."

"Sounds like we need to speak to this Carly Wolf," Watson said. "Did he have an address for her?"

"He did," replied Carmichael. "She lives in Haig Avenue, in Southport, but apparently, we will be able to find her, Swift and the other lady, a woman called Gabby Johns, at Harri's Bar this afternoon. According to Swift they've all arranged to meet there at two-thirty."

"That's all very convenient," Rachel remarked. "With a bit of luck, we will be able to speak to Harriett Hall too, to verify what Gavin Michelson told us."

"Assuming they all turn up," added Watson cynically. "If one of them killed him, they could be half-way to god-knows-where by now."

Carmichael looked up at the large flashing digital clock on the wall. It read 13:47.

"Well, we'll find that out in just over forty minutes. If we act sharply, we should be able to get to Harri's Bar at about the time their little gathering is due to commence."

Chapter 11

The pair had just finished their lunch when Cooper spotted the unmistakeable figure of Carmichael entering Harri's Bar, followed closely behind by Watson and Rachel Dalton.

"I wonder what they're here about?" remarked Julia, her curiosity plainly aroused.

"It won't be for a social, I can tell you that," observed Cooper who watched as the trio made their way towards the centre of the large bar.

As he walked, Carmichael's eyes scoured the room trying to locate Martin Swift amongst the mass of people decked out in their Steampunk finery.

"They're looking for someone," remarked Cooper as they watched the three officers cross the floor, their ordinary clothing making them stand out in a sea of Victoriana.

"And I think they've just found him," replied Julia, as Carmichael ushered his two colleagues to where the man who had made such an unremarkable talk that morning was sitting, still clad in his long, union-flag decorated trench coat. Sat next to him was a fresh-faced woman with long blond plaits, wearing a brown suede dress and leather boots. She had a leather flat cap perched backwards on her head, and, to complete the ensemble, a pair of flying goggles rested ornamentally on her forehead.

"I wonder what Carmichael wants with them?" Cooper remarked.

"It must be serious," Julia observed, "otherwise they wouldn't all be here."

Cooper nodded. "You're right, my dear," he concurred. "It must be pretty important."

* * * *

"Good afternoon, Mr Swift," said Carmichael as he arrived at his table. "These are my colleagues, Sergeant Watson and DC Dalton. Do you mind if we join you?"

Martin Swift rose from his seat and held out his right hand, which Carmichael grasped firmly. "This is Gabby Johns, she was one of the ladies Kendal and I had dinner with last night."

As he spoke, the young woman, who Carmichael estimated to be in her early thirties, also stood up, greeting Carmichael with a smile. It was not a broad grin, but a polite, forced smile, as one would expect from someone trying to bear-up after receiving some very sad news.

Carmichael looked directly into Gabby Johns's eyes. "Pleased to meet you," he said, before offering her the hand he'd just extracted from Swift's rather feeble grip.

Neither Watson nor Dalton were greeted with the same formal handshake; they had to make do with a gentle nod and a faint, acknowledging smile. Although this mild rebuff was patently unintentional, it clearly demonstrated to both Watson and Rachel Dalton that they were already perceived, by both Martin Swift and Gabby Johns, as less important than their boss; not that either officer cared that much.

"I'm sorry about the death of your friend," Carmichael added as soon as all five of them were safely seated. "I understand from Martin that you all had dinner last night."

"That's correct," replied Gabby, her accent indicating that she certainly hadn't been born in Lancashire. In the noisy atmosphere of Harri's Bar, Carmichael couldn't detect precisely where Gabby Johns hailed from, but it sounded like it was the east midlands.

"We had a Chinese at the China Garden on Kirkwood Road," Gabby continued. "We met there at about nine and we all left the restaurant at around eleven forty."

"And Martin told me you both drove home in separate cars, leaving Kendal and Carly Wolf to walk back to the Fairfax."

"That's correct," replied Gabby once again.

"And that was the last time you saw or spoke with Kendal?" Carmichael asked.

"That's right," Gabby replied, "I drove home and went to bed."

"I understand that you and Kendal were once partners," continued Carmichael. "Is that correct?"

Gabby Johns shot a fierce glare in Swift's direction, as if to demonstrate her displeasure at him for disclosing that piece of information to Carmichael. Swift got the message and looked suitably chastened, but he said nothing.

"We were for about five years," replied Gabby, "but that was ages ago. We're just good friends, or at least we were."

"I'm surprised neither you, nor Martin, hadn't taken Carly and Kendal back to their hotel after the meal," Carmichael remarked. "Did you not offer them a lift? It couldn't have been that far out of your way."

Gabby Johns smiled. "I didn't offer, but, even if I had, they wouldn't have accepted."

"And why do you say that?" Carmichael enquired.

"Because I know... rather, I knew Kendal well and, knowing him, I'm certain he welcomed having twenty or so minutes alone with Carly. It would have been his opportunity to try and sweet-talk her into giving him another chance."

"Another chance?" repeated Carmichael. "What do you mean?"

Gabby exhaled theatrically. "After we split up, Kendal had quite a few dalliances, Inspector. I suspect few, if any, of the poor unsuspecting women he managed to lure under his spell meant much to him, but Carly was different. I think he really did love her. However, in true Kendal style, he couldn't help himself and, after a while, Carly, like me, suddenly realised what sort of man he was, and she dumped him. It was clear, over dinner last night, he was desperate to rekindle the relationship, so a twenty-minute walk alone with Carly would have been a godsend to Kendal."

"I see," replied Carmichael. "Kendal was a bit of a ladies' man, then?"

"It's true; Kendal had an eye for the fillies," interjected Swift, his use of language plainly not to Gabby Johns' taste, by yet another angry look she shot over in his direction, "but he wasn't a malicious person and he always treated women with the utmost respect."

Gabby Johns rolled her eyes. "That's a matter of opinion," she remarked tersely. "It's true that Kendal was always the perfect gentleman, Inspector. In fact, I'd liken him to a lovable, attractive, cuddly tomcat. He would purr and charm the pants off you all day, but at night, when he was out of sight, he'd take his pleasures when and wherever he could find them. A secretive opportunist, just like every other tomcat out there. It took me over five years to work that out Inspector, more fool me."

Carmichael said nothing. He'd not expected to be given such an unflattering synopsis of the dead man by someone who was a friend of Michelson, and certainly not so soon after his murder. It was most likely his shocked expression that prompted Gabby to further remark, "If you don't believe me, ask Carly."

As she spoke, Gabby Johns moved her eyeline in the direction of an attractive young woman who'd just entered the bar.

"She's clearly brighter than I was," continued Gabby, "it only took her a year to twig his game."

Carly Wolf had spotted Martin Swift's extravagant two-handed wave as soon as she'd entered the room and, as Carmichael looked up, she had already managed to strut confidently almost half-way to their table.

Carly Wolf was twenty-five years old and unquestionably attractive, not even her fiercest critics could deny her that. She had a jet-black bob, wore knee-length, brown boots, and had a brown corset so tightly bound that it was hard to fathom what was preventing some of her God-given attributes from bursting out of the top. Her outfit was completed by a small brown hat and her short white cotton skirt, which, in a certain light, re-enacted the infamous photo that had embarrassed young Diana Spencer decades earlier. In the way she dressed and the way she walked, Carmichael's first impression was that Carly Wolf was a confident young woman and a woman who wanted to make a statement. And, from the varying looks he observed on the faces of the people she passed by, not to mention the ones she joined at their table, it was quite clear that Carly was, what he'd later describe to Penny as, a *marmite girl*, either loved and admired or resented and detested.

"You must be the law," she remarked assuredly as she reached where the three officers were sitting. Carmichael found the term not only inappropriate, given the circumstances, but also years out of date. He'd not personally been referred to as the law since his early years on the beat in London. However, he knew from experience that sudden grief could make people behave oddly, so, given Carly's age and that fact that her ex-boyfriend had just been brutally murdered, Carmichael decided to allow the shapely young women with the elfin face the benefit of the doubt.

"Good afternoon," Carmichael said, his right hand stretched-out to greet his new acquaintance.

"Nice to meet you," replied Carly, who elected not to shake his hand and confidently positioned herself on a stool situated in between Rachel Dalton and Watson, much to Watson's obvious delight.

After introducing his team, Carmichael decided to dispense with any frivolous small-talk and get straight to the point.

"I understand that, after the Chinese last night, you and Kendal walked back to the Fairfax Hotel. Can you tell me what happened after both Martin and Gabby had headed off home?"

With her black, fingerless leather gloves, Carly Wolf smoothed down her white, frilly skirt against her thighs and took a few seconds to look at each of the five-people sitting around the large, round table.

"I could do with a drink," she said as her eyes eventually found a resting place on Carmichael. "Why don't we go to the bar and I'll let you know what happened."

Carmichael nodded. "Of course," he replied, before standing up and escorting Carly Wolf to the furthest end of the long, wooden bar, where he hoped there would be less noise and more room for them to talk without being overheard.

* * * *

"Looks like Inspector Carmichael has pulled," remarked Julia, with a wry smile and a slight movement of her head, which alerted Cooper to the rather amusing sight of Carmichael in his customary sombre suit and tie, guiding a

43

trendy but eccentrically-dressed young woman, little more than half his age, to the bar.

Cooper smiled broadly. "Yes," he replied as quick as lightning, "if we didn't know better, we could be forgiven for thinking he was a Westminster MP just about to start spending some of his generous maintenance allowance."

Chapter 12

Even though there were several people who'd been waiting before them, Carly lent confidently on the bar and, after nodding her head in the direction of the nearest barman, she managed to become the next customer to be served.

"I'll have a Jack with a splash of coke, Luke," she announced confidently. "What do you want, Inspector?"

Carmichael smiled. "I'll have the same, but without the Jack Daniels," he replied.

"Ice?" asked the barman.

"Not for me," replied Carly.

Carmichael shook his head., "Me neither," he said.

As the barman walked away to the impressive array of optics that lined the wall behind the bar, Carmichael put his hand in his jacket pocket to extract his wallet.

"No need," replied Carly firmly, a faint conceited smile breaking out on her face. "This will be on the house. I'm related to Harri, the owner, so my drinks are always free."

Carmichael nodded his head. "Lucky, you," he remarked, although in truth he wasn't even remotely impressed.

"So, what is it you want to know?" Carly enquired, as soon as their drinks had been delivered.

"I understand that after you'd finished the Chinese meal last night you and Kendal walked back to the Fairfax Hotel," Carmichael remarked. "Can you tell me what happened after both Martin Swift and Gabby Johns had headed off home?"

With one elbow resting on the bar, Carly looked up at Carmichael. "We walked back towards the Fairfax and chatted," she replied.

"About what?" Carmichael asked.

"Nothing really," Carly replied. "Just the usual stuff."

Carmichael nodded. "Did you both walk all the way back to the hotel?" he enquired.

Carly took a large swig from her glass tumbler. "No," she replied, her lips glistening wet with the remnants of her Jack Daniels and coke. "We parted company before we got to the Fairfax."

"Why was that?" Carmichael probed.

Carly Wolf eased herself up onto a barstool and, once seated, smoothed down her frilly skirt just as she had done when she'd entered the bar. "He stopped to take a call on his mobile."

"Who was it from?" Carmichael asked.

Carly shrugged her shoulders. "I've no idea," she replied.

"So why didn't you just wait while he finished the call?" Carmichael asked.

"I did, for a while," replied Carly. "But when it didn't look like it was going to end any time soon, I just said bye and left him to it."

"And that was the last time you saw Kendal?" Carmichael confirmed.

Carly nodded. "Yes, that was it."

"And what time would that have been?" Carmichael asked.

Carly Wolf shrugged her shoulders and put on an expression that suggested she had no idea. "Eleven forty-five, maybe a little later," she replied vaguely. If you check Kendal's calls, it'll be about two or three minutes after he received that call," she continued.

"I'll do that," replied Carmichael.

Carly smiled an arrogant smirk of a smile, which irritated Carmichael. Whether it was her manner or her apparent complete lack of sorrow at the death of her friend, he wasn't sure. But what was for certain was that Carmichael couldn't warm to Carly Wolf. And, as such, as far as he was concerned, she was firmly on his list of suspects.

"I understand you and Kendal used to be an item," he remarked.

"An item!" replied Carly, contemptuously. "You make it sound like we were royalty."

"Answer my question, please," Carmichael instructed, his voice controlled, but his words were delivered to ensure Carly was in no doubt that he wasn't prepared to take any nonsense from her.

From the irritated look on her face, it was clear Carly wasn't used to being told what to do and it was even more evident that she didn't like it. "We were an item," she replied, her enunciation childishly and deliberately extenuating the words *an item*. "But that ended months ago, when I realised he was a serial cheat. Does that answer your question?"

Carmichael nodded. "It does," he replied. "But I understand Kendal was still interested in you. Did he talk about you getting back together when you were walking to the Fairfax Hotel?"

Carly rolled her eyes. "I can only imagine you got that idea from sad-boy Swift over there," Carly remarked indignantly. "However, if you must know, he did, but I was having none of it, Inspector. And, to be honest, when he got that call, I was happy for the excuse to leave him there and head off back on my own."

"I see," replied Carmichael. "And when you got back to the hotel, what did you do then?"

"Who said I went back to the hotel?" replied Carly, her conceited poise having once more returned.

"So, what did you do?" Carmichael enquired.

"I came here," replied Carly. "I had a few drinks and then, at closing time, I took young Luke over there back to my room at the Fairfax and, well, I'm sure I don't have to share all the details."

As she spoke, a smug grin returned to Carly's face, as if she was revelling in her attempt to shock Carmichael.

Carmichael looked over at the barman, who was serving another customer, but found time as he did to shoot a friendly smile in Carly's direction.

"Who do you think killed Kendal?" Carmichael asked.

"Other than me, it could be anyone of the so-called friends of his," she replied matter-of-factly, and without taking any time to consider the question. "Of course, Luke will vouch for me, but if I were you, I'd have a chat with Martin and Gabby. For different reasons, they both have reasonable grounds to want him dead."

"Which are?" Carmichael enquired.

"Well, Martin's been in his shadow for years," replied Carly. "Other than his knack for making money, Martin's a bit of a waste of space and has always been in awe of Kendal. And, to be honest, Kendal knew it and could be quite patronising with him at times."

Carmichael listened intently but remained silent.

"As for Gabby," she continued, her tone changing to one of even more distain, "she's just like some love-struck twelve-year-old, patiently waiting for Kendal to get back with her."

Carly paused, took a sip of the yellowish-brown liquid from her glass and then stared directly into Carmichael's eyes, with a slight smirk on her face.

"Maybe one of them finally had enough of him and did something uncharacteristically audacious for once."

Carmichael stared intently into Carly Wolf's eyes. "I can assure you, Miss Wolf," he said abruptly, "there's absolutely nothing audacious about murder."

Chapter 13

Carmichael left Carly Wolf and made his way back to the table where Marc Watson, Rachel Dalton, Martin Swift, and Gabby Johns had remained while he'd been at the bar. Upon his arrival, he remained standing.

"We'll need formal statements from you both," he said, his eyes fixed first on Swift then moving slowly onto Gabby Johns. "You can either come into the Police Station to do that or you can do it now, with my officers, if that's easier."

Martin Swift and Gabby Johns exchanged a sideways look then nodded in unison.

"We may as well do it now," replied Gabby Johns.

"Good," said Carmichael with a smile. "Then I'll leave you to it."

As he spoke, Carmichael finally noticed Cooper and his wife, who were sat together some distance away. "I'll see you both back at Kirkwood," he added, his last remark aimed at Watson and Dalton, although his attention was firmly on their colleague and his wife in their striking, yet unusual, outfits.

"Right you are, sir," replied Watson, who had already made his mind up that he'd be taking the statement of the attractive Gabby Johns and leaving Rachel to interview Martin Swift.

"And while you're about it, I'd also like you to take statements from Carly Wolf and the barman Luke," added

Carmichael, his comments directed in a hushed voice at his two officers.

Watson nodded and smiled back at his boss, again having taken no time at all to decide which one he was going to interview.

* * * *

"Good afternoon," Carmichael remarked with a smile as he reached the Coopers' table. "I'd heard you were both interested in Steampunk, but I hadn't expected to see you here."

Julia Cooper smiled up at her husband's boss who loomed over them as they sat at their table. "We were just remarking on how surprised we are to see you here as well," she replied.

"I assume it's a case?" Cooper added as soon as his wife had finished talking.

Carmichael nodded. "Yes," he replied. "There's been a murder. A man called Kendal Michelson. His body was found on the beach this morning."

The Coopers exchanged a look of surprise.

"We were supposed to be given a talk by him earlier today," remarked Julia, her voice trembling. "That explains why he never showed."

"When was that?" Carmichael enquired.

"This morning," replied Cooper. "We had to make do with a rather boring talk about Jules Verne from that guy, Martin Swift, who Rachel seems to be ushering over to another table. Is he a suspect?"

Carmichael turned his head to watch as Rachel Dalton and Martin Swift made their way towards one of the only empty tables left in Harri's Bar.

"Yes," replied Carmichael as soon as he'd returned his attention back on the Coopers. "He, the woman with Marc

51

Watson, and the young lady I was speaking to few minutes ago, were friends of the dead man. In fact, they all had dinner with him last night, shortly before he was murdered."

"How was he killed?" Cooper asked.

Carmichael took a deep breath. "Gruesomely," Carmichael replied. "He was found this morning on the beach, impaled by his own sword."

"How awful," remarked Julia.

"Do you want me to report back to help out?" Cooper asked.

Carmichael shook his head. "No need," he replied with a smile. "We're going to have a debrief later once we have statements from those three, but I can update you on that in the morning. You both enjoy what's left of your day."

With relief etched across her face, Julia Cooper smiled. "Thanks, Inspector," she said. "We've one more event to attend today, so that's good news."

"Have we?" Cooper said, the surprise in his voice suggesting his wife's announcement was news to him.

"Yes," Julia replied firmly. "That author chap's giving a talk later at the library. I think he'll be very entertaining."

Cooper glanced in his wife's direction and nodded slowly, a resigned nod that indicated clearly to Carmichael that his trusty sergeant would far rather be involved in the murder investigation than attend the talk.

"Anyway," Carmichael said, with a broad smile on his face, "it was nice to see you again Julia, and I'll see you in the morning Paul."

The Coopers watched as Carmichael made his way towards the exit of Harri's Bar.

"I thought you said you didn't want to attend any more events today," remarked Cooper.

Julia Cooper rolled her eyes skywards. "I don't, but it's your day off, Paul," she replied resolutely. "You spend most of your life with those three. And, anyway, I thought it would be nice to go out together for a meal somewhere tonight."

Cooper leant over and kissed his wife's cheek. "That's a relief," he said. "And a meal this evening sounds perfect, just as long as I can go home and get changed first; these tight trousers are killing me."

Chapter 14

The main seating area at Harri's Bar was too crowded and far too noisy for Watson and Dalton to take statements so, after brandishing their identity cards at Luke, the barman, they made use of the bar manager's office and the staff canteen to conduct their interviews.

"After we've finished talking with Ms Johns and Mr Swift, we'll also need to talk with you two," Watson had advised Luke and Carly Wolf as they passed by them into the back office.

Luke obediently nodded in an instant and, despite a look of petulant indignation, Carly Wolf also made a slight movement of her head, which suggested to Watson she heard, understood, and would begrudgingly consent to his command.

* * * *

Carmichael figured it would be an hour or two before Watson and Rachel arrived back at the Kirkwood Police Station, so he decided to take a walk back to the murder scene, which was no more than ten minutes away from Harri's Bar.

It was 3:15pm on a beautiful bright Sunday afternoon and, had his thoughts not been so focused on the case, it would have been a perfect day to take a leisurely stroll along the seafront and down onto the beach.

The wide pavement that skirted the flat, sandy beach was busy with holidaymakers, day trippers, young couples hand-in-hand and, of course, more than the odd Steampunk enthusiast – who, to Carmichael's surprise, no longer seemed out of place in the sunny seaside town.

When he finally arrived at the steps leading down onto the beach, Carmichael paused and took a few moments to survey the scene. In front of him, the flat, sandy beach stretched out far into the distance with no apparent end and not a hint of sea on the horizon, although he knew it was out there, somewhere. Michelson's body, the small tent that had shrouded him and Stock's small, white-suited army of crime scene investigators had long since departed, leaving the beach looking none the worse for the tragedy that it had witnessed less than twenty-four hours earlier.

To Carmichael's right, the North Coast Road continued, a straight road, which Michelson would have walked down from the China Garden on his way to the Fairfax Hotel, that crumbling edifice, which stood across the road behind him.

What struck Carmichael was just how open it was. It would have been dark when Michelson went on to the beach the night before and, at such a late hour, there would have been few people around. However, even taking account of both factors, Carmichael found it hard to believe the murderer hadn't been observed. If not a passer-by, surely someone staying at one of the hotels on the front, or a resident of one of the many balconied flats that looked out onto Southport beach would have seen something.

He was just about to make his way down onto the beach when his mobile rang.

"It's Sergeant Newman," announced the caller. "I just thought you'd like to know, we've got a man here who's just walked into the station and confessed to the murder on Southport beach."

Carmichael froze as he absorbed Newman's message. "I'll be straight over," he replied, before turning on his heels and heading back down the North Coast Road in the direction of his parked car.

Chapter 15

Carmichael sat up and gazed across into the unshaven face of the shabbily-dressed man who was claiming to be Kendal Michelson's assassin.

"Mr Carr," Carmichael remarked, looking down at the few scribbled notes he'd made on his notepad, "let's just recap. You were sleeping rough in the doorway of one of the houses opposite the seafront when the dead man approached you and started shouting at you and kicking you."

"That's correct," replied the scruffy man who nervously fidgeted across the table.

"You then followed the man down onto the beach where you confronted him and, in the struggle that ensued, you killed him," Carmichael added.

"It was self-defence," said Carr in a loud voice. "It was him that had the knife."

"And tell me, Mr Carr," continued Carmichael, "how many times did you stab your attacker?"

Bernard Carr took a few seconds to consider his answer. "I don't recall," he replied. "It all happened so quickly."

"Then what did you do?" Carmichael asked.

"What do you mean?" replied Carr his voice emphasising his apparent confusion.

Carmichael held out his arms in Carr's direction with

the palms of his hands facing upward. "Did you take away anything from the dead man? Did you run away? What did you do, Bernard?"

"I don't remember," replied Carr vaguely. "I suppose I just ran away."

"And where did you stay last night?" Carmichael enquired.

"I went back to the doorway and kipped down there until about six this morning, then I jumped on the train and came over to Kirkwood," continued Carr. "It was when I was on the train I realised I needed to hand myself in."

Carmichael shook his head. "Do you know what I think, Bernard?" he remarked. "I think this is a complete and utter tissue of lies. I don't think you had anything to do with the murder. In fact, I would not be surprised, when I check the CCTV footage, to discover that you were nowhere near where the murder took place. Isn't that the truth?"

Bernard Carr gazed ruefully at the table top between him and Carmichael and shrugged his shoulders.

Carmichael shook his head despairingly. "Why are you confessing to a crime you had nothing to do with, Bernard?" he enquired. "No court in the land would convict you of the murder, but wasting police time is another matter."

"How long would I get for wasting police time?" Bernard asked.

Carmichael shook his head for a second time, but this time with more feeling. "Officer," he said, addressing the uniformed policeman standing behind him. "Get this time-waster out of my sight."

As the tall, broad-shouldered PC escorted Bernard Carr out of the interview room, Carmichael rested his head in his hands. It never failed to amaze him why anyone would confess to crimes they hadn't committed, but over the years he must have met dozens of would-be-offenders and most of them were like Bernard Carr, hopelessly inadequate liars.

* * * *

Watson had finished taking statements from Gabby Johns and Carly Wolf for a good fifteen minutes before Rachel Dalton arrived at the door to the manager's office, where she spied her colleague leaning back in the luxuriant red-leather chair, gazing at the ceiling with his hands folded behind the back of his head.

"Penny for them," she said, a comment which didn't alter her colleague's relaxed demeanour, but prompted him to move his head slightly to make eye-contact with Rachel.

"Do you ever feel that you've missed your vocation?" he enquired rather obtusely.

Rachel's forehead creased as she tried to absorb her colleague's question. "Like being a captain of industry," she replied, assuming that that was where Watson was going.

"Precisely," Watson replied with enthusiasm. "I'm sure that if I'd taken a different track I could be MD somewhere by now, managing hundreds of people and responsible for millions of pounds of sales."

With a look of scepticism etched across her face and eyebrows raised, Rachel walked over to the chair previously occupied by Gabby Johns and then Carly Wolf, and sat down.

"Dream on Lord Sugar," she remarked before placing her notebook on the table in front of her and leaning back in the chair. "So how did it go with those two?"

With his delusions of power dissipated, Watson sat upright. "They went fine," he replied. "Nothing earthshattering though. Neither claim to have had any lingering designs on Kendal Michelson. To be honest, I believe Carly Wolf but

I got the impression that Gabby Johns still had the hots for him."

"What gave you that impression?" Rachel asked.

"Years of experience of women and interviewing people," replied Watson vaguely. "She's trying hard to retain the impression that his death hasn't had any effect on her, but inside she's in bits, in my view."

"But you don't think Carly Wolf is bothered?" Rachel added.

Watson shook his head. "Nah," he replied instantly. "She's a tough little cookie. She's moved on from her relationship with Kendal, and from how she talked, Carly's not the slightest bit upset by his death."

Rachel shook her head. "It's really weird, isn't it," she remarked. "These are two women that have had relationships with the dead man. Not one-night-stands or brief dalliances, but serious long-term relationships. They are still friends with him, share his passion for Steampunk, they go out for dinner with him on the evening that he dies, but neither seem to show, or want to show, any signs of being remotely upset by his gruesome death. That's not normal behaviour."

Watson nodded. "You're right Rachel," he concurred. "It is a bit strange."

"Do you think either of them could be our killer?" Rachel asked.

Watson shrugged his shoulders. "Who knows?" he replied nebulously. "Ex-partners have to be prime suspects, so I'd not rule either of them out at this stage. Gabby doesn't have an alibi for the time he was killed, so it could be her, I suppose. Carly, on the other hand, is adamant she was with the barman Luke at the time of Kendal's death. So, depending upon what he says, she could well be in the clear."

Rachel nodded. "I see," she replied.

"Anyway, how did you get on with Martin Swift and Carly's latest conquest?" Watson asked.

"I had an interesting discussion with Martin Swift," Rachel remarked. "Again, he showed little sign of emotion regarding Kendal's death, but it's clear he did have a strong affection for the dead man. To be honest, I got the impression he idolised him."

"Really," replied Watson. "What made you think that?"

"It was just the way he talked about him," continued Rachel. "They had been friends for years and I got the impression Kendal was Martin's hero."

"So, you don't think he's the killer then?" Watson asked.

Rachel paused for a few seconds before responding. "I wouldn't rule him out," she replied. "I can't think of a motive for him killing Kendal, but like Gabby Johns, he's not got an alibi for the time of Kendal's death."

"And what about Luke?" Watson enquired. "What did he have to say for himself?"

Rachel took a deep breath before referring to the notes.

"His name is Luke Barrett-Hobbs, he's nineteen years old, lives at home in Southport with his parents and has worked in Harri's Bar for about six months."

"With a name like that he sounds like one of your country-set," remarked Watson in an insulting, off-hand manner, sadly all-too-familiar to Rachel. "Did he verify Carly's story from last night?"

Rachel ignored Watson's acidic aside. "He maintains that Carly got to the bar just before twelve last night," she replied. "Luke's sure about the time as his shift was due to end at one and when Carly arrived she came straight up to him, ordered a Jack Daniels and asked him when his shift finished. He says he checked his watch and told her in just over an hour."

"And does Luke Barrett-Knobbs corroborate Carly's

claim that they spent the night together at the Fairfax Hotel?" Watson enquired.

Rachel elected to ignore her colleague's infantile alteration of Luke's surname. "Yes, he maintains they went straight there after his shift finished and he left this morning at around 7am."

Watson leaned back in the leather chair and nodded. "So, it looks like Carly is in the clear."

As he spoke, Rachel's mobile beeped to indicate the arrival of a message. She took the phone from her pocket and looked at the screen with an expression suggesting to her colleague that she'd just received something of significance.

"What is it?" Watson enquired.

Rachel looked back at Watson. "Martin Swift told me that they'd had a few photos taken at the restaurant last night by the waiter. I asked him to send them through to me and they've just arrived."

Watson shrugged his shoulders. "And will they help us solve the case?"

"Maybe not," replied Rachel as she turned the screen to show him the photo she was looking at, "but they do beg a big question," she continued.

Watson gazed at the photo, but by the expression on his face, he clearly couldn't work out what Rachel was referring to.

"I don't get it," he remarked. "What's so significant about this photo?"

Rachel allowed herself a self-satisfied smile. "Look at Kendal Michelson," she remarked. "What's noticeable about him?"

Watson looked intently again at the photograph on the small screen then shook his head. "I've no idea what you're talking about, Rachel," he conceded. "What is it that's so important?"

"His helmet," replied Rachel. "His bright, shiny silver helmet with that trumpet contraption. As I recall, there wasn't a helmet near his body, which suggests that either he left it somewhere after these photos were taken or, more likely, someone has taken it. Possibly his killer."

Chapter 16

It was just after 5pm when the three officers assembled at Kirkwood Police Station for the debrief.

Carmichael had received a copy of Dr Stock's autopsy report and, having read it, conveyed the gist of it to his two colleagues. He then updated Watson and Dalton on his interview with Bernard Carr, before listening intently to their summaries of the statements of Gabby Johns, Carly Wolf, Martin Swift, and Luke Barrett-Hobbs.

Much to Watson's annoyance, Carmichael instantly spotted the helmet Kendal Michelson was wearing in the photograph at the Chinese Restaurant and, like Rachel, wondered why it wasn't near the body when they found him.

"His mobile wasn't on him either," Carmichael remarked. "So why would the killer take his mobile and his helmet, but leave his wallet and his expensive gold pocket-watch?"

For a few seconds, both Watson and Rachel pondered Carmichael's rhetorical question.

When neither was able to give any possible answer, Carmichael expanded further. "And why would Michelson lie on his back and allow someone to ram his own sword into him like that."

With perplexed expressions, his team once more remained silent.

"From Stock's report, there appears to be absolutely no

sign of a struggle," Carmichael continued. "You'd expect him to, at the very least, move slightly to try and escape before the sword entered his body. But Stock's report is clear. The sword was driven straight down vertically into him and it looks like he just lay there and let it happen. That doesn't make any sense."

"Maybe it was some sort of assisted suicide," suggested Rachel, although by the sound of her voice it was evident that she wasn't completely convinced about the hypothesis she was making.

Carmichael shrugged his shoulders. "Maybe," he remarked, "but that's one hell of a way to die. If he wanted to commit suicide, surely there are less painful ways to do it."

"But these Steampunk people are weirdoes," announced Watson, glibly. "Maybe dying like this isn't so strange to them."

Carmichael looked up at Watson with a mystified expression on his face.

"I feel I should disagree with you, Marc," he remarked, "but, in fairness, I know so little about this movement, I actually don't know what to think."

Rachel shook her head. "I certainly couldn't see myself being interested in Steampunk," she conceded, "however, from what I've seen, I don't think they're dangerous. They're just interested in all that Jules Verne-type stuff."

Carmichael nodded. "As always, we keep an open mind," he remarked, "but our prime focus must be on this being a murder, plain and simple."

Watson and Rachel suspected what was coming next, and they weren't wrong.

"Okay," continued Carmichael, "let's record what we know, what we've still to find out and start to make a list of our potential suspects."

Rachel stood up, trying hard not to look at Watson, whose expression, she knew, would have almost certainly made her snigger. She moved quickly towards the whiteboard and grabbed the blue marker-pen. "Which list do you want us to start with?" she enquired.

"Let's start with the things we know," replied Carmichael, which was no surprise to his two officers, as for every murder case they'd ever conducted with Carmichael, they'd always make these lists and the facts always came first.

It took the three officers less than thirty minutes to complete their three lists, which read as follows:

Facts (written in blue):
1. Kendal Michelson died between Midnight and 2 am.
2. He'd spent that evening at the China Garden, a Chinese restaurant on the North Coast Road with Carly Wolf, Gabby Johns, and Martin Swift.
3. He took a call on his mobile, shortly before he died, less than ¼ mile from where his body was found.
4. He didn't struggle with his killer.
5. Between leaving the restaurant and his body being discovered, he'd lost his helmet and his mobile phone was not recovered at the scene.

Unknowns (written in green):
1. Who killed Kendal Michelson?
2. Why was he killed?
3. Who called him on his mobile shortly before he died?
4. Where is his helmet?
5. Where is his mobile?

Potential suspects (written in red):
1. Gabby Johns (no firm alibi)
2. Martin Swift (no firm alibi)
3. Carly Wolf & Luke Barrett-Hobbs (would have to be jointly involved)
4. Bernard Carr (doubtful, but has confessed)

"Have we missed anything?" Carmichael asked.

Watson and Rachel shook their heads.

"In that case," Carmichael continued, "your main task tomorrow, Rachel, is to check with Kendal's mobile provider the activity on his mobile in the forty-eight hours prior to his death. I particularly want to know who it was he was speaking to when Carly Wolf left him last night."

Rachel Dalton nodded.

"And I want you to check out the CCTV footage in and around that area," Carmichael added. "Find out who went down on that beach last night. I also want you to look for anyone wandering around with Kendal's helmet and see if there's any footage of Carly Wolf and Luke. I want to know if their story about last night is accurate or just some concoction of lies to cover-up for one or both of them."

"Will do," replied Rachel with enthusiasm.

"What about me?" Watson enquired. "What do you want me to focus on?"

Carmichael rubbed his chin with the palm of his hand. "I want you to speak with Cooper," Carmichael replied. "I want you both to go to Kendal's workplace and do some digging. Find out what sort of person he was and see if there's anything from his working life that could have led to his death."

"No problem," replied Watson. "I'll call him tonight and set it up."

"What are you going to focus on?" Rachel enquired, her eyes fixed on her boss.

"I'm going to speak with Kendal's father, I want to find out from him what sort of son Kendal was. Then, if I've time, I'm going to track down the owner of Harri's Bar," announced Carmichael. "I want to double-check the alibi Gavin Michelson gave you and Marc."

"Surely you don't suspect Kendal's father of killing him?"

Rachel remarked, her puzzled expression confirming her doubts.

Carmichael smiled. "Not strongly enough to add him to our suspects list, but we all know family members are, sadly, too often the perpetrators of crimes like this, so we need to make sure his alibi is completely water-tight."

Carmichael looked at his watch. It read 5:50pm.

"Which leaves us with this evening," he remarked. "I suspect most will have already gone home by now, but for the rest of this evening, I want to know as much as I can about Kendal Michelson's involvement with Steampunk. We need to get ourselves back over to Southport and if there are any of those people still around, we need to talk with them. It may have no bearing at all on his murder, but while these people are still here, let's see if they can tell us anything new about Kendal."

Chapter 17

It was close to midnight by the time Carmichael arrived home.

Having decided to split up to maximise the number of Steampunk enthusiasts they could speak to before they departed, Carmichael had sent Rachel to the train station while he and Watson scoured the bars and restaurants in Southport. His sergeant took responsibility for everything east of Lord Street, while he worked his way through the surprisingly numerous inns and eateries located between Southport's main thorough-fare and the seafront.

Other than the common response of genuine grief and a sense of shock and disbelief that something so heinous could have taken place during the event, Carmichael learned nothing in the four hours he'd wandered from pub to bistro. Nobody claimed to have known Kendal Michelson, although a few did know of him and had seen him about at previous events. And, from his mobile phone conversations with Rachel and Watson as he drove home along the winding country roads, Carmichael learned that they'd had a similar response. The only small potential piece of evidence they found was uncovered by Rachel, when a young couple from Wigan thought they may have seen Kendal with someone walking in the town at about midnight. The couple maintained that they were just coming out of a small restaurant when two people, one of them matching Kendal's description, marched past them. According to the prospective witnesses, the couple were walking very quickly and, although they couldn't remember much about the person with him, they said his companion was wearing jeans and a hoodie. They thought it was a female, as they both recalled commenting to each other on the strong smell of a distinctive perfume shortly after their paths had crossed, which the young woman identified as Coco Channel, one of her own favourite fragrances. However, they were much more certain about the man whose striking red tunic and shiny silver helmet they remembered vividly. And, when they also mentioned that the man they saw had wispy dark sideburns, Rachel was certain that the man the couple had seen was Kendal Michelson.

"You're really late," remarked Penny, as her husband flopped down into his favourite comfortable armchair. "Is it really Gavin Michelson's son that's been murdered?"

Carmichael looked up in astonishment at his wife. "Is that how it's being reported?" he enquired. "I'd never heard of him before today. Is the father that renowned?"

Penny nodded. "Yes," she replied, her expression suggesting she was, not for the first time, amazed at how uninformed her husband was about well-known local people. "He's a self-made multi-millionaire confectioner," she continued. "He was born and raised in Barton Bridge and has a massive chocolate empire. You must have heard of The World of Chocolate, it's one of the premier brands of hand-crafted chocolates available."

Carmichael shook his head. "I can honestly say that I've never heard of either Gavin Michelson or The World of Chocolate," he confessed. "Mind you, I've learned quite a few things today. Up until this morning, I'd never heard of Steampunk, but now I'd fancy my chances on mastermind with it as my specialist subject."

"So, what happened?" Penny asked.

Carmichael puffed out his cheeks. "It's a weird one," he replied. "Kendal Michelson was found this morning with a sword embedded in his chest. His own sword at that. He was taking part in the Steampunk convention in Southport, which is apparently an annual event."

Penny nodded. "Yes, it's a massive event," she confirmed. "They've been going there for a good few years. Southport gets packed when it's on."

"So I found out," added Carmichael. "Anyway, there are no signs of a struggle and, apart from a few suspicious friends of the dead man as possible suspects, we've not got many leads so far."

"Do you think it was a random killing or was it planned?" Penny enquired.

Carmichael shrugged his shoulders. "It's not clear," he confessed, "but I'm leaning towards it being premeditated. I think he knew his killer, which is why there wasn't any sign of a struggle. But, of course, I could be wrong."

"Do you want a drink?" Penny asked with a friendly smile.

Carmichael shook his head. "No thanks," he replied before planting a kiss on his wife's lips. "I'm going to head on up to bed. I've got to get up early in the morning and do a bit of research into The World of Chocolate before I go to talk with Gavin Michelson, the king of chocolate. And, besides which, I'm absolutely shattered."

Chapter 18

Monday 15ᵗʰ August

By 7:40 am, Carmichael was up, showered, dressed, and sitting at the kitchen table with a coffee and a couple of slices of marmalade-laden toast, which he devoured rapidly, hardly chewing at all. He was engrossed in the information he was reading on the small tablet in front of him about Gavin Michelson and The World of Chocolate.

He didn't want to get to Michelson's house too early, so he'd figured that, if he left at 8:15am, he'd be there around 8:45am; a reasonable time, in his mind, to make a house call to the recently bereaved Michelson senior.

As his pupils flickered from left to right, scanning the information about the globally-renowned, locally-based chocolatier who, less than twenty-four hours before, Carmichael had never even heard of, the doorbell rang.

Carmichael rose and walked slowly down the hallway towards his front door. He was only half-way there when the unmistakable heavy sound of his son's size twelve feet resonated down the corridor.

Stopping in his tracks, Carmichael observed Robbie quickly open the door and usher his two best friends into the house.

With a quick, "Morning Mr Carmichael," from one

of Robbie's friends, the three teenage boys quickly rushed upstairs, leaving Carmichael as perplexed as his wife had sounded when she'd made him aware of this uncharacteristic early-morning behaviour.

Having returned to the kitchen table, Carmichael then spent the next thirty minutes genning up on the person who he planned to interview in more detail later that morning, interrupted only by the sound of Robbie's friends, some twenty-five minutes after they'd arrived, heading down the staircase and the sound of the front door closing shut as they presumably made their exit.

* * * *

It was another bright summer's morning. The sun had been up for almost two hours and, as his car glided down the narrow country lanes, Carmichael's thoughts about the case were briefly interrupted by the sight of a skein of maybe twenty or thirty geese flying no more than twenty metres off the ground, in an almost perfect v-formation. He switched off the radio and drew down the window so he could hear the piercing sound of their calls to each other as they made their way, presumably, to Martin Mere, the wildlife sanctuary a little over ten miles to the west.

Carmichael had seen this early morning migration before, but never with so many members in one regimented flyby and he was taken aback by the noise these large, yet graceful creatures made as they headed off to their daytime feeding place.

It took him twenty-five minutes to arrive at Gavin Michelson's house, an impressive modern-style building, set back from the road with strong, angular lines and large, gleaming windows.

The large, expensive-looking wooden gate was open,

allowing Carmichael to drive onto the gravel drive, where his car came to a rest. He walked slowly up to the front door, his shiny black shoes making a noisy crunching sound with each step he took on the deep, polar-white Cotswold chippings below.

Before he had a chance to ring the bell, the door opened and a young, slightly-built, dark-haired, young woman greeted him with a welcoming smile.

"Good morning," Carmichael remarked with as friendly a smile as he could muster. "My name is Inspector Carmichael. I'd like to speak with Mr Gavin Michelson."

As he spoke, Carmichael took out his identity card and pushed it towards the young woman at the door.

Having taken the identity card from his hand, she studied it carefully for a few seconds before handing it back to Carmichael. The young woman then smiled and shook her head.

"Mr Michelson is at work," she replied in a thick Spanish accent. "He left very early."

Carmichael had wondered whether Michelson senior would have gone to work that day, but had concluded that this was highly unlikely, given he'd only, the day before, been given the news regarding his son's murder.

"I assume he's at the factory?" Carmichael remarked.

"Yes," replied the woman enthusiastically, and with a broad smile. "It's on the high street." As she responded, she raised a tiny, thin arm and pointed in the direction Carmichael needed to take. "It's just five minutes away by car."

Carmichael smiled at the young woman and, without saying anything more, turned on his heels and walked back towards his black BMW.

He'd covered no more than ten paces when Carmichael stopped and turned to face the young woman who had answered the door.

"I take it you are the same person who my colleagues spoke to yesterday at Kendal Michelson's house?" he enquired.

"Yes," replied the woman. "I'm Carmen Martinez. I am the housemaid for both Mr Michelsons."

Carmichael nodded. "Do you live in one of these houses?" he asked.

Carmen nodded. "Yes, I have a room here," she replied.

Carmichael smiled again, turned back around to face his car, and carried on walking.

Carmen Martinez remained stationed at the open door until Carmichael's car had driven out of the drive and had disappeared down the lane. Once he was out of sight, the young housemaid closed the front door gently and picked up her mobile phone from the glass-topped table in the hallway.

* * * *

Rachel Dalton had arrived at Kirkwood Police Station at 8:45am. After purchasing a bacon roll and a large mug of skinny latte from the canteen, she made her way back to the office. Unlike her male colleagues, Rachel didn't mind doing desk-based investigations, particularly when she was left alone. So, when Carmichael had instructed her to check out the CCTV footage and the activity on Kendal Michelson's mobile, she was more than happy with her assignment. Settling down at her desk, Rachel decided to focus her efforts on finding the dead man's network provider, a relatively simple task, given that she'd noted down his number during her interview with Martin Swift the day before.

* * * *

Michelson's Antique Restoration Ltd was located in a small industrial unit tucked away down a road behind the old bank on a site that had, in years gone by, been a village basket works.

"It would have made much more sense if Carmichael had taken on this job," pronounced Watson, as Cooper's clapped-out Volvo came to rest under the huge sign which proclaimed Michelson's Antiques as 'The Premier Furniture Restorer, French Polisher and Antique Sourcing Agents in the North West'. "Carmichael only lives about a hundred yards down the road."

Cooper glanced sideways at his cantankerous colleague. "I think we've got the prime assignment," he remarked. "You hate desk work, so you wouldn't have liked Rachel's task and, if the boss has two interviews like you told me earlier, I reckon we've got the easy assignment."

Watson shrugged his shoulders before clambering out of the car. "Doesn't look much of an empire," he muttered under his breath before trudging towards the office door.

* * * *

Based upon the research he'd conducted that morning, Carmichael had discovered that The World of Chocolate was Gavin Michelson's brainchild. Lavishly heaped with praise, the business he'd built up from nothing was lauded by a host of reputable bodies as a text book example of a British entrepreneurial success. Located in a state-of-the-art, 30,000 square foot, modern, purpose-built, air-conditioned factory, The World of Chocolate was a far cry from its humble origins at the Michelson family kitchen table, almost four decades earlier.

Carmichael's online investigation had also informed him that Gavin Michelson's business employed up to 150 staff during peak production times. On its website, the company boasted about winning numerous awards and having been ranked in the Top 10 Chocolate Manufacturers in Europe, in eight of the last ten years.

It was, therefore, no surprise to Carmichael, when he drove through the gate, to discover the impressive façade of The World of Chocolate, with its ultra-modern, floor-to-ceiling, glass-walled reception area.

Carmichael parked his car in one of the visitor spaces in front of the imposing, glass entry door, clambered out of the car and, having passed through the revolving glass door, walked over to the reception area.

"Good morning, sir. How can we help you?" enquired the immaculately-presented young woman behind the front desk.

We, thought Carmichael, the use of the plural being clearly as important an element of the receptionist's training as her smart business suit, her carefully-painted fingernails and the fresh, welcoming smile that no doubt greeted every visitor presenting themselves at The World of Chocolate.

"Inspector Carmichael," he replied as he placed his identity card on the counter. "I'd like to speak with Gavin Michelson please."

"One moment, Inspector," the receptionist replied without bothering to look at his identity card. "I'll tell him you're here."

From her response and the fact that she'd not enquired whether he had an appointment, Carmichael surmised that the receptionist was expecting him, which probably meant Michelson's housemaid had called them.

"If you'd care to take the lift to the second floor," announced the receptionist, with her left hand, palm facing upward, motioning towards the polished-glass door to Carmichael's right, "Mr Michelson will meet you as you arrive."

Impressed with her efficiency, albeit a little robotic for his liking, Carmichael smiled, turned 90 degrees, and sauntered over to the lift.

* * * *

Michelson's Antique Restoration Ltd consisted of just four people; the late Kendal Michelson, a lady in her late-fifties called Kim Bolton, who appeared to run the office and manage all the administrative work, and two furniture restorers, dressed in well-worn, long brown overcoats, who introduced themselves as J.C. Palmer and Zorik Daniels.

At first sight, of the three, only Kim Bolton appeared to be distressed at the news of her employer's demise; her puffed eyelids and reddened eyes giving her grief away. When questioned, it became obvious that the death of Kendal Michelson also affected the two technicians, but they were clearly better at masking their feelings.

Each of the three work colleagues had been interviewed privately and each asked in turn the same questions.

"Do any of you know anyone who might have wanted to hurt Kendal?"

Each one had shaken their heads and said "no".

"What sort of person was he?" they'd all been asked. And again, their answers were similar.

"A lovable, friendly, but eccentric person," Kim Bolton had replied.

"A nice guy, although he was a bit of an oddball," Palmer had remarked.

"A good boss, but peculiar," was Daniels's response.

When asked about Kendal's friends, and whether there was anyone particular in his life, J.C. Palmer and Zorik Daniels appeared to be in total synch, with both remarking that Kendal had an impressive record in finding partners, but that Carly Wolf had been the main woman in his life, most recently.

Kim Bolton was more guarded in her response. "Kendal was a popular man," she'd initially replied, "but I never talked to him much about his friends outside work." When pushed by Watson, she'd confirmed that Kendal had several girlfriends and that Carly Wolf appeared to be the most recent lady in his life, although her description of Carly as "that cocky little nurse" made it plain what Kim Bolton thought of her.

They all remarked that they'd last seen him on Friday at 5pm when he'd left them to close up, so he could sort himself out for the Steampunk gathering that weekend.

"And what did you think of his involvement in Steampunk?" they were all asked.

"Strange, but harmless," was Kim Bolton's response.

"A totally bizarre thing for an adult to do," Palmer had replied.

"Weird, plain weird," was Daniels's summation, much to Watson's amusement and Cooper's evident, but discreetly-suppressed, embarrassment.

Having spent almost an hour gaining very little, the two officers looked sideways at each other as Daniels, the last of Kendal's colleagues, was leaving the room. With almost synchronised head movements, they agreed it was time to depart.

As they reached the door, Cooper turned to face the dead man's colleagues. "With Kendal passed on," he said as sensitively as he could, "who will now own the business?"

It was now the three colleagues' turn to exchanged furtive glances.

"Why, we all will," replied Kim Bolton. "Kendal has left this place to the three of us, as equal partners."

"That's if his will is true to what he told us," added J.C. Palmer.

"Which it will be," remarked Kim Bolton, curtly. "Kendal

was always true to his word." A comment that was received by both Palmer and Daniels with gentle nods, indicating they agreed with the group's spokeswoman on the matter.

"Really," Watson replied. "That was very generous of him."

"I'd also say that it's very unusual," whispered Cooper as the two officers headed off to the car.

"Why do you say that?" Watson asked.

"Well, for someone as young as Kendal, with no wife and no children, I'm surprised he'd have even thought about making a will?" replied Cooper.

Watson nodded. "Now you mention it," he remarked, "that is strange. Mind you, the more I get to know about Kendal Michelson the weirder he seems."

Chapter 19

Just as the receptionist had told him, when the doors of the lift opened on the second floor, Carmichael was greeted by Gavin Michelson.

"Good morning, Inspector," he remarked in a business-like fashion and with his right arm stretched out to shake Carmichael's hand.

"Good morning," Carmichael responded, as he took hold of Michelson's hand and shook it firmly for a few seconds. "I have a few more questions if that's okay with you?"

Gavin Michelson smiled and nodded gently. "Of course," he replied, "I'll help you as much as I can, although I have to say it's still not really sunk in."

"I can understand," replied Carmichael, sympathetically. "To be honest, I was surprised to see you at work today."

"Life must go on," Michelson replied.

Although he found Gavin Michelson's apparent stoicism a little bemusing, Carmichael didn't want to make any snap judgement of Michelson senior just because he'd gone back to work. Over the years, he'd seen countless people shortly after they'd experienced the shock of bereavement and, in his experience, the grieving process affected people in very different ways. He concluded that it was likely Kendal's father had yet to really accept his son had been murdered and was, in effect, still in denial.

"Follow me," Gavin Michelson instructed Carmichael. "We can use Ecuador."

The slightly greying but trim fifty-something marched Carmichael down the carpeted corridor at a pace, passing Peru, Dominica, Ghana, Nigeria and then eventually arriving at the door with Ecuador written in swirly, brown letters.

"I take it your offices are all named after the main cocoa producing countries," Carmichael remarked.

"Yes," replied Michelson as he opened the door to Ecuador. "We have ten meeting rooms so we named them after the ten major countries we deal with."

Carmichael entered the room, which was constructed with floor-to-ceiling walls of frosted glass. The only exception being the glass wall opposite the door, which looked down on the factory floor, an impressive well-ordered amalgamation of highly-polished hoppers, spotlessly-clean conveyors and a small army of workers beavering away in their crisp, white uniforms, matching white hats and white wellington boots.

"Now, what can I get you to drink?" Michelson enquired.

"White coffee with two sugars, please," replied Carmichael.

Michelson smiled, then without another word, departed, shutting the door behind him.

* * * *

"Well, they were a bundle of laughs and not a great deal of help either!" remarked Watson as he and Cooper sat together in Cooper's motionless Volvo.

"Apart from them all benefiting from Kendal's death," replied Cooper. "That's got to be a potential motive for murder."

"Maybe," replied Watson, who didn't sound convinced, "but can you really see any of those three being up to killing anyone, and certainly not with a sword."

Cooper smiled. "Shall we get back to Kirkwood and see how Rachel's getting on with Kendal's mobile and the CCTV images?"

Watson puffed out his cheeks and nodded. "I suppose we should," he replied, "but let's find a café first. I haven't eaten this morning and could murder a bacon bap and a large cappuccino."

* * * *

Carmichael only had to wait a matter of minutes before the door opened and Gavin Michelson returned with a small tray carrying two The World of Chocolate mugs of steaming coffee.

"Yours is the one on your right," announced Michelson as he thrust the tray towards Carmichael.

Carmichael took the mug and placed it down on the glass table.

"It's a very impressive facility you have here," he remarked, his head motioning towards the window overlooking the factory floor.

"Thank you," replied Gavin Michelson. "It has to be. The competition in our industry is fierce and unless you can manufacture efficiently, even at the high-quality end where we play, you'll not survive for too long."

"I'd like to ask you a few questions about Kendal if I may," said Carmichael, his considerate but firm gaze directed into Michelson's eyes. "What sort of person was he?"

Gavin Michelson leaned forward in his chair and fixed his stare on the coffee mug in front of him.

"He was a complicated young man," replied Michelson, his words spoken as if to excuse rather than in celebration. "He was bright and, with people and things he liked he was as passionate as anybody I have ever met."

"How do you mean?" Carmichael enquired.

"At his studies at Nottingham University, Kendal was totally absorbed. He got a first-class degree in classics," replied Michelson with pride in his voice. "And at his work, at the antiques business he set up, he was doing so well," continued Michelson. "But he was awful at relationships, although given what he'd been through, it's hardly surprising."

"And what had he been through?" prompted Carmichael.

"The death of his mother when he was so small," replied Michelson. "She died, when she was just thirty-five, from a sudden aneurysm. He was just seven years old. He took that so badly, as of course we all would if the same had happened to us at such a tender age."

Carmichael nodded, sympathetically.

"Then, to make matters even worse," continued Michelson, "his nanny, who I'd taken on after his mother died and with whom he'd built a very close bond, committed suicide when Kendal was just twelve."

"I see," replied Carmichael. "And you feel these events made him awkward socially?"

Michelson shook his head. "Not awkward," he replied. "Kendal was always the centre of attention and he could charm the birds from the trees, but he was careful never to get too friendly with people and when he felt he was getting close he'd abruptly cut them from his life."

"I was told he had many female friends," Carmichael continued. "Did this behaviour apply to them?"

"Especially to women," replied Michelson. "He could find a girlfriend easily enough, but few lasted."

"But a few did, though?" Carmichael remarked. "Like Carly Wolf, and I also understand Kendal had a reasonably long relationship with Gabby Johns."

Gavin Michelson shuffled uncomfortably in his seat. "Yes,

he was very keen on both, but for different reasons those relationships didn't last," he replied.

"And what about your relationship with your son?" Carmichael enquired. "How was that?"

To Carmichael's surprise, Gavin Michelson took a while before answering, as if he was searching for the right words.

"We got on rather well most of the time," Michelson finally replied. "We were more like friends than father and son, really, but not close friends."

"And did Kendal have no desire to join the family business?" Carmichael enquired.

"God no," responded Michelson. "Kendal made it abundantly clear from the age of about twelve that he had no interest whatsoever in joining me at The World of Chocolate. He maintained that business life was against his socialist principles. But, ironically for someone so set against the life his capitalist father had carved out for himself, my son had not done too bad a job building up his own little empire, albeit in antiques rather than chocolate."

Carmichael smiled. He'd spoken often to his own children about their chosen careers and, although none of them seemed too sure what they wanted to do, they'd made it abundantly clear to Carmichael that they did not want to join the police. So, in that respect, Carmichael could empathise totally with the man sat across the table from him.

"You told me yesterday that you last spoke with your son on Saturday morning and I understand from one of my officers that you were at home with a lady friend on Saturday evening; a woman called Harriett Hall."

"That's correct," Michelson replied. "We jointly own a bar in Southport. We had dinner at my house to talk about some ideas she had about growing the business."

"That will be Harri's Bar," remarked Carmichael.

"Yes," replied Michelson. "It's named after Harriett, although I'm the major shareholder."

"And when did Harriett leave?" Carmichael enquired.

"Did your officers not tell you that?" replied Michelson, his reply indicating a degree of frustration at Carmichael's questioning being directed at him, as if he was a possible suspect.

"Sergeant Watson and DC Dalton said you told them it was at around twelve," replied Carmichael without a flicker of a reaction to Michelson's apparent annoyance. "Is that correct?"

"It is," Michelson responded firmly. "But no doubt you will be asking Harriett in due course, too."

Carmichael nodded. "Yes," he replied. "I'll be going to see her directly after I've finished here. I assume I'll find her at Harri's Bar."

"I would expect so," replied Michelson, "but I'm not her keeper."

"I totally understand," remarked Carmichael.

"Now, if that's everything," Michelson abruptly announced, rising to his feet. "I have a business to run here and I imagine you've got more important things to do, like find my son's murderer."

Carmichael stood up, too and stretched out his hand. "You've been most helpful," he remarked. "I'll keep you fully informed on our progress and I can assure you, Mr Michelson, that we will catch the person who killed Kendal."

"Be sure you do, Inspector," Michelson replied, who shook Carmichael's hand, but only briefly, before gesturing with his left arm that his visitor should make his way to the exit.

Carmichael did as he was told and started to leave.

"One last thing," Carmichael said before he reached the door. "Your highly efficient receptionist appeared to be expecting me when I arrived this morning. Or did I just imagine that?"

Gavin Michelson smiled. "We were expecting you," he conceded. "Carmen called me after you'd left the house and I advised Rebecca that you'd be arriving."

"You have two very loyal and efficient employees there, in that case," replied Carmichael.

Gavin Michelson smiled broadly. "Trustworthiness, ingenuity, loyalty and competence are the four minimum requirements to work for me, Inspector," he said. "Without these four qualities you'd not last a day in my team."

"Really," replied Carmichael, who felt he was not only starting to understand Michelson senior a little better, but also appreciate how it was that father and son had chosen not to work together.

Chapter 20

It took Rachel less than an hour to identify Kendal Michelson's network provider and, within a further thirty minutes, she had his mobile activity statement on her screen, including all his most recent calls and transcripts of his last incoming and outgoing texts.

With a perplexed expression, Rachel slumped back in her chair, her hands clasped behind her neck as she read, then re-read several times the information in front of her. Unable to make any sense of it, she leant forward again, puffed out her cheeks and took a sip of her now stone-cold, skinny latte, which she quickly banished to the far end of her desk.

* * * *

They were still in Hazel's Coffee Break, one of only two cafes in Moulton Bank, when Watson's mobile started to buzz and vibrate on the table, with Carmichael's name emblazoned clearly on the small screen.

"It's the boss," remarked Watson as he picked up the mobile and placed it next to his ear.

"We've just this minute left," Watson lied, in answer to Carmichael's opening question.

"Nothing much," Watson then added, before listening to Carmichael's next question.

As he did, Cooper moved his head so that he was in Watson's eyeline. "Tell him about them inheriting the business," he whispered.

"Actually, there was one thing," Watson said as soon as Carmichael stopped speaking. "The three employees at Michelson's Antiques maintain that Kendal promised to leave the business to them in his will."

Carmichael listened intently to this as he sat in his car, which was still parked in The World of Chocolate's car park.

"Assuming there's some value in the business, I suppose that would be a motive for one of them to murder Kendal," he surmised aloud. "Did any of them strike you or Cooper as being potential murderers?"

"I'd have to say no," replied Watson. "But I guess it's possible."

"And what did they say when you asked them about their movements on Saturday evening?" Carmichael continued.

Watson's facial expression indicated to his colleague, sat opposite him, that he was struggling.

"I'm losing you, sir," he replied. "I think you might be in a bad reception area."

"I can hear you fine," replied Carmichael, his voice now slightly raised. "I'm not moving, I'm sat in the car in a car park."

"I'm really sorry, sir," Watson continued. "I don't know if you can hear me, but I'm only picking up every third or fourth word you're saying."

Frustrated by Watson's apparent inability to hear him properly, Carmichael raised his voice even louder.

"Look," he shouted, "I'm going to interview Harriett Hall. You and Cooper get yourselves back to Kirkwood and help Rachel out. We can have a debrief at two this afternoon."

"I think I got most of that," replied Watson, who was now speaking more loudly. "A debrief at two."

Irritated by his inability to finish his conversation with Watson, Carmichael ended the call, switched on the car's engine, and headed out of the car park in the direction of Southport.

Watson exhaled loudly, placed the mobile in his pocket and smiled at Cooper. "We forgot to ask them about their alibis for Saturday," he said. "The boss wants us in a debrief at two, so we better get back there and talk with them again."

Cooper raised his eyebrows. "So, that's what all that 'I can't hear you' nonsense was about," he said, although he was secretly impressed with his partner's resourcefulness.

* * * *

As Rachel Dalton finished her call, the office door opened and PC Dyer entered the room. "Here's the images the team have collected so far from the various private CCTV cameras in the seafront area of Southport from Saturday evening," he remarked with a playful grin, "and the recordings from the fifteen street cameras in the area, between nine o'clock on Saturday evening and two o'clock on Sunday morning, have all been set up for you to look at in the IT suite."

Rachel looked up from her desk.

"Thanks," she replied with a smile, "that was quick."

Chapter 21

At 11:30am on a Monday morning, Harri's Bar proved to be a very different place from the crowded, vibrant, noisy watering hole Carmichael had encountered less than twenty-four hours earlier. And, with a total absence of Steampunk aficionados, it appeared more calm, relaxed, and inviting, as far as he was concerned.

Luke Barrett–Hobbs, the young barman who had, by both their admissions, been Carly Wolf's conquest on the night of the murder, was the only member of staff in view, standing behind the smoothly-polished bar, fiddling with the positioning of the brightly-coloured beer towels.

"I'm looking for the manager," Carmichael announced as he reached the bar. "Is she available?"

Luke nodded. "Yes, she's out back in her office," he replied. "I'll get her for you."

Without bothering to wait for a response from Carmichael, the tall young man departed through the small, arched opening that led to the manager's office.

As he waited, Carmichael turned, lent his back on the bar and gazed around the large room. Except for two men sat alone at different tables, both with what looked like recently-started pints of lager, and a couple of women sat in the far corner leaning forward over their glasses of latte absorbed in their conversation, the place was practically deserted.

"Good morning," came a friendly, confident female voice from behind him.

Carmichael turned to be greeted by the warm smile of an attractive, late-thirty-something with shoulder-length, straight, strawberry-blond hair, piercing blue eyes and sparkling-white teeth, which seemed to glisten as she smiled. "I'm Harriett Hall. I believe you'd like to speak with me."

"My name's Inspector Carmichael," he replied. "I would like to talk to you, if I may, about Kendal Michelson's murder."

"Of course," she said with another smile. "Why don't we sit over there? It's always dead here on Monday mornings, so I'm sure we won't be disturbed."

As she spoke, Harriet Hall gestured with her arm in the direction of a table in the far corner of the room, yards away from any of the bar's four customers.

* * * *

Equipped with the information of the alleged whereabouts of Kim Bolton, Zorik Daniels, and J.C. Palmer on the evening of Kendal Michelson's murder, the two sergeants sat together in Cooper's trusty old Volvo.

"If any one of them murdered him, I'll eat your underpants," announced Watson.

Cooper glanced briefly at his colleague in the passenger seat. "You could be right, Marc," he concurred, "but they all have a motive for wanting Kendal dead and, until we check out their alibis, they have to be on our suspects list."

Watson gazed out of the side window. "Shall we verify their stories before we go back to the station?"

Cooper checked the time on the dashboard clock, it read 11:40am. "As we only have to be at Carmichael's debrief at two this afternoon, it should give us enough time," he replied.

"Let's go and talk with Mrs Palmer first, as the home address he gave us is just around the corner."

* * * *

"How can I help you, Inspector?" Harriett enquired, her polished smile lighting up her face.

"Well," replied Carmichael, "I understand that you had dinner with Gavin Michelson on Saturday evening. Is that correct?"

"Yes," confirmed Harriett, without hesitation. "We had dinner at his place. I have some ideas about expanding the business that I wanted to talk through with him."

"I understand you are partners?" remarked Carmichael.

"That's correct," Harriett replied.

"What time did you arrive?" Carmichael enquired.

"It was about eight-thirty," replied Harriett.

"And what time did you leave?" Carmichael continued.

"It was just before twelve," she replied.

"Thank you," said Carmichael. "That's pretty much what Mr Michelson told us too."

"Surely, he's not a suspect," remarked Harriett, her voice emphasising her surprise that the police could even consider her partner to be his son's killer. "They weren't particularly close, but there was no bad feeling between them, and Gavin wouldn't hurt a fly."

Carmichael shook his head. "No," he replied, "I can assure you that Mr Michelson is not a suspect, but we do need to verify where he was at the time Kendal was killed. It's just standard procedure."

By the changed expression on her face, it was clear that Harriett was now suitably reassured. "Well, if poor Kendal died between eight-thirty and twelve, it couldn't have been Gavin as he was most certainly with me."

"How well did you know Kendal?" Carmichael enquired.

Harriett Hall ran her fingers through her hair, pushing it away from her face. "I knew Kendal very well," she replied. "For a few years, Gavin and I lived together. It was when Kendal was in his late teens, so, in a way, you could even say he was family."

"Really," remarked Carmichael, who was somewhat taken aback by Harriett's admission. "But surely you're not that much older than Kendal?"

Harriett smiled. "I'm very flattered," she replied with another glint of her perfect teeth. "I'm forty in three weeks, Inspector, so there was nearly nine years' difference in our ages. When I first moved in with Gavin, Kendal was seventeen and I was a few weeks short of my twenty-sixth birthday. And before you ask, I can confirm that, at first, my age was a problem for Kendal."

"And how long were you and Gavin together?" Carmichael enquired.

"About four years," Harriett replied. "I left him after he'd had one-too-many affairs. That was a trait father and son had in common, I'm afraid. Part of their shared DNA, I guess you could say."

Once more, Harriett smiled broadly while again pushing back her hair.

"But you kept friends after the split?" Carmichael remarked.

"With both of them, yes," replied Harriett. "Gavin and I had already opened up this place before I left and part of the agreement we had was that we'd share the profits fifty-fifty, but that I'd have sole control over the running of it and I'd live upstairs in the flat rent-free."

"But Gavin mentioned to me that he was the majority shareholder," Carmichael added.

"Technically that's true," replied Harriett. "He bought

this place initially and was only prepared to allow me to own thirty per cent when we went our separate ways. However, in the contract I had him sign when we split, it states clearly that he cannot sell this business or make any material changes without my consent. So, if we were to sell, he'd get seventy per cent of the sale price, but he can't sell without my agreement."

Carmichael took a few seconds to look around the bar. "I'd say you managed to get yourself a great deal," he remarked with a wry smile.

"Oh yes," replied Harriett in a tone suggesting to Carmichael that the woman sat in front of him was a great deal more than just a pretty face.

* * * *

Rachel Dalton gazed up at the clock on the wall high above the large screen in the IT suite, it read 11:55am.

Having spent the last hour and a half pouring over multiple recordings of CCTV footage from the cameras in the area around where Kendal Michelson's body was found, Rachel decided to take a short break. She walked over to the water fountain, poured herself a small cup of ice-cold water, took a tiny sip, then returned with the cup to her desk. She was contemplating calling Carmichael to update him when she noticed a text on her mobile.

HI RACHEL – WE'RE CHECKIN OUT ALIBI'S OF KENDALS WORK COLLEAGUES. CARMICHAEL WANTS US ALL IN A DEBRIEF AT 2PM. JUST THOUGHT I'D LET YOU KNOW. ENJOY LOOKING THOUGH ALL THOSE CCTV IMAGES. MARC

Rachel sighed, placed the mobile next to her plastic cup of water and returned her gaze to the CCTV images on the screen in front of her.

* * * *

"So, tell me about Kendal," Carmichael asked. "What sort of man was he?"

Harriett Hall considered the question for a few seconds before responding. "He was a nice guy, really," she replied. "He could be as obstinate as his father and he was also a bit of a control freak, too, but I got on pretty well with him."

"Even when you were living with his Dad?" Carmichael enquired.

"As I said before, at first it was really tricky," Harriet conceded, "but I made a massive effort with Kendal back then and after about three or four months our relationship improved and, in the end, it was fine. In fact, when Gavin and I spilt up, Kendal was great with me, he even helped me out here for a short while in his vacations when he was at Uni."

Carmichael nodded. "And, of late, did you see much of Kendal?"

"Not since he and Carly split up," Harriet replied. "When they were together, they'd often come here in the evening, but since that all fizzled-out I've not seen him at all."

"That's right," remarked Carmichael. "I understand that Carly Wolf is your niece."

Harriett nodded. "She's my eldest sister's girl," replied Harriett. "Have you met her?"

Carmichael nodded again. "I met her here yesterday," he replied. "She's quite a character."

Harriett let out a loud roar of laughter. "That's one way to describe her," she replied.

"So, did you approve of their relationship?" Carmichael asked.

Harriett puffed out her cheeks while she considered how to answer. "I liked them both," she replied. "So, on one level, it was nice to see them together, but I did worry a little about

96

whether they'd last. Kendal was a lovely guy, but he was like his father, a serial womaniser. He was never going to be faithful to Carly and with her personality being so strong, she was never going to stand for it."

"Sounds like it was doomed from the outset," observed Carmichael.

Harriett smiled and nodded her head. "That's about the long and the short of it," she replied. "I was just glad they'd remained on good terms afterwards."

"Like you and Gavin?" Carmichael said.

Harriett put her head slightly to one side and shrugged her shoulders. "I guess so," she replied.

Carmichael took a deep intake of breath. "Do you know anyone who'd have wanted to kill Kendal?" he enquired.

Harriett folded her arms in front of her and leaned back in her chair. "At times, I suspect most of the women he'd ever dated," she remarked rather flippantly, "but he was such a likable guy, I can't see how anyone would want to hurt him."

"How did he and Carly get into this Steampunk craze?" Carmichael asked.

"It's not a craze in their eyes," Harriett replied. "It's more like a way of life to those people who are involved."

"Who was interested first?" Carmichael enquired, "Carly or Kendal?"

"Kendal has been actively involved since he was at university," replied Harriett. "He goes to the Lincoln asylum every year, that's the big annual event. And he does about three or four smaller gatherings, too, every year, including here in Southport."

"So, he introduced Carly to Steampunk then?" Carmichael continued.

"No," replied Harriett. "She got involved independently of Kendal, but I think she goes for an altogether different reason."

"Which is?" prompted Carmichael.

"To have the excuse to dress-up," replied Harriett. "She's a fashion nutcase, so Steampunk is like a dream come true for Carly. And if you hadn't noticed, my beautiful niece, who I love to bits, adores being the centre of attention, so Steampunk is a perfect medium to strut her stuff."

Carmichael allowed himself a wry smile. "I understand," he replied, remembering how effectively Carly had turned the heads of most of the people in the bar, the day before, when she made her entrance. "You've been a great help, Harriett," he continued before standing up and offering his hand to the manager of the bar.

"No problem," replied Harriett before rising herself and then, with a final glint of her trademark smile, gently but warmly shook Carmichael's hand.

Chapter 22

It was 1:40pm when Cooper and Watson appeared at the doorway to the IT suite. Rachel Dalton had spent the last few hours with her eyes glued to the nine separate pieces of surveillance footage on the large screen in front of her.

"How's it going?" Watson enquired with an impish grin on his face.

Rachel turned her head to the left so she could make eye contact with her colleagues. "It's slow going, but I've found a few images that may prove useful," she said.

"So where are these cameras located?" Cooper asked, as he pointed at the screens.

"The top three are of the coast road," replied Rachel. "One from the top end near the sailing club, one at a few hundred metres from where Kendal's body was found and the other is from further down the road, near the funfair. The three middle images are from cameras located on Lord Street and the bottom three are from a few of the side roads leading from Lord Street to the coastal road."

"So, what is it you've found?" Cooper enquired.

Rachel stopped the recordings and turned her chair to face her colleagues.

"We've got the debrief in fifteen minutes, why don't we wait until then?" she suggested. "It will save me repeating myself and give me another ten minutes to check these recordings."

"Suits me," replied Watson, "I want to grab a coffee anyway, do you want anything, Paul?"

Cooper shook his head. "No, I'm fine."

"I'll have a latte, if you're offering," Rachel shouted as her colleague disappeared down the corridor.

* * * *

As always, Carmichael started his meeting at precisely the time he'd set, on this occasion it was 2pm.

"Right then," he announced energetically, "who wants to start?"

"We better start with Rachel," remarked Watson sarcastically, "as she's been very guarded about what she's discovered on those CCTV recordings and the suspense is killing me."

"That's fine by me," replied Rachel, "but it may be easier if we went to the IT suite so I can show you."

"Ok then," continued Carmichael, "let's go through there and you can show us what you've found."

A few minutes later the four officers had relocated themselves in the IT suite and were facing the nine screens.

Rachel expertly reset the time of the images to 11:44pm.

"If you recall," she announced confidently, "the only potential sighting we have of Kendal that evening was from that young couple from Wigan who I talked to last night. They said they might have seen Kendal as he and someone else, who we presumed to be Carly Wolf, were walking into the town at about midnight."

"That's right," concurred Carmichael. "It was when they were leaving a restaurant."

Rachel nodded eagerly. "So, initially, I looked to see if I could find some images from around that time."

"Makes sense," Carmichael remarked.

Rachel started the recordings. "The image on the right, in the middle row, is from a camera just ten yards from the restaurant," she announced. "If you look carefully you'll see what is, unmistakably, Kendal Michelson walking quickly down the road."

Rachel Dalton's three colleagues looked intently at the surveillance images. There was no doubt that the person they were looking at was Kendal Michelson resplendent in his Steampunk regalia.

"Well he's wearing that unmistakeable helmet in these images," remarked Carmichael.

"Hang on," said Watson. "I thought your witnesses said he had someone with him. He appears to be alone here."

"Well remembered," replied Rachel, with a hint of sarcasm in her voice. "And they also said they saw him walking towards the seafront. In this clip, he's clearly alone and walking away from the coastal road."

"That doesn't make any sense," remarked Cooper.

"Unless the images we're looking at here aren't at the time the couple saw him," Carmichael observed.

That was exactly my thinking, too," replied Rachel, "and, if you move the images forward by just seven minutes, you can see Kendal walking back down the street but in the other direction. However, this time he appears to be with someone else."

Rachel reset the time to 11:51pm and started the recording.

The group of officers looked intently at the screen. Although the pictures weren't particularly clear, the distinctive image of Kendal Michelson was obvious for all to see, however the person with him was less clear.

"Is that a man or a woman?" Carmichael asked, straining hard to see. "Can you enlarge that image?"

Rachel froze the frame and expertly zoomed in on the

image of the two individuals. However, the picture was very poor and, with them walking away from the camera, it was impossible to get a good look at Kendal's companion, who was wearing jeans and trainers and had the back of their head covered with a hoodie top.

"I'm assuming that it's a female," remarked Rachel, "as, if you recall, my witnesses did remark on the strong smell of Coco Channel perfume when the couple rushed past them, but the image could be male or female."

"I think it's a woman," Cooper remarked. "That walk looks more like a woman's walk than a man's."

"I agree," added Rachel.

Carmichael wasn't so sure. "Run it forward a little," he remarked.

Rachel did as she was told and, having viewed the couple walking together, Carmichael found himself concurring with his colleagues. "You're probably right," he remarked. "It is more likely to be a woman than a man, but, at this stage, I'm not prepared to exclude it being male."

"Have you found any other images of Kendal?" Cooper enquired, as soon as the figures disappeared from sight.

"Not yet," replied Rachel, "but I've still got tons of images to go through."

Carmichael nodded. "Good work so far, Rachel," he acknowledged. "How about Kendal's mobile activity, any developments on that?"

Rachel raised her eyebrows. "There are," she responded with a puzzled expression, "and what I found doesn't make sense."

"Why?" Carmichael enquired.

"Because," Rachel replied, "according to his network provider's report, Kendal's last call was made on Friday at four thirty in the afternoon. He didn't receive any calls after two thirty-five on Saturday and, although he received three text messages on Saturday evening, and a couple yesterday morning, the last text message he sent was also on Friday."

"So, either he had two mobiles," suggested Carmichael, "or Carly Wolf's story about him receiving a call when they were walking into town late on Saturday evening was a lie."

"Exactly," replied Rachel.

"So, who was he talking to in the last texts and calls he received?" Carmichael asked.

"Judging by the numbers, the calls all appear to be work related," Rachel explained. "Two of the incoming texts on Saturday are from people he went to dinner with on Saturday evening, Martin Swift and Gabby Johns. They were sent at five thirty and six twenty and were both basically saying the same thing, namely that they were looking forward to seeing Kendal that evening at China Gardens."

"What about the other one on Saturday?" Carmichael enquired.

"That was from Harriett Hall, sent at ten to seven," replied Rachel. "That one seems to have been sent to Kendal by mistake. I think she meant to send it to his father."

"Why, what did that one say?" Carmichael enquired.

Rachel picked up the report she'd printed out and read the text message.

HI, LOOKING FORWARD TO SEEING YOU LATER. I THINK YOU'LL LIKE MY PROPOSAL FOR HARRI'S BAR. I'LL BRING THE WINE. LUV HARRI X

"I see," replied Carmichael, who was deep in thought. "And I assume the two texts from yesterday morning were both from Martin Swift?"

Rachel looked surprised. "How did you know that?" she enquired

Carmichael smiled. "When I met him for the first time at

the Fairfax Hotel, he mentioned that he'd tried to text Kendal, to find out where he was when he hadn't turned up for that talk he was supposed to be giving."

Rachel nodded. "That all ties-in," she remarked. "Both messages were basically just asking where he was."

"Is that everything?" Carmichael enquired.

"Yes," replied Rachel.

"Good work," he said, his eyes gazing deep into hers and his head nodding positively. "You've achieved a lot this morning."

"Thank you, sir," replied Rachel, who as usual felt energised when the boss took the time to express his appreciation. "Do you want me to continue wading through these CCTV tapes this afternoon?"

"Definitely," replied Carmichael. "Let's see if they tell us anything more about Kendal's movements on Saturday. And hopefully we'll get a better picture of that person he was with."

Carmichael turned to face Cooper and Watson. "So, what did you guys find out from Kendal's work colleagues?" he asked.

"The main thing we discovered was what Marc told you on your call," replied Cooper. "His three work colleagues told us that they now inherit the business."

"And in your view, is the business worth anything?" Carmichael enquired.

Cooper shrugged his shoulders. "It's hard to say," he replied. "I suspect that Kendal's contacts and knowledge were the main driver, so I'd say no. But I think we need to check that out."

Carmichael nodded. "And what about their movements on Saturday?"

"Well, two of them appear to have good alibis," replied Watson. "the one called Zorik Daniels was out bowling in Chorley and maintains he left at around ten thirty, drove the fifteen miles back home and was tucked-up in bed with his wife at around eleven fifteen, which she has corroborated."

"And the other guy, a bloke called J.C. Palmer," added Cooper, "maintains he was watching a live two-hour programme on BBC2 about some rare astronomical event that was going to be visible at around midnight. It went on until twelve thirty and his partner has confirmed they both watched the programme at home, going out into the garden at twelve to try and see it."

"Sounds enthralling," remarked Carmichael cynically.

Cooper laughed. "Kendal's other colleague, a lady called Kim Bolton, has nobody other than her two cats to vouch for her," he remarked. "She maintains she spent the evening alone at home on Saturday, and saw nobody."

"And where does she live?" Carmichael asked.

"That's the thing," added Watson, "she's a middle-aged woman and doesn't strike you as having it in her to commit a murder, but she lives in Southport, no more than a ten-minute walk from where we found Kendal's body."

Carmichael's eyes opened wide. "So, could that figure in the CCTV footage be her?"

"The person in the recording looks too slightly-built to be Kim Bolton," Cooper remarked, "but it might be her."

"I'd definitely say no," added Watson. "Kim Bolton, in my view, is a fair bit bigger than that person."

Carmichael puffed out his cheeks. "Nevertheless," he said, "from what you've said, we need to add her to our list of potential suspects. If she has the motive, has no corroborated alibi, and lives so near to where Kendal was found, she has to be on our list."

Cooper and Watson exchanged a brief glance at each other before both nodding that they agreed.

"How was your morning, sir?" Rachel asked.

"Interesting," he replied. "I found Gavin Michelson a

little abrasive. He's clearly still in shock about his son's death, but he's not someone I warmed to and it's clear that he and Kendal weren't particularly close."

"What about Harriett Hall?" Cooper enquired.

"Now she was an altogether different character," Carmichael replied. "Friendly, co-operative and very helpful."

"In what way?" Rachel asked.

"To start with," replied Carmichael, "she corroborated Gavin's alibi. She maintains they were together from eight until twelve. She also told me that she and Gavin had once lived together, and she also gave me some insight into Kendal's relationships, especially with her niece, Carly Wolf."

"Really," remarked Cooper. "What did she say?"

Carmichael rubbed his hand across his chin. "She described Kendal as a lovely guy, but like his father, a serial womaniser who, in her view, was always going to be unfaithful to Carly. I got the impression that Kendal and Carly's relationship was a tempestuous one."

"Do you think we can scrub Gavin off our suspects list?" Rachel asked.

Carmichael thought for a few moments. "I suppose it's still technically possible for him to have got himself to Southport after Harriett Hall had left the house on Saturday, but it would be cutting it fine and I can't think of any serious motive for him killing his son, at present."

"In that case, by the same token, Harriett could have got herself to Southport, too, after she'd left Gavin's house," observed Watson.

Carmichael shrugged his shoulders. Having met her, there was no way he saw Harriett as being a serious candidate, but technically Watson was, of course, correct. "I think that's unlikely, Marc," he replied rather dismissively, "but theoretically she could have killed him, like just about anyone in the Southport area on Saturday evening."

"So, what's the plan now?" Rachel enquired.

"Well," replied Carmichael, "as we've agreed, I want you to plough through the rest of the CCTV recordings. Marc, you can help her, as we need to get through them all this afternoon and I think two pairs of eyes will be needed."

Watson wasn't overly happy to be given this assignment but didn't offer any objections.

"I'd like you to also find out who paid the bill at the restaurant on Saturday evening," Carmichael added. "Even if they split it, I'd expect at least one of them will have paid by card, so there must be an exact time recorded on the transaction document, which should help us work out exactly when they left the China Garden."

Watson nodded. "Good idea," he replied. "It might also make sense to get a uniformed officer to walk the journey from the restaurant to town, so we know exactly how long it would have taken him and Carly."

Carmichael nodded. "Good idea," he replied. "Leave that with me, Marc. I'll get that organised.

"What do you want me to focus on?" Cooper enquired.

"You and I are going to go and have another word with Carly Wolf this afternoon," Carmichael replied. "I want her to tell me exactly where they were when Kendal took this so-called telephone call. Once we have that, we can try and calculate the timings between there and the restaurant."

"Assuming there was a call," remarked Watson.

"You're right." replied Carmichael. "Unless Kendal had two mobiles, that part of young Carly's story is looking more than a little shaky."

Carmichael looked at his watch. "Let's reconvene back here at six," he announced. "Hopefully, by then we'll have a much better idea of what really happened on Saturday evening."

Chapter 23

"We'll take my car," Carmichael announced, as he and Cooper entered the station car park. "I'm never quite sure we'll make the journey when we're in that clapped-out car of yours."

Cooper shrugged his shoulders. He was used to taking insults about his car, but he didn't care. He'd had it over ten years and it had never let him down.

"Fine by me, sir," he replied with a smile, before walking over to the passenger side of Carmichael's black BMW.

Carmichael's car glided out of the office compound onto the A59 and headed south.

"Tell me about Steampunk," Carmichael enquired. "What's the attraction?"

Cooper took a massive slug of air through both nostrils. "As far as the attraction, it was Julia's idea," he replied, almost apologetically. "At first, I thought she was crazy, but to be honest, I really like it. I know it's a bit outlandish, but it's great, harmless, fun and you meet some interesting people."

By the unconvincing glance from Carmichael, it was clear that his boss wasn't sold on the movement in any shape or form. However, Cooper carried on regardless.

"I'd describe Steampunk as just a different way of looking at the world. It's a movement against convention, but a peaceful one. It encompasses creativity and celebrates a person's individuality, be it through style, gadgets, or attitude."

"So, like the true punk generation from the late eighties, but more grown up and less aggressive," remarked Carmichael.

"In a way, I suppose so," replied Cooper with a smile. "At one of the first meetings I attended, someone called it a chemistry of unorthodoxy. I think that sums it up quite well."

Carmichael kept his eyes firmly fixed on the road ahead, but the slight shake of his head signalled his continuing bewilderment.

"Do you think Kendal's death could be due to his association to the movement?" he enquired.

Cooper shrugged his shoulders. "I've no idea," he replied honestly. "I've never seen any sign of trouble when I've attended a Steampunk event, but I can't vouch for everyone that takes part."

* * * *

Gavin Michelson looked up from his screen to be greeted by the sight of Rebecca Graham, walking towards him with a large mug of coffee in her hand. As their eyes met, the elegant receptionist smiled warmly at her boss.

"I thought you could probably do with a drink," she remarked before getting in close to Michelson and placing the mug on the desk. a matter of inches from his right arm.

Michelson smiled. "Thanks, my dear," he replied before sending a smile back in Rebecca's direction.

"If you'd like," said Rebecca, "after work, I could cook you dinner at my place."

Michelson tenderly took hold of Rebecca's wrist. "That's really tempting, Becs," he replied, "but I doubt I'd be very good company this evening, and I'm going to have to work late tonight as I have loads to do before I go to Belgium on Saturday."

"But, surely, you'll be letting someone else take the reins at the exhibition," suggested Rebecca, her eyes wide open, expressing her consternation. "Isn't Janet Sutherland supposed to be the Marketing and Sales Director? Can't she handle the meetings with the retailers?"

It was clear from her tone that Rebecca wasn't a fan of Janet Sutherland.

"The exhibition itself, maybe," replied Michelson, "but Janet's not established the relationships yet with the bigwigs at the retailers. I still need to go."

Rebecca shook her head. "I think you're mad Gavin," she reprimanded. "In the circumstances, nobody would expect you to go."

Michelson looked sternly up at his attractive, young scold. "Maybe so," he remarked, "but the world moves on; I'm working late this evening and I am going to Belgium as planned. Your kind invitation is much appreciated Becs, but let's delay our next evening together until after Belgium, and after I've sorted out Kendal's funeral, whenever that will be."

For a split-second Rebecca's poise slipped and her expression changed from oozing sympathy to one of the jilted teenager. However, the lapse was momentary.

"Well, the offer remains open," she replied, before smiling again at her boss and strutting away to the exit, like a seasoned model on the Milan catwalk.

Michelson allowed his eyes to briefly enjoy the sight of Rebecca, as she sashayed out of the room, before once more returning them to the information on his computer screen.

Chapter 24

Carly Wolf worked as a nurse at Southport Royal Hospital, a modern building based at the northern end of the seaside town.

"Do you know which department she works in?" Cooper enquired as Carmichael's BMW pulled into the visitor car park.

"We may not need to," replied Carmichael as he gestured with his head to the figure of a young nurse dragging hard on a cigarette as she sat alone on a bench on the small patch of grass that edged onto the car park.

"What are the chances of that?" Cooper remarked as Carmichael's car came to rest a matter of a few feet from Carly Wolf.

As Carmichael climbed out of the car, the warm afternoon heat engulfed him, making him loosen his tie before walking over to where Carly was sitting.

"Inspector Carmichael," announced Carly with a broad smile before taking a last drag on her cigarette and crushing the butt under her flat, black shoes. "What can I do for you?"

"I thought nurses weren't supposed to smoke," Carmichael remarked.

"Just like fat ones can't tell you you're overweight," replied Carly cheekily, and as quick as a shot. "To be honest, they don't like us smoking, but nurses are probably the worst when it comes to stuff like that. I only smoke a few each day, but I don't see any great need to kick the habit, not yet anyway."

"This is Sergeant Cooper," continued Carmichael. "We'd like to ask you a few questions, if we may, about Saturday evening."

Carly looked at Cooper with a frown on her face. "Weren't you at the hall on Sunday when Martin did that naff talk about Jules Verne?"

Shocked that she should mention it, Cooper took a second to respond. "Yes, I was there with my wife. I'm impressed that you noticed us," he replied.

"You're a tall guy," Carly replied, "and I remember you 'cos you were sat at the end of the row with your long legs sticking out into the gangway. Also, I remember the woman sat next to you as I really liked her royal-blue dress with that matching bonnet and her frilly umbrella."

"You were one of the organisers, as I recall," Cooper remarked.

"Yeah," replied Carly, but it was Kendal who was supposed to give the talk, not monotonous Martin."

"You mentioned, yesterday," said Carmichael, who was keen to get the interview going, "that when you and Kendal were walking into Southport, he received a call."

"That's right," Carly replied. "What of it?"

"Can you tell me again precisely where you were when he received the call, and roughly what time it was?" Carmichael asked.

"It was like I told you yesterday," replied Carly. "We were about five minutes away from the Fairfax. It was outside that other hotel, the big one opposite the entrance to the marina."

"The Grove," suggested Cooper.

"Yeah," replied Carly. "The Grove."

"And remind us what time that would have been," Carmichael enquired.

"Like I said yesterday," replied Carly sharply, "I'm not certain. It was probably about eleven forty-five. If you check Kendal's mobile, it'll tell you when he received that call."

"You see," said Carmichael with deliberate calm in his voice, "that's our problem. Kendal's mobile activity suggests he didn't receive any call that evening."

"That's wrong," replied Carly angrily. "He did get a call, I heard the mobile ring and he spent at least two to three minutes talking before I left him. He was still on the phone when I left. He definitely received a call."

"Could he have had two mobiles?" Cooper enquired.

Carly shrugged her shoulders. "I suppose so," she replied, "but I can't recall him mentioning having two mobiles."

"And you have no idea who he was talking to?" Carmichael asked.

Carly shook her head. "No," she replied, "but I think it was a woman."

"Why do you say that?" Carmichael enquired.

Carly shrugged her shoulders and rolled her eyes. "Because, for the previous twenty minutes, he was like a dog on heat trying to get me to go back with him to the Fairfax," she replied. "Then he gets a call, goes all mysterious on me, tries to stop me from hearing what he's saying and couldn't give a monkey's about me when I told him I was off. What do you think?"

Carmichael smiled. "I see," he replied.

Carly stood up. "Is that everything?" she asked. "I need to get back to the ward."

Carmichael nodded and turned to walk back to the car. He'd only taken a few steps, when he spun around.

"There is one thing more," he said. "Do you know if Kendal kept a spare key to his house?"

Carly had already travelled four or five steps away from

the bench by the time Carmichael spoke, but stopped and looked back over her shoulder.

"Round the back, under the upturned plant pot, near the sundial," she replied. "There's usually one under there."

Carly turned back again and headed off leisurely towards the hospital entrance.

"That's handy," Carmichael remarked in Cooper's direction. "I'd like to take a look at Kendal's house for myself, before we go back to the station, so that saves us the job of breaking in."

Chapter 25

Penny's mind was still trying to work out why Robbie's two best friends had started to visit him so early each morning. Not only was it unusual, but it had been going on for days, with the same pattern; Ben and Jason arriving at the house at around 7:40am, rushing upstairs with Robbie to his bedroom, only to then depart about twenty to thirty minutes later.

She'd asked her son that morning what was going on, only to receive a bland and dismissive, "Nothing. They're just coming round to play computer games."

Penny had no reason to disbelieve her son, he was basically a good lad and she had no evidence to suggest he was lying to her, but her instinct told her that something was going on, and she was determined to find out what.

* * * *

"What did you make of Carly Wolf?" Carmichael enquired as the two officers travelled together down the winding country lanes that led to Barton Bridge.

Cooper thought for a few seconds before replying. "Confident, strong-willed and very observant," he said. "She's sticking to her guns about that telephone call, and I was amazed she recognised me from the hall on Sunday.

There must have been dozens of people in there, so that was astonishing."

Carmichael glanced briefly in Cooper's direction and smiled. "Particularly with you being in costume," he remarked.

Cooper nodded. "Yes, very impressive."

"But, Paul, do you think she'd be capable of killing Kendal?" Carmichael added.

Cooper again took a little time before answering. "I wouldn't rule her out," he replied. "Having seen her at the hall yesterday, and then at Harri's bar with you and the team, it's clear she relishes being the centre of attention; and I image she could get quite annoyed if she felt she'd been wronged. So, yes, given certain circumstances, I could see her killing someone."

Carmichael nodded. "Me too, but she has a very strong alibi. So, unless Rachel finds something on the CCTV footage to incriminate her, she's a long shot."

Cooper nodded. "But if there was no call on his mobile, why would she lie to us?"

"Why indeed," replied Carmichael. "Why indeed."

* * * *

Penny rarely set foot into her eldest children's bedrooms. She'd decided several years before that the more privacy her children had in their rooms the better it was for all concerned, a strategy that had, to date, worked very well for her.

However, she allowed, within this unwritten agreement, to venture into Robbie's room every couple of weeks to strip down the bed and change the sheets. Strictly speaking, Robbie's sheets were probably not due for changing for a few more days, however, Penny decided that she'd do it today while he was at the chicken farm and, at the same time, take the opportunity to see if there were any clues to the strange early morning behaviours of the three young men.

116

Having stripped off the bed and piled the old used sheets on the landing, Penny started to take a more detailed look at Robbie's cluttered, untidy room.

There were two things that struck Penny as being odd. Firstly, her son's laptop was shut and, with a single screwed-up sock and what appeared to be the contents of his quickly-emptied pocket sat on top of the lid, it certainly didn't suggest that there had been any computer games played on that piece of equipment for a good while. On closer inspection, Penny noticed, amongst the screwed-up bank notes and change, that Robbie appeared to have rapidly set down on the laptop lid his return train ticket from Southport on Friday evening, when he and a group of the lads had been out at a bar playing pool.

The second thing that seemed out of place to Penny was Robbie's desk chair, which was not by or under his desk, as was normal, but had been moved to the window and was turned as if the last occupant had been sitting on it, looking out into the Carmichael's back garden.

Penny sat on the chair for a few moments and peered out into her garden.

"That hedge at the back needs trimming," she muttered to herself, before standing up and, still non-the-wiser, switching her attention to completing the task of changing Robbie's bed sheets.

Chapter 26

The spare key was exactly where Carly Wolf had told them; in the back garden under the upturned flower pot near the stone sundial.

Except for the kitchen, which faced southwards over the small, but well-kept garden (and was modern with large floor-to-ceiling windows letting in a huge amount of light), the rest of Kendal's house was as Watson and Dalton had described... decidedly eccentric, looking like it had been trapped in a nineteenth century time warp.

"Wow," remarked Cooper in wonder at what he was seeing, "Julia would love this place."

Carmichael looked over at Cooper's awestruck expression. "It's not my cup of tea," he remarked rather scathingly, "but it's certainly striking and in-keeping with their shared love of Steampunk, I suppose."

All three of the downstairs rooms and the hallway, which led to the kitchen, with the staircase heading to the first floor, were immaculately tidy and covered in furniture, carpets, paintings and ornaments that all looked to have been created in the nineteen hundreds.

"It is like a museum," Carmichael remarked, "just like Marc said."

As they walked slowly from room to room, the distinctive character of the house grew ever more apparent.

"These paintings in here alone will be worth a fair amount," Carmichael observed. "I wonder who inherits this."

"It is all left to me," replied a voice from the top of the staircase.

Surprised by this unexpected reply, the two officers looked upwards into the dimness to see the figure of Martin Swift standing at the top of the staircase.

"Good afternoon," said Carmichael. "We didn't expect anyone else to be in. What are you doing here?"

"Carmen kindly let me in," replied Swift, who remained at the top of the stairs, but was then joined by the bird-like frame of the young housekeeper, her expressionless face giving no sense of what was going on behind those dark brown, Latin eyes.

Carmichael looked across at Cooper for a split second then, with a slight-but-sudden move of his head, indicated to his colleague that he should join him as he ascended the stairs.

"So how do you know that you inherit the house?" Carmichael enquired as he reached the half-way point of the staircase.

Martin Swift smiled. "I was not only Kendal's friend," he replied, "I'm also his solicitor. He made his will with us about six months ago, and I looked at it this morning. I wasn't involved in the preparation or witnessing of the will, which was done by one of my colleagues, but, to my surprise, Kendal has kindly left the house and its contents to me."

Carmichael arrived at the landing, closely followed by Cooper.

"That's very generous of him," remarked Carmichael. "This house and its contents must be worth a fair amount of money."

Martin Swift shrugged his shoulders. "I'd imagine it could, quite possibly, come to over a million," he replied, his tone and expression suggesting he was rather embarrassed at the fact. "I guessed he'd left me something when he requested I was not involved in the drafting or witnessing of his will, but I never dreamt he would be so kind."

"I will leave you gentlemen alone," announced Carmen respectfully, once Martin Swift had finished talking. "I need to get back to my jobs at Mr Gavin's house." As soon as she'd finished talking, the tiny cleaner descended the staircase and disappeared through the front door, closing it quietly behind her.

"So, who else benefits from Kendal's will?" Carmichael enquired, turning back to face Martin Swift.

"It's actually quite simply divided," he replied. "I get the house and contents, Kendal's three colleagues at Michelson's Antique Restoration Ltd get his business in equal shares, the Steampunk Society gets a legacy of ten thousand pounds, KADAS gets a similar size legacy, and any monies left over from his various bank accounts and anything he is due from the sales of his shares and his life insurance are split equally between Carly and Gabby."

"And those assets, are they significant?" Carmichael enquired.

Swift shrugged his shoulders once more. "To be honest I'm not sure," he replied, nonchalantly. "My colleagues will start to work on that, but knowing Kendal, he will have taken out life insurance, he was that sort of bloke, so again it could be a hefty amount."

Carmichael nodded. "For a man of, what, thirty," he remarked, "Kendal seemed to be quite wealthy."

"He was thirty-one," replied Swift, "he'd inherited a good deal of money from his Mum, which helped him get started with the Antiques company, and I dare say his dad will have helped him out, too, but he'd done pretty well for himself, that's certainly true."

"I also believe that you've been fairly successful

financially," remarked Carmichael, as he recalled part of the conversation he'd had with Carly Wolf at Harri's Bar the day before.

"I've done all right, I suppose," replied Swift modestly and with a faint shrug of his shoulders.

"You just mentioned KADAS as being in his will," Carmichael remarked, his brow slightly furrowed, "What's that?"

Martin Swift smiled. "It stands for the Kirkwood and District Astronomical Society, another one of Kendal's obsessions."

Carmichael and Cooper exchanged a quick look.

"Kendal seems to have had several unusual hobbies," Carmichael remarked.

Swift smiled broadly, "Kendal used to say he had four great passions, antiques, astronomy, Steampunk and women."

"Really?" said Carmichael. "And which was his favourite passion?"

Swift laughed aloud. "I think that fluctuated depending upon his mood," he replied.

"Do you mind if we continue to look around your house?" Carmichael enquired, his ironic question aimed at Swift.

"Of course not," Swift replied, pointing to one of the doors over Carmichael's left shoulder. "Kendal's bedroom is the door over there. The room next to it is the guest room. This door behind me is to the bathroom and that door over there is to the planetarium."

"Well, I propose we have a look at the planetarium first," Carmichael suggested.

Swift looked at his watch. "Look, I'm going to have to rush," he said, "I've a client meeting at five."

Carmichael smiled and held out his hand. "No problem, Mr Swift," he remarked. "Cooper and I will only be here for a short while, we'll let ourselves out."

Swift shook Carmichael's hand firmly and did the same with Cooper before making a hasty exit.

"So," exclaimed Cooper, "we've now got motives for not only Kendal's work colleagues, but also Swift, Gabby Johns and Carly Wolf."

Carmichael nodded. "Yes," he replied, "but what baffles me is that his father and his ex-stepmother got nothing in his will, if we are to believe Swift."

Cooper shrugged his shoulders. "I assume Kendal would have thought he'd outlive both," he suggested, "and, at any rate, I suspect both are already fairly well off."

"You could be right," Carmichael replied. "Anyway, let's have a good look at this planetarium and then do a bit of poking around in Kendal's bedroom."

Chapter 27

At 6 o'clock precisely, Carmichael started the debrief with the team in the main meeting room at Kirkwood Police Station.

"How did you get on this afternoon?" he asked, his question directed at Rachel and Watson.

The two officers exchanged a sideways glance of mutual self-satisfaction before Watson responded. "Pretty good, actually," he replied. "We've not managed to view all the CCTV footage, but I think we have a much better idea of what went on Saturday evening."

"Really?" remarked Carmichael, his tone of voice suggesting he was pleasantly surprised. "Tell us more."

"We've documented the timings for Saturday evening based upon what we've noticed on the CCTV footage, and from what the China Gardens were able to tell us," continued Watson. "Do you want to run through it, Rachel?"

Rachel Dalton nodded, stood up and walked over to the white board.

"We've established that the bill was paid at the restaurant at eleven twenty-five," Rachel announced. "There's no footage around the restaurant, but if we assumed they all departed between five and ten minutes after the bill had been paid, that would take us to around eleven thirty or eleven thirty-five, when the four went their separate ways."

As she spoke, Rachel pointed to the whiteboard where she'd already written *left China Garden at 11:30 to 11:35*.

"The direct route from the China Garden into town is the North Coast Road," continued Rachel. "It's almost exactly half a mile between the restaurant and the Fairfax Hotel. So, at a walking speed of three miles per hour, the journey, had they made it, would have taken no more than ten minutes."

"But he didn't make it," remarked Carmichael. "So, when do you first pick Kendal up on the CCTV footage?"

Rachel smiled and pointed to the second time she'd written on the whiteboard.

"At eleven thirty-seven, we see Kendal and Carly on the CCTV footage, walking very briskly down the North Coast Road," Rachel announced. "They are about halfway between the China Garden and the Fairfax Hotel."

"If that's the case, they must have left the restaurant at around eleven thirty-three," remarked Cooper.

Rachel nodded. "Yes, that's probably about right," she concurred.

"So, when do you see Carly and Kendal again?" Carmichael asked.

"Together, we don't," replied Rachel. "We do see Kendal walking alone at eleven forty, still on the North Coast Road. And, at about the same time, we see, on a separate piece of footage, Carly walking slowly alone down Seabank Road, heading towards Lord Street."

Cooper nodded. "That would tie in with Carly's story about her and Kendal splitting up outside the Grove," he remarked. "Although Carly maintained they parted at around eleven forty-five."

"In fairness to her, she said she wasn't sure," Carmichael added, "so I'd not be too concerned about her being ten minutes out."

"I suppose so," replied Cooper.

"When is the next sighting?" Carmichael enquired.

"Of Kendal? It's the footage you're aware of," replied Rachel, "of him walking alone down Nevill Street towards Lord Street at eleven forty-four, then back again in the opposite direction at eleven fifty-one, with the figure in the hoodie."

"What about Carly?" Carmichael enquired.

"We have just one more image of her walking down Lord Street towards Harri's Bar at eleven forty-eight," replied Rachel.

"So, there's no way the perfumed companion of Kendal's was Carly?" Carmichael enquired.

"No way whatsoever," replied Rachel resolutely.

"What was the next sighting of Kendal?" Carmichael asked.

"We have two more sightings of him," Rachel continued. "The first is at eleven fifty-three, running up the North Coastal Road, chasing the figure in the hoodie, who appears to have his helmet in their hand."

"Are you saying he'd been mugged?" Cooper enquired.

"From the footage, that's what it looks like," Watson confirmed. "We've looked again at the footage of them walking together down Nevill Street and we're fairly sure they weren't actually together. We think the hoodie figure was walking close to Kendal, but they weren't together."

"She was just intent on robbing him," remarked Carmichael.

"Yes," confirmed Watson, with an affirmative nod of his head. "That's exactly what it looks like."

"You said you had another sighting of Kendal," Carmichael reminded them. "When and where was that one?"

Rachel again pointed at the whiteboard. "That was at eleven fifty-eight," she replied. "It's of him crossing over the

North Coastal Road, not far from the Fairfax Hotel, and going down the steps that lead to the beach."

"Was he alone?" Carmichael enquired.

"Yes," replied Rachel firmly, "and we've no footage of anyone else going down those steps within twenty minutes of Kendal."

Carmichael sat back in his chair and placed his clasped hands behind his head.

"That's good work," he remarked. "Well done, you two."

"That's not everything," Rachel remarked.

Carmichael looked intently at his young DC. "So, what else have you got?" he enquired.

"We have another image of the hoodie person at eleven fifty-six," replied Rachel. "On this one we see her, helmet in hand, entering the homeless people's hostel near Avondale Road."

"Really?" asked Carmichael. "And do we see her leave at any stage?"

Rachel shook her head. "We've checked until twelve thirty and whoever it was didn't leave. In fact, nobody left the hostel during that time."

"At least not through the front door," Watson added.

"What about later that evening for any of the other suspects?" Cooper enquired. "Anything more on the tapes regarding Carly and Luke's movements when Harri's Bar closed?"

Rachel shook her head. "We've still got more footage to look at," she replied, "but so far we've seen nothing."

"Good work you two," announced Carmichael. "At last we might be getting somewhere."

"How did you get on this afternoon?" Watson enquired, his question directed at Carmichael and Cooper.

"It was interesting," replied Carmichael, "we met Martin Swift at Kendal's house. He informed us that he's now the owner; a generous legacy from his mate Kendal."

"He also confirmed that Kendal's three colleagues at Michelson's Antique Restoration Ltd get his business in equal shares," added Cooper, "and that the Steampunk Society and the local Astronomical Society both get ten thousand pound legacies."

Carmichael nodded. "And let's not forget the money that's raised from sales of his shares, the contents of his bank account and his life insurance," he remarked. "According to Swift, all of that, whatever it's worth, is to be split equally between Carly and Gabby."

"Nothing for Dad?" Rachel commented.

"No," replied Carmichael, who was impressed his young DC had picked-up on that. "Nothing for Dad."

"Well that's a fair amount of people with a motive to kill him," remarked Watson.

"Correct," replied Carmichael, his hands still clasped behind his head.

After a brief pause, he continued. "What I think we should do now is to update our three lists. Will you be our scribe again, Rachel?"

Rachel Dalton smiled and resumed her position by the white board.

* * * *

For the next hour, the four officers discussed what they needed to add or modify on their three lists. When Carmichael was satisfied that they were as complete as they could be, he instructed Rachel to print off four copies from the whiteboard and hand one to each of them to mull-over that evening.

"Get yourselves off home," he said at 7:30pm exactly. "You've all done a great job so far, but we've still a great deal to do before we can identify Kendal's killer. I'll see you all, bright and early, in the morning. Don't be late."

Carmichael remained in the incident room for a further fifteen minutes, alone with just his thoughts and a copy of Rachel's hand-written summary of their progress so far.

Chapter 28

Penny was pleasantly surprised when she heard the familiar sound of her husband's car as it pulled-up outside their house. It was only 8:25pm, which was incredibly early given he was only just ending day two of his latest murder enquiry.

"How's the case going?" Penny asked as soon as Carmichael entered the kitchen.

"We are making progress," he replied, while at the same time putting his arm around his wife's waist and tenderly kissing her forehead. "But we've got a whole list of suspects and, at the moment, I'm none the wiser about who our killer is."

"Well it's early days," Penny replied reassuringly.

"What's strange," he continued, "is that, as far as I can gather, the dead man was a reasonably popular guy, but so far I've not seen any major outpouring of grief. According to Marc, his colleagues at work appeared to be slightly upset, but apart from them, nobody else seems that emotional, including, I must say, his two ex-partners and his father."

Penny smiled. "Maybe he just wasn't as popular as you're being told."

Carmichael nodded. "Anyway, where are Natalie and Robbie this evening?" he enquired.

"Natalie's in her room and Robbie's out with Ben somewhere," Penny replied.

Carmichael opened the fridge door and peered inside. "Have we any cheese?"

"Yes," replied Penny. "Well, at least I think we have some."

Penny gently levered Carmichael to one side and looked for herself. "Actually," she replied after a few seconds of searching, "it would appear we haven't. I suspect Robbie may have used it up making himself a sandwich when he came back from work this afternoon."

Carmichael shut the door with a despondent look on his face.

"I see what you mean about him and his pals," he remarked. "They couldn't get up the stairs fast enough this morning; it's definitely suspicious."

Penny was pleased her concerns were now shared by her husband. "He told me this morning that they were playing computer games," she confided, "but I had a look in his room this afternoon and the laptop hasn't been used since Friday and his chair has been positioned as if they're looking out of the window."

"How do you know he hasn't used the laptop since Friday?" Carmichael enquired.

"He had an old train ticket, amongst other stuff, lying on top of it," replied Penny. "It looked like he'd just emptied his pockets when he came home last Friday night, putting everything in them on his laptop, and they'd remained there ever since."

"Impressive detection, Holmes," he remarked sarcastically.

"So, what do you think?" Penny asked.

"I've absolutely no idea," Carmichael replied, with a flippant shrug of his shoulders, "and it may be wise for us to remain in the dark on this one."

Penny took a step back in amazement. "No way!" she exclaimed. "He may be getting involved in something like…"

Carmichael laughed. "Like drug running or people smuggling?" he asked dismissively.

"I'm worried, Steve!" replied Penny, her face looking serious and troubled.

Carmichael put his arms around her shoulders and kissed her lips. "You're bonkers," he said, "but if it's so important to you, I'll have a word with him."

Penny smiled. "Will you?"

Carmichael nodded his head again. "But it will cost you a Chinese takeaway," he replied, while at the same time removing the printed menu of the Mandarin House from the notice board and handing it to his wife. "Mine's the usual," he remarked, "and plenty of prawn crackers, please."

* * * *

Having eaten his takeaway, Carmichael retired to his attic study, where he sat behind his desk with a large glass of Monkey Shoulder, his favourite blended malt whiskey.

He took out the copies of the three lists that he had prepared with the team at that evening's briefing and, having laid them on the desk in front of him, started to read them repeatedly.

Unknowns
1. Who killed Kendal Michelson?
2. Why was he killed?
3. Why did he go down to the beach on his own?
4. Did anyone call him, as Carly claims, shortly before he died?
5. Who stole his helmet?
6. Where is his mobile?

Facts

1. Kendal Michelson died between Midnight and 2am.
2. He'd spent that evening at the China Garden, a Chinese restaurant on the North Coastal Road with Carly Wolf, Gabby Johns and Martin Swift.
3. He and Carly walked from the restaurant towards town (left China Garden at 11:30 to 11:35pm).
4. Kendal and Carly had parted company by eleven forty.
5. He didn't struggle with his killer.
6. Between leaving the restaurant and his body being discovered, he'd had his helmet stolen and his mobile phone has yet to be recovered.
7. Kendal leaves (details need to be verified) significant legacies in his will to Martin Swift, Gabby Johns, Carly Wolf, Kim Bolton, J.C. Palmer and Zorik Daniels, giving all motives.
8. Kendal is seen on CCTV going down to the beach alone at eleven fifty-eight. No other persons seen going down to the beach down those stairs within 20 minutes of Kendal.
9. There are no records of any mobile phone activity by Kendal on the day he died.

Potential suspects

1. Gabby Johns (no firm alibi)
2. Martin Swift (no firm alibi)
3. Carly Wolf & Luke Barrett-Hobbs (jointly involved)
4. Bernard Carr
5. Kim Bolton from Michelson's Antiques (no firm alibi)
6. CJ & Zorik from Michelson's Antiques (both appear to have alibis)
7. Gavin Michelson (no alibi after 12 midnight)
8. Harriett Hall (no alibi after 12 midnight)

It was almost midnight before Carmichael went to bed, and almost an hour later before he could get to sleep; his head was a whirl with theories, questions and, to his frustration, very few answers.

Chapter 29

Tuesday 16ᵗʰ August

"That's your mobile," protested Penny as she stabbed her husband hard in the ribs with her elbow.

"What time is it?" Carmichael replied, his eyes blinking hard as he tried to rouse himself.

"Six thirty," Penny remarked grouchily.

Carmichael picked up the mobile, which had been resting on the small cabinet by his bed, and put it to his ear. "Carmichael," he said, his voice gruff and dry.

As he listened intently, Carmichael swung his legs out of the bed and sat facing the full-length mirror on his bedroom wall.

"I'll be forty minutes," he announced. "Contact Cooper and Watson and tell them both to meet me there."

Carmichael placed the mobile back on the bedside cabinet and half turned to face Penny, who was now sat up in bed, her curiosity having been aroused by her husband's rapid transformation from deep slumber to a man now seemingly ready for action.

"There's been another murder," he announced.

* * * *

On his journey, over to Barton Bridge, Carmichael called Rachel Dalton to update her on the latest development and inform her of his revised plan. Rachel had just emerged from the shower when she took the call and had no issue going through the rest of the CCTV footage without Watson's help. In fact, she preferred the new arrangement.

"I'll ask the duty sergeant if he can spare me one of his PCs to help," Rachel remarked, in a typically pragmatic style, her hair dripping onto the bedroom carpet.

"While they're doing that," Carmichael continued, "see if they can find any footage of Gabby Johns or Martin Swift in their cars after they'd left the restaurant on Saturday evening. I want to make sure they're both telling us the truth."

"Fine," replied Rachel before Carmichael abruptly ended the call.

* * * *

At the main entrance to The World of Chocolate, two burly looking uniformed officers had been placed on guard duty, blocking the passage of anyone they didn't know from entering. However, they immediately recognised Carmichael, in his black BMW, and stood to one side to allow his car to pass under the large wrought-iron gates.

Carmichael abandoned his car as close to the main entrance as he could and quickly pushed through the revolving glass door.

As he entered the lobby, he spotted Cooper crouched down next to the sobbing figure of Rebecca Graham, the ultra-efficient receptionist, who was sat frantically trying hard to stem the flow of tears cascading down her cheeks. Carmichael couldn't be sure she'd even noticed him as he walked passed, her head remaining bent downwards and her puffy eyes staring at the floor.

Cooper saw him, though, and after a quiet reassuring word to Rebecca and a gentle squeeze of her arm, he stood up and walked swiftly to join his boss.

"He's through here," Cooper remarked as he guided Carmichael through a set of double doors that led to the production area.

"Good god!" exclaimed Carmichael as he caught sight of the unmistakeable figure of Gavin Michelson, sitting naked on a chair covered from head to toe in chocolate.

At his side, with a perplexed look on his face, stood Dr Stock.

"I thought I'd seen everything," Stock remarked, "but this is most definitely a first for me."

"Me too," replied Carmichael, who took a few steps closer to the chocolate encased body of Gavin Michelson.

Carmichael looked closely at the figure in front of him for several seconds.

"The chocolate's set hard," he announced, "and by the expression on his face, it doesn't look like he was in the least bit alarmed when all this was happening."

Stock nodded. "Two very pertinent observations," he remarked approvingly. "I'm no expert on the time it takes for chocolate to set, but my initial thoughts are that he was killed, or at least sedated somehow, then stripped, tied to this chair and immersed in chocolate. He was found here, but I think he was moved here after the chocolate had set, as there's no sign of any drips around him."

Carmichael nodded. "Have you an idea of the time of death?" he enquired.

Stock shook his head more vigorously. "Absolutely none, at the moment," he replied. "I'll need to get him back to the lab and do some research into the science of chocolate making first. My guess is that it will be later today, or even tomorrow morning, before I can give you anything more definitive."

For once, Carmichael didn't push his old friend to be quicker, he just frowned, and shook his head gently from side to side before turning to face Cooper.

"So where do we think he was dipped in chocolate?" he asked.

Cooper nodded towards the opposite end of the factory. "There's a large vat over there," he replied. "Marc's there now. We think that's where it must have happened."

"Let's go and have a look," remarked Carmichael, who, still confounded by the nature of Gavin Michelson's death, marched purposefully in the direction Cooper had indicated.

* * * *

Fortified with a steaming plastic cup of canteen coffee and a bacon roll, DC Rachel Dalton continued to pour over the CCTV footage from Saturday evening. She had managed to persuade the normally less than helpful Sergeant Butterworth to allow her to co-opt the services of PC Dyer and WPC Twamley for the morning, which she considered a result, albeit that it had cost her a large cappuccino and a sausage baguette, with an extra sausage, to seal the deal.

"Carmichael is particularly keen for us to identify anyone going down onto the beach between the hours of midnight and 2am," she announced to her seconded aides. "Can you both focus on that, please? I'll try and find anything that will help us understand whether Martin Swift and Gabby Johns did just head off home from the China Garden, as they maintain."

Her two helpers nodded and started to get on with their allotted tasks.

* * * *

"So, what have we got, Marc?" Carmichael enquired as soon as he'd clambered up the impeccably-clean metal steps to the platform overlooking the equally-spotless, stainless steel vat of liquid chocolate below them.

Watson pointed up above their heads. "I reckon if someone threw a rope over that beam," he said, his eyes fixed on the steel support strut located above the chocolate silo, "it would be relatively easy to lower a body strapped to the chair down into the chocolate."

Carmichael and Cooper both looked up at the metal beam and then below at the liquid chocolate.

"That would take a fair bit of effort, even if Gavin was sedated or unconscious," remarked Cooper. "I can't see it being a one-man job."

Watson shook his head. "Actually, I disagree," he remarked. "I reckon one person could have done it. They'd have had to be quite strong, but I reckon it's possible."

Carmichael surveyed the area around where they were standing, then leaned over the side of the gantry to look at the floor around the vat.

"But there's no sign of any spillage," he remarked. "If it happened as you suggest, Marc, the chocolate would have been dripping all over the place. It's absolutely spotless."

Watson shrugged his shoulders. "Maybe they tidied up afterwards."

"They?" remarked Cooper. "So, you're starting to think this was a two-man job now, too?"

"If that is what happened," interrupted Carmichael, "then this was a well-planned and impressively-executed murder. It would have to have been committed by someone who knew about making chocolate, as I doubt vats of chocolate are left bubbling away all night. So, whoever did this must have been here a good few hours preparing the vat. Then, after they'd killed Michelson, they must have spent a good deal of time cleaning-up."

Both sergeants nodded in unison.

"What do we do next?" Watson asked.

Carmichael considered Watson's question for a few seconds.

"I want you, Marc, to find out as much as you can about chocolate production," he replied. "Find whoever is the chief chocolatier, if that's what they call themselves. I want to know how long it would have taken to prepare this vat, how long it would take for the chocolate to set, and I also want to know how many people here have the skills to be able to do this."

Watson nodded. "No problem," he replied.

"And while he's doing that," Carmichael added, "I'd like you, Paul, to interview whoever it was that found Michelson senior's body this morning. I'd also like to understand what the security arrangements are here at night, and what Michelson was doing here so late."

Cooper nodded, too. "I'll get on to it right away," he remarked with enthusiasm.

"What about you, sir?" enquired Watson. "What are you going to be doing this morning?"

Carmichael looked back into his sergeant's eyes.

"I'm going to meet some homeless people in Southport," he replied, before heading down the metal stairs towards the factory exit.

Chapter 30

As he walked back through the reception area of The World of Chocolate, Carmichael again noticed the forlorn figure of Rebecca Graham, no longer sobbing uncontrollably, but clearly in shock. He walked slowly over and sat down beside her.

"Are you going to be alright, Ms Graham?" Carmichael asked with genuine sensitivity. "This must have been a terrible shock for you."

Turning her head so her swollen, red eyes could make contact with his, the receptionist started to cry once more. "Why would anyone do such a thing to Gavin?" she enquired. "He was such a nice man."

"I take it you were close," Carmichael remarked.

The distraught receptionist nodded.

"Now he's gone, I don't suppose there's any need to keep it quiet," she remarked, her voice trembling, "but we were in a relationship. We had to keep it quiet because of the issues it may have caused here at work, but we'd been seeing each other for the past six months."

"I see," replied Carmichael. "In that case, I can understand why you're so upset. I'm very sorry for your loss."

Rebecca Graham conjured-up the best small smile she could muster, under the circumstances. "Thank you," she responded.

"So, tell me, when did you last see Gavin alive?" Carmichael enquired.

"It was yesterday evening," she answered. "I offered to cook him dinner at my place, but Gavin blew me out. He said it was tempting, but that he needed to work late as he had loads of stuff to do before his Belgium trip on Saturday."

"Ah, the convention," remarked Carmichael. "He mentioned that to me, too, when we spoke yesterday. I have to say, I was surprised he was still going given that his son had just been murdered."

Rebecca raised her eyebrows and gave the slightest of sniggers.

"That's what I thought, too," she remarked," but Gavin was adamant that he should go. I'd suggested that he send Janet Sutherland in his place, but I don't think he trusted her to handle the various meetings he'd set up with the retailers."

"Janet Sutherland," remarked Carmichael. "Who's Janet Sutherland?"

"She's supposed to be the Marketing and Sales Director," responded Rebecca, her answer suggesting quite clearly that she had little regard for the woman.

"I see," replied Carmichael. "So, roughly, what time was it when you last saw Mr Michelson?"

Rebecca thought for a few seconds. "It would have been about six thirty last night. I popped my head into his office and said goodbye." As she spoke, Rebecca started to sob uncontrollably. "That was the last time I saw him."

Carmichael put a comforting arm on Rebecca's shoulder before beckoning over a WPC who was standing a few feet away.

"Can you sit with Rebecca for a while?" he said to the WPC, a question posed in a way that made it clear the only acceptable answer was yes.

"One of my officers will need to take a statement from

you, Rebecca," Carmichael announced sympathetically, "but in the meantime WPC…" He paused, realising he'd forgotten the WPC's name.

"Hammond," remarked the WPC, with no sign of any annoyance at her superior's inability to remember her name.

"Yes, WPC Hammond will look after you," Carmichael declared, as if his hesitance was merely a trivial oversight.

Carmichael stood up, his place on the chair swiftly being occupied by WPC Hammond, who's immediate, comforting embrace was noticeably more robust than the half-hearted one that Carmichael had shared.

Carmichael walked briskly towards the exit before stopping and turning back to face Rebecca once again.

"When you met with Gavin," he remarked, "was that always at your place?"

Rebecca nodded. "Mostly," she replied. "We did occasionally stay late together here, but it was mostly at my place."

"I thought you wanted to keep it a secret," Carmichael remarked. "Surely meeting here would have been very risky?"

Rebecca Graham shook her head. "When we met here we'd always do so after work, when Gavin was supposedly working late. When he did that, he'd invariably tell Wayne, the night security guard, he could have the night off."

"I see," replied Carmichael, "but what about at his house?"

"We never met there," replied Rebecca instantly. "His live-in cleaner, Carmen, was almost always around, so we couldn't risk meeting there."

Carmichael smiled, before turning and walking hurriedly towards the exit door.

* * * *

With the now-established morning ritual at the Carmichael's house over, and Robbie already on his way to work, Penny sat in the kitchen drinking her coffee. After only a few seconds' deliberation, Penny decided to take a further look in her son's bedroom to see if she could uncover any sort of clue as to what the three boys were up to each morning. She was as certain as she could be that there would be a perfectly innocent explanation, but this was becoming almost like an obsession for her, and a mystery she was absolutely determined to solve.

Chapter 31

It was a beautifully fresh, bright summer's morning and, despite the circumstances, Carmichael was enjoying the drive from Barton Bridge through the pretty Lancashire countryside en route to Southport.

Although he had yet to get anything back from Dr Stock's team to support his theory, he was as sure as he could be that the murders of the two Michelson men were linked. They had to be.

As he drove, Carmichael couldn't help thinking about the women in both their lives. Kendal, who in his mind was certainly no Brad Pitt, had been in relationships with two head-turners in Carly Wolf and Gabby Johns, while Gavin, who was well into his fifties, had once lived with the unquestionably attractive Harriett Hall and, if her earlier admission was correct, was now in a relationship with Rebecca Graham. She could not yet have reached the age of thirty and could quite easily pass herself off as the current Miss Lancashire.

Having considered the scenario for most of the journey, Carmichael concluded that Gavin and Kendal provided strong support to a view he'd long held. Namely that, for many women, if a man was wealthy, powerful, and confident, these traits would adequately compensate for mediocre looks or the wear and tear from the passage of time.

He was still considering this highly subjective theory when his car arrived outside the homeless hostel in Avondale Road.

"Right," he said to himself, "it's time to meet Coco Channel."

* * * *

Steve would be proud of me, Penny thought to herself as she departed her son's bedroom, a wry smile on her face. *But knowing what they do each morning is one thing, understanding why is another.*

With the three boys meeting at such a precise time each day, Penny figured that the time was key to the conundrum. But how was she going to get the total picture, without being in the room with them herself?

Penny sat at the breakfast table, pensively considering what her next move should be.

* * * *

Avondale Hostel was a brick-built building with a gentle dog-leg ramp leading up to a large glass door encased in a bright-green metal frame.

It had been built no more than ten years earlier by the Liberal-dominated council, who had wanted to do something about the growing numbers of homeless people attracted to Southport and who had taken to kipping-down at night in the large doorways of its prestigious shopfronts on the west side of Lord Street. There was no way they'd wanted Southport to start mirroring the homelessness problem associated with Blackpool, their larger cousin, a matter of an hour's drive north.

Carmichael entered the lobby, where he was greeted

by the sound of a young, rather bulbous, tattoo-festooned woman, who had her short, cropped hair dyed red and green in a rather haphazard sort of way.

"Well, if she never nicked it, where the hell is it?" she was shouting at the thin, middle-aged man standing patiently behind the reception desk.

"As I've told you, Mandy, I'll speak to her," he replied eventually in a calm, authoritative voice. "If she did take your mobile, I'll make sure you get it back, but I'm sure you've just mislaid it somewhere."

Mandy was clearly unimpressed with his response, but elected to curtail the discussion with a vigorous shake of her head, a few unsavoury words about Chantelle, the person she believed had stolen her mobile, and a few further expletives to describe her opinion of the establishment she was making a hasty exit from.

"Can I help you?" enquired the man, with a warm, welcoming smile extended in Carmichael's direction.

Carmichael strode a few paces forward and presented his identity card. "I'm looking for a young person who stayed here on Saturday evening," he announced. "She was wearing a hoodie and arrived at around 11.56pm."

"That's very precise," remarked the receptionist. "Is she in any trouble?"

Carmichael shook his head. "Not really," he replied vaguely. "However, it's important that I speak to her."

The receptionist paused, as if he was considering whether his loyalties should lie with the person who had been staying at the hostel or with helping the police.

"Well, we do keep records of who is staying," he replied, "but, to be honest, if they told us their name was Micky Mouse we'd sign them in as Mickey Mouse and say no more. We're very conscious to avoid putting up barriers that prevent people coming here."

Carmichael nodded. "I understand," he replied, "but if you could check your list of residents for Saturday evening, that would be really appreciated."

"I'm Colin, by the way," replied the receptionist. "I wasn't here on Saturday, but let's check the register."

Colin extracted a large, tatty, red book from under the counter and placed it between him and Carmichael, before flicking over the pages until he reached Saturday 13th August.

"It wasn't that full on Saturday," Colin remarked as he reached the correct page. "Just fifteen."

"May I take a look?" Carmichael enquired.

"Of course," replied Colin, who obligingly swivelled the book 180 degrees so Carmichael could read the names.

To Carmichael's relief, there were only five female names in the register and, more importantly, there was a time against each registration.

"Jackie Donnelly, 11:57pm," said Carmichael as he pinpointed the only female to have registered within a thirty minute radius of the time the CCTV had spotted the hoodie entering the hostel. "Do you know her?"

Colin raised his eyebrows. "Oh yes," he remarked. "Jackie stays with us quite often."

"Does she wear a hoodie and is she fond of wearing expensive perfume?" Carmichael enquired.

Colin ignored the question. "Are you sure she's not in any trouble?" he asked. "It's strange that a Police Inspector is interested in her if she's not in any bother."

Carmichael smiled. "We think she may have something belonging to the poor man who was murdered on the beach on Saturday," he replied with a reassuring smile. "We are certain she had nothing to do with his murder, but we do need to talk with her."

Carmichael's words seemed to mollify Colin's fears. "Oh good," he remarked. "Jackie's well known for being a bit of

147

a magpie, but she's harmless and I'd hate to see her in any trouble."

"Rest assured, Colin," Carmichael replied, "I'm not going to arrest Jackie, but I do need to talk with her. Do you know where she'll be?"

Colin nodded. "As it happens, she stayed here again last night," he said. "I suspect she'll be in the dining area having some breakfast before she gets turned out."

Seeing the expression on Carmichael's face, Colin decided to provide further clarity. "We only allow people here overnight," he replied. "Guests can register from 5pm, when we serve an evening meal, but need to be out by 11am, after we've served breakfast."

"I see," replied Carmichael who, as he spoke, gazed down at his watch. "So, in a few hours' time?"

Colin nodded. "Jackie stays most nights and is always one of the last to leave in the morning," he remarked. "I'd be amazed if we didn't find her in the dining area."

"And where's that?" Carmichael asked.

Colin shut the registration book, placed it under the counter then pointed to the double doors to his left.

"If you go through those doors," he announced, "the dining area is right at the end."

Carmichael smiled. "Thanks, Colin, you've been very helpful."

Chapter 32

It took Carmichael no time whatsoever to pick out Jackie Donnelly. There being only two women in the dining area was a major help, but her identification was sealed when Carmichael spotted Bernard Carr, the down-and-out who'd confessed to Kendal's killing, sitting next to her, the two deep in conversation.

"Can I join you Bernard?" Carmichael asked, as he sat down opposite the couple. "This must be Jackie Donnelly."

Carmichael's arrival startled the pair.

"Oh, good morning, Inspector," responded Bernard, who made it obvious that he wanted to alert his companion to the fact that the man joining them was from the police. "What are you doing here?"

"I've actually come to speak with Jackie," replied Carmichael. "I think you both know why." As he spoke, the strong aroma of Jackie's perfume reached Carmichael's nostrils. He had no idea what Coco Channel smelt like, but he knew an expensive perfume when he smelt one, and this one smelt expensive.

* * * *

Despite it being still mid-morning, Watson had already gleaned a colossal amount of information about the manufacture of high quality chocolate confectionary, so much so that he was already contemplating trying his hand at making some at home over the weekend.

Jean-Paul Mercier, Gavin Michelson's long-serving, half-Belgian, half-English, Senior Chocolatier, had spent almost two hours educating Watson on the complexities of chocolate manufacturing. This included the importance of controlling the temperature during the process; the meticulous detail they went to in order to ensure the correct combination of cocoa solids, cocoa butter, sugar, milk powder, caramel, salt, sugar and stabilisers were introduced into the process; and the importance of managing the cooling after the chocolate had been made.

"I had no idea it was such an exact science," Watson had remarked, with genuine enthusiasm. "So, tell me, would your vats normally be empty at night?"

Jean-Paul nodded. "Unless we were doing an evening production, which we weren't last night, the equipment would have all been cleaned and empty, ready for today's production."

Watson listened intently. "So how long would it take someone to have prepared a full vat of chocolate, as they did last night?" Watson enquired.

Jean-Paul considered the question. "The mix looks like a simple milk chocolate blend," he remarked, "around forty-five percent cocoa solids and around fifteen percent milk solids would be my guess. So...."

Jean-Paul took a long dramatic pause while he contemplated his answer.

"So, in my view, about two hours to get the mix correct then about two hours setting time afterwards."

"Four hours!" exclaimed Watson. "Are you sure?"

Jean-Paul again considered the question.

"Maybe three in total," he replied, "but certainly no less

than three hours. Whoever did this was certainly no master chocolatier, but he was no novice either. The chocolate he produced would never have passed our rigorous quality control processes, but it was of reasonable quality and certainly as good as you'd get if you bought a bar of chocolate in the supermarket from one of those cheap and cheerful mass-production companies."

Watson smiled. It was clear that Jean-Paul was a perfectionist in his work – so much so that Watson couldn't help wondering whether there was any room in Jean-Paul's life for anything other than chocolate.

* * * *

"Tell me, Jackie," said Carmichael, his voice calm but firm, "what have you done with that helmet you acquired from Kendal Michelson on Saturday evening?"

The pale young woman with hollow dark eyes and a haunted expression on her face, simply shrugged her shoulders.

"Look, we know you took the helmet," continued Carmichael. "We have it all on CCTV footage. We also saw you coming here with the helmet at just before twelve midnight. So where is it now?"

Jackie Donnelly glanced sideways in Bernard Carr's direction, as if she was looking for his guidance.

"We sold it," remarked Carr. "We took it to Arnie's Cash Converter down Markwell Road yesterday morning. We got forty quid for it."

"We," remarked Carmichael. "You went together?"

Jackie Donnelly's eyes fixed their stare on the table between her and Carmichael, and her lips remained shut tight. It was clear she was frightened and it appeared to Carmichael that she was more than happy to allow Bernard Carr to do her talking.

"We're mates," replied Carr. "We look out for each other."

"Really," replied Carmichael. "But you must have been aware that the helmet belonged to the man that was brutally murdered. A murder you actually confessed to."

As he spoke, Carmichael shot a steely glare in Bernard Carr's direction.

This didn't seem to faze Carr in the slightest.

"Look, you'd already sussed I hadn't killed that bloke," Carr remarked. "So, I figured it was no big deal in us getting a few quid for that helmet. Let's face it, he doesn't need it anymore."

Carmichael sat back in his chair, folded his arms in front of his chest and exhaled deeply.

"You are priceless," he remarked. "This is a murder enquiry; didn't it occur to you that the helmet might be important to the police?"

"I told him that," snapped Jackie, her eyes firing-off an angry look in the direction of Carr. "But you never listen to me."

Bernard Carr seemed taken aback by Jackie's pronouncement, as if it was totally out of character.

"I was just looking out for us both," Carr responded in a condescending, yet tender, tone, "like I always do."

"Well, I can't remember you giving me any of that forty quid yet," she retorted irately.

"That's bloody charming," replied Carr, his voice now loud and full of bitterness. "I bloody confessed to the murder when I thought it was you."

"Well, you're a dick, aren't you?" said Jackie. "How could you think I killed that bloke? I hold my hands up, I nicked his stupid helmet, but I never touched the bloke. In fact, if he'd have caught me, I reckon it was him that would have murdered me."

Bernard Carr, clearly furious, stood up, knocking his chair

backwards and stormed off, muttering a stream of obscenities aimed at his so-called mate as he exited the dining room.

Carmichael waited for Carr to depart before returning an intimidating stare at Jackie. "Now he's gone," Carmichael remarked. "Tell me exactly what happened on Saturday evening."

Chapter 33

It was 11:30 before Cooper and Watson had finished their allotted assignments. They stood together in the warm sunshine, just inside the gates of The World of Chocolate, and watched as Stock's team carefully-but-hastily manhandled the chocolate-encased body of Gavin Michelson from the entrance into the refrigerated van, which Dr Stock had ordered to transport the body to his pathology lab without it melting.

"I suspect that's most women's fantasy," remarked Watson flippantly, "a naked man smothered in chocolate."

Cooper couldn't help but smile, although he found his colleague's comment crass and inappropriate, but in total keeping with Watson's usual, irreverent behaviour.

"What did you learn this morning?" Cooper enquired.

Watson considered the question. "I learnt that coffee praline is the top selling chocolate at the moment," he replied facetiously. "I also know just about all I'd ever need to know about setting-up my own chocolate factory. So, if I ever get bored of the exciting world of crime detection, I now have another career possibility to fall back on. How about you?"

Cooper shrugged his shoulders.

"Michelson's body was found this morning by the cleaning company at about 5:45am," he replied. "He was universally adored by the people I spoke to; and the night security guard, Wayne McBride, informed me that he got a call from Michelson at about 6pm last night, telling him he didn't need to come in."

"Really?" said Watson. "That is interesting."

Cooper nodded. "What's more interesting," he continued, "is that this was not the first time he'd been told by Michelson he could have the night off. According to McBride, it's become a regular thing, around a dozen times in the last six months."

* * * *

Without her so-called friend by her side, Jackie Donnelly seemed much more self-assured.

"I know it was wrong," she confessed, "and I know I should have come forward, but it's him. He never told me he'd confessed to that murder until after he'd seen you. I think he thought he was doing me a favour, taking the blame for the murder. I have no idea why he'd think I could kill anyone, but that's just Bernie."

Jackie Donnelly paused, shrugged her shoulders and held out her hands, palms upwards to emphasise her comments.

"He's harmless really," she continued, "and his intentions are always good, I suppose, but he is a dick. I shouldn't have let him sell that helmet either, but we're skint and forty quid is a load of money to us. Not that I've seen any of it yet."

Carmichael smiled. "What happened on Saturday?" he asked for the second time.

Jackie sighed. "Steampunk weekend is always a good weekend to nick stuff," she remarked, with unabashed candour. "The people who come are always rich types and are normally off their guard, so dead easy marks. I saw the guy and followed him down Nevill Street. When his mobile rang and he got it out, I thought I'd grab it from him and make a dash for it. There was nobody about and I'm a quick runner, so I figured I'd be safe. But when I got to him, he saw me and pulled his mobile away from his ear. He must have moved his head at the same time, as that stupid helmet fell off as I reached him and, just before it landed on the ground, I caught it. Then I was off."

"And he chased you," Carmichael suggested.

"Yeah," replied Jackie, "he was pretty quick, too. Faster than he looked, but not fast enough. I ran without looking back 'til I got here. I figured he'd run out of breath a few hundred yards after I took off. Anyway, he never followed me into here, so I was safe."

"So, he had a mobile?" Carmichael reiterated. "Are you sure?"

"Yes," Jackie replied, with a trace of astonishment in her voice. "I reckon it was the latest iPhone, a nice-looking one, for sure."

Carmichael took a few seconds to consider what Jackie had just told him, before standing up.

"Are you going to arrest me?" Jackie enquired, her eyes looking anxious.

Carmichael shook his head. "Not this time," he replied with a smile. "But my advice to you is to stop stealing people's mobiles, or anything else for that matter, otherwise you will be in trouble. Not all the policemen you'll meet are as sympathetic as me."

Carmichael walked slowly towards the door of the dining room before turning back.

"I'd also dump Bernie Carr, if I were you," he remarked. "I reckon you could do a lot better than him."

Jackie stared back at Carmichael with a look of indignation. "He isn't my boyfriend," she replied brusquely. "That's all in his stupid, peanut brain."

Chapter 34

Carmichael was just getting into his car when he received the call from Cooper.

"Hi Paul," he said, before making himself comfortable and closing his car door. "What have you and Marc managed to find out?"

Carmichael then listened intently as Cooper gave him a summary of his interviews that morning.

"Did you talk with Rebecca Graham?" Carmichael enquired.

"Yes," replied Cooper. "She was probably the most upset of anyone, and they all seemed genuinely distressed by Michelson's murder."

"Unlike his son," remarked Carmichael. "Very few people seemed that saddened about his death."

"She told me she'd mentioned to you that she was in a secret relationship with Gavin Michelson," continued Cooper.

"Do you believe her?" Carmichael enquired.

Cooper considered the question for a split second. "I know there's a pretty big age difference," he observed, "but I do. Whether he was as keen on her as she obviously was on him, I guess we'll never know, but yes, I reckon she's telling the truth."

Carmichael smiled, comfortingly he'd already come to the same conclusion.

"How did Marc get on?" Carmichael asked.

"I'll pass you over and he can tell you himself," replied Cooper, who handed over the mobile to Watson. "The boss would like a quick update on your findings this morning," he said.

Carmichael listened intently as Watson filled him in on the crash course he'd had from Jean-Paul Mercier regarding the manufacture of chocolate.

"Three to four hours!" exclaimed Carmichael, when Watson advised him of Jean-Paul's estimate of the time it would have taken Michelson's assassin to prepare the chocolate, immerse the murder victim and for the chocolate to set.

"Yes," replied Watson, "whoever did this knew how to make chocolate and must have spent half the night in the factory."

"They must have also known that there would be no guard on duty that evening," added Carmichael. "So, somebody very close to Michelson."

There were a few seconds of pause before Watson spoke again.

"What do you want us to do now, sir?" he enquired.

Carmichael looked at his watch.

"I'd like one of you to get over to the pathology lab and relay back to me anything Dr Stock is able to discover about Michelson's murder from his autopsy," instructed Carmichael. "I'd like the other one of you to interview Carmen Martinez. We never talked with her about her movements when Kendal was murdered and, as she knew both men, we need to consider her as a potential suspect also."

"But she won't know how to manufacture chocolate," Watson quickly pointed out.

"True," replied Carmichael, "but we need to talk with her even if it's just to eliminate her from our enquiries. Also,

Gavin and Kendal's relationships may prove to be important in this case, so ask her about their various lady friends. If anyone will know about them, it will be Carmen, being their cleaner; she'll probably have the low-down on all the women that came and went in both men's lives."

"Will do," replied Watson.

"Let's all plan to meet back at the station at 2pm," added Carmichael. "Hopefully. by then Rachel will have been able to finish looking at the CCTV footage too."

"What are you going to be doing?" Watson enquired.

With his left hand, Carmichael straightened his hair in the rear-view mirror. "I'm still in Southport so I'm going to have another talk with Harriett Hall," he replied. "She was close to both of them, so I need to interview her again."

Carmichael abruptly ended the call and switched on the engine of his black BMW.

Watson passed back the mobile to Cooper.

"The boss wants us all to meet up at the station at two," he said. "But, beforehand, his instructions are that I need to find and interview Carmen, the cleaner, and he wants you to get over to the pathology lab and relay anything Stock discovers during the autopsy."

Oblivious to his colleague's deliberate adaptation of Carmichael's actual instructions, Cooper shrugged his shoulders. "I'll see you later in that case," he remarked nonchalantly, before strolling over to his Volvo to head off to Stock's pathology lab in Kirkwood.

* * * *

Carmichael switched on the Satnav and keyed in Markwell Road. Despite him having lived in the North-West for several years, he was still unfamiliar with the roads in many of the towns and villages in the area, Southport was a prime example.

When the Satnav's irritating voice, that sounded like a computerised version of Fiona Bruce, indicated his next destination was a matter of a couple of hundred yards away, Carmichael decided he'd leave his car where it was and walk to the pawn shop where Bernard Carr and Jackie Donnelly claimed to have sold Kendal's helmet. And with Harri's Bar being no more than five minutes' walk beyond the cash converter store, abandoning his car where it was seemed a logical decision.

As he strode down the wide pavement, Carmichael's thoughts centred chiefly on Kendal's mobile. Despite the dead man's network provider maintaining that there had been no activity on Kendal's mobile on the day of his murder, Carmichael had from the beginning tended to accept Carly Wolf's claim that Kendal had received a call when they were walking into town on Saturday evening. In Carmichael's mind, Carly could well have had something to do with the murders, but she wasn't stupid. She would have known that the police would check Kendal's mobile activity, so she'd have known that any lies she told about the call would have easily been detected. What's more, she'd suggested on two separate occasions that they should check the timing of Kendal receiving the call, to help verify the timing of their parting that night.

So now that Jackie Donnelly had also confirmed that she saw Kendal on his mobile, Carmichael was convinced that both calls had taken place and, in all likelihood, Kendal must have had two mobile phones. The question was, why had they been unable to find a trace of either of them?

Carmichael was still contemplating this point when he arrived at the entrance to Arnie's Cash Converter, the pawn shop on Markwell Road.

Carmichael allowed himself a wry smile. It would not take him long to repossess Kendal's helmet, given that it was being prominently displayed in the centre of the shop window with a price of £190 attached to it on a small white label.

Chapter 35

It was just after noon when Watson arrived at Gavin Michelson's house.

He rang the doorbell and, as he'd expected, the door was opened by the diminutive figure of Carmen Martinez, dressed in a blue apron that looked at least two sizes too big for her.

"May I come in?" Watson enquired.

"Mr Michelson is not home," replied Carmen, her Spanish accent seeming more pronounced than when they met previously, but her English was very clear. "He's been working all night again at the office."

Watson smiled his best reassuring smile, "No, it's you I've come to see," he said. "Can I come in?"

* * * *

With the help of two willing hands in WPC Twamley and PC Dyer, Rachel Dalton had made great progress with the CCTV footage. By the time the three officers had decided to break for lunch, they'd established beyond any doubt that Gabby Johns and Martin Swift had both, as they'd said in their statements, travelled directly to their respective homes after leaving the China Garden restaurant on Saturday evening.

CCTV cameras identified Gabby's red fiesta on three

separate occasions during her twenty-five minute drive to Linbold, the last just two minutes from her house, giving her estimated time of arrival home at almost exactly midnight. Martin Swift's conspicuous white Audi TT was even easier to spot. It was picked up on four separate occasions by cameras, with his estimated time of arrival at his remote country home being just a few minutes before Gabby Johns's arrival home.

As if this wasn't enough, Rachel, being Rachel, had asked WPC Twamley to also look at the CCTV footage for the thirty minutes after each of the two friends had arrived home to see if there was any indication that either of them had returned to Southport. And as Carmichael's highly resourceful officer had fully expected, WPC Twamley couldn't find any evidence that either of their cars had made the journey back to Southport.

As for corroborating the stories of Carly Wolf and Luke, namely that they left Harri's Bar just after closing, CCTV cameras picked them out clearly on two occasions as they made their way, arm in arm, from Harri's bar towards the Fairfax Hotel. Although, to Rachel's annoyance, there wasn't any footage of them entering the hotel, she was as confident as she could be that their story had been fully endorsed by the footage. If the couple had gone down to the beach, the earliest they could have done so was 1:20am, and although they did not have CCTV footage that covered the entire coastal road, by the time she broke for her lunch, Rachel was convinced that the two lovers must have walked directly from Harri's Bar to the Fairfax Hotel.

"Let's get back here in half an hour," she suggested to PC Dyer and WPC Twamley. "When we get back, I think we each need to look at a couple of those six CCTV tapes from the North Coast Road, focusing on the time between ten thirty and one thirty in the morning. If we view them at double speed, we could have this all done and dusted by two."

* * * *

With Kendal's shiny helmet safely in a plastic carrier bag, Carmichael left Arnie's Cash Converter on Markwell Road and headed on foot towards Harri's Bar. He'd had no resistance from the plump, ginger-haired woman, with the sweaty brow and ruddy complexion, when he'd announced who he was and that he was commandeering the item in the shop window. She'd denied having any knowledge of where the item had originated, stating that the purchasing was Mr Anderson's sole domain and that he'd popped out for half an hour to have his lunch. Carmichael had no reason to disbelieve the woman behind the counter, who gave the impression that she was, as she maintained, simply a hired hand.

"Ask Mr Anderson to get himself over to Kirkwood police station this afternoon," he'd instructed her. "He'll need to make a formal statement regarding how he came by the helmet and what checks he did to ensure that the item wasn't stolen before he bought it."

Carmichael knew that, in truth, the law didn't stipulate in any meaningful detail the lengths establishments like Arnie's Cash Converter had to go to when checking the true ownership of items they bought, and he could have allowed the owner to make his statement at the local station; however, Carmichael wanted to make the proprietor's task as awkward as he could, to emphasise how dimly he viewed those sorts of premises buying stolen goods. Also, the extortionate margin the shop was trying to make on the helmet had significantly amplified Carmichael's annoyance.

* * * *

Carmen Martinez sat upright in the middle of the large, expensive, black-leather sofa that dominated the room, her tanned, spindle-thin legs crossed as she sat on her employer's settee.

"I'm sorry to give you such dreadful news," Watson said, his voice hushed and his words being selected with uncharacteristic care and sensitivity. "When did you last see, or speak with Mr Michelson?"

Carmen's eyes remained transfixed on a point over Watson's shoulder.

"I last saw him yesterday morning," she replied, "before he went to the office."

"And what time would that have been?" Watson prompted.

Carmen remained still and impassive.

"About seven thirty," she replied. "But he called me at five o'clock last evening to say he would not be home. He was working late at the office."

"I see," said Watson. "Was that common?"

Carmen moved her head a few centimetres, her eyes meeting his for the first time since she'd been delivered the bombshell about Gavin Michelson's death. "What do you mean?"

"Did Mr Michelson often work through the night?" elaborated Watson.

Carmen nodded. "Sometimes," she replied, her answer vague, but in keeping with what Cooper had been told by the night security guard earlier in the day.

"So, what did you do yesterday evening, knowing that your employer wasn't coming home?" Watson enquired.

Carmen's gaze again became fixed over Watson's shoulder.

"I stay here and finish my work," she replied in broken English. "Then I slept for a few hours. Then, at about eleven, I walk to the train station and take train to Southport."

Taken aback by her response, Watson's eyes widened. "Why did you go into Southport?" he asked.

Carmen once more moved her head so she could make eye contact with Watson. "I started a new job last night with Mrs Hall," she replied. "I now do cleaning at Harri's Bar after it closes."

Watson nodded. "I see," he replied, "And have you been doing that job long?"

Carmen shook her head. "No," she replied. "It was my first night. Mrs Hall said I could do that job since Mr Kendal died. She has always been very kind to me. She knows I need the money to send back home."

Watson nodded. "And what time did you return home after work?"

"It is a big bar and a big job," replied Carmen. "I start when the bar closes at 1am and was finished at 6am. I then got train back here."

"Did you do the cleaning on your own?" Watson enquired.

"No," replied Carmen. "Mrs Hall stayed with me until about 2:30am, then she went home."

Watson paused for a few seconds. "What about on the night that Kendal Michelson was killed?" he asked. "What did you do that evening?"

Carmen thought for a few seconds. "Mrs Hall came over that evening," she replied. "Mr Michelson was going to cook something for them. He gave me the evening off, so I stayed in my room."

"All evening?" Watson probed.

Carmen nodded. "Yes, I was in my room from about six and did not come down until around seven, when I started to clear away the dishes from the night before."

Watson nodded. "I see," he replied.

"So, both Mr Michelsons have been murdered," Carmen remarked. "Did the same person kill them both?"

Watson shrugged his shoulders. "We aren't sure," he replied candidly, "but we are seriously considering that as being a possibility."

"It is unbelievable," Carmen continued. "They were both so kind to me. Why would anyone want to kill them?"

Watson suddenly felt sad and concerned about Carmen.

"Is there anyone who you could call and ask to come over and sit with you?" he enquired.

Carmen shook her head. "No, I will be all right, but I don't know where I will live from now on, now Mr Michelson is dead too," she replied, her accent once more sounding pronounced, as if to emphasise her vulnerability following the murders of her two employers.

Watson smiled. "For the time being, you'll still be able to stay here, I suspect," he replied. "I guess it depends upon who inherits Mr Michelson's house."

Carmen nodded. "Yes," she replied. "I suppose I will just wait and see."

Watson rose from his chair and walked slowly towards the door. However, before he'd got even half way there he turned back.

"One last question," he said. "Do you know if Kendal Michelson had two mobile phones?"

Carmen shook her head. "Not that I am aware of," she replied. "He had just the one, as far as I know. He was always mislaying it. In fact, he lost it on Friday last week before he went to Southport. I found it yesterday, down the side of his chair in the planetarium at his house."

"Really?" replied Watson. "We'll need to go over to his house in that case, as I'll need to take the mobile away with me."

Carmen smiled. "No need," she replied. "I have it in my

room upstairs. I was going to give it to Mr Michelson when I next saw him."

As she spoke, Carmen's words trailed away as if it dawned on her that she was never going to see Gavin Michelson again.

Chapter 36

Carmichael's first boss in CID had once given him some advice about interviewing suspects. "Whether they are fat or thin, black or white, rich or poor, drop-dead gorgeous or physically repulsive, you must treat them all the same," DI Chatfield had said. Wise words, Carmichael had thought all those years ago; and a mantra he'd often repeated to new officers, as if it was his own.

His problem, however, was keeping to it. The fat/thin, black/white, and rich/ poor bit he was OK with, and with men, if he was honest he hardly cared whether they were attractive or not. However, he struggled badly to maintain Chatfield's doctrine when it came to interviewing attractive women suspects. In short, as Penny had told him many times, he was a sucker when it came to a pretty face.

The good news was he knew full well that this was his Achilles heel, and as a result, Carmichael was always very conscious to retain a detached professionalism when interviewing women he found attractive, but boy did he have to work hard at it.

Harriett Hall fitted this weak-spot profile like a glove. In his eyes, she was unquestionably good-looking, intelligent, easy to talk to and had a smile that Carmichael couldn't avoid warming to.

As Harriett Hall returned to the same table they'd

used at their previous meeting, carrying two large coffees on a small circular black tray, Carmichael took a deep breath. He was about to break the news to her that Gavin Michelson, her business partner, and a man with whom she'd previously had a lengthy, loving relationship, had been murdered.

Carmichael waited until she'd placed the tray on the table and had made herself comfortable before he told her the bad news.

"I'm really sorry to tell you," he began, Harriett's face already starting to look pensive and slightly concerned as he delivered those first few words. "Unfortunately, earlier today, we found the body of Gavin Michelson, who appears to have died late last night or in the early hours of this morning," continued Carmichael.

With the bombshell well and truly dropped, Harriett shook her head from side to side with a look of total disbelief on her face. "Where, how..." her voice cracked and she stopped after those two short words, her left hand shooting up to cover her mouth.

"I'm so sorry to give you such dreadful news," repeated Carmichael sympathetically, "his body was found this morning at the office."

"I can't believe it," said Harriett, who looked understandably shaken, but dry-eyed and, in the main, still in control. "How did he die? Surely it wasn't suicide?"

Carmichael shook his head. "We are still trying to piece together all the facts, but we doubt it was suicide," he replied, keeping the details firmly to his chest.

"Murder then?" Harriett remarked, her blue eyes now wide open. "Was he murdered like Kendal?"

It was precisely at that moment when Carmichael's mobile started to ring. He removed it from his pocket and saw the name Watson appear on the tiny screen.

"I'm sorry," he said to the still-dazed-looking Harriett, "I'm going to have to take this call. I'll only be a minute."

Carmichael turned in his chair and, looking away from Harriett, put the mobile to his ear.

"Hi, Marc," he said, "I'm just with Ms Hall; is it important?"

Carmichael listened intently as Watson updated him on his meeting with Carman, her claim that she'd been at Harri's Bar last night and the fact that he'd now located Kendal's mobile phone.

"Thanks, Marc," replied Carmichael, who was conscious not to inadvertently allow Harriett to know any of the information he'd just been given. "I'll see you at 2pm, as we agreed."

Without any further comment, Carmichael ended the call and turned back to face Harriett Hall, giving her his best reassuring smile.

* * * *

Having established the nucleus of an idea as to what Robbie and his two pals were up to each morning, Penny's next step was to test her theory. To do that, she needed to make sure that she could be in Robbie's room at the precise time when he, Ben and Jason met each morning.

Penny had spent the morning pondering this dilemma while she did her housework and over a couple of cups of coffee. Having established what, she considered, was a workable plan, Penny picked up the phone and dialled her old school friend to ask a favour.

* * * *

"Please don't jump to any conclusions, but I have to ask you where you were last night," Carmichael enquired, his stare fixed firmly on Harriett Hall's attractive blue eyes.

Harriett looked shocked. "I was at home until about eleven," she replied, "then I came here. I was here until about two thirty in the morning, then I went home again."

Carmichael nodded. "And can anybody vouch for you?" he enquired.

Harriett nodded. "The staff on duty last night will all be able to confirm what I'm saying is correct," she replied, "and Carmen was here last night after closing. We started her in a cleaning role, so she'll be able to confirm that I left at around two thirty."

Carmichael gave Harriett a reassuring smile. "That's fine," he said. "I just needed to clarify your movements, it's standard procedure."

Harriett nodded, but said nothing.

"Do you know of anyone who would have wanted to kill Gavin Michelson?" Carmichael asked.

Harriett shook her head. "He was in business for many years, so I suppose there may have been people who he'd upset along the way, competitors or maybe ex-employees with a grudge, but I'd not know them."

Carmichael nodded gently, a tactic he often used to try and coax information from the person he was interviewing. "What about ex-lovers or their partners?" he enquired.

Harriett smiled wryly and nodded. "I suppose if I had to speculate," she replied, "I'd probably guess that he'd be more likely to be harmed by an ex than anyone else. But I'd not expect any of them to murder him. Mind you, I don't know half of them, so maybe one was the murdering type."

"There were many then?" Carmichael asked.

Harriett rolled her eyes skywards. "Over the years, scores of them to my knowledge," she replied.

"Any names you'd care to share with me?" Carmichael asked.

"Have you got a large piece of paper?" she replied, "and plenty of ink?"

Carmichael took out his note pad. "I'm ready," he remarked.

Without needing to stop for breath, Harriett Hall reeled out eight names from Gavin's past, none of whom meant anything to Carmichael. However, the ninth name did cause him to take notice.

"Really?" Carmichael asked. "Gavin had a relationship with Gabby Johns, but she was one of Kendal's ex-girlfriends?"

Harriett nodded. "Oh yes," she replied wryly. "And, to make matters worse, their fling, as I think that's all it ever was, was when she was still seeing Kendal."

"Really?" asked Carmichael for a second time. "That must have been awkward."

"Awkward," repeated Harriett, her tone making it clear that Carmichael's choice of word was totally inadequate. "It was catastrophic. Up until then, Gavin and Kendal had been inseparable, but after Gavin and Gabby had slept together, their relationship was never the same. Kendal maintained he wasn't that bothered, but he was. They didn't fall out completely, but the bond that had been so strong before was shattered and it never mended."

"I assume that's what caused Gabby and Kendal to break up," Carmichael suggested.

Harriett nodded. "The silly cow tried so hard to repair the damage," replied Harriett, "but it was futile. Kendal maintained a friendly relationship with her, but as a couple they were finished."

Based upon what Harriett had just revealed to him, Gabby Johns had suddenly climbed to the top of Carmichael's suspects list, assuming what Harriett had told him was true.

"And what's your relationship like with Gabby Johns?" Carmichael enquired.

Harriett smiled, "Let's just say we give each other a wide berth."

"What about Gavin's current relationships?" Carmichael enquired.

Harriett shrugged her shoulders. "I don't know for certain," she replied, "but I think he was seeing that pretty young thing on his reception desk."

"Rebecca Graham," said Carmichael.

"Yes, Rebecca," confirmed Harriett. "I suspected there was someone else, too, possibly Janet Sutherland, his new sales and marketing director. She's a bit plain for his normal tastes, and I've only met her once, when I went to an open day they had at the factory a few months ago. However, from the body language between Janet and Rebecca, I detected there was a bit of rivalry between those two, which I always took to be associated with them vying for Gavin's affections. But of course, I could be wrong."

Whether she was right or wrong, Carmichael sensed that Harriett was very keen for him to be aware of these two women.

"Do you think either of them could have killed Gavin?" he asked.

Harriett smiled and shrugged her shoulders once more. "Why not?" she replied. "There's nothing more dangerous than a woman who doesn't get her man."

Chapter 37

The four officers assembled in the incident room at 2pm on the dot.

"Can you update us on how you've got on with the CCTV footage, Rachel?" Carmichael asked.

Rachel was more than happy to oblige.

"We've established that Gabby Johns and Martin Swift both went home directly from the China Garden, as they'd maintained," she announced.

"Are you sure?" Carmichael asked.

"Absolutely," replied Rachel. "We checked the CCTV footage after they'd arrived home and there's absolutely no evidence of either of them leaving their houses for at least thirty minutes. The earliest either of them could have arrived at the beach was 1am, which is an hour after we have footage showing Kendal going down onto the sand. In my opinion, neither of them are our killer."

Had it been Watson making this statement, Carmichael would have probably been less inclined to trust such a categorical view, however as it came from Rachel Dalton, he had no issue in accepting what he'd just been told.

"What about Carly Wolf and Luke Barrett-Hobbs?" Are their statements supported by the CCTV footage?"

Rachel nodded. "They were clearly seen walking from Harri's bar in the direction of the Fairfax Hotel by a couple of CCTV cameras," she announced. "We estimate that they arrived at the hotel at about 1:20am and there's no evidence of them leaving. There's certainly no CCTV footage of them going down to the beach. In fact, apart from Kendal, and a young couple who went down the same steps at 11pm before re-emerging fifteen minutes later, we could find nobody else who went down to the beach between 10:30pm and 1:30am."

Carmichael puffed out his cheeks. Having learned about Gabby John's relationship with both dead men, he'd not expected Rachel to be so conclusive regarding her movements. With Gabby Johns seemingly out of the frame, to then also be told that the alibis of Martin Swift and Carly Wolf were both seemingly robust and that nobody appeared to follow Kendal down to the beach was a huge, confusing blow to him.

"Well, he didn't commit hari-kari," Carmichael remarked irritably. "Someone was down there, someone rammed that sword into him; and with him putting up no resistance at all, it must have been someone he knew."

Rachel shrugged her shoulders. "I suppose we could have missed something," she offered in the way of a potential explanation for the conundrum they found themselves in, "but I'm as certain as I can be. We were really thorough in looking at the CCTV footage, and we had loads of it, too."

Carmichael nodded. "I'm not suggesting for one minute that you haven't been diligent, Rachel," he replied. "It just doesn't make sense."

"If the footage you looked at didn't spot anyone going down to the beach," interjected Cooper, "that means they were either down there before 10:30pm or they made their way down to the beach from a point further north or further south."

"And their exit, too," Carmichael added.

"Either that or they arrived from the sea," remarked Watson.

Rachel nodded. "We've no cameras located beyond the ones we've already looked at," she replied, "so there's no way of checking."

"But how far north or south would the killer have had to enter the beach for them not to be detected by CCTV?" Cooper enquired.

Rachel shrugged her shoulders. "About half a mile in each direction," she replied.

"So not that far," Carmichael remarked.

"Not really, sir," replied Rachel.

"So, who does that now leave us as potential suspects for Kendal's murder?" Watson enquired.

"Assuming it is someone he knew, it just leaves Harriett Hall, Carmen and Kendal's colleagues at work," replied Cooper.

Carmichael shook his head. "We can probably remove Harriett Hall from our list, as if what she and Gavin told us is correct, she didn't leave his house until around twelve. For her to have travelled from Barton Bridge to Southport, then gone down onto the beach at a point beyond the range of the CCTV footage, that Rachel's been scrutinising so closely all morning, it would take her the best part of an hour. I really don't see that being likely."

"Dr Stock did say the time of death could have been anything up to 2am," Rachel reminded her boss.

Carmichael nodded. "I know," he conceded, "but I think he died nearer midnight, as I can't see any reason why he'd have remained down on the sand on his own in the dark for over an hour. No, I'm convinced he died quite soon after he went down onto that beach."

"That just leaves us with Carmen or one of the people from Kendal's Antiques company," Cooper remarked. "And, if it was Carmen, how did she get from Barton Bridge to Southport? I don't think she has a car."

"By train, maybe," offered Rachel as an explanation.

"Maybe," replied Carmichael, "but, if so, she'd have had to have walked a fair way from the station to get down onto the beach without being detected by the CCTV cameras."

"And I suppose there's also the question of how she'd have got back home afterwards," remarked Cooper.

"Do you want me to see if there's any footage available from the train station that I can check to see if Carmen travelled to Southport on Saturday?" Rachel asked.

Carmichael nodded. "Yes, please," he replied with a dry smile, "as you're such an expert now at analysing CCTV images."

Rachel returned the smile. If the truth was known, she had enjoyed studying the tapes that morning, so doing a little more of the same wasn't an issue for her.

"Can you also contact the taxi companies in Southport and see if anyone remembers picking up anybody in the early hours of Sunday morning and taking them back to Barton Bridge," continued Carmichael.

What about Bernard Carr and the hoodie who stole his helmet?" asked Watson. "Aren't they still potential suspects?"

Carmichael shook his head. "No," he replied definitively. "I'm certain they had nothing to do with his death. They were in the hostel all night. The hoodie, a woman called Jackie Donnelly, has admitted taking the helmet, which they both later sold to a dodgy local pawn broker, but they didn't kill Kendal."

As he spoke, Carmichael lifted a carrier bag from beneath his desk and extracted Kendal's shiny silver helmet.

"They only got forty pounds for it, too," he said.

"But Bernard Carr did confess," remarked Watson.

Carmichael nodded. "He's not the sharpest tool in the

box," he replied, "I'm convinced he thought Jackie might have done it so was trying to take the blame for her. However, when I dismissed his feeble confession he saw that as the all-clear to sell the helmet."

"So, they were a bit of a waste of time then," remarked Watson.

"Well, not really," replied Carmichael. "We've located the helmet now, we've eliminated the perfume-smelling hoodie, and Jackie Donnelly did tell me one important fact."

"What was that?" Rachel enquired.

"That Kendal was on his mobile when she stole the helmet," replied Carmichael. "She was absolutely certain. In fact, she told me it was the mobile that she really wanted to steal."

"So, where the hell is his mobile?" Cooper remarked.

"And why didn't the statement from his network provider show any activity?" Rachel added.

Watson smiled broadly and held up a clear-plastic bag with the mobile he'd retrieved from Carmen.

"I can answer one of those questions," he remarked smugly. "Carmen claims she found Kendal's mobile down the side of a chair in his planetarium room when she was cleaning yesterday. She gave it to me earlier. According to her, Kendal was always mislaying his mobile."

"As for the lack of any recorded call activity," added Carmichael, "I reckon Kendal must have had two mobiles."

* * * *

The phone rang on Martin Swift's desk at Hathersage, Marlow and Swift, the small solicitors' practice he'd been a partner in for the last five years.

"Martin Swift," he announced in a voice that seemed to start as if he was an alto but ended as a soprano.

"It's Carly," continued the voice from the other end of the phone. "Have you heard about Kendal's dad?"

"No," replied Swift. "What about Gavin?"

"It sounds like he's been murdered, too," Carly said, her voice animated as she broke the news to her friend. "That Inspector Carmichael was round at Harri's Bar earlier on and told Harriett. He didn't tell her how or where he died, but it sounds like he was killed some time last night."

"How dreadful," replied Swift, his throat suddenly becoming dry as he spoke.

Chapter 38

Penny knew her plan was taking shape, when her son arrived back from the chicken farm at 3pm.

"You're home early," she remarked, as if it was a total surprise.

Robbie nodded. "Yes, Mr Hayley wants us in at eight in the morning, so he let us off early today."

"Really," replied Penny. "That means you'll have to be out the house before 7:30am. You better set your alarm a bit earlier."

Robbie nodded before opening the fridge door and extracting a carton of milk. He didn't notice his Mother's wry, self-satisfied smile.

* * * *

Carmichael leaned back in his chair, arms folded in front of him. He was starting to wonder whether any of the potential suspects they'd identified so far would go on to prove to be Kendal Michelson's murderer. Maybe his assumption that the killer was known to Kendal was wrong. Maybe the killer had a grievance with Gavin, not Kendal and, as such, was not yet on their radar. Whatever the truth was, one thing Carmichael was sure of was that whoever killed Kendal had also killed Gavin.

"As we don't appear to have made that much progress in identifying Kendal's killer," he remarked to the team, "let's now focus on Gavin's murder."

The nods around the room indicated that his three officers felt this was a sound idea.

"I know we've already discussed this on the phone, but why don't you kick off, Marc," Carmichael suggested. "I'd like to hear what Paul and Rachel make of what you learnt this morning."

Watson smiled. "Put it this way," he said, "after spending several hours with Jean-Paul Mercier, I am now well-versed in the art of chocolate making."

"But the question is," interrupted Carmichael, "does any of this information help us with the case?"

Watson gave a faint shrug of his shoulders. "About ninety-nine percent doesn't," he conceded. "However, what I did discover from Jean-Paul was that the vats were empty at 5pm yesterday when they finished the day's production; that it would have taken in total a minimum of three hours, and more likely four, to have prepared the chocolate mixture and for the chocolate Michelson was encased in to have set; and, very importantly in his view, whoever made the chocolate in that vat knew exactly what they were doing. They must have been someone that either works there now or has previously worked at The World of Chocolate."

"Maybe a bitter ex-employee?" suggested Rachel.

Watson nodded. "I'm on to that already, Rachel," he replied. "I spoke with the HR manager there just before I left and she's sending me over a list of ex-employees who had knowledge of making chocolate. I've asked her to indicate which, if any, were fired."

"How far back did you ask her to look?" Carmichael enquired.

"Five years," replied Watson.

Carmichael nodded. "Good work, Marc. That should be far enough," he confirmed. "What about your meeting with Carmen. How did that go?"

"Well, apart from her disclosure about Kendal's mobile," Watson replied, "she also told me that she received a call from Gavin at five o'clock yesterday evening to say he would not be home as he was working late at the office. She also confirmed that this was not uncommon. She then told me that she finished her work at the house, had a few hours' sleep, then, at about eleven, she took the train to Southport to start her new job as a night cleaner at Harri's Bar."

"She's a hard worker is our Carmen," Rachel remarked, with a hint of admiration in her voice.

"She may also be a killer," observed Carmichael, "but, in fairness, that story does tie-in with what Harriett Hall told me. She said she stayed with Carmen until about two thirty, then she went home."

Watson looked at his notes. "Yes, two thirty is the same time Carmen said Harriett left," he confirmed. "She also told me that she finished the cleaning at six in the morning and she then got the train back to Barton Bridge."

Carmichael turned to face Rachel Dalton, but before he could speak, she nodded and smiled.

"More CCTV footage for me to check, I take it," she remarked.

Carmichael shrugged his shoulders. "You've got it in one, Rachel," he replied.

Watson waited for the team's attention to return to him.

"I also asked Carmen about her movements on the evening Kendal was killed," he announced. "Carmen maintains that on that evening Harriett Hall came over for dinner with Gavin Michelson..."

"Which we know," remarked Carmichael.

Watson nodded. "But what she also told me was that it

was Gavin Michelson who did the cooking, so she basically had the evening off and, according to her, she just stayed in her room from about six and did not come down until around seven the next morning, when she started to clear away the dishes from the night before."

"Well, hopefully, when Rachel looks at the CCTV footage from Saturday evening and talks with the local taxi companies, we'll be able to see whether she slipped away and got herself to Southport," Carmichael remarked.

Watson nodded. "I agree," he replied, "but, to be honest, my money says Rachel won't find anything. With both Michelsons being killed, she's potentially lost her income and a roof over her head, so I don't quite get why she'd kill either of them."

"And, of course, she's got an alibi for the time of Gavin's death, if she was at Harriett Hall's bar cleaning all night," added Cooper.

Carmichael nodded, "You may both be right," he replied, "but let's not jump to conclusions. As I've just said, until Rachel looks at the CCTV footage and checks out the local taxi companies, she's still got to be a suspect."

Cooper and Watson nodded, to indicate their agreement.

"That's great work, Marc," Carmichael remarked. "Did you learn anything else from Carmen?"

Watson shook his head. "Not really," he replied. "I did ask her if Kendal had two mobiles. She seemed vague when she answered, but she thought he only had one."

Suitably impressed with the information Watson had supplied the team, Carmichael then fixed his eyes firmly on Cooper.

"What about you, Paul?" he enquired. "Why don't you start by filling everybody in on the interviews you had this morning, then give us an update on Dr Stock's findings so far."

Cooper nodded and took out his note book.

"I spoke with four people at The World of Chocolate," Cooper announced. "Rebecca Graham, the receptionist; Janet Sutherland, the sales and marketing director; Wayne McBride, the night security guard; and Martin Bailey, the caretaker who found Gavin Michelson's body."

"Of these, who was the last one to see or speak with Michelson?" Carmichael enquired.

Cooper looked at his notes for a few seconds.

"It would be Janet Sutherland," Cooper replied. "She worked late with Michelson last night, preparing for the meetings he was due to be having next weekend in Belgium. According to Ms Sutherland, she left at about six forty-five, but told me that he was planning to work through the night."

"What sort of person is she?" Carmichael enquired. "Harriett Hall suggested she and Gavin Michelson may have been having a relationship."

"She's a woman in her late twenties or early thirties," replied Cooper. "Quite quiet and unassuming really. Maybe it was the shock of Michelson's death, but she did not strike me as being the sort of person you'd expect to be heading up sales and marketing. If I didn't know what she did, I'd have said she was more likely to be a bookkeeper, or some such job where she'd be tucked away in the back office somewhere."

"And what about her relationship with Michelson?" Carmichael enquired. "Did she mention much about that?"

Cooper shook his head. "No," he replied. "She was certainly upset about his death, but she held herself together really well considering; and I didn't ask her specifically about any personal relationship she may have been having with Michelson as, frankly, it never crossed my mind that that was remotely likely."

"Even with them working late alone together in the office?" interjected Watson.

Rachel Dalton shot a disapproving sideways look at her

colleague. "I've worked late with you dozens of times," she remarked, "but it doesn't mean we're sleeping together."

"That's only because I've got strong willpower," Watson replied with a wide grin on his face.

Carmichael ignored their comments, his focus remaining with Cooper.

"It would appear Gavin Michelson regularly worked through the night," he remarked.

Cooper nodded. "Yes," he concurred, "this was confirmed by all four people I spoke to. Wayne McBride, the night security guard, reckoned in the last six months Michelson had called him several times to tell him he wouldn't be needed that night as he was working late. And Martin Bailey, the caretaker told me he'd opened up the factory at five thirty on numerous occasions to find Gavin Michelson still working."

"I assume they must have showers in the building, then, in that case," Rachel suggested.

Cooper nodded. "Oh yes," he replied. "The World of Chocolate has a few showers. According to Bailey, Michelson encouraged his staff to keep fit. You know, go for runs at lunchtime and cycle to work. He'd even installed a small gym in the building, so yes, they have showers."

"That seems in keeping with him," remarked Carmichael. "Anything else we need to know from these interviews?"

Cooper shook his head. "Only that Rebecca Graham confirmed what she'd told you, about being in a relationship with Gavin," he remarked. "But other than that, there's nothing else that struck me as being particularly relevant from my interviews. However, one of the findings from Dr Stock's autopsy on Gavin Michelson is very significant given what we know."

"And what's that?" Carmichael enquired, his attention now even more heightened.

"According to Stock, there was clear evidence that Gavin

Michelson had been sexually active not long before he died," Cooper announced.

"How long before?" Carmichael asked.

Cooper shrugged his shoulders. "Within three to four hours of him being killed," Cooper replied, "and Stock reckons Gavin Michelson died between eleven last night and two this morning."

Carmichael raised his eyebrows. "It looks like we may have a new suspect in Janet Sutherland," he remarked. "I'd certainly like to talk with her."

Chapter 39

Carmichael and his three officers remained in the incident room for a further forty-five minutes. For the first ten of these, Carmichael updated the team on his discussions with Harriett Hall, including her comments about there being friction between Janet Sutherland and Rebecca Graham, her revelation about Gabby Johns's affair with Gavin Michelson, and the fact that Harriett herself didn't seem to have much time for Gabby.

They all then updated the list of knowns, theories, and suspects for both murders, adding to the suspects list a note indicating the perceived strength the team gave to the alibis they'd been given so far.

Before the meeting broke up, Carmichael confirmed the actions he wanted each of the team to undertake for the rest of the afternoon.

Rachel's task was to study the CCTV footage and to find out if Carmen had used a taxi on Saturday evening or in the early hours of Sunday morning.

Carmichael had instructed Watson to get in touch with Kim Bolton, J.C. Palmer and Zorik Daniels, the three colleagues from Kendal's work, to find out if they knew Gavin Michelson and what their movements had been on the previous evening. Watson was also tasked with chasing up the list of ex-employees from The World of Chocolate and to start looking to see if anyone on the list looked as though they could be a potential murder suspect.

As for Carmichael and Cooper, their assignment was to locate and interview the two suspects at the top of their revised list; Gabby Johns and Janet Sutherland.

* * * *

Since receiving the call from Carly Wolf that morning, Martin Swift had been troubled. He had known Kendal and Gavin Michelson almost his entire life; and, although even he'd have to admit they'd often been a little indifferent towards him, they were still, in his eyes, two of his closest friends.

The murder of Kendal had been a massive shock to him, but in isolation he'd not even considered it to have been linked to events several years before. However, with Gavin now murdered, and so soon after Kendal's death, one event loomed large in his mind. As he slowly recounted the part he'd played, his throat became dry and his palms started to feel moist with sweat.

Swift slumped back in his chair, his forehead cold and clammy. He could feel his heart beating faster in his chest and his pulse quickening in his wrists, as it dawned on him that he may be the next one to suffer from the killer's vengeance.

Chapter 40

Carmichael decided they'd interview Gabby Johns first.

Gabby worked at Logan-Lane Labs, a pharmaceutical company on the outskirts of Moulton Bank, very close to where Carmichael lived.

As he was keen to look at the three lists they'd just refreshed, he elected to allow Cooper to drive. He wasn't a great fan of Cooper's driving and was even less impressed with his clapped-out car, however, Carmichael didn't want to waste any time. He needed to use the next twenty minutes to study and review the notes they'd jointly updated, so, reluctantly, he decided to brave Cooper behind the wheel.

As they got underway, he lay the three sheets of paper with the thirty-two bullet points on his lap.

Facts
1. Kendal Michelson died between Midnight and 2am.
2. He'd spent that evening at the China Garden, a Chinese restaurant on the North Coastal Road with Carly Wolf, Gabby Johns and Martin Swift.
3. He and Carly walked from the China Garden towards town.
4. Kendal and Carly had parted company by eleven forty.
5. He didn't struggle with his killer.
6. Kendal had a mobile on the night he died.

7. Martin Swift, Gabby Johns, Carly Wolf, Kim Bolton, J.C. Palmer and Zorik Daniels, all benefit financially from Kendal's death.
8. There are no records of any mobile phone activity by Kendal on the day he died (even though two independent witnesses maintain he used a mobile).
9. Gavin Michelson died between 10pm and 2am
10. Gavin had been sexually active shortly before he died.
11. Whoever killed Gavin knew how to make chocolate (maybe a current or ex-employee).
12. Both Kendal and Gavin appear to have had several partners – Gabby Johns apparently had relationships with both.

Unknowns
1. Who killed Kendal Michelson?
2. Why was he killed?
3. Why did he go down to the beach on his own?
4. Who did he talk with on the two calls he is alleged to have had shortly before he died?
5. Did he have a second mobile? If so, where is that mobile?
6. Who killed Gavin Michelson?
7. Why was he killed?
8. Is his death linked to Kendal's?
9. Why did Gavin regularly tell the night security guard he didn't need to come in? Was he meeting someone?
10. Who did Gavin have sex with on the night he died?

Potential Suspects / Alibi matrix
1. Gabby Johns – Kendal (highly unlikely), Gavin (Possible).
2. Martin Swift – Kendal (highly unlikely), Gavin (Possible).
3. Carly Wolf & Luke Barrett-Hobbs – Kendal (no), Gavin (Possible).

4. Kim Bolton – Kendal (possible), Gavin (Possible but no link).
5. CJ – Kendal (possible), Gavin (Possible but no link).
6. Zorik – Kendal (Possible), Gavin (Possible but no link).
7. Harriett Hall – Kendal (Possible but unlikely), Gavin (Highly unlikely).
8. Carmen Martinez – Kendal (Possible but unlikely), Gavin (Highly unlikely).
9. Rebecca Graham – Kendal (Possible but no link), Gavin (Possible).
10. Janet Sutherland – Kendal (Possible but no link), Gavin (Possible).

By the time Cooper's car arrived at Gabby Johns's place of work, Carmichael had circled points 4 and 10 of the unknown list. His gut told him that if he could get answers to these questions, he'd know who the killer was. He wasn't sure how he was going to discover who Kendal had been talking to on the mobile before he was killed, but hopefully finding the identity of Gavin's late-night lover would prove to be a much less arduous task. After a quick call to Stock, to verify there was sufficient DNA to identify who Gavin Michelson had been with before he was killed, Carmichael allowed himself a small, but satisfied grin.

"Let's see what Gabby Johns has to say for herself," he said cheerily to Cooper, before clambering out of the car.

* * * *

Unlike her boss, Rachel Dalton was not prone to hunches. She always tried to stick with the facts and, as such, was more than happy to once more be given the task of investigating the facts that would either support or contradict Carmen's story.

As she waited for the CCTV footage to be brought to her from Southport train station, Rachel started to make calls to the five registered taxi companies located in Southport and the two companies based out of Barton Bridge.

* * * *

Carmichael and Cooper waited in the reception of Logan-Lane Labs for Gabby Johns to arrive.

"Do you still think it was a two-person job, the killing at the factory last night?" Carmichael enquired, his voice hushed so the receptionist could not overhear him.

Cooper nodded. "Yes," he replied, also in a whisper. "Marc's right, of course, that it may have been one person, but I think it would have been really hard for someone to have managed to sedate Gavin, strip him naked, tie him to the chair, dip him in chocolate, then move the chair to the far end of the factory. And then to clean everything up themselves afterwards." Cooper shook his head. "No, in my opinion it has to be a two-man job."

Carmichael shrugged his shoulders. "Maybe he didn't need his clothes taken off," he remarked, "if he'd been having sex maybe he was already naked. And if that person killed him, you have to ask yourself, is it likely they'd have an accomplice with them?"

Cooper pondered for a while. "You could be right," he conceded. "But I still think it would have been really difficult for one person to have managed everything that went on last night on their own."

Carmichael smiled. "Well, hopefully, Ms Johns can help us," he replied. "She had affairs with both father and son, both are now dead. And if she turns out to be Gavin's mystery lover from last night, she'll elevate herself to the top of my list of suspects."

Cooper nodded. "Well, here she comes. Let's see what she says."

* * * *

Watson fully expected his discussions with Kim Bolton, Zorik Daniels and J.C. Palmer to confirm that none of them knew Gavin Michelson, and that they'd all been tucked up in bed at home last night, with nobody other than their partners, the ones that had them, to verify their alibis.

His hunch was wrong. All three had met Kendal's father on several occasions, and, as for their alibis, they maintained that they'd been together the night before at an antiques restoration convention, which had taken place at a hotel seventy miles away. An event that had not finished until well after midnight, which meant they'd stayed over and travelled back together that morning; leaving at 8am, they'd had breakfast in full view of the other guests and staff, in the hotel's dining room.

Armed with the details of where they'd stayed, Watson left Michelson's Antiques and strolled back to his car to call the hotel. If the hotel confirmed their story, they'd be totally in the clear, which would also mean a tidy, quick and easy result for him; a thought which pleased him greatly.

Chapter 41

"Good afternoon, Ms Johns," Carmichael said loudly, with his right hand firmly held out.

"Good afternoon," she replied, as she tentatively took hold of Carmichael's hand, but only for a few seconds before her lukewarm grip was released and her arm returned to her side. "How can I help you?"

"This is Sergeant Cooper," said Carmichael, his free right hand now motioning in Cooper's direction, "I don't think you met the other day."

Gabby Johns smiled and nodded at Cooper. "How can I help you both?" she asked again.

"Is there somewhere private we can go?" Carmichael enquired.

With a nervous look on her face, Gabby Johns pointed in the direction of a door to the right of them. "We can use one of the small meeting rooms, if you'd like," she suggested.

* * * *

It took no more than ten minutes for the manager of Long Meadow Park Hotel, the venue where Kim Bolton, J.C. Palmer and Zorik Daniels had claimed to have stayed the night before, to substantiate their story.

"They were seated on table seven for dinner," he

confirmed. "They all signed separate chits for their drinks bill at twelve forty-five and they all checked out at around the same times this morning; two minutes past eight, five minutes past eight and then seven minutes past eight."

"Thank you," replied Watson. "You've been most helpful."

* * * *

"I'm afraid I've some bad news for you," Carmichael remarked once he, Gabby Johns and Cooper were all safely seated and the door had been closed in the tiny meeting room.

Gabby Johns looked genuinely concerned, her large, brown eyes open wide as she waited for Carmichael to enlighten her.

"It's Gavin Michelson," continued Carmichael. "He's been murdered."

Carmichael looked intently at Gabby as he delivered his message, trying hard to gauge her reaction to the news of her ex-lover's death; but her expression told him nothing.

"How did he die?" Gabby enquired calmly.

"We're still trying to establish the details of his death," replied Carmichael, "but it happened at the factory last night."

"Poor Gavin," replied Gabby. "Do you think he was murdered by the same person who killed Kendal?"

Carmichael gave a slight shrug of his shoulders. "It's a possibility," he replied, "but we are looking at all other avenues."

Gabby Johns nodded. "Would you like a coffee?" she asked. "I could certainly do with one."

"I'll sort that out," said Cooper, who rose quickly to his feet. "What would you like?"

"White with no sugar," replied Gabby, without any attempt to make eye contact with Cooper.

195

Carmichael looked up at Cooper and shook his head, to indicate he didn't need a drink, which Cooper acknowledged with a quick nod before hastily leaving the room.

"I understand that you and Gavin once had a relationship," Carmichael remarked. "Is that correct?"

Gabby looked straight into Carmichael's eyes and nodded. "It was hardly a relationship," she replied, "a one-night stand, and one I'm not proud of; but it's true."

"And was this at the time you were also with Kendal?" Carmichael enquired.

Gabby Johns nodded. "Unfortunately, yes it was," she replied. "It was what eventually broke us up, not so surprisingly."

"And after you broke up with Kendal," continued Carmichael, "did you then continue to have a relationship with his father?"

Gabby Johns squirmed uneasily in her seat. "God no," she replied. "I was drunk, when we…"

Her voice tailed off as if she was uncomfortable in describing her dalliance with Gavin Michelson… "It happened only once, but of course it was once too many and…"

Again, Gabby Johns appeared to find it hard to articulate the circumstances.

"I see," remarked Carmichael, in an attempt to spare Gabby any further embarrassment. "I need to ask you about your movements yesterday evening and last night," he continued.

Gabby Johns sat back in her chair and looked back at Carmichael in amazement. "Surely you don't think I did it, do you?" she remarked firmly, with a hint of irritation in her voice. "Why on earth would I want to kill Gavin?"

"You've just told me that he was the reason you and Kendal split-up," replied Carmichael. "For some people, that would be reason enough."

"Not me," Gabby replied angrily. "If I was going to kill anyone, it wouldn't have been Kendal or Gavin."

"Really," observed Carmichael. "So, who would you like to kill?"

Gabby Johns straightened her posture before answering.

"I've no intention of killing anyone," she replied. "It's not in my nature. However, it was that spoilt little madam, Carly Wolf, and her interfering ever-so-bloody-trendy aunt, Harriett bloody Hall, who told Kendal about me and Gavin. So, if I was going to murder anyone, Inspector, it would be one of those two."

As she finished her sentence, Cooper returned, holding a steaming, brown plastic cup in his hand. Without a word, he placed it carefully on the low table just in front of Gabby Johns.

"Anyway," continued Carmichael, "you were about to tell me what you were doing last night."

Gabby Johns picked up the plastic cup and took a tiny sip.

"I was here until about eight thirty," she replied, "then I headed off."

"So, what time did you arrive home?" Carmichael enquired.

Gabby shrugged her shoulders.

"It would have been about nine fifteen," she replied.

"And did you remain at home all evening?" Carmichael asked.

"Yes," replied Gabby. "I was at home all evening and all night, on my own. I got up this morning at about seven thirty and left to come here at about eight twenty."

"Did you call anybody or have any contact with anyone?" Carmichael enquired.

Gabby Johns shook her head before suddenly opening her eyes wide.

"Actually, that's not totally true," she remarked. "I ordered a Chinese and about twenty minutes later, went to pick it up."

"And at what time was that?" Carmichael enquired.

"I guess it would have been at about ten thirty," she replied.

"Seems very late to be eating," Carmichael suggested.

Gabby Johns shrugged her shoulders once more. "I often eat late. I know it's not what they recommend, but it's how I am."

Carmichael nodded. "Can you tell me which Chinese you called?"

"It's called the Canton House," replied Gabby. "It's about fifteen minutes' drive from my house."

Carmichael nodded. "Can you remember what you had?"

Gabby Johns smiled. "Of course," she replied. "Vegetarian spring rolls and vegetarian spicy noodles. I always order the same thing."

Carmichael nodded again. "One last thing," he remarked, "would you be willing to allow us to take a DNA sample?"

"Why?" Gabby enquired.

"Well, we believe we have the DNA of the person who killed Gavin," replied Carmichael. "So, if we had yours, we could hopefully eliminate you from our enquiries."

Gabby Johns took a few seconds to consider the question.

"Why not," she replied eventually. "I've nothing to hide."

Chapter 42

It was almost 5pm when Watson finally arrived back at Kirkwood Police station.

"Any word from Carmichael or Cooper?" he asked.

Rachel Dalton shook her head. "How did you get on this afternoon?" she enquired.

Having spent little time completing the main element of his assignment, Watson had been at home for a few hours, but wasn't about to admit that to Rachel.

"It took a while," he replied with a sigh, "but I've spoken to all three and have checked out their alibis and it's abundantly clear that none of them could have murdered Gavin Michelson. Their alibis are water tight. They did know him though."

Rachel nodded. "The boss will be pleased you've managed to eliminate them from our suspects list, not that they were ever very strong candidates."

Watson nodded. "Well, it does narrow the field down a little," he remarked.

"That reminds me," Rachel added. "The HR lady at The World of Chocolate called earlier. She says she's emailed you the list of ex-employees. They should be in your inbox."

"What about you?" Watson asked as he started to log onto his computer. "How have you got on with the CCTV footage and calling all those taxi companies?"

Rachel shook her head. "Her story all checks out," she replied, rather despondently. "The image of Carmen, at Southport train station, getting off the last train from Barton Bridge at eleven fifty-six last night is crystal clear. She's also visible on the CCTV at Southport station boarding the six twenty-five train this morning. None of the seven taxi companies I called had any record of taking a fare from anyone matching Carmen's description to Barton Bridge at any time between six o'clock last night and three o'clock this morning."

"So, that means she's not our killer either," remarked Watson.

Rachel nodded. "That's certainly what it looks like," she replied.

* * * *

"What did you make of Gabby Johns?" Carmichael enquired as soon as the two officers were seated in Cooper's Volvo.

"Her alibi's pretty weak," he replied, "but if we can establish that she had a take-away at about ten thirty, that does shed some doubt on her being our killer. I guess she could have had her take-away and then gone to the factory, but that would mean her getting there at about eleven thirty to midnight at the earliest."

Carmichael nodded. "I didn't buy her protestation about being incapable of killing the two Michelsons; she has a clear motive in my opinion," he replied, "but if this take-away claim can be confirmed by the Chinese restaurant, then I'd have to agree with you."

"Do you want me to check that out?" Cooper enquired.

Carmichael shook his head. "No," he replied, "I suspect either Marc or Rachel will have concluded their tasks already, so I'll get them to check out Gabby's story. I'll call them while you drive us back to The World of Chocolate. We need to try and catch Janet Sutherland before she leaves for the evening."

Cooper nodded. "Sounds like a plan," he replied, mimicking one of Carmichael's well used phrases.

* * * *

Rachel Dalton had just taken a large bite of the apple she'd brought from home that morning, when her mobile rang. "It's Carmichael," she remarked, before quickly chewing and swallowing what was in her mouth.

Watson grinned, but continued to stare at the details of the five ex-employees that had been sent over to him.

"Hi, sir," announced Rachel as soon as her mouth was empty.

"Are you busy?" enquired Carmichael – his way of questioning why it took her so long to pick up his call.

"No," Rachel replied. "I'm with Marc. We were just updating each other on our findings from this afternoon."

"How've you got on?" Carmichael asked.

"To cut a long story short," replied Rachel, "Marc's been able to rule out the three people from Kendal's work as Gavin's killer. He's now looking at the list of potential disgruntled ex-employees the HR woman from the factory has just sent him."

"I see," replied Carmichael. "And why's Marc so certain that Kendal's colleagues are all innocent?"

Rachel looked over in Watson's direction. "It would appear that all three of Kendal's colleagues were at a business function of some sort, at a hotel seventy miles away, last night. Marc's checked out their story with the hotel and he's sure they couldn't have carried out Gavin's murder. They wouldn't have had time."

"And what about you?" Carmichael enquired. "How have you got on?"

"After viewing the CCTV footage," Rachel replied, "it's clear that Carmen's telling us the truth about her movements last night."

"What about the taxi companies?" Carmichael remarked. "Did you check them out?"

"Yes," replied Rachel, "I called them all, seven in total. None of them took a fare last night from Southport to Barton Bridge. And none of them remembers seeing anyone who looked remotely like Carmen's description."

Carmichael paused for a few seconds to consider what Rachel had just told him. "We've finished talking with Gabby Johns," Carmichael told her, "and we're now off to The World of Chocolate again to talk with Janet Sutherland. If we can catch her, I also want to try and speak with Rebecca Graham again."

"How did your interview go with Gabby Johns?" Rachel asked. "Do you think she's got anything to do with the murders?"

"She doesn't have much of an alibi for last night," replied Carmichael. "She reckons she was home all night by herself. She does, however, maintain that she called in, then collected, a take-away from a Chinese restaurant near her called the Canton House. She says it's about fifteen minutes' drive from her house. Can you check that out for me, please? She also says it was at about ten thirty and she ordered vegetarian spring rolls and vegetarian spicy noodles. According to her, she goes there quite often and always orders the same thing."

"No problem," replied Rachel. "I'll get onto it straight away."

"Also," added Carmichael, "I want you and Marc to get someone from Stock's team down to the station in the morning to take DNA samples from the six women who might have been Gavin's late-night partner last night. I've already arranged for Gabby Johns to come in first thing in the morning and I'll be asking Janet Sutherland and Rebecca Graham to join her. If you can do that and, between you and Marc, contact Carmen Martinez, Harriett Hall, and Carly Wolf. I want them all to give us DNA samples, too."

"What if they refuse?" remarked Rachel.

"Well, we can't force them," admitted Carmichael, "but I'm sure you and Marc can impress upon them the importance of giving us what we need."

"What about the list of ex-employees?" Rachel enquired. "Do you still want Marc to follow those up?"

"Absolutely," replied Carmichael, as if she'd asked him the most ridiculous question in the world. "But the immediate priority is to get DNA samples arranged. So, for the time being, tell him to help you sort that out."

"No problem," replied Rachel. "Marc and I will get that organised before we finish this evening."

Upon hearing Rachel's final comment to Carmichael, Watson looked over to his colleague, sensing his hopes of an early finish had just been scuppered.

Chapter 43

As soon as Carmichael clapped eyes on Janet Sutherland, he practically scrubbed her from his list of suspects.

The decidedly plain-looking young woman with the clammy handshake and a decidedly timid demeanour didn't match the template he'd created in his head of the type of woman Gavin Michelson would have gone for. To be thorough, though, he would still ask her to give a DNA sample, but he'd have wagered a month's salary against Janet being Gavin's partner on the previous evening.

"It's absolutely terrible," Janet remarked, when they'd finished the normal pleasantries in the Kenya room, the location of their meeting. "This will create serious problems for the business as Gavin had a hand in all the decisions here. He never felt the need to appoint a deputy."

"What sort of relationship did you have with Gavin?" Carmichael enquired.

"Very good, I think," replied Janet. "He was starting to give me much more latitude in making marketing decisions and we worked well together."

"I believe you're quite new here?" Cooper added.

"Yes," replied Janet, "I joined about six months ago. I finished my combined honours degree at Hertfordshire University last year, did six months at a marketing agency in London, then came here in February."

"Quite a sudden promotion then," remarked Carmichael. "There can't be many graduates who become Sales and Marketing Director within a year of finishing University."

Janet Sutherland's cheeks blushed slightly. "My father knows... sorry, knew Gavin," she replied rather sheepishly. "He helped me get the position here."

"Really," remarked Carmichael. "What does your father do?"

Janet's cheeks reddened even more. "Er, he's the Managing Director of one of our biggest retail outlets," she replied. "They go back ages."

Carmichael and Cooper exchanged a quick knowing look.

"Can you share with us the details of your movements last night?" Carmichael enquired.

"Of course," Janet replied, her willingness to help plainly evident in the speed of her response and in her body language. "I finished work last night at about six, then I went to my flat in Barton Bridge, had a bath, had some dinner, then I spent most of the rest of the evening skyping Barry."

"Barry," repeated Carmichael. "And who's Barry?"

"He's my boyfriend," replied Janet. "We met at Uni. He's currently on a gap year in South America. He's been in Rio for the last three months, working in a bar just off Copacabana Beach, so he's about four hours behind us."

"What time did you have your skype call?" Cooper enquired.

"It was at ten our time," Janet replied, "six local time in Rio."

"And how long were you on the call for?" Carmichael enquired.

"It was Barry's night off last night," Janet replied, "so we talked for most of the evening."

Carmichael shrugged his shoulders. "Can you be a bit more specific?"

Janet looked slightly puzzled. "I'll check my tablet when I get home to see," she replied, "but we must have been talking for at least three hours."

"Until about one in the morning?" Carmichael asked, trying to get some clarity into her story.

Janet nodded. "Yes, it would have been about then," she replied. "We'd have been talking for longer, but I was tired and wanted to get some sleep. We have the convention coming up this weekend in Belgium, so I wanted to make sure I wasn't late in the morning, especially as Gavin was planning on working through the night."

Carmichael raised his eyebrows. "So, you knew he was planning on working through the night?" he asked. "How come you didn't join him?"

Janet frowned, as if Carmichael's question was absurd.

"Gavin never wanted anyone to join him when he worked late," she replied. "In fact, he'd normally tell the night security guard not to bother coming in when he did a late-one."

"And was he prone to doing late-ones?" Carmichael asked.

Janet shrugged her shoulders. "Not every week," she replied, "but at least two or three times a month, I'd say."

"Do you know anyone at the factory who'd want to harm Gavin?" Carmichael enquired.

"Nobody," replied Janet, "absolutely nobody. He was liked by everyone."

"And was there anyone who he was particularly close to?" continued Carmichael.

Janet's cheeks again began to redden. "There's Rebecca, of course," she replied.

"Rebecca Graham," Carmichael confirmed.

Janet nodded. "Yes," she replied, "I think she and he may have had something going on. If not, it certainly wasn't for the lack of trying on her part."

"She fancied him, did she?" Carmichael remarked.

"Oh, I'd say so," replied Janet. "And she made it quite clear that she didn't want me making a play for him."

As she spoke, Janet hunched her shoulders and screwed-up her face. "I ask you," she continued, "he's almost old enough to be my grandad. Hers, too, come to think of it."

Carmichael once more exchanged a quick glance in Cooper's direction.

"We'll need to see the record on your tablet regarding the call you made last night with Barry," he remarked, "and I'd also like to ask you to come into the police station tomorrow morning to provide a DNA sample, if that's OK with you."

Janet looked back at Carmichael with a mystified look on her face. "Why do you need my DNA?" she enquired nervously.

"It's just to help us eliminate you from our enquiries," he advised her. "We believe we have DNA that might be his killer's, so we want to eliminate as many people as possible."

Janet nodded. "OK, I'll come over in the morning, and I'll bring my tablet with me."

Carmichael stood up and smiled. "Thank you for your time, Ms Sutherland," he remarked. "You've been really helpful."

"Not at all," Janet replied.

Carmichael was just about to exit the room when he turned around and looked back at the young woman.

"You mentioned you'd done a combined degree," he remarked. "What subjects did you take?"

Business Studies with Spanish," she replied, with a smile. "The plan is to one-day work in Barcelona, but I may have to wait a few years until I get around to that."

Carmichael smiled politely before turning away again and exiting the meeting room.

* * * *

Having learned from Rachel the additional tasks that Carmichael had set them, Watson decided to pull rank and pick the two that were the least bother for him. He had no desire to go back over to Southport, so he had elected to delegate the job of contacting Harriett Hall and Carly Wolf to Rachel, leaving him the tasks of dropping in on Carmen Martinez once more and also checking-out the Chinese restaurant where Gabby had allegedly bought her take-away the evening before. Both calls were on his way home, and as he quite fancied a Chinese for his evening meal, Watson had a smile on his face and a spring in his step when he left Kirkwood police station.

Rachel, on the other hand, wasn't so pleased with her assignment. Neither Harriett Hall or Carly Wolf were answering their mobiles, so a thirty-minute drive over to Harri's Bar and Carly's house in Haig Avenue, were now required to ensure they could be informed about Carmichael's request for a DNA sample.

Rachel left the office ten minutes after Watson, annoyed and frustrated with her senior colleague.

* * * *

"Looks like daddy has pulled a few strings to get Janet her job," Cooper remarked, as soon as they had left the room.

Carmichael nodded. "Wheels within wheels, I think they call it."

"I assume we now speak to Rebecca Graham again," Cooper remarked.

Carmichael nodded. "And as long as she's not gone home early, she should still be on reception; we can talk with her about a DNA sample on our way out."

* * * *

The land line rang for several seconds before Martin Swift picked it up. It was now 7:30pm and he was already on his third large scotch when he answered the call.

"Oh, it's you," he remarked.

He paused for a few seconds while he listened to the voice at the other end of the line.

"I'm bloody sure their deaths are linked," he remarked anxiously.

Martin Swift again listened intently to the person who'd called him.

"I'll be here all evening," he replied, "but I'm not sure what there is to discuss."

The call ended abruptly, with a worried-looking Swift placing the receiver down and taking another large swig from his whiskey tumbler.

Chapter 44

By the time Carmichael arrived home, it was 8:30pm.

He'd spoken personally with Rebecca Graham, Gabby Johns and Janet Sutherland and had managed to get all three women to agree to come into the station the next morning to provide their DNA samples. And, having been informed by Rachel that both Harriett Hall and Carly Wolf had also agreed, albeit reluctantly in Carly's case, to come to Kirkwood Police Station the following morning, all that Carmichael was now waiting for was another update from Watson.

He'd already spoken to his sergeant, who'd informed him that the Canton House clearly remembered Gabby Johns ordering a take-away by phone at around 10:30pm the evening before, which she'd then collected at about 11pm. According to Watson, the person he'd spoken to at the Canton House said he knew Gabby well as she had deliveries from them most weeks and would always place the same order. However, at the time they'd spoken, Watson had informed Carmichael that he'd not yet managed to locate Carmen, despite leaving a message on her mobile and calling at both Michelson houses.

Not wanting to allow Carmen to avoid providing her DNA, Carmichael had informed Watson, in no uncertain terms, that he was to locate her that evening and make sure she provided her sample the next morning, just as the other five women were doing.

As he opened the front door, Carmichael, for the first time, felt that the team were making progress with the case. In his mind, the DNA would surely identify who Gavin had sex with just before he died. And, if it was one of the six women they'd asked to provide DNA material, which he fully expected, the likelihood was that they were involved in Gavin Michelson's murder, and in all probability, Kendal Michelson's too.

"Hi Dad," remarked Robbie, who swiftly passed by his father in the hallway before rapidly ascending the stairs up to his bedroom.

"Hi son," replied Carmichael as the fleeting apparition disappeared from view.

Carmichael carried on walking towards the kitchen.

"Hello," pronounced Penny with a warm smile as her husband appeared through the open kitchen door. "How's your day been?"

Carmichael walked over to Penny and gave her a hug before moving towards the refrigerator. "I'm famished," he remarked as he opened the fridge door.

"What's new?" Penny replied sarcastically, her hands on her hips and her head shaking slowly from side to side. "I know where your son gets it from."

Carmichael ignored his wife's observations.

"The second murder," he remarked, his head now embedded inside the open refrigerator. "It's the father, Gavin Michelson."

This was not news to Penny, as the local radio had been giving updates every half hour since 11am, not that they had revealed much other than a man had been found dead that morning at The World of Chocolate. From about 1pm the news reports had changed slightly indicating that, although the police had not formally revealed who the man was, sources at The World of Chocolate had indicated that the dead man was Gavin Michelson.

"How did he die?" Penny enquired.

Carmichael extracted a small pork pie from out of the fridge and bit into it. Turning back to face his wife, his mouth still partially full, Carmichael rolled his eyes to the ceiling.

"All the indications are that he was drowned in chocolate," he replied. "I'm waiting on Stock's detailed report, but it looks like he was sedated then submerged in liquid chocolate."

Penny's expression of disbelief spoke volumes.

"Really," she exclaimed. "What an awful way to die."

Carmichael smiled and took a second bite of the pie.

"I suspect there are millions of people who'd disagree with you," he remarked flippantly. "I would guess it's a dream way to die for most chocoholics."

* * * *

It had been well over an hour since Marc and Susan Watson had finished their Chinese take-away.

"I better go and find Carmen," he announced after checking the time on his watch. "Hopefully, she's home now."

Susan Watson smiled back at him. "Yes," she replied, with a hint of ridicule in her best fake German accent, "you better not fail in your assignment or you'll be sent to the Russian front."

Watson shrugged his shoulders, gave his wife a lingering kiss on her lips, then jumped up from the sofa and headed for the door.

"I'll not be long," he replied. "Well I hope not."

* * * *

"So, are you any wiser about who this killer is?" Penny enquired as she and Carmichael sat together at the kitchen table.

Carmichael shrugged his shoulders.

"I'm convinced our murderer is one of six women that the Michelsons knew," replied Carmichael. "It may even be a couple of them in cahoots. That's what Cooper suspects, and I'm starting to think he may be right."

"Which of them are your prime suspects and what's their motive?" continued Penny.

Carmichael's embarrassment, at having to admit that he had precious little in the way of an answer to his wife's question, was spared when his mobile rang.

"Hi sir," came the familiar tone of Watson at the end of the line. "I've managed to locate Carmen. I'm in the car outside Gavin Michelson's place now. I've just this minute left her."

Carmichael gazed up at the clock on the kitchen wall, it was 9:30pm.

"Great," he replied, "where was she?"

"I don't think that woman ever sleeps," remarked his sergeant. "I passed her as she was coming out of the train station. She was weighed down with bags. Apparently, she'd been shopping in Sheffield this afternoon."

"Sheffield!" exclaimed Carmichael. "That's miles away."

"I know," replied Watson. "She had to get three trains, which is why it was about nine fifteen by the time she arrived home."

Carmichael shrugged his shoulders. "So, is she going to provide us with a DNA sample in the morning?" he enquired.

"Yes," replied Watson, "She says she'll come in after she's done her night cleaning at Harri's Bar."

"I see what you mean about her not needing much sleep," Carmichael remarked. "She'll need to catch the

213

train in less than two hours to get herself over to Southport."

"I know," replied Watson, "She's clearly wonder woman."

As they spoke, Carmichael could see that someone else was trying to call him.

"Look Marc," he said, "I'm going to have to go, but good work. I'll call Rachel and ask her if she can get to the office early in the morning to ensure the DNA tests go without a hitch. That should leave you free tomorrow morning to start to make contact with the ex-employees from The World of Chocolate. I appreciate you working late this evening, so don't feel you have to be into the office first thing."

Both Watson, at the end of the phone and Penny, listening a few yards away from her husband, were taken aback by Carmichael's gesture, as it was almost unheard of for Carmichael to ever allow an officer any leeway when it came to their work start times.

"Thanks, sir," replied Watson with genuine gratitude. "Have a good evening."

Penny waited for her husband to end the call before giving him one of her best admonishing looks.

"Did I hear you correctly?" she remarked. "Marc Watson can arrive a bit later in the morning, but poor Rachel Dalton has to be in early. If I didn't know you better, Inspector Carmichael, I'd have thought you were sexist."

Carmichael's brow furrowed. "Marc worked late this evening," he replied. "Anyway, it's her rank not her sex that prompted my decision. And besides, she'll be much better at dealing with the DNA samples than either Watson or Cooper. Especially as the people coming in are all women."

"Good recovery," Penny remarked sarcastically.

Carmichael nodded and smiled. "I thought so, too," he replied with a wry grin.

As he spoke, Carmichael's mobile beeped to indicate he had a voice message.

"Sorry, I need to listen to this," he remarked, while at the same time pressing 121 to retrieve his message.

Penny stood up. "I need to talk to you about Robbie," she whispered. "I've arranged for him to be out of the house early in the morning, which will give us a chance to work out what he's been up to."

Carmichael looked up at his wife with a sense of unease.

"Ok, we can talk about it in a minute," he replied.

"There's a programme starting at ten on channel four I want to catch," Penny remarked, as she walked towards the hallway, "so don't take ages on your call."

As his wife disappeared, the voice message kicked in. It was Martin Swift, sounding decidedly edgy.

"Hello, Inspector Carmichael. It's Martin Swift here. I need to talk with you. Could you please either call me back this evening or maybe we could meet at my office in the morning. I think I have some information that may be important regarding the deaths of Kendal and Gavin."

At that point, Carmichael could hear a doorbell ringing on Swift's message.

"Damn," Swift continued, "I'm going to have to go as I've got someone at the door. If you can't call back this evening, I generally get into work at about eight in the morning, so please pop over when you can."

The message ended.

Despite trying three times, Carmichael was unable to reach Martin Swift. Before he went to bed, he'd toyed with going over to Swift's house, but he finally decided that he'd wait until the morning before finding out what it was that Martin Swift believed to be so important.

Chapter 45

Wednesday 17ᵗʰ August

After contacting Rachel Dalton on her mobile, then spending the next hour half-watching the programme Penny had been so keen to see (a documentary looking at the arguments for and against nature and nurture as the main influence on human development) it was after 11pm before Penny had the chance to tell her husband about the call she'd made to Nigel Hayley, an old school friend whose father owned the farm where Robbie was working. With Nigel's help, she'd managed to contrive for Robbie to be told to report for work early the next day.

Although impressed by her ingenuity, Carmichael couldn't help feeling a little treacherous in being part of his wife's machinations. Given a choice, he'd have much preferred to have just sat Robbie down and had an honest conversation with him.

However, that option was not the course of action Penny had chosen, which is why, at precisely 7.35am, he found himself with his wife seated in his son's room facing the window.

"This is exactly where they sit," announced Penny, "I'm sure of it."

Carmichael peered through the window and over their back garden.

Pretty much all he could see was the tall green leylandii trees, which had been there when they bought the house and almost totally obscured the large detached houses of Lancaster Lane, which backed onto their rear gardens.

"Maybe they've suddenly taken up nature watching," Carmichael announced sarcastically. "You never know; there may be a rare bird nesting in one of those trees."

As he spoke, he picked up the binoculars Penny had extracted from their loft the day before and scoured the leylandii bushes searching for anything that would solve Penny's obsession. It was then he saw it, or rather her.

Carmichael turned the wheel slowly on the eyeglasses so that he could get the image into focus.

"I think I know why they've been so excited," he remarked. "And to be honest, my theory wasn't that far adrift."

"What is it?" enquired Penny with an eager but, at the same time, slightly wary tone to her voice.

Carmichael maintained his concentration on the image he was spying through his binoculars for a few seconds more, before handing them to his wife.

"Between the middle two leylandii," he announced pointing in the direction of a small break in the greenery.

It took Penny a few seconds to home in on the exact position her husband had described. However, Carmichael could tell when she'd found the target by the way her jaw dropped and she uttered the words "good god."

Penny placed the binoculars down on the window ledge.

"What on earth does she think she's doing?" she remarked.

Carmichael shrugged his shoulders and giggled. "Early morning naked exercises is my guess," he replied.

"But why would she do that in full view of her bedroom window?" Penny continued.

Carmichael laughed even louder. "To be fair to her," he replied, "she probably has no idea that there's a gap in the

217

leylandii, so she probably thinks she can't be seen. And, to be honest, apart from Robbie, his mates, and now me and you with our binoculars, she's probably not far wrong."

"But surely that's a criminal offense," protested Penny.

"I'm not sure," replied Carmichael. "I'll probably need to take one more look to make a judgement." As he spoke, he moved his hand forward in the direction of the eyeglasses.

"No way," replied Penny, who seized the binoculars and placed them out of her husband's reach.

Carmichael found the whole scenario hilarious and started to laugh uncontrollably.

"I'm serious," Penny remarked. "She has to be breaking some law posing naked like that each morning right in front of her window."

Carmichael, still laughing, shrugged his shoulders.

"I can't remember exactly what the law states," he replied, "but I'd imagine that it isn't unlawful to be naked in your own home, even in full view of the public, so long as the person concerned isn't performing an indecent act, which she's not. As far as I could see, before you hid the binoculars, she's just doing some stretching exercises. I can't see how she's breaking the law."

"Surely, she's in breach of public decency laws," argued Penny.

Carmichael shook his head. "To be honest," he remarked, "it's probably Robbie, his mates and now me and you that are more likely to have committed a crime," he replied. "Again, I'm no expert, but I expect a good brief could make a decent enough argument about us breaching her privacy, if she were to take us to court."

The colour drained from Penny's face. "Do you really think so?" she remarked.

Carmichael sniggered. "Look, leave it with me and I'll talk with Robbie tonight," he said. "Once he knows we know what he's been up to, I'm certain he'll stop," Carmichael added. "Well, I'm certain he'll stop inviting his pals around, although I wouldn't be surprised if he still has a quick peak now and again."

Penny's mouth opened wide. "I can't believe you're being so nonchalant about this," she remarked. "I think it's depraved of her to flaunt herself like that, and it's immoral of our son to be inviting his mates round for a cheap peep show."

"You're quite right," replied Carmichael, not wanting to heighten his wife's concern by taking a contrary stance, "but I can't see any real harm being done here, so as long as the peep show, as you call it, stops then surely that's all that's required."

Penny nodded. "Ok, but make sure you speak with him tonight," she announced sternly.

Carmichael nodded and stood up. "Anyway, who is that young woman?" he enquired. "Surely that's Mr and Mrs Harper's, those teachers from that public school near Kirkwood."

"The Boys Priory," confirmed Penny. "Yes, I think you're right; that's the Harper's house."

"Well, I know Mrs Harper's in reasonable nick for her age," he added, "and, of course, I've never had the pleasure of seeing her in the buff, but I can't imagine she's as…"

Carmichael paused as he tried to think of a word he could use to describe the naked young woman he'd just seen through the binoculars.

"I think 'conditioned' is the word you're struggling to find," suggested Penny with an admonishing expression on her face.

"Yes, 'conditioned'," repeated Carmichael.

Penny shrugged her shoulders. "I've not met her, but I did hear they had taken on a Nanny to help with their son,

Ethan," she remarked. "I suspect it's the Nanny we've been watching."

Carmichael nodded. "That would explain it," he replied.

Chapter 46

As instructed, Rachel Dalton had arrived at Kirkwood Police Station even earlier than normal.

Confident that neither the lab technician from Stock's team or any of the six ladies invited to give their samples would be at the station at 7:50am, she made her way directly to the canteen where she purchased a large black coffee, a slightly-over-ripe banana (the best she could find in the bowl) and a medium-sized tub of granola.

With her purchases in her hand, she then made her way upstairs. Having called down to the front desk to make them aware that when the ladies arrived they were to let her know, Rachel sat at her desk and started to nibble at her breakfast.

* * * *

The offices of Hathersage, Marlow and Swift were located about fifteen minutes' drive from Carmichael's house; so, traffic permitting, Carmichael expected to arrive at about 8:10am. He was curious to discover what Martin Swift wanted to discuss with him as, by the tone of his voice message, it did seem to be important; at least in Swift's eyes.

As he made his way along the windy, but thankfully almost empty, country roads, Carmichael's thoughts drifted. He tried desperately to retain focus on the case and to methodically work through the facts he and the team had so far assembled, but he couldn't help recalling the vision of the young woman they'd spied-on earlier, stretching naked at her bedroom window. As he did, he smiled. He would definitely have a quiet word with Robbie, Penny would be livid if he didn't, but he wasn't going to go over the top. In a perverse way, he was quite proud of his son, with part of him even hoping Robbie had had the commercial sense to charge his mates, say £5, for the privilege of sharing his early morning visual spectacular. However, now he was aware of what was going on, he'd have to make sure his message to his son was clear and that, after they'd spoken, Robbie would curtail his early-morning viewing.

As his black BMW arrived at Swift's office, Carmichael allowed himself a small smile before turning his thoughts back to the case.

He'd expected Swift's offices to be one of those old, dated solicitors' buildings with crumbling pointing, a large, sombre front door and maybe a badly-tended wisteria invading the outside. Then, once inside, he'd expected to find lots of pokey rooms with austere rows of ancient law books on sturdy, wooden bookcases. He couldn't have been more mistaken.

Outside the brand-new building, there was a large, tarmacked parking area with ample spaces for dozens of cars. There were large windows, bright and shiny as they reflected the sun, which was now beaming down from the east; a glass front door with the name Hathersage, Marlow and Swift etched deeply in the middle; and not a climbing plant in site.

Carmichael parked his black BMW in the first available space he could find, between a bright red Porsche 911 Turbo and an extremely large, brand-new-looking Range Rover.

"I bet they'll belong to two of the partners," muttered Carmichael as he clambered out of the car and made his way to the front door.

At exactly 8:15am, the Technician from Stock's team arrived at Kirkwood Police Station and was escorted by Rachel Dalton to the small room she'd booked out for him to conduct the tests.

"Will you just be doing saliva tests?" Rachel enquired.

The Technician smiled. "Yes," he replied. "Just a quick scrape with my magic wooden instrument, then into the test tube and we're done."

"I haven't seen you around before," Rachel remarked, "have you just started with Stock?"

The young man smiled again, a broad smile that showed-off his perfectly-symmetrical white teeth. "Yes," he said. "I started a few weeks ago. I was working in Leeds before. I was at university there, which is where I qualified."

Rachel moved her tongue quickly across her own teeth, to ensure she'd not left any granola debris.

"And how do you find working for Dr Stock?" she enquired.

"He can be a miserable old sod at times," replied the technician candidly, "but I can cope with him."

Rachel, confident that her teeth were a granola-free area, smiled back at the technician. "He's a brilliant pathologist," she remarked, "but he can be a little crabby. Inspector Carmichael and he often have a few verbal sparring matches."

The technician smiled again. "That sounds like Uncle Harry," he replied.

"Uncle?" repeated Rachel, "Stock's your Uncle?"

The technician held out his right hand. "Yes, I'm Matthew Stock," he said with another beaming smile. "I'm really pleased to meet you."

Carmichael had been sitting in the waiting room for nearly twenty minutes before he decided to call Martin Swift's mobile. Whether he'd had a problem with traffic or whether his claim to be an early starter was slightly exaggerated, Carmichael wasn't sure. What he was certain about, though, was that it was now 8:30am and Martin Swift had yet to arrive at the office.

After five rings, Swift's mobile went to answer machine as it had done the evening before when Carmichael had tried to return his call.

Carmichael hated leaving voice messages, but reluctantly did so on this occasion.

"Hello, this is Inspector Carmichael," he said, "I'm at your office and have been so for over twenty minutes. Can you please call me on this number and let me know what time you expect to arrive in this morning?"

The receptionist could see Carmichael's frustration building as he ended the call and started to pace up and down the reception area.

"This isn't like Mr Swift," she remarked, as if to defend her boss. "He's normally here by now. I can only think he's slept in."

Carmichael's expression remained unsympathetic to the receptionist's unsuccessful attempt to defuse the situation. "Do you have his address?" he enquired, his exasperation evident in his stern facial expression.

The receptionist nodded and tapped on her keyboard.

"It's 2 Cedar Court, Barton Bank," she replied. "It's at the other end of the village, but no more than five minutes, even if you walked."

Carmichael knew where Cedar Court was, he'd been there once before when another resident, a golf chum of Chief Inspector Hewitt, had complained about an alleged break-in, which turned out to be his drunken son smashing a window to get in after losing his key.

Carmichael, in a conscious effort to mask his frustration, squeezed out a forced smile. "Thanks," he replied, "I'll make my way over there."

* * * *

To Rachel's surprise, three of the six women arrived at the station before 8:30am, and by 8:45am, Matthew Stock had successfully taken swabs of saliva from Rebecca Graham, Gabby Johns and Carmen Martinez.

"We should take bets on which one gives us a match," remarked Matthew mischievously, once Carmen Martinez had departed.

Rachel laughed. "So out of the three so far which, if any, do you think will give us a match?" she enquired.

Matthew smiled. "The first two were very nervous," he replied, "so it could have been one of them. But definitely not the last one. I got the impression she knew she was fine."

Rachel shrugged her shoulders. "That's hardly scientific," she remarked, "and I think picking two people from the first three is a bit of a rip-off."

Matthew Stock smiled again. "You may be right," he conceded. "As Uncle Harry would say, we should let science give us the answer."

* * * *

As soon as Carmichael pulled-up outside Swift's house, he had a feeling that all was not well.

The fact that the curtains were still drawn and that there was a gleaming Audi TT sat on the drive, made Carmichael feel nervous. Then, as he walked up the drive and saw the end of the Daily Telegraph poking out from the letter box, he started to fear that something untoward had happened in the house.

Remembering that in his voice message he'd heard the doorbell ring and Swift had said he had to answer the door, Carmichael decided not to touch it. Instead he rapped heavily, with his clenched fist, on the large oak door. As he had expected, there was no answer. After repeating the exercise three further times, with the same conclusion, Carmichael decided to wander around the back.

Chapter 47

A large bank of floor-to-ceiling windows dominated the rear of Swift's house, looking out upon his long, well-maintained garden. In the centre of this wall of glass was the back door.

Carmichael tried the handle and, to his surprise, it opened.

"Hello," he shouted as he took a step into the kitchen. "It's Inspector Carmichael. Are you home, Mr Swift?"

Carmichael's question was answered with silence. Except for a faint ticking, presumably from a clock in the hallway or one of the rooms deeper inside the house, the place was hushed and still; and appeared to be unoccupied.

Carmichael took a few paces further into the kitchen and quickly surveyed the room. It was a big, open-looking room, expensively kitted-out with shiny black kitchen units, gleaming stainless-steel appliances, and a large, oak butcher's block in the centre, presumably used as one of those fashionable islands, which Penny always remarked about whenever the subject of a potential kitchen refurbishment came up in the Carmichael household.

"Mr Swift!" Carmichael shouted again, now loudly.

Once more his call was greeted with silence.

Tentatively, Carmichael made his way through the house, checking every room as he did so. It was in the room to the right of the front door where he found Martin Swift, sat upright in

227

his armchair, eyes bulging, with a wad of bank notes, mainly in £20 denominations, rammed tightly into his mouth.

* * * *

The next two arrivals at Kirkwood Police Station were Harriett Hall and Carly Wolf, who'd travelled together. Neither of them looked too pleased to be there when Rachel met them in the reception area.

"Is this really necessary?" asked Carly Wolf, her exasperation palpable in her voice.

Rachel returned a conciliatory smile. "It's just standard procedure," she assured her. "The more people we can eliminate from our enquiries, the quicker we'll be able to apprehend whoever killed Kendal and Gavin."

"We understand," responded Harriett, although her facial expression could not hide the fact that she was rather irritated also. "Will this take long? I need to be in Southport at nine thirty and Carly's shift starts at ten."

Rachel smiled again and shook her head. "It will take no more than five minutes," she assured them. "It's a really quick exercise."

Then, gesturing with her left arm towards the double door, Rachel invited the two women to follow her down the corridor.

* * * *

It took Cooper no more than fifteen minutes to arrive at Swift's house, having been summoned by Carmichael, and within ten more minutes there were two further police vehicles at the crime scene. Dr Stock and his team arrived a few moments later.

"It has to be said, Carmichael, that even by your

standards these three deaths are bizarre," remarked Stock with his customary acidity. "Three deaths in five days and all three carried out as if they were part of some huge theatrical extravaganza."

"I'd hardly call murder artistic," responded Carmichael.

Stock shrugged his shoulders. "It depends upon your point of view," he remarked. "Being run through by your own sword, being drowned in your own vat of chocolate and what looks like somebody choking to death by having twenty-pound notes thrust down their windpipe, strikes me as being extremely melodramatic. There's certainly nothing humdrum about the modus operandi in these cases."

Although Carmichael wasn't comfortable with the unerringly detached view Stock could bring to the murders, he had to admit that the pathologist's words rang true. Whoever had committed the murders of Kendal Michelson, Gavin Michelson and now Martin Swift, had done so with a great deal of planning, and it did appear that the manner in which the murders were conducted was as important to the killer as the end result.

"Do you really think he was choked to death?" Cooper enquired. "Could he not have died some other way and the notes just be placed in his mouth afterwards?"

Dr Stock maintained his hawk-like attention on the mouth of the dead man.

"It's possible," he replied. "I'll only know for certain when I open him up. However, looking at the amount of saliva on the notes in his mouth, he was certainly alive when they were thrust in there. But, you are right Sergeant, the cause of death could be something else."

"What about a time of death?" Carmichael enquired.

Stock shook his head while he considered the question.

"Judging by the temperature of the body and the stage of rigour mortis, I'd say he's been dead for between ten to fifteen hours," he replied, "but I'll only know for sure once I start to examine him properly back at the lab."

"Well, I received a voice message from him at just after nine thirty last night," announced Carmichael, "so that means he must have died between then and twelve forty-five this morning."

Stock puffed out his cheeks. "I don't want you to take this as the gospel truth," he remarked, "as I'll not be able to be definite until I've completed a full autopsy, but if you want my opinion, I expect we'll find this man probably died within an hour of leaving you the voice message."

Chapter 48

"Hello, Inspector Carmichael. It's Martin Swift here. I need to talk with you. Could you please either call me back this evening or maybe we could meet at my office in the morning. I think I have some information that may be important regarding the deaths of Kendal and Gavin. Damn, I'm going to have to go as I've got someone at the door. If you can't call back this evening, I generally get into work at about eight in the morning, so please pop over when you can."

"How could I have been so lax?" remarked Carmichael when he'd finished playing back Swift's message to Cooper, as they sat together in Carmichael's BMW. "If I'd have gone over to Swift's straight away, I may have been able to prevent his murder."

Cooper shook his head. "I doubt it," he replied. "For starters, it would have taken you a good fifteen to twenty minutes to find out where he lived and then another fifteen to twenty minutes to get over here. If the person at the door was the killer, he'd probably be long gone before you arrived."

Carmichael looked across at Cooper and smiled. His sergeant's honest attempt to lessen his guilt was welcome and totally in keeping with Cooper's character. And, although it certainly put some perspective to the true consequences of Carmichael's decision to delay calling on Martin Swift until that morning, he knew in his heart that, had he acted more

231

promptly, there was a good chance that Martin Swift would still be alive, a fact that weighed heavy on his shoulders.

"I wonder what he wanted to tell you?" Cooper remarked. "And I wonder if what he knew was the reason he was killed?"

Carmichael stared into the distance. "I suspect there's a good chance it was," he replied wistfully.

* * * *

With Janet Sutherland, the last of the six women to have given a sample of DNA, now departed from Kirkwood Police Station, and having checked her tablet and established that she had indeed been on a mammoth two-and-a-half-hour skype call to her boyfriend late into the evening when Gavin Michelson had been murdered, Rachel's latest assignment was now completed. Back in the office, she stood at the window and watched as the good-looking lab technician walked across the police carpark and clambered into his bright-red Ford Fiesta.

Watson, who had taken Carmichael up on his offer and only arrived at the station at 9:50am, was pouring over the list of names and exit interview notes that the HR lady at The World of Chocolate had sent him, so wasn't paying much attention to his young female colleague.

"I reckon there are only two of these worth following up," Watson remarked. "One of the others on this list was fired five years ago, so if he'd killed Gavin Michelson he's taken an age to reap his revenge, and looking at the exit interviews with two of the others, they seem to be delighted to be leaving."

"Sorry," remarked Rachel as she turned slowly from the window. "Were you talking to me?"

Watson looked up from the computer screen, his brow furrowed, displaying his evident exasperation. "Try and keep up, Rachel," he said sarcastically. "I was saying there's only two people on this list worth following up."

"Right," Rachel replied, still only paying a half-hearted interest in what Watson had been saying. "Do you want me to do one?"

"Yes," said Watson, almost immediately, "Why don't you take this one, he's called Ivan Stoller. He's an Austrian with an address in Barton Bank. At least that was his address when he was fired from The World of Chocolate in February; for persistent absenteeism and for being found drunk at work on two separate occasions."

As soon as she read the details on Ivan Stoller, Rachel started to regret having been so quick to offer her support.

"I might take someone from uniform with me," she remarked. "Judging by the language in his exit interview, I'd say Mr Stoller may have a bit of a temper on him."

Watson smiled. "Yes, that's probably a good idea," he concurred. "Saying 'you can stuff your job where the sun doesn't shine' and 'I hope Michelson rots in hell', does suggest he may be a bit of a tricky customer."

"And what about yours?" Rachel enquired. "Who are you going to try and interview?"

Watson shrugged his shoulders. "She could be equally difficult," he remarked. "Mine's a lady called Beverly McKnight, she worked in accounts for about fifteen years. She was fired for syphoning off about £500 from the petty cash over a period of two to three years. She was equally scathing in her exit interview, claiming that Gavin was firing her due to her age and that he just wanted to replace her with, in her words, a young slip of a lass who he could drool over."

With her arms tightly folded and mouth wide open, Rachel started to shake her head from side to side.

"You're unbelievable," she remarked. "I get the

potentially-violent drunkard and you get the little old lady who was caught with her fingers in the till."

Watson shrugged his shoulders and beamed broadly. "Just look upon it as yet another important career-enhancing experience," he replied.

* * * *

"How do you want to proceed from here?" Cooper enquired as the two officers remained seated in Carmichael's black BMW.

"A good question," replied Carmichael. "I guess, to start with, we need to establish the movements of Harriett Hall, Carly Wolf, Rebecca Graham, Janet Sutherland and Gabby Johns at the time Stock thinks he was killed. After all, if we are talking about the same person for all three deaths, they've got to be our main focus as Swift's murderer."

"And Carmen Martinez, too," Cooper added.

Carmichael shook his head. "No, not Carmen, she's got a perfect alibi," he remarked. "It was Marc I was talking to when Swift tried to call me last night and left that voice message. When I was on the call with Marc, he told me he'd literally just come out of Gavin Michelson's house, where he'd left Carmen. So, if the person who rang Swift's bell was his killer, we know it definitely couldn't have been Carmen."

Chapter 49

Although Penny had no doubts that her husband would speak with Robbie, and she was reasonably sure that, when he did, their son would be so embarrassed that they knew what he and his chums had been up to that he'd almost certainly stop, Penny just couldn't help herself when she saw Mrs Harper, her son Ethan and that young woman (now fully-dressed) enter the minimarket across the road from her house.

Penny knew Mrs Harper reasonably well, certainly well enough to engage with her in polite conversation; so, without hesitation, she grabbed her shopping bag, threw her purse inside and quickly slipped into the nearest available shoes by the front door, a battered pair without heels that she used when she was pottering about in the garden.

Within three minutes of Mrs Harper, Ethan and his nanny entering the minimarket, Penny was already half-way across the road, and a minute later, she was in the store.

* * * *

Carmichael instructed Cooper to stay with Dr Stock and his team at Swift's house for the rest of the morning and to report back to him and the team whatever Stock was able to uncover between then and the next team meeting, which he scheduled for 12:30pm.

Once Cooper had clambered out of Carmichael's car and re-entered Swift's house, Carmichael made separate calls to Watson and Rachel Dalton.

Having brought both officers up-to-speed with the news of Swift's murder, received a quick update from them on their activities that morning, and advised them about the debrief he had called for 12:30pm, Carmichael considered what he should do for the ninety minutes before he'd have to head back to the Police Station.

He took a few moments to deliberate who of the five remaining suspects he thought most likely to have murdered Martin Swift. To his knowledge, neither Rebecca Graham nor Janet Sutherland knew Swift, so he discounted them. He also dismissed Harriett Hall. She would have almost certainly known Swift, but he didn't think she'd have known him that well. That left only two serious suspects, Gabby Johns and Carly Wolf; Kendal's two Steampunk chums and the two ladies who'd dined at the Chinese restaurant with Swift and Kendal on Saturday evening.

However, he only had time to interview one of the ladies, so he decided to visit Carly Wolf.

Despite her apparent cast-iron alibi for Kendal's murder, she had yet to be asked to provide details of her whereabouts for the evening Gavin Michelson was killed and, of all the women involved in the case, Carly was the one that Carmichael found the most irritating. That, of course, was no reason to elevate her above the other female suspects, but enough to sway Carmichael to head in the direction of Southport Royal Hospital.

* * * *

"Hello, Mrs Harper. Hello, Ethan," said Penny cheerily as they met each other coming in opposite directions down the biscuit aisle.

236

Mrs Harper looked up at Penny and smiled. "Oh hello, Penny," she replied cheerily, "are you just looking for something for dinner, too?"

Penny strategically positioned herself in the centre of the aisle to make it as difficult as possible for either Mrs Harper, Ethan or the (as she now observed) extremely attractive nanny to get past her.

"And who's this?" she enquired with a welcoming look in the nanny's direction.

"Oh, I'm sorry," replied Mrs Harper, as if she'd committed a major social misdemeanour. "This is Marie-Claire, she's helping me out with Ethan."

Marie-Claire smiled at Penny and nodded cheerily. "Hello," she said in a confident but quiet voice that had a tinge of a French accent.

"Nice to meet you," remarked Penny before turning to face Mrs Harper again.

"Actually, I knew you had someone staying with you as my son remarked only the other day that he'd seen a young woman in the upstairs window when he was getting ready for work at about seven forty-five. That must have been you Marie-Claire."

As she finished her sentence, Penny gazed back in the direction of the young nanny, whose friendly expression had evaporated completely and who was now sporting a bright-red pair of cheeks.

"Maybe," she replied, her French accent now much stronger, her voice shaking and the confident poise she'd displayed a few seconds earlier now completely vanished.

"Anyway, I must dash," continued Penny, who now stepped aside with as broad a smile as she could muster. "Nice to see you again, Mrs Harper. Nice to see you, too, Ethan and so very nice to meet you, Marie-Claire."

Oblivious to the significance of Penny's comments, Mrs

Harper continued down the aisle with Ethan in tow. Marie-Claire remained motionless, staring over her shoulder at Penny who'd picked up a packet of chocolate digestives and was striding away triumphantly towards the till.

* * * *

To say that Carly Wolf was annoyed at being summoned to the reception to meet with Carmichael would have been an understatement; and she did nothing to hide her anger as she marched purposefully down the long corridor that led to where Carmichael was waiting.

"What is it with you police?" she remarked angrily. "I gave you a statement on Sunday, I gave a written one later that day. You came here the other day asking questions and less than three hours ago I gave a DNA sample. What's going on?"

"There's been a development," replied Carmichael calmly. "I'd like to talk with you somewhere private, if I can."

Carly took a few seconds to study the expression on Carmichael's face before nodding towards the entrance. "The best place for privacy will be out there," she remarked. "There's nowhere in here."

Carmichael smiled and gestured to Carly to lead the way, which she duly did with Carmichael walking a couple of steps behind her.

Once outside, Carmichael and the now less-animated Carly Wolf located an empty bench and sat down together in the warm, summer sunshine.

"So, what's this new development?" Carly enquired, her piercing eyes fixed on Carmichael's face.

For a woman so young, Carmichael found Carly disturbingly aggressive in her manner and, despite her stunning looks, he found her unattractively overconfident. He had no doubt that she was a smart individual, but he found little about her that made him warm to her. She certainly lacked the endearing qualities he'd encountered when he'd met her Aunty Harriett. However, irrespective of his opinion of Carly as a person, whether she was a killer was another matter entirely.

"I'm afraid there's been another murder," Carmichael replied, his eyes retaining contact with Carly in an attempt to gauge her reaction as he told her the news. "It's your friend, Martin Swift. He was killed last night."

He was sure Carly had the capacity to fake her emotions. If she had murdered Swift, she could quite easily have manufactured the look of surprise on her face and the horror in her eyes. However, Carmichael's first instinct, though, was that Carly was genuinely in shock, the news being a bombshell and not what she was expecting to hear.

"That's three in four days," she muttered. "All of them I knew really well. Who the hell's doing this? And, more importantly, why?"

Carmichael's eyebrows raised. "I was hoping you might be able to help me answer those questions," he replied. "That's why I'm here."

"No, no," replied Carly firmly. "This has nothing to do with me. I was pissed-off with Kendal, I admit it, but I'd never kill him. And I really liked his dad. As for Martin…" As she mentioned his name, she paused and sighed deeply. "The guy was an utter prat," she continued, "but a harmless prat. Why would I want to kill him?"

"Do I take it you had little time for Martin Swift?" Carmichael added.

"Most of the time, I found him irritating," replied Carly. "He certainly seemed to have the ability to make tonnes of money all the time, with deals here and there, but I found him a bit wet, if you really want to know."

Carmichael shrugged his shoulders. "So, if it wasn't you, who do you think murdered them?" he enquired.

"Gabby," replied Carly without hesitation. "It has to be that warped cow."

"Why Gabby?" Carmichael asked.

Carly sighed. "Well, she was besotted with Kendal," she replied. "He wanted nothing to do with her after she screwed his Dad, unsurprisingly. She had a motive to kill him. Then, with Gavin being the reason she and Kendal broke-up, she probably blamed him. I'd say that's a good motive for doing away with him, wouldn't you?"

Carmichael nodded. "But what about Martin Swift?" he added.

"That's more of a tricky one," Carly replied. "Maybe he knew she'd killed Kendal and Gavin, so she had to kill him, too. Or, maybe she's just a bloody nutter who wants us all dead. Maybe I'm next."

Although Carly's last remark seemed to be a throw-away comment, Carmichael thought he saw a slight glimmer of concern on her face, as if the thought of her being next was a possibility.

"I'm afraid I'll need a statement from you regarding your movements on Monday evening, when Gavin was murdered, and yesterday evening, when we believe Martin Swift died."

Carly puffed out her cheeks. "On Monday evening, I was in Harri's Bar until about eleven, then I went home. Luke and Harriett can vouch for me. Last night, I stayed in and watched TV."

"What did you watch?" Carmichael enquired.

Carly shrugged her shoulders. "Mainly stuff I'd got on record."

Carmichael nodded. "So, after eleven on Monday and for yesterday evening, you've nobody who can confirm your story?"

Carly's eyes widened and she shook her head slowly from side to side.

"It's not a story," she replied angrily, "Had I known there were going to be two more murders, I'd have asked Luke back with me or picked up another hunk of beef somewhere. But, I didn't know, so I'm afraid you'll just have to take my word for it."

Carmichael smiled and stood up.

"Thanks for your time," he replied calmly. "You'll need to come into Kirkwood station in the next twenty-four hours to make a full, written statement, but for now I'll leave you."

As she watched Carmichael walk away, Carly lit up a cigarette and inhaled deeply.

Chapter 50

With the team assembled in the main incident room at Kirkwood Police Station, Carmichael started the meeting. It took almost thirty minutes for his three officers to enlighten the rest of the team with the details of their morning's activities; with Carmichael, for once, mainly listening.

First up was Cooper, who told the team that Stock had confirmed Swift had indeed died from choking on the wad of notes thrust down his gullet, £220, to be exact. Stock had also concluded that the unfortunate Swift had been sedated with an injection to his neck and, although Stock had still to identify the exact material administered to the dead man, he believed it to be a morphine-based substance, which would have almost certainly left him paralysed, allowing his killer to slowly stuff his oesophagus with bank notes.

"According to Stock," Cooper told them, "the process could have taken up to thirty minutes to complete, with note after note being pushed into his mouth and down his throat."

The time of death was now clearer. Stock believed it would have been before 11pm, so within ninety minutes of Swift leaving the voice message on Carmichael's phone; a development that did little to ease Carmichael's already weighty conscience.

Next up was Watson, who reminded the team that it was impossible for Carmen Martinez to have been Swift's mystery caller, given the fact that he'd only left her in Gavin Michelson's house two minutes before calling Carmichael, and that the time it would have taken to walk the distance between Gavin Michelson's house and Martin Swift's house was at least fifteen minutes.

Watson then confirmed that he'd met with Beverley McKnight, one of only two ex-employees of The World of Chocolate who, in his view, could have held a grudge against Gavin Michelson.

"She was shedding no tears over his death, that's for sure," remarked Watson. "In fact, she was quite laid back about it. She couldn't have done it though," he added, "as she was only released from hospital on Tuesday morning, after having a hip replacement operation. She still can't stand-up."

On hearing this, Rachel shrugged her shoulders. "It's not your other potential ex-employee either," she added, "as according to his old landlady, Ivan Stoller went back to Austria a month ago."

"So, your efforts this morning were largely fruitless," Carmichael remarked. His words echoed some frustration and were directed at Watson and Rachel Dalton.

"Not totally," Watson replied. "I did learn from Mrs McKnight that all employees at The World of Chocolate are shown how to make chocolate as part of their induction. So even admin and office people, like Rebecca Graham and Janet Sutherland, would have some knowledge of how to get the vats working."

Carmichael raised his eyes skywards. "Now that is interesting," he remarked.

Rachel slowly shook her head. "I can say for certain it wasn't Janet Sutherland who killed Gavin Michelson," she announced. "I saw her tablet this morning when she came to give DNA. It showed she did have a long Skype call with her boyfriend as she'd maintained. It started at just before 10pm and finished at ten minutes to 1am. Unless she was skyping while she killed Gavin, then she's in the clear."

"And how did you get on with the DNA tests?" Carmichael enquired.

Rachel nodded. "They were all done and Stock's assistant reckoned they'd have the results early this afternoon," she replied.

For about ten seconds the room became hushed, until eventually Carmichael spoke. "Let's remind ourselves of what we have here," he stated, his voice slow and deliberate. "We've got three murders, all men. The murders were carried-out in the space of less than 72 hours and all were committed late in the evening or in the small hours."

Carmichael's team listened in silence.

"What's more," continued Carmichael, "the three victims were very close to each other, and they were all murdered in very specific ways. As Stock correctly observed, it's almost as if the killer had a sense of theatre about his handiwork."

Carmichael's three officers exchanged glances with each other, but remained silent.

"I'd welcome your comments," he said by way of a prompt. "You're not usually this shy."

"I still think it's two people," remarked Cooper. "The more I think about it, the more I'm certain of it."

"Why?" Rachel enquired.

"Firstly," replied Cooper, "I cannot see Gavin Michelson being murdered by just one person. I know in theory it's possible, but his murder was so elaborate and required so much time and effort; I think it more likely that two people were involved. Then secondly, if we are to believe that the killings were all committed by the same person, and it was one of the nine prime suspects we've been working on, then every one of them has a cast-iron alibi for one or other of the murders. So, in my mind, it's got to be two of them working together."

Rachel nodded. "That does make sense, I suppose," she conceded.

"If we are to accept your theory," Carmichael said, "and for what it's worth, I'm starting to come around to your way of thinking, who would be our most likely murderers?"

"Harriett Hall and Carly Wolf, maybe?" remarked Cooper. "They're related and both benefited from Gavin and Kendal's death."

"But what about Martin Swift?" Watson remarked. "Neither benefited from his death."

Cooper shrugged her shoulders. "Maybe they just killed him because he knew something."

Carmichael shook his head in frustration and pointed to the suspects list they'd compiled on the white board the previous day. "You're all forgetting, we've already established that neither could have killed Kendal," he remarked. "So, it can't be that pairing."

Carmichael's three officers looked at the white board.

"If we follow through with your assumption, Paul, the three suspects for Kendal's murder, without an alibi, are Kim Bolton, Rebecca Graham and Janet Sutherland."

"I'd add Carmen Martinez to that list, too," Rachel added, "but I'm not sure how she'd have got to the beach in Southport and back home without being detected on the CCTV."

"And she doesn't have a car," added Watson.

Although Carmichael doubted Carmen was Kendal's killer, he didn't want to be too negative.

"Ok," he said. "So, our most likely suspects for Kendal's murder are Kim Bolton, Rebecca Graham, Janet Sutherland and Carmen Martinez,"

"We don't have any motives for Rebecca, Janet or

Carmen," Cooper pointed out. "But Kim Bolton stood to gain from Kendal's murder. In my mind, she has to be the most likely killer."

"Maybe," replied Carmichael calmly, "but the point is we now have four prime candidates.

"So, what about Gavin Michelson?" Watson asked. "Who is the most likely killer for him?"

"Let's take it step by step," remarked Carmichael. "Let's first look at who, from our list of nine potential killers, could have killed him."

"Well, we can rule out Kim Bolton from that one," remarked Watson assuredly. "She, J.C. Palmer and Zorik Daniels are in the clear. They have watertight alibis."

"Harriet and Carmen too," added Rachel. "They were both cleaning at Harri's Bar when he was being dipped in chocolate. Carmen all night and Harriett until about two thirty. I think they are both in the clear."

Carmichael nodded. "You're right, Rachel," he concurred. "So, who can we put on our list?"

"And we can also rule out Janet Sutherland too," Rachel added. "She was talking on skype to her boyfriend when Gavin was being killed."

"With Gabby Johns's alibi about getting that Chinese take-away confirmed," remarked Watson, "I'd say we're just left with two people on our list for Gavin's murder; Carly Wolf and Rebecca Graham."

Carmichael nodded. "But we've no evidence of them even knowing each other," he remarked, "but maybe their paths have crossed."

"Rebecca will know how to make chocolate," added Watson.

"But why would she kill Kendal and Martin Swift?" Rachel asked. "I can't see her having a motive for their murders."

"Me neither," Cooper added, "but, she does appear to be the only person who's in the frame for both murders; and if she is in cahoots with Carly, then maybe it's Carly who has a motive for Kendal and Swift's murders."

Carmichael nodded vigorously "And, if the DNA results indicate that it was one of them who Gavin was with on the evening he died, then they'll both have a lot of questions to answer."

"We should be getting the results any time now," announced Rachel, remembering the promise the handsome Matthew Stock had given her just before he'd left that morning.

Chapter 51

Carmichael stood alone, staring out of the window of the briefing room, his team now despatched to carry out their latest instructions.

Whether Cooper's theory, that there were two people responsible for the murders, was true or not, he'd decided that the five women with dodgy alibis for any one of the first two murders needed to be their prime focus. Having already spoken to Carly and established that she didn't have a good alibi for the time Swift was killed and, knowing that Carmen Martinez was with Watson literally seconds before Swift answered the door to his potential killer, Carmichael had instructed the team to focus on Rebecca Graham, Kim Bolton and Janet Sutherland.

He'd given Rachel Dalton the task of talking with Kim Bolton, Cooper had been assigned Rebecca Graham, and Watson had been asked to interview Janet Sutherland.

It was one of those rare, hot, windless summer afternoons that, in his experience, were few and far between in that part of Lancashire. Through the second-floor window, Carmichael gazed at the tops of a row of tall poplar trees standing motionless to attention with, what seemed like, geometrically-calculated distance between them.

He turned his eyes downwards onto the Police car park, where he could see his three officers clamber into their cars and head off to their allotted assignments.

He was not totally convinced that Cooper was right, but he couldn't build a sufficiently strong argument to test his sergeant's hypothesis; and the simple truth was that, apart from Rebecca Graham, none of the major suspects on their list appeared to have the opportunity to kill both Kendal and Gavin.

To make matters worse, he couldn't see why Rebecca would have murdered any of the three men, particularly Gavin, who she clearly adored.

Carmichael remained at the window, his thoughts moving away from possible suspects and potential motives to more practical questions.

"Who called Kendal on the night he died?" was one they'd not managed to answer. *"Where is the mobile that Kendal used that night?"* was another unanswered, but important question. *"Why did Kendal go down to the beach so late on Saturday evening? Was he meeting someone? And, if so, who?"* Each of these questions needed to be answered; and equally as important as any of these unexplained conundrums was *"Why is the killer (or killers) intent on murdering in such a theatrical fashion?"*

As Carmichael considered these challenging questions, his mobile rang. It was Rachel.

"I've just received a call from the forensic team," she announced excitedly. "They've got a match with one of the DNA samples."

Carmichael listened intently as his young officer eagerly conveyed her news.

"We'd better bring her in then," he replied.

"Do you want me to do that?" Rachel asked; her tone clearly indicated that was what she had hoped to be told.

Carmichael took a few seconds to consider her request.

"No," he replied decisively. "I still need you carry on and interview Kim Bolton. But once that's completed, get yourself back here as quickly as you can."

Chapter 52

It was almost 4pm by the time Carmichael started the formal interview with their new prime suspect.

"Ms Sutherland," he said, his words delivered slowly and clearly, with an emphasis on the Ms, something Carmichael had been accustomed to doing over the course of the years when he interviewed a single young woman. "As you are aware, our forensic team have matched the DNA sample you provided this morning to the evidence they collected at the scene of Gavin Michelson's murder. Do you have any comment to make regarding this finding?"

Carmichael and Watson, who was sitting to his left, looked across the table at Janet Sutherland, who glanced briefly at the duty solicitor at her side before answering.

"Yes, it's true," she replied, her voice faint, faltering and highlighting her nervousness. "We were together that evening."

"So why did you tell us that you weren't in a relationship with him?" Carmichael enquired, his voice still calm and controlled.

Janet Sutherland shook her head. "It was no relationship," she replied in a firm, matter-of-fact way. "It was more of a business arrangement."

Carmichael sat back in his chair, his forehead wrinkled, suggesting a degree of puzzlement at the answer he'd just heard. "I'm not sure I understand," he remarked. "Can you explain what you mean?"

Janet took a gulp of breath. "It was just an agreement we had," she replied glibly.

"What sort of agreement?" Carmichael asked. "Had he threatened to fire you, if you didn't…"

Before he could finish his sentence, Carmichael could see Janet shaking her head vigorously, which caused him to stop.

"Oh no, it was nothing like that," replied Janet dismissively. "I wasn't forced to do anything I wasn't willing to do. It was just an arrangement between us."

"I see," replied Carmichael, his eyes fixed on the young woman in front of him. "And how long had this 'business arrangement' been going on?"

Janet shrugged her shoulders. "It was the third time it had happened," she replied. "And I told him, and he agreed, that it was to be the last time."

Carmichael paused for a moment. "I can see what he got out of the arrangement," he remarked, "but what was in it for you?"

Janet once more shrugged her shoulders.

"To be honest I did quite well, as it happens," she replied with the hint of a triumphant smirk on her face. "I have a new company Jaguar on order, I've had a six-month notice period inserted in my contract and, had he not been murdered, I was also due to be put on a new, quite lucrative, incentive plan."

"I take it that wasn't confirmed in writing before his death?" enquired Carmichael.

Janet shook her head once more, this time more ruefully. "The deal was that he'd confirm what we agreed the day after we'd… Well, after I'd delivered my part of the agreement, so to speak."

"I see," said Carmichael. "So, in a way, his death coming when it did was quite unfortunate for you."

Janet forced a faint smile. "Yes," she replied, "but, in a way, I suppose the bonus not being agreed yet in writing is quite fortuitous, too, as it should demonstrate to you that I had absolutely no involvement in his death."

Carmichael chose to ignore Janet Sutherland's final remark.

"In your earlier statement to me yesterday," he continued, "you said that you'd finished work that night at about six, went to your flat in Barton Bridge, had a bath, had some dinner, then spent most of the rest of the evening skyping your boyfriend, Barry, who's been employed for the last three months in a bar just off Copacabana Beach, in Rio. Given that we now know what you told me before wasn't totally correct, would you care to tell me exactly what happened on Monday evening?"

Janet shrugged her shoulders again. "Everything I told you was true," she replied, "apart from the fact I had sex with him before I left."

"What about the time?" interjected Watson. "Was it six when you left The World of Chocolate?"

Janet thought for a moment.

"It may have been slightly later," she conceded, "but it was certainly no later than six fifteen. Our arrangement didn't take long."

Carmichael and Watson exchanged a quick look of shared incredulity.

"I see," Carmichael replied slowly, his eyes moving back to fix their glare on the young woman a few feet across the table.

Carmichael was trying hard to appear calm and controlled, but inside his mind was working overtime. His first impressions of Janet Sutherland had been, quite clearly, well off target and he was now totally confused as to whether she was a genuine suspect or not.

"Can you tell me about that last meeting with him?" Carmichael asked. "How did he seem?"

Once more Janet shrugged her shoulders. "To be honest, he'd actually forgotten our arrangement was for that evening," she remarked. "I guess with his son dying it must have, understandably, slipped his mind. But, apart from that, he seemed as he always was."

"Which was?" probed Carmichael.

"Sorry?" replied Janet, "I don't get what you're asking."

"What was Gavin normally like?" clarified Carmichael.

"I see," replied Janet with a nervous, almost adolescent giggle, "a power mad, control freak, as always."

Carmichael rubbed the palm of his hand around his chin as he considered how to proceed.

"I'd like you to tell me what you were doing last Saturday night and last night," he asked.

Janet thought for a few seconds. "Last Saturday evening, I was at one of my Uni friend's birthday parties in North London," she replied. "And last night I was home alone, although I had another long Skype call with Barry until he started his shift in the bar in Rio. So, from about six thirty to about ten."

Carmichael nodded. "That's all for now," he remarked abruptly, standing up as he spoke. "However, before you leave, I'll need you to produce a new statement for the night Gavin Michelson was killed. You can do that now with Sergeant Watson. In that statement, I'll need you to provide confirmation about this party on Saturday, too, with contact details of your friends for us to check out your story. I want you to also leave Sergeant Watson with the contact number of Barry in Rio, as we'll need to talk with him, too."

At the mention of her boyfriend's name, the colour drained from Janet's face.

"You won't mention anything about my agreement with

Gavin, will you?" she asked, her eyes watery and pleading, and her voice trembling as she spoke.

Carmichael looked back at her and shrugged his shoulders. "Not unless I think it will help us apprehend the person who killed Gavin Michelson," he replied. "But I'm not prepared to give you any guarantees, Ms Sutherland. My job is to catch a killer, not to protect your reputation."

Chapter 53

Carmichael was already half way down the long corridor that led from the interview room to the stairs when Cooper and Rachel Dalton caught up with him. They'd been watching his interview with Janet Sutherland intently from the room next door.

"What do you make of her story, sir?" enquired Rachel, who was first to arrive at his side.

Carmichael continued walking briskly.

"If she's telling the truth," he replied, "which she may well be, then it's very unlikely that she's involved. But, she's lied before so I want her alibi claims checked out thoroughly."

"I've already checked her tablet about the skype call she had with her boyfriend, on Monday evening, when Gavin Michelson was killed," remarked Rachel. "That matched her story."

Carmichael stopped suddenly.

"That's maybe what it looks like," he replied, "but I want someone to talk with her boyfriend. I'm not an expert on social media, but I want to be certain that call happened and, if it did, I want to know whether they had visual contact. The same goes for the other call she claims she had last night."

"Do you want me to get onto that?" Rachel enquired.

Carmichael shook his head. "No, let Marc do that," he replied. "I've got another job for you."

"We've spoken with Kim Bolton and Rebecca Graham," announced Cooper. "Neither have particularly strong accounts for where they were last night. Rebecca maintains she was at home on her own."

"And Kim Bolton said the same," interjected Rachel.

Carmichael thought for a few moments.

"Do you still think we are looking for two murderers?" Carmichael enquired, his eyes fixed firmly on Cooper.

"I'm absolutely convinced of it," replied his sergeant.

"In that case, I'd like you to spend the next couple of hours working out who the two could be," continued Carmichael. "Focus mainly on the first two murders, as apart from Carmen Martinez, any one of the other suspects could have killed Martin Swift. So, just look at the murders of Kendal and Gavin."

Cooper nodded enthusiastically before turning to leave.

"Have you both any plans for this evening?" Carmichael enquired.

"Not really," replied Rachel, slightly guardedly.

"Me neither," added Cooper.

"That's good," replied Carmichael, "as I'd like to take you both, and Marc, of course, for a nice Chinese meal."

Having expected to be asked to undertake something relating to the case, Rachel and Cooper were both slightly taken aback by the offer.

"That's great," remarked Rachel, "which Chinese are we going to?"

"The China Garden in Southport, of course," replied Carmichael, as if his answer was obvious. "I'll meet you all there at eight forty-five. I think that's about the time Kendal and his friends would have gathered together on Saturday."

Chapter 54

"He's late!" exclaimed Watson as the three officers sat at the bar of The China Garden. "Five-to-nine and he's not here. That's unheard of. Do you think he's had an accident?"

Although his comments were spoken in jest, it was so unusual for Carmichael to be late that the thought of an accident wasn't as ridiculous as it seemed.

Cooper smiled. "Well, as Rachel has so gallantly volunteered to drive us both home, I think we should order a beer."

Watson nodded. "Good idea, I'll have a cold pint of draught lager," he replied, "but put it on a tab. I know he didn't say as much, but my understanding was that this was on him."

"You're terrible," Rachel remarked, "but I'll still have a diet coke."

As Cooper tried to catch the eye of the barman, Rachel, her forehead screwed-up as if she was trying to focus on something out the window, continued. "Isn't that him walking towards us along the beach?"

Cooper and Watson both turned their heads in the direction of the distant figure, that must have been at least 200 metres away, marching purposefully towards them.

"I think you're right," remarked Watson. "I'd recognise that walk anywhere."

The three officers watched for the next couple of minutes as their boss strode towards them over the flat expanse of sand.

"Sorry I'm late, guys," said Carmichael with a smile as he at last entered the restaurant, his clothes the same as he'd worn that day and his shoes now covered in sand. "I've been retracing the possible steps of our killer."

* * * *

Penny had been less than impressed when her husband had called her to say he'd be very late home and that he was having a Chinese with his team. She'd hoped he'd be having a quiet word with Robbie about their son's morning ogling, but as she'd already marked the card of the subject of Robbie's pre-work attraction, Penny was reasonably sure that the boys would be disappointed when they all gathered at the window the following morning. Nevertheless, she was going to make sure Steve was going to keep his promise and talk with their son, as she felt he needed to know his parents were aware of what he was up to and didn't approve.

Having eaten a cheese sandwich and a small slice of chocolate cake for her evening meal, Penny sat back in the comfort of her favourite armchair with a glass of Prosecco by her side. *It's my second glass… but who's counting?* she thought to herself.

* * * *

"Actually, this really is a spectacular-looking restaurant," Carmichael remarked as he stared up at the modern, arched beams above their heads. "I can see why it's so popular."

"I've been here a few times with Julia," remarked Cooper. "She particularly likes the dim sum selection here."

Watson's look of incredulity indicated he had no idea what dim sum was.

"It's like Chinese tapas," remarked Rachel, trying to help her colleague. "I might try that as a starter."

Watson shrugged his shoulders. "I'm sticking to my trusted favourites: a large spring roll, Singapore-style noodles, a portion of sweet and sour chicken balls and as many prawn crackers as I can eat."

"Were you serious when you said you were tracing the killer's footsteps?" Rachel enquired as the four officers scoured the menu.

"It's a possibility," replied Carmichael. "You've already pretty much established that the killer, or killers, didn't go down to the beach anywhere near where Kendal was killed, so they must have either come down from about here or from the south side of the town near the funfair."

"Unless they arrived by boat," remarked Watson cynically.

"That's got to be another possibility," replied Carmichael with a faint smile, "but I'd say it's probably a long shot."

"I take it you've not been home yet?" Cooper remarked.

Carmichael shook his head. "No, I had a few things I wanted to do," he replied, rather ambiguously. "Anyway, how did you three get on after I left you?"

"Well, I checked out Janet Sutherland's story," replied Watson, "and it's watertight. Her boyfriend swears blind that she was on Skype with him when Gavin and Martin Swift were murdered. He says she skyped him from her apartment, he verifies the times she gave us and confirmed they had visual contact during the call. What's more, her pal in North London confirms that she was with her at the party on the night Kendal was murdered. So, I think she's out of the frame completely. To be absolutely sure though, I've commandeered her tablet and the forensic guys are going to check it over, just to see if they can work out if her apparent Skype calls could have been doctored in some way."

Carmichael puffed out his cheeks. "To be honest, that's taken the wind out of my sails a little," he remarked, "I really thought the DNA would find our killer. But it looks like it was a false avenue, which is disappointing to say the least."

"I managed to talk with Gabby Johns and Carly Wolf on the phone, like you asked," announced Rachel, "and they confirmed that Martin Swift had picked up Carly and Kendal from the Fairfax and had driven them here. Gabby came alone."

"And who got here first?" Carmichael enquired.

"It was Gabby Johns," replied Rachel. "She arrived at about ten to nine and the others arrived together about five minutes later."

As soon as she'd finished talking, the waiter arrived to take their order, which prompted Carmichael to look seriously at the menu for the first time. Fortunately, his three officers had all decided what they were having, which gave him a couple more minutes to select something.

"And what about you?" Carmichael asked, turning his head in Cooper's direction. "Have you managed to find two potential partners in crime?"

Cooper smiled. "With Janet Sutherland out of the equation, I'm pretty sure I have one of them identified," he remarked. "And I've two potential cohorts for her."

Carmichael, Watson, and Rachel all stopped what they were doing to listen carefully to what Cooper was about to share with them.

"For Kendal's murder, it's clear that Kim Bolton could be the killer and assuming Carmen could get herself here somehow, it could be her, too." Cooper announced. "But for the second murder, there are only two people who appear not to have a plausible corroborated alibi. Carly Wolf and Rebecca Graham."

"So, what are you saying?" remarked Watson.

Cooper smiled. "Well, my theory is that it was Carly and Rebecca who carried out the murders. I think they both killed Gavin, but I think Rebecca was the one who killed Kendal."

Cooper's three colleagues all took a few seconds to absorb what Cooper had said.

"When you look at it as them being a pair, it all fits," Cooper continued. "Carly could have briefed Rebecca on Kendal's movements on Saturday night, right down to when he took the first call."

Watson nodded. "And Rebecca would know how to get the vat working at The World of Chocolate."

"It does make sense, I suppose," admitted Carmichael, "but what about their motive?"

"And what about Swift's murder?" added Rachel.

"As far as I'm aware, neither Carly or Rebecca have an alibi for last night," continued Cooper.

"Well, apart from Carmen Martinez and Janet Sutherland, nobody has a very good alibi, to be honest," remarked Watson.

Carmichael nodded. "I'd like to try and understand what their motives would be, though," he repeated. "And although they are about the same age, I'm not sure they even know each other."

"But if we do find a link between them," said Cooper, "then surely we've got to look at this as being a strong possibility."

Carmichael nodded slowly as he considered what Cooper had said.

"As they are about the same age, maybe they were at school together," remarked Rachel; a comment which received another sage-like nod from their boss.

"It's food for thought," remarked Carmichael after a few

moments of consideration, "and certainly worth following-up."

"Shall we bring them both into the station in the morning?" Cooper asked.

"Let's just bring Rebecca Graham in for now," Carmichael replied. "We've talked with Carly a fair amount over the last few days and, until we have something more definite to put to her, I doubt she'll say much more than she's said already. My suggestion is we leave Ms Wolf for now. Rebecca, on the other hand, has yet to be put under too much pressure, so I think it's time we got a bit firmer with her."

By the united nods that followed Carmichael's recommendation, it was clear the team were all in agreement.

"You didn't say what you'd been doing this afternoon," said Rachel.

Carmichael took a sip from his glass. "I've been quite busy, as it happens," he remarked with a smug, self-assured expression on his face. "I've spoken to Mr Marlow, one of the partners at Hathersage, Marlow and Swift, and asked him to send over copies of Gavin Michelson and Martin Swift's wills, which he promised to have with me in the morning. But, more importantly, I think I now know why Kendal Michelson went down to the beach on Saturday night."

Cooper, Watson, and Rachel all stopped eating in sync and looked back at their boss in silence.

Carmichael smiled. "It was so obvious; I can't understand why we hadn't twigged it before now."

Chapter 55

"Say that again?" said Penny, turning her head to the right to make sure she could see her husband's face as he recounted his hypothesis.

Carmichael smiled. "He was a nut about the stars," Carmichael replied, "he left money in his will to the local Astronomical Society and he even had a planetarium in his house. To be honest, I'm annoyed I didn't pick up on this sooner."

It was almost 12:30pm and all Penny really wanted to do was turn over and go to sleep, however, she always took a keen interest in her husband's cases and his sudden pronouncement that Kendal Michelson, the first of the three murdered men, had gone down to the beach at midnight to lie on his back and gaze up at the heavens, was so strange that even her desire to get to sleep couldn't overcome her need to know more.

"So, you really believe that Kendal was looking at some star in the sky when he was run-through with his own sword?" she remarked with a note of surprise in her voice.

"Not just some star! It was Vega, the brightest star in the constellation Lyra the Harp," replied Carmichael, trying hard to mimic the words he'd been told by Harry Parker, the President of the Kirkwood and District Astronomical Society, who he'd spoken to late that afternoon. "I'm reliably informed that on Saturday, thirteenth of August, the night Kendal was killed, it was visible clearly with the naked eye and I think Kendal went down to the beach so that he could view Vega."

"But it would be dark down there," Penny remarked. "Couldn't he have just looked up at the heavens from the main road?"

Carmichael shook his head and theatrically exhaled vigorously through pursed lips. "Light pollution, my dear," he replied, again in his best anorak voice. "You can't properly appreciate the stars when there's light pollution."

"Sounds a bit weird to me," Penny remarked.

Carmichael smiled. "Maybe so," he replied, "but I'm convinced Kendal went down onto the beach specifically to look at the night sky. It would explain why he was on his back when he was found and, to an extent why he didn't put up any resistance when he was stabbed so viciously with his own sword."

"So, he was just looking up into the sky, oblivious to anything else around him when he was killed?" enquired Penny.

"I suspect so," replied Carmichael.

"And you believe that whoever killed him, knew he was going to go down to the beach?" enquired Penny.

Carmichael shrugged his shoulders. "I couldn't be certain," he replied, "but that would be my guess."

Penny slowly shook her head before rolling over with her back to her husband.

"It still sounds weird to me," she remarked, the last words she uttered before falling into a deep sleep.

Chapter 56

Thursday 18ᵗʰ August

Carmichael was making his way downstairs when, at 7:40am, the doorbell rang.

"No prizes for guessing who that is," he muttered to himself.

But, before he could get anywhere near the door, Robbie had burst out of his bedroom and had come hurtling down the stairs, pushing past his father as he rushed to the door.

"Morning son," remarked Carmichael who, having reached the ground floor, turned, and made his way towards the kitchen. "I'll be heading out in about thirty minutes if you'd like a lift to work."

Robbie didn't reply, which came as no surprise to his father, who carried on into the kitchen, where he found Penny, still in her dressing gown, filling up the kettle.

"I'll drop him off on my way to work," remarked Carmichael. "I'll speak to him then."

The noticeably-relaxed, smug expression on his wife's face immediately sparked Carmichael's curiosity.

"Why do I think I'm missing something," he enquired.

Penny shrugged her shoulders.

"I didn't have a chance to tell you last night," she said with a wry smile, "but, as it happens, I bumped into

Mrs Harper, Ethan and her Nanny in the store yesterday afternoon."

"Really," replied Carmichael, who could tell by the way Penny was recounting the tale that the chance meeting was probably no such thing.

"Well," continued Penny, who was clearly very pleased with herself, "I just happened to remark to Marie-Claire, the Nanny, that our son had mentioned seeing someone he didn't recognise in the morning when he was looking out of his window; and that it must have been her."

Carmichael shook his head. "And was nudity, or the fact that our son invites the neighbourhood to join in with him for his early morning peep show mentioned?"

"No, no," replied Penny, "to be honest, I didn't think that was necessary. By the devastated look on the poor girl's face, there was no need to go into all the details; she got the message."

"I'm sure she did," remarked Carmichael as he placed two slices of bread into the toaster.

Within five minutes, the undeniable sound of Jason, Ben and Robbie descending the stairs could be heard, followed a few seconds later by the thud of the front door as, presumably, two disappointed young men left the Carmichael house.

"I'm going in fifteen minutes," Carmichael shouted through into the hallway. "If you want a lift, you need to get a shift on."

Once again Carmichael's offer of a lift appeared to be ignored.

* * * *

It was 7:55am and Watson and Rachel Dalton continued to wait patiently in Watson's car outside the main gates of The World of Chocolate.

"Do you think it's Carly Wolf and Rebecca Graham behind these murders?" Watson enquired.

Rachel opened her eyes wide and shrugged her shoulders.

"Cooper's theory does hold water," she confessed. "Rebecca Graham doesn't have much of an alibi for either of the deaths, Carly doesn't have an alibi for Gavin's death and she could have quite easily fed Rebecca all the information she needed to kill Kendal. It also would stack-up with the lack of any evidence of Kendal receiving the call she says he received."

Watson nodded. "But what about the call that homeless woman reckons she saw Kendal make when she nicked his helmet?" Watson remarked. "Surely that suggests Kendal did have a mobile."

"Maybe," replied Rachel, "but she didn't sound the most reliable of witnesses from how the boss described her."

Watson nodded. "I guess that's true," he conceded.

"Then there's the making of the chocolate," continued Rachel. "Now that's certainly something Rebecca would be able to do."

Watson nodded again, but this time in the direction of the small, red Peugeot which had just pulled into the carpark.

"Well here she is," he remarked. "We'll have a better idea of things once we've had a chat with her."

Rachel smiled back at her colleague, and both officers clambered out of the car.

* * * *

"How's the summer job going at Hayley's Chicken Farm?" Carmichael enquired, as his black BMW sped towards his son's place of work.

"It's fine," replied Robbie, who was clearly not keen to

talk, his head facing away from his father, staring out of the side window.

"I've been having a bet with your Mum about what you and the lads get up to every morning before you go to work," continued Carmichael.

On hearing what his father just said, Robbie turned his head back a little, but not enough to enable the pair to make eye contact.

"Really," he replied. "And what do you think?"

"Your Mum reckons you're all playing computer games," Carmichael lied.

"And what do you think?" replied Robbie in a tone aimed to suggest he wasn't really that interested in the answer his Dad was about to share with him.

"Actually, I think you're all peeking at that young woman who you can see naked in the house behind us," Carmichael remarked. "But your Mum won't hear of it. She's adamant that you'd never do anything like that."

Robbie turned his head back towards the window.

"Well, neither of you are right, as it happens," he replied, "but I'll let you both carry on guessing!"

As he finished his sentence, Carmichael's BMW arrived at Hayley's farm.

Robbie quickly opened the door and clambered out.

Turning back to face his father, Robbie gave him a wry smile. "But we've decided to knock it on the head, as it happens," he remarked. "So, I guess you'll both never know."

"That's probably for the best," replied Carmichael.

Robbie smiled again. "Thanks for the lift, Dad," he added, before closing the car door and sauntering away.

Chapter 57

Carmichael's natural inclination was to lead from the front, particularly when it came to interviewing suspects. However, occasionally he did allow his team to question suspects without him; and, in the case of Rebecca Graham, he decided that they may achieve more if he let Rachel and Watson conduct the interview, while he observed her body language and facial reactions out of the suspect's sight, hidden behind the two-way glass.

Rachel Dalton turned on the recording equipment.

"The time is nine twenty-five am on Thursday, eighteenth of August. Interview with Rebecca Graham at Kirkwood Police Station," she announced in a clear voice. "Sergeant Watson and DC Dalton in attendance. Ms Graham has been offered the opportunity to be accompanied by a solicitor, but has declined that request."

Carmichael looked closely at the smartly-dressed, well-presented young woman who sat opposite Rachel Dalton and Watson. The distinctive poise that had abandoned her just after the discovery of Gavin Michelson's body, had returned once more.

"As you are aware, we are investigating three murders," Watson announced. "Kendal Michelson, who was killed in the early hours of Sunday morning; Gavin Michelson, who died on Monday evening or in the early hours of Tuesday morning; and now a gentleman called Martin Swift, who died on Tuesday evening. We, of course, know you knew Gavin Michelson very well, but can you tell us how well you knew his son, Kendal and whether you knew Martin Swift?"

Rebecca Graham sat bolt upright in her chair with her hands neatly clasped together on the desk in front of her, her carefully-manicured and meticulously-painted fingernails an outward display of tidiness and efficiency.

"I had met Kendal on a few occasions," replied Rebecca. "His father had mentioned him a couple of times when we were together, but I didn't know him very well. As for Mr Swift, I knew him slightly better. He was the company's solicitor, so he did have reason to come to the factory on many occasions. I sometimes took the minutes at their meetings."

"And what sort of meetings were these?" Watson enquired.

"They varied," replied Rebecca with a faint shrug of her shoulders. "They could be to do with personnel issues with senior employees, they could involve contract discussions with some of our major distributors, or maybe to do with supplier contracts or the cocoa producer partnerships we have around the world."

"The World of Chocolate part-owns some of the farms that produce the cocoa beans for you?" interjected Rachel.

"That's right," replied Rebecca. "I don't know how many there are, but I'd say at least half a dozen partnerships and there are actually a couple of farms in Ecuador that Gavin, sorry, The World of Chocolate, owns outright."

Carmichael could see from Watson's expression that he wasn't happy with Rachel butting-in. True to his character, and with Carmichael not being in the room, it was clear that his sergeant wanted to take the dominant role in the interview.

"I'd also like you to tell us where you were when the three

men were murdered," Watson said. "Can you start with your movements on the thirteenth of August? That's Saturday evening."

"From six thirty until eight, I was visiting my Grandma in hospital," replied Rebecca. "After that, I drove back home, had a bath, watched an old film and went to bed."

"Is your Grandma very ill?" Watson enquired.

"Considering she's eighty-seven, she's doing brilliantly," replied Rebecca, "but she fell a week ago and is recovering from a broken hip."

"Which hospital?" Rachel asked.

"It's in Southport," replied Rebecca. "The new one on the north side of the town."

"The Royal?" asked Rachel.

Rebecca nodded. "Yes, that's right, the Royal."

Watson and Rachel exchanged a brief look.

"Which ward is she in?" Rachel enquired.

"Why are you interested in my Grandma?" Rebecca asked, her expression emphasising her apparent bewilderment.

"To eliminate you from our enquiries we'll have to verify your story," replied Watson. "So, if you can be so good as to answer my colleague's question."

"She's in Stanley Ward," replied Rebecca.

"And the evening Gavin Michelson was murdered," said Watson, "remind us about your movements that night?"

From behind the glass, Carmichael could see Rebecca's eyes start to glint as they filled up with water. She pulled out a tissue from the box strategically-placed to her right and started to gently dab her eyes. There was no dramatic outpouring of grief as there had been two days earlier, but Carmichael could see Rebecca was clearly still distressed.

"As I told Inspector Carmichael and as I put in my statement," replied Rebecca slowly, in a slightly faltering voice, "it would have been about six thirty. I went to his office and said goodbye. That was the last time I saw him."

Watson allowed Rebecca a few seconds to dab her eyes again before continuing with his questioning.

"Then you went home alone," he remarked. "Is that correct?"

Rebecca nodded. "That's correct," she repeated. "I didn't go to see my Grandma that evening as her friend was due to visit. I had an evening alone at home."

"And what about on the evening of Tuesday, sixteenth of August," enquired Watson. "What were your movements that evening?"

"Again, from six thirty until eight I was visiting my Grandma in hospital," replied Rebecca. "And again, after that I drove back home, had some dinner, had a bath, watched TV, and went to bed," replied Rebecca.

"On your own?" Watson enquired.

Rebecca nodded. "Yes," she replied. "I went to see my Grandma on my own and was at home that evening on my own."

"What about your parents?" enquired Rachel. "Do they not join you when you visit your Gran?"

Rebecca shook her head. "My parents are on a cruise," she replied. "They're coming back at the weekend, but at the moment they're somewhere between the Caribbean and Southampton. Until they get back, it's down to me to be Grandma's main visitor in hospital."

Watson paused for a few seconds before continuing with his questioning.

"Do you know a lady by the name of Carly Wolf?" he enquired.

Rebecca shrugged her shoulders and made a face that suggested the name meant nothing to her.

"Sorry," she replied. "I don't know anyone by that name."

Rachel Dalton took out a photograph of Carly Wolf from

the buff folder that she'd previously placed on the table in front of her.

"This is Carly," she announced as she pushed across the desk a photograph of Carly taken at the China Garden Restaurant on the night Kendal Michelson had been murdered.

Rebecca studied the photograph carefully.

"She does look familiar, but I can't place where I've seen her," said Rebecca eventually, her eyes half-closed as if she was scrutinising the photo meticulously. "Looking at the way she's dressed, I take it she's one of those Steampunk enthusiasts that were down in Southport over the weekend."

"Take your time," remarked Rachael reassuringly. "Take a good look at the photo."

* * * *

Having been the one who'd been arguing the case for Carmichael to consider there to be two killers working together, and having put forward the theory that the most likely candidates for the murderous duo were Carly Wolf and Rebecca Graham, Cooper had been assigned the task of trying to find a link between the two women.

He'd initially discovered that there was an age difference between Carly, who was 24 and Rebecca, who was 3 years older. This ruled them out as being classmates at school, but didn't necessarily mean they could not have met at school, which was an avenue that he was starting to follow when the door opened and Carmichael entered the incident room.

"How's Marc and Rachel doing with their interview with Rebecca Graham?" Cooper enquired as soon as he caught sight of his boss.

"It's only just got started," replied Carmichael, "but, her alibis for all three murders are really flimsy. So, in short,

Rebecca could have been involved and, coupled with the fact that she will know how to make chocolate, she's now got to be our prime suspect."

Cooper nodded. "Well, as yet, I've not been able to find a link between Rebecca and Carly," he said, "but I'm going to check which schools they went to."

"I'd leave that line of enquiry for now," announced Carmichael. "What Marc has discovered is that Rebecca's Grandmother is currently in the hospital where Carly works. She's in Stanley Ward. Why don't you see if you can find out which ward Carly's on?"

"Will do," replied Cooper. "I'll get on to it straight away."

Carmichael smiled. "I'm going back up to see how they're getting on with the rest of the interview. Let me know if you discover a link between our two ladies."

Cooper nodded again. "I will, sir," he replied.

Carmichael was almost at the door when Cooper shouted across at him. "I almost forgot," he called, "copies of Gavin Michelson and Martin Swift's wills were delivered about twenty minutes ago." As he spoke, Cooper pointed to the documents that were lying on the desk next to where Carmichael was standing.

"Excellent," replied Carmichael as he picked them up. "I'll read them upstairs while I eavesdrop on the rest of Marc and Rachel's interview with Rebecca Graham."

Chapter 58

When Carmichael returned to his inconspicuous post behind the two-way mirror, it was clear that in the short time he'd been away, Watson had started to turn up the pressure on Rebecca Graham.

"You've got to look at it from the perspective of a jury," Watson was saying firmly as Carmichael took his seat by the glass. "You've got nobody who can corroborate where you were when all three of the murders were committed. You knew all three victims and, by your own admission, you're more than capable of getting those chocolate vats working at the factory. You have to admit that it doesn't look good for you."

Rebecca Graham's body language was no longer one of a self-assured woman, as it was when Carmichael had left his observation point. She remained sitting upright with her hands in front of her, but her face was red and the way her hands were tightly gripped together suggested she was becoming decidedly anxious.

"Why would I kill them?" she replied irritably. "I loved Gavin. Martin Swift was just the company solicitor and I hardly knew Kendal Michelson at all."

A fair point, thought Carmichael as he started to read the last will and testament of Gavin Michelson; a document that intriguingly was dated only one month earlier.

"People commit murder for a whole host of reasons," replied Watson offhandedly, his eyes fixed firmly on Rebecca.

After a pause of no more than fifteen seconds, Rachel Dalton smiled across at the increasingly nervous-looking interrogee.

"Have you been able to think any more about the young woman in the photo?" As she spoke, Rachel pushed the image of Carly Wolf back across the table towards Rebecca Graham.

Carmichael didn't see Rebecca Graham pick up the photograph. He didn't see the look of puzzlement on her face or hear the response she gave her questioners. He didn't see the look Watson and Dalton exchanged on hearing Rebecca's repeated vague remark that the person looked familiar but she was not sure where she'd seen her; and he was oblivious to Watson suggesting that they all took a ten-minute break and asking Rebecca if she'd like a drink.

Carmichael's attention was focussed entirely on the beneficiaries listed in Gavin Michelson's will.

"Now that is interesting," he said to himself, before setting down Gavin's will and picking up the copy of Martin Swift's last will and testament.

* * * *

Within minutes of Watson and Rachel Dalton vacating the interview room, they had joined their boss in the adjoining room where they could also observe Rebecca Graham in secret, as she nervously fidgeted in her chair, occasionally taking sips of coffee from the plastic container she'd been given by WPC Twamley, who remained in the interview room standing quietly on guard at the door.

"She's definitely involved," remarked Watson, "I can sense it."

Rachel pulled a face that suggested she wasn't as certain. "Maybe," she replied, with a note of caution in her voice, which suggested her *maybe* was more a *maybe not*. "But I can't understand what her motive would be and, until we can find a definite connection between her and Carly, I'm still quite unsure about both, to be honest."

Carmichael smiled. "Read this," he suggested, pushing the copy of Gavin's will towards his two colleagues.

* * * *

"Are you sure?" enquired Cooper to the Senior Registrar at the end of the phone.

"Yes," came back the reply. "Nurse Wolf is working, and has always worked, in our children's unit. She's never worked in Stanley Ward, that's at the opposite end of the building and is solely for our geriatric patients."

"Thanks," replied Cooper, slightly crestfallen. "You've been most helpful."

Cooper sat for a moment, puffed out his cheeks, then decided to find Carmichael to give him the frustrating result of his discussion with the woman at Southport Royal.

* * * *

"Actually," announced Rebecca Graham to WPC Twamley, "can you advise Sergeant Watson and DC Dalton that I would like to talk with a solicitor."

WPC Twamley smiled and slipped out of the door, locking it behind her as she made her way to find the two investigating officers.

* * * *

As Cooper passed the Duty Sergeant's desk, he was accosted by his colleague, Sergeant Butterworth.

"One of the forensic team left this," the portly Duty Sergeant remarked, pointing to a bright-pink tablet to his right. "He asked me to deliver it to Watson or DC Dalton. He reckons they've checked it out and they believe the Skype calls made in the last five days are all genuine."

Cooper hardly broke step as he picked up the tablet and marched on towards the interview room.

* * * *

"There's our motive," remarked Watson. "I'd say inheriting ten percent of the business is more than enough incentive to bump off her sugar daddy."

Rachel nodded as she read the crucial portion of the will again.

"So, Rebecca gets ten percent of The World of Chocolate," she remarked, "but so does Martin Swift and the Senior Chocolatier, Jean-Paul Mercier. And the biggest beneficiaries are Kendal, who inherits fifty percent and his cousin Hillary Lindsay, who gets twenty percent. So, there's a few others still alive that benefit from Gavin's death."

Carmichael nodded. "True," he replied, "and they probably get even more, given that Kendal died before Gavin.

"We shouldn't forget the part-owners of the cocoa co-operative farms in Africa and South America," continued Rachel. "They get to wholly own their farms. And, of course, Harriett Hall gets Gavin's share of Harri's Bar, so she now owns it outright."

"We've already established that Harriett Hall could not have killed either Kendal or Gavin," Watson announced, his voice slightly raised, "I reckon it's got to be Rebecca. Maybe she's in it with Jean-Paul Mercier rather than Carly Wolf, but surely she's got to be our prime suspect still."

Carmichael paused for a few seconds before looking over at his two subordinates.

"The other thing that does tend to suggest that it might be Rebecca," he added, "is the fact that whoever killed Gavin most probably knew that the night watchman had been told to take the evening off. If we assume that Janet Sutherland is not involved, that does just leave Rebecca Graham."

As he finished his sentence, WPC Twamley entered the room, with DS Cooper a few paces behind her.

"Rebecca Graham is asking to speak with a solicitor," the WPC announced.

"That's even more proof of her guilt in my opinion," remarked Watson, his arms out wide to emphasise his frustration."

Carmichael looked up at WPC Twamley.

"Can you get Sergeant Butterworth to sort that out for her, please," he replied. Then, turning to his team, he added, "Which will give us a bit of time to take stock on where we are and decide how we should proceed."

Chapter 59

It was just before 11am when the four officers started the debrief in the incident room at Kirkwood Police Station.

"So," commenced Carmichael in a loud, authoritative voice, "what did you find out from the hospital, Paul?"

Cooper shook his head. "If Carly and Rebecca do know each other, it's unlikely to be through the hospital. I'm assured that Carly Wolf nurses kids and has never had anything to do with geriatrics."

"That doesn't necessarily mean they aren't in it together," added Watson. "Rebecca's 'I think I may recognise her' ploy suggests to me she's trying to give herself an out."

"What do you mean?" enquired Rachel.

"I just think she's boxing clever," continued Watson. "By being a little less certain about not knowing Carly, when we eventually do make an association between the two of them Rebecca can say that she'd never categorically said she didn't know Carly."

Carmichael shrugged his shoulders. "What do you think?" he asked, his question aimed at Cooper. "Do you still think Rebecca and Carly are our murderers?"

Cooper puffed out his cheeks and exhaled loudly. "I still think it's a possibility, especially now we know the details of all three wills. However, Gabby Johns and Harriet Hall are also big winners, so I'm not sure."

"I agree," Rachel remarked, keen to ensure her views were heard. "If the inheritance is the motive, then it's got to be either Gabby, Carly or Harriett who are in on it with Rebecca."

"The fact that Harriett has concrete alibis for the first two murders surely means we can rule her out," remarked Watson.

Cooper reluctantly nodded. "And, I suppose, the fact that Swift's will leaves everything he owns equally to Kendal, Gabby, and Carly, with the caveat that if any of them die before him then their shares are divided between the surviving beneficiaries, certainly gives both Gabby and Carly a very strong motive to kill Kendal first then Martin Swift."

Carmichael considered what he'd heard for a few seconds.

"Given what we now know, from the three wills, I reckon the legacies of Carly and Gabby are phenomenal," he remarked. "They'll each get tens of thousands from Kendal's will alone, then when you take everything that Kendal left to Swift and also the ten percent of The World of Chocolate business that Swift inherits..."

"And," interjected Cooper, "with Kendal already being dead when Gavin died, his fifty per cent will be shared between the other beneficiaries, so Swift would have got..."

Carmichael held the palm of his hand up to silence his colleague. "I was just coming to that, Paul," he remarked with a hint of frustration in his voice. "So, when you add everything up, it's got to run into many hundreds of thousands each, and most likely into the millions."

"A good enough reason for some people to kill," concurred Watson, seemingly oblivious to Carmichael's earlier gesture.

"I'd say so," added Cooper.

"How do you think we should proceed from here, sir?" Rachel enquired.

Carmichael thought for a few seconds.

"I think we should stick to the theory we had before we saw the wills for now and bring in Carly Wolf for questioning, too," he replied. "Why don't you and Marc go and pick her up? When you're back, we'll decide who continues the interview with Rebecca and which of us has Carly. But let's get them both in."

* * * *

Within minutes, Watson and Rachel Dalton were on their way to Southport to pick up Carly Wolf. Cooper, still keen to try and establish some link between Carly and Rebecca, headed back to his desk; which left Carmichael alone.

Figuring that it would be at least an hour before Rebecca would have been able to be allocated a brief and to have had a chance to discuss her predicament with him, and allowing about the same amount of time for Rachel and Watson to return to Kirkwood with Carly Wolf in tow, Carmichael decided to walk over to the canteen and get himself a sandwich for lunch.

On his way, he passed Janet Sutherland, who had come into the station to collect her tablet.

"I take it I'm in the clear now?" Janet asked, her tone suggesting more than a hint of indignation.

"You are," replied Carmichael decisively. "I don't think we'll be needing to talk to you again."

This seemed to satisfy the young woman, who forced a smile before scurrying away.

"Actually," shouted Carmichael at the departing figure. "There is one more thing I'd like to ask you."

Janet Sutherland stopped abruptly in her tracks, then turned to face Carmichael, who strode slowly towards her.

"You mentioned that you and Gavin Michelson met on

three occasions to conduct your business arrangement," he remarked as tactfully as he could, upon his arrival at Janet Sutherland's side. "You also indicated that on one occasion you did so at his house."

"That's correct," replied Janet rather nervously.

"Well, when you were with Gavin, either at home or in the office, did anyone see you?"

Janet shook her head. "His Latino housemaid was at the house the time we were together there, but Gavin told her we were having a business meeting, and I saw her leave the house well before anything happened."

"That's fine," replied Carmichael. "Thanks again for your help with our enquiry."

Carmichael watched as Janet Sutherland scampered away. He still could not see Janet as being Gavin Michelson's type, but fully accepted that he wasn't an expert in such matters.

Chapter 60

It was a beautiful, warm and bright summer's afternoon and, as Watson's car sped down the A59 that connected Kirkwood and Southport, Rachel gazed pensively through the side window at the green fields beyond the higgledy-piggledy hedgerow that skirted the road.

"I can't help thinking we're missing something obvious," she remarked, without bothering to turn her head to make eye contact with Watson.

"That wouldn't be the first time," replied Watson scathingly, "but Rebecca Graham's feeble attempt at making out she didn't know Carly, suggests to me that, not only was Paul right to think we have two murderers, but they are Rebecca and Carly Wolf. Once we get positive proof they know each other, then I reckon we'll have cracked it."

"I'd love you to be right," replied Rachel sceptically, "but I'm not so sure. I'd certainly say that Rebecca is a strong candidate, but for some reason I don't see Carly as the other person. I'd be more likely to pick Gabby Johns than Carly, or even her aunt, Harriett Hall. They both inherit from the wills, and in Gabby's case, just as much as Carly."

"Maybe they are all in it together?" suggested Watson, mischievously. "Maybe it's Carly, Rebecca, Harriett and Gabby."

"No chance," replied Rachel with a strong shake of her

head and a disdainful look. "From what they've told the boss about each other, it's highly unlikely that either Harriett or Carly will be in league with Gabby. They both seem to detest her, from what they've been saying about her."

"Which brings us back to Rebecca and Carly," Watson remarked, with a wry smile.

As he spoke, Rachel's mobile rang. She pulled the mobile from her trouser pocket and looked at the small screen. The number displayed was not one she recognised.

"DS Dalton," announced Rachel, as she placed the mobile next to her ear.

"Oh hi," she then said in a far friendlier voice, before moving the mobile from her right ear to the left ear – the ear furthest from Watson.

"Well, it is a bit tricky now," she replied vaguely, which her companion in the car assumed was her answer to *'are you free to talk right now?'*

"Ok," continued Rachel, "I'll speak to you then."

DS Rachel Dalton ended her call and placed her mobile back in her trouser pocket.

"Anyone I know?" enquired Watson with an inquisitive, impish grin.

Rachel shot him a discerning look before turning her head to look out of the side window once more.

* * * *

Carmichael stood alone at his office window, looking out over the car park below. The cheese and ham baguette he'd purchased from the canteen lay, half-eaten, on his desk next to the half-empty coffee cup.

Just like DS Dalton, he was struggling to come to terms with Rebecca Graham and Carly Wolf being the perpetrators of the three murders. He had no doubt that they were strong candidates, but he found it difficult to accept that these two young women were capable of such acts of violence and with such premeditated intent. For certain, Carly had a motive, her potential inheritance running into hundreds of thousands was incentive enough to convince most juries. And, as for Rebecca, a twenty percent share in The World of Chocolate was a significant inheritance, so it wouldn't take a barrister worth his salt five minutes to get a jury to buy that as a motive, either. However, Carmichael's gut told him it was not that simple.

Then there was the question of the mobile that Kendal was using on the night he died. Had the hoodie mugger, Jackie Donnelly, not also maintained she'd seen Kendal on the phone, Carmichael may have been content to accept that Carly Wolf had made the whole story up. However, Jackie Donnelly had been very certain about Kendal using his mobile. Without any prompting or coercion, she'd suggested it was his mobile she'd really wanted to steal. So, in Carmichael's eyes, there had to have been a mobile. *But where is that mobile now?*

Then, to compound the confusion, there was also the sense of theatre with all three murders. Kendal, run through with his own sword while gazing up at the stars; Gavin, naked and drowned in his own vat of chocolate; and, finally, Martin Swift, choked to death by a large amount of bank notes. Why would the perpetrators go to such lengths?

Carmichael wandered back to his seat and took a tiny sip of the now lukewarm coffee. He then scribbled down three words on the scrap of paper in front of him;

PASSION, REVENGE, MONEY

Chapter 61

It was 2.15pm by the time the interview with Rebecca Graham restarted and, in Interview Room 2, which was just five metres down the corridor, Carly Wolf sat with the duty solicitor waiting for her interview to commence.

Once again, Carmichael had decided to step back from conducting either interview. From his position in the room in between the two interview rooms, he could observe both interviews simultaneously, which he felt may enable him to glean more than if he'd been focussed on just one of the interrogations.

Armed with their respective lists of key questions, compiled by Carmichael, Watson and Rachel Dalton restarted their interview with Rebecca Graham.

"Have you been able to remember where you've seen this woman before?" Rachel enquired, again pushing the photograph of Carly Wolf across the table.

Rebecca shook her head.

"My client has advised me that she isn't certain if she knows this woman," interjected her brief. "She merely indicated earlier that the face looked familiar. She's not sure why."

"Is that correct?" Rachel asked, her eyes on Rebecca rather than the legal adviser.

Rebecca glanced sideways at her solicitor before replying.

"I don't wish to hinder your enquiries," she said. "However, unless you are officially charging me with an offence, I'm not prepared to answer any more of your questions."

Rachel Dalton smiled and sat back in her chair.

"You've got to look at this from our perspective, which will also be how a jury will see it," continued Rachel. "You stand to gain considerably from Gavin's death and you have nobody to corroborate your account of where you were at the time any of the three murder victims were killed."

"What do you mean I 'gain considerably from Gavin's death'?" enquired Rebecca angrily, her eyes glaring at Rachel and her forehead creased enough to suggest this news was a major shock to her. "I loved Gavin, I have gained nothing from his death."

"Oh, but you have," replied Rachel calmly. "Did you not know he'd left you ten per cent of the business, and with Kendal having been killed before Gavin, your share now doubles to twenty per cent. Surely Gavin told you this?"

"No, he didn't" replied Rebecca, who had clearly decided to ignore the advice of her legal representative to remain silent. "He never mentioned anything to me about a will."

Rebecca's eyeline shifted downwards for a few seconds, as she took on board what she'd just learned.

"But, it does prove what I'd been saying about our relationship," she continued, her eyes now returning to meet those of her inquisitor, with a look of relief and the faintest glint of joy. "We were in a relationship and he did love me."

From behind the two-way mirror, Carmichael observed Rebecca Graham's reaction to the news of her legacy. Unless she was an actor of Shakespearian proportions, her response suggested to him that their potential murder suspect hadn't the slightest inkling of the inheritance. And that faint smile she gave out, after her latest remark, was a sure sign to Carmichael that Rebecca valued the news of the legacy more for its significance in terms of Gavin's affection towards her rather than the substantial monetary benefit it would now bestow on her.

Then, out of the corner of his eye, Carmichael noticed Cooper entering Interview Room 2. He swivelled around in his chair, muted the microphone to Interview Room 1, and then turned on the other microphone, which would allow him to listen to Cooper's interrogation of Carly Wolf.

"Good morning, Carly," Cooper began with a warm smile. "Thanks for coming in to see us."

"I hardly had a choice, as I recall," replied Carly Wolf, her arms folded tightly across her chest, a clear sign of her displeasure at being brought to Kirkwood Police Station.

"I can totally understand that this is an inconvenience for you," continued Cooper, who retained his smiling, friendly disposition. "However, information has recently come to light that we'd like to talk to you about."

Carly Wolf shook her head from side to side to emphasise her exasperation.

"And what information is that?" she enquired dismissively.

"Well, firstly there is the inheritance from the wills of Kendal Michelson and Martin Swift," remarked Cooper. "Were you aware that they both left generous legacies to you?"

Carly's brow furrowed slightly.

"I knew that Kendal had left me some money," replied Carly, "Martin told me that the other day. But I wasn't aware of Martin leaving me anything. How much do I get from him?"

Cooper paused for a short while.

"A considerable amount," he replied. "More than enough to lead some people to commit murder."

"I have to protest," interjected Carly's solicitor. "My client is here of her own free will. She is not under arrest and your

289

insinuation that she has murdered someone to benefit from their will is totally unfounded."

Cooper smiled again.

"So, you had no idea about the inheritance from Martin Swift?" he enquired for a second time.

From behind the two-way mirror, Carmichael observed as the normally brash, over-confident young woman started to look a little nervous. Carly's tightly folded arms loosened, and she shuffled uneasily in her chair.

"I didn't know he'd actually gone and changed his will," replied Carly. "I thought he'd just treat it as another one of Kendal's stupid ideas. That's what the rest of us did... Well, I can't speak for Gabby, but I'd be amazed if Kendal changed his will, and I haven't even made a will."

Cooper's expression was one of puzzlement. "Can you explain what you're talking about?" he enquired.

Carly puffed out her cheeks. "It was at the Steampunk Asylum last year in Lincoln," replied Carly. "I was still with Kendal and Martin was trying, as he always did, to make out that we were some sort of gang. I'm not sure why, I guess he was just lonely and wanted to belong. Despite him being very successful at work and loaded, socially he was quite inept and Kendal was probably his only real male friend."

"But what about you and Gabby Johns?" Copper remarked. "Weren't you his friends too?"

Carly shrugged her shoulders. "Again, I can only speak for myself," she replied, "but I found him a real bore to be honest with you. That sounds a bit harsh now as he's dead and I do feel guilty saying it, especially as you say he's left me some money, but I didn't consider him a close friend. He was a hanger-on at best."

"I see," replied Cooper. "So, what happened in Lincoln?"

"Well," continued Carly, "Martin was banging on one

evening about how we four were a great team and how we were like blood brothers and Kendal, or maybe it was Gabby, said something flippant, along the lines of… *if we're so close we need to prove it.* The conversation then went on to suggest that we should all make wills leaving almost everything we owned to the other three."

Carmichael listened intently from behind the two-way mirror.

"And Martin acted upon it?" Cooper enquired.

Carly shrugged her shoulders.

"I didn't," she replied, "and I suspect Gabby hasn't either, but from what you're saying, Martin did."

"And Kendal did too," remarked Cooper. "He left money to you, Gabby, and a big inheritance to Martin."

Carly's eyes widened as she listened to Cooper's pronouncement. "I'm amazed," she remarked. "Kendal must have liked him more than I realised."

"So, who was it that suggested the details of this pact?" Cooper enquired.

Carly shrugged her shoulders. "It certainly wasn't me," she replied. "I suspect it was Kendal, but I couldn't be sure. Maybe Gabby will remember."

Cooper leaned back in his chair.

"Does the name Rebecca Graham mean anything to you?" he enquired.

Without hesitation, Carly nodded. "Yes, she was at my school," she replied. "She'd have been three years above me, so I suspect she wouldn't remember me, but she was Head Girl. So yes, I know her. Why do you ask?"

"So, when was the last time you saw her?" Cooper enquired.

Carly smirked. "As it happens, I saw her in the car park at the hospital where I work the other night," Carly replied. "I assumed she was visiting someone as it was at normal evening visiting time, but apart from that I've not seen her since she left school, so it must be eight years."

"Did she recognise you?" Cooper enquired.

Carly shook her head. "I don't think so," she replied. "To be honest she probably didn't know I existed when we were at school, given I was three years below her. Anyway, what's the big deal about her?"

Cooper looked back at Carly Wolf, his eyes stern and piercing, but he didn't answer her question.

After checking the time on the clock which hung directly behind where Carly was sitting, Cooper stood up.

"I need to consult with Inspector Carmichael," he remarked, "but unless he wants another word with you, you'll be free to go. If you could just wait here a moment."

Not for the first time that afternoon, Carly Wolf puffed out her cheeks. "Surely, he's not going to have anything else to ask me," she remarked as Cooper made his way through the door. "He must have exhausted all the questions he has, given the amount of time he's been hassling me over the last five days."

Cooper heard her, but didn't look back or reply.

Chapter 62

It was precisely 3pm when Carmichael, Cooper, Watson, and Rachel Dalton reconvened in the small viewing room between the two interview rooms.

"What do you think, boss?" Watson enquired.

Carmichael took a deep breath before answering.

"I think there's a chance one of these two could be involved," he replied, "but I don't see them being in it together."

All four officers spent a few seconds looking at the two suspects as they sat with their briefs in the two adjoining rooms.

"I'm sure Rebecca is telling the truth about Carly," Rachel added. "I don't think she knows her."

Reluctantly, Watson nodded his agreement. "That's the conclusion I came to as well," he remarked.

"What do you think, Paul?" Carmichael asked, turning to face Cooper.

Cooper shrugged his shoulders.

"I'm still sure we have two murderers," he replied. "And between them, these two could have killed all three. But I did believe Carly when she said she knew nothing about Swift making her a beneficiary in his will and, in my view, she was telling the truth when she said she'd not seen Rebecca Graham for eight years, other than the other day at the hospital."

"Where does that leave us?" Rachel asked, her query directed at Carmichael.

"That's a very good question," replied Carmichael thoughtfully.

"Do we let them both go?" Watson asked.

Carmichael gave a reluctant nod of his head. "Yes," he replied, "but let's release them together. I want them to leave the station at the same time. I want to see how they react when they see each other."

* * * *

Fifteen minutes later, Carly Wolf, accompanied by Cooper, exited the police station through the rear door, which took them to the car park. She was closely followed by Rebecca Graham, escorted by Watson.

Carmichael and Rachel Dalton looked on from the first-floor office.

The two women could not have avoided seeing each other, but gave no indication to suggest they were in any way partners in crime.

As soon as the two cars transporting the women out of the car park had disappeared from their sight, Carmichael turned to face Rachel.

"It's not them," Carmichael remarked, his tone one of emptiness and disappointment. "I'm certain of it. I know they technically could have managed the three murders between them, but I'm pretty sure it's not them."

Carmichael walked back to his desk and turned over the scrap of paper to reveal the three words he'd scribbled down at lunchtime.

PASSION, REVENGE, MONEY

"What's that, sir?" Rachel asked, her eyes having caught a brief glimpse of the three words on the note.

"Just some scribblings," Carmichael replied, rather evasively, before folding the paper and placing it in his pocket. "Random ideas I've had regarding potential motives."

Rachel waited for a few seconds, expecting her boss to elaborate more on the note he'd hastily tucked away out of sight. But Carmichael remained tight-lipped.

"Do you have some ideas on what's behind these murders?" continued Rachel, her strong desire to have some insight into what was going on in Carmichael's head evident in her voice.

Carmichael fixed his eyes on his young colleague and smiled, realising she'd probably clocked the three words he'd written.

"It could just simply be for money. That would appear to be the most obvious reason," replied Carmichael. "However, I'm not sure, it could also be for a few other reasons."

"Like what?" Rachel enquired.

Carmichael took a couple of seconds before he replied.

"My hunch is that they're either crimes of passion or they're carried out as some form of revenge," he remarked.

"So, in your view, nothing to do with Steampunk?" Rachel enquired.

Carmichael looked directly into Rachel's eyes. "I very much doubt it," he replied. "Gavin wasn't into that world and Martin Swift died after the event was over, so although Kendal was killed while attending the Steampunk weekend, I'm fairly confident these deaths aren't driven by their involvement in Steampunk."

Rachel nodded to indicate she agreed.

"Of the three reasons you've mentioned, I'd probably favour money as being behind all this," suggested Rachel.

Carmichael found it hard to argue with Rachel's supposition.

"The legacies in those three wills are huge," he conceded, "certainly large enough to tempt a lot of people to commit murder."

"I'd say so," Rachel replied. "And, apart from Carmen Martinez, all our suspects gain significantly from those wills."

"You may well be right, Rachel," Carmichael remarked, "but we'd be foolish to jump to conclusions. The truth is we just don't know what the motivation is in this case."

Expecting there was more Carmichael was about to tell her, Rachel kept her eyes firmly on her boss.

"However, I am certain that if we can find that mobile Kendal used on Saturday evening we'll be much closer to understanding what's going on," continued Carmichael.

"Do you think there are two killers?" Rachel asked.

Carmichael shrugged his shoulders. "Who knows?" he replied vaguely, "but I have to confess that it's becoming increasingly hard to believe that this was the work of just one person."

Rachel nodded. "Then there's the way the murders have been committed," she added. "They were so dramatic, almost as if they'd been stage-managed to reflect the main hobbies and interests of the dead men. Steampunk and the stars in the case of Kendal, the manufacture of chocolate in the case of Gavin…"

"And money in the case of Martin Swift," Carmichael added.

"Yes, for him it was the love of money," remarked Rachel.

Carmichael smiled. Despite her limited experience as a detective, he had a high regard for Rachel Dalton, especially when he could see her mind was working in parallel to his own.

"You're right," Carmichael agreed, "carried out

meticulously as if to reflect the driving forces behind the victims."

"Their true passions," Rachel remarked.

Carmichael nodded. "Precisely," he replied. "Passion murders."

"So, what now?" enquired Rachel.

Carmichael puffed out his cheeks.

"I'm going to have another talk with the Kirkwood and District Astronomical Society," he replied, "and, while I'm doing that, I'd like you to do some more digging for me."

Then, after looking at his watch, Carmichael continued. "And if you're quick, you may have the information I need before the day's out."

Chapter 63

It was just after 6pm when Carmichael emerged in a buoyant mood from the tiny office of Kirkwood and District Astronomical Society.

Having spent the last two hours in the company of Harold Parker, who he'd met the day before, Carmichael was certain he, at last, had the breakthrough he'd been looking for.

Parker was a tall, thin, slightly eccentric man in his late sixties with a wiry, gingery-grey beard and, although Carmichael found him to be a bit of a bore, he was able to provide some very useful information. So much so that, as he strode confidently towards his car, Carmichael was certain he knew who had killed Kendal Michelson. And if Rachel's investigations yielded the information he was expecting, he'd have enough evidence to caution his suspect and bring her in for questioning.

* * * *

Rachel Dalton had just received the last piece of information she needed when her mobile rang.

A smile of glee appeared on her face when she recognised the voice on the end of the line.

"I said I'd call back," announced Matthew Stock, "are you free to talk now?"

Rachel's smile remained on her face. "As it happens I am," she replied.

* * * *

It was a magnificent, warm, dry, summer's evening and, for once, Carmichael welcomed the journey time. Normally, he found the drive home through the narrow country lanes tedious, but today it was different.

Almost certainly, the glorious weather was a factor, but of greater significance was the information he'd just been given by Harold Parker.

The road bent sharply to the right, sending the sun streaming through his windscreen, making Carmichael squint and move his head slightly to the left. He slowed down, quickly adjusted the sun visor above his head then, with his eyes safe from the sun's strong glare, he leaned back in his seat and pressed his foot hard on the accelerator.

* * * *

"Seven thirty may be pushing it a little," replied Rachel. "If you can make it eight, then you're on."

"Eight it is," replied Matthew Stock. "Now if you can give me your post code I'll see you then."

Rachel Dalton recited her postcode slowly, so her date would not get it wrong, before adding, "I'll see you later then," in an affectionate voice and resting her mobile phone on the table in front of her.

Rachel had a good feeling about Matthew Stock, but quickly pushed any thoughts of potential romance from her mind. She still had work to do.

Picking up the print-outs, she started to look for the specific information her boss had requested.

* * * *

Carmichael's car had just come to a halt on his drive when he received the call from Rachel Dalton.

"So, what did you find?" he asked eagerly.

Rachel, who was still at her desk at the station, paused for a second before answering.

"Well," replied Rachel, "it's a little disappointing."

Carmichael listened intently as Rachel provided a summary of the reports on the calls made by and from the mobile phones of the main suspects on the evening Kendal Michelson was murdered.

"So not one of them made a call out at the times Carly Wolf and Jackie Donnelly maintain they saw Kendal on his mobile?"

"No," replied Rachel, "but there is one strange thing."

"What's that?" Carmichael enquired.

"Well," continued Rachel, "at about those times, Gavin Michelson appears to have called Carmen Martinez on her mobile from his land line at home."

"Why would he do that?" remarked Carmichael. "Particularly as, according to both Gavin and Carmen's accounts, Carmen was in her room in the same house all evening."

"That's exactly what I was thinking," replied Rachel. "It doesn't make any sense."

Carmichael thought for a few seconds.

"Actually," he remarked in a sage-like tone of voice, "on the contrary, I think this is all starting to make perfect sense."

Chapter 64

Rachel was relieved when Matthew Stock didn't arrive at the allotted time of 8 o'clock. She'd only got home at 6:55pm then, having to spend a further fifteen minutes on the phone with Carmichael, receiving her new instructions for the following morning, that extra ten minutes she'd gained, by her date being late, was just enough time to get herself half-decent.

"You look wonderful," remarked Matthew reassuringly when she opened her door. "I'm so sorry I'm late. I got waylaid by my uncle, who decided, when I was just about to leave, that he needed fresh blood results on some poor soul who was killed this morning in a motor cycle accident. I swear he knew I was in a hurry to get away. He can be a miserable old sod at times."

Rachel smiled. "We know Dr Stock very well," she replied, "he can be a bit awkward. Mind you, my boss has his moments, too."

* * * *

After speaking with Rachel, Carmichael then spent almost an hour on the phone talking first with Cooper then with Watson. Having issued his team with their respective instructions for the following morning, Carmichael finally decided to vacate his stationary BMW and join the family inside the house.

"Where is everybody?" he enquired, when it was only Penny he found in the lounge.

"Robbie's gone out and Natalie's in her room," Penny replied.

Carmichael walked over to the sofa and plonked himself down next to his wife.

"I spoke with Robbie this morning," he remarked. "I'm not sure whether it all went in, but I think I got the message across."

Penny snuggled up beside her husband. "Even if it didn't, I don't expect Mrs Harper's Nanny will be quite so brazen from now on."

"Brazen!" repeated Carmichael, the pitch of his voice slightly higher than normal to accentuate the word. "Now that's a word you don't hear that often."

Penny directed a hard, swift jab of her elbow into Carmichael's side.

"I don't think you have taken all this as seriously as you should," she remarked, trying hard to conceal the smile that was trying to break out on her face.

"Ow," yelled Carmichael, although the pain was nowhere near as great as he made out. "Maybe not," he replied, "but I think it's safe to say that little episode in the annuls of the Carmichael family is now over."

"How's the case going?" Penny enquired.

"As it happens, it's just taken a turn for the better," replied her husband with a glint of glee on his face. "Based on a conversation I've just had with Rachel, and a meeting I had earlier with a man, who has to be one of the front runners for this year's *most boring man of the year award*, I'm now pretty sure that there are two murderers. And what's more, I think I know who they are."

Penny sat up straight and turned so she could look directly into Carmichael's eyes.

"Tell me more," she remarked enthusiastically.

* * * *

The Auberge Brasserie was already getting busy by the time Rachel and Matthew arrived.

"I've never been here myself," announced Matthew, "but I know my uncle comes here, so it's got to be good."

Rachel smiled. She'd never been to the restaurant before either, but she knew it would be good as her father often dined there, and her father was a very discerning man who would never return to a restaurant unless he was absolutely satisfied with the food, the service, and the atmosphere.

"I'm told it's very good," she replied encouragingly.

Having been shown to their table, the two diners ordered their drinks and sat facing each other.

"So, tell me about Carmichael?" Matthew enquired. "He's got quite a reputation amongst the team down at the pathology lab."

Rachel took a sip of her white wine and raised her eyebrows.

"So, you've invited me out to find out more about my boss?" she teased.

Matthew's smile evaporated. "Oh no," he replied, apologetically, "but he does have a reputation and I was just curious."

Rachel smiled reassuringly back at Matthew.

"He can be very demanding, he's often full-on and when he's unhappy he lets you know about it," she remarked. "However, he's a brilliant detective and I really like working with him. I've learned so much from him."

Matthew nodded. "No more questions about Carmichael,

I promise," he pronounced with a glint of his fine, white teeth. "Let's talk about you."

* * * *

Having listened intently, Penny gently nodded; her way of signifying she endorsed the logic her husband had used to create his theory.

"It makes sense, I suppose," she remarked. "And from what you've said, it does sound like all three murders were carefully choreographed to highlight each victim's main interests."

Carmichael nodded sagely. "The way the victims died appears to have been as important as the act of killing them, to the killers."

"That's frightening," remarked Penny. "So, what are the team's tasks before you make the arrests in the morning?"

"I've asked Rachel to do more CCTV checking on the night Gavin was killed," replied Carmichael. "I've told Cooper to get back to The World of Chocolate to dig deeper into the co-operatives that Gavin set up. And while they do that, I'm picking up one of our ladies and Watson's going to arrest the other at the same time."

Penny smiled. "You're pretty certain those two are your killers," she remarked.

Carmichael smiled. "I would hesitate to claim I'm certain," he replied, "but I am pretty confident I'm right. And I'm hopeful that, after Rachel and Cooper have completed their assignments, we'll be able to not only confirm their motives, but also demonstrate that between them they had the ability to commit these three murders. And we'll have irrefutable proof they've both been lying to us."

"Sounds like you've got it all sewn up," remarked Penny, before planting a kiss on her husband's lips.

Carmichael rolled his eyes. "I sincerely hope so," he replied.

"Does Hercule Poirot need anything to eat?" she continued, "for those little grey cells..." Her French accent was so poor it brought a frown to Carmichael's already weary brow.

"Mais oui," replied Carmichael, which was about the limit of his French vocabulary.

Chapter 65

Friday 19th August

Carmichael woke up early, but remained in bed listening to the dawn chorus outside his bedroom window.

He wasn't exactly sure what time it was, but the lack of any noticeable sound of traffic from outside suggested to him that it was certainly well before 7am.

As he lay there silently, his gaze fixed on the ornate circular plasterwork that surrounded the light fitting on their bedroom ceiling, Carmichael's thoughts never deviated from the woman he was planning to meet and arrest later that morning.

He could not help but ponder on how, out of the six or seven potential suspects, she was the one he'd warmed to the most. *Maybe Penny's right*, he thought to himself. *Maybe I am a soft touch with some women.*

Carmichael considered this thought for a few seconds. It was certainly true he'd taken a bit of a liking to the attractive-looking owner of Harri's Bar, but he was sure his judgement and objectivity had never been in any doubt. Now he was going to arrest her and charge her on two counts of murder and, on being an accessory to a third, there would be absolutely no favouritism afforded to Harriett Hall, no matter how beguilingly she smiled.

****

Rachel Dalton had managed less than five hours' sleep. Her date with Matthew at the French restaurant had gone really well. So much so, that after their meal they'd decided to move on to a bar just off Lord Street, where they remained talking and laughing until well into the early hours.

Slightly hung-over and extremely tired, Rachel could not believe it when her alarm rang, indicating so violently that it was already 6:25am.

"Bugger," she shouted as she smashed her right hand heavily onto the plunger at the top of the offending time-piece, sending it swiftly into silence.

****

The more Carmichael thought about Harriett Hall and Carmen Martinez being their two murderers, the more it made sense.

Despite it being impossible for Harriett to have killed Kendal, as she was with Gavin at the time they believed that murder was committed, she could have still played her part in Kendal's death. If, as Carmichael surmised, it was indeed Harriett who had made those two calls to Kendal from Gavin's house, she could have quite easily been guiding the poor victim, her fellow amateur astronomer, down to the beach and his death at the hands of Carmen Martinez. She could have also probably even driven Carmen there earlier that evening before she went to see Gavin, he thought. Then picked her up later, after the gruesome deed had been committed. What's more, Carmen could have quite easily taken the mobile Kendal had been using after she'd killed him, which would explain its absence at the crime scene.

Even that apparently mistakenly sent call from Harriett to

Kendal, on the evening Kendal died, which they'd all assumed Harriett meant to make to Gavin, could have been part of their wicked plan. Although, no matter how hard he tried, Carmichael could not work out how that call fitted in.

As for the murder of Gavin Michelson two days later, the two women had effectively given each other an alibi by maintaining they were together at Harri's Bar until Harriett left at two thirty, and in the case of Carmen, that she'd been there cleaning until after sunrise. If they were in it together, they could have easily slipped away from Harri's Bar and driven to The World of Chocolate in Barton Bridge, after everyone else had departed. They would have had ample time to carry out the macabre, theatrical murder of Gavin Michelson and still get Carmen back to the bar well before dawn, and in plenty of time for her to catch the early train from Southport to Barton Bridge; thus, supporting her version of events that night, and eliminating her from suspicion.

As for the killing of Martin Swift, Carmichael concluded that his murder could have quite easily been carried out by Harriett working alone. With Watson having only just left Carmen when the mystery visitor, who they all believed to be the murderer, arrived at Swift's house, it would have been impossible for Carmen to have killed Swift. However, they'd not yet spoken to Harriett about her movements on that evening, and Carmichael was quietly confident that when he questioned her later, she'd struggle to provide a convincing alibi for the time Swift was murdered.

Suitably pleased with these versions of events, Carmichael slowly eased himself out of bed and gingerly made an exit from the bedroom, his wife sound-asleep and completely oblivious to the finer details of the great detective's deductive powers.

Chapter 66

In line with Carmichael's instructions from the evening before, both Harriett Hall and Carmen Martinez were arrested at precisely 9:00am.

Their apprehension went flawlessly and by 10:30am both women were safely in custody at Kirkwood Police Station and in deep conversations with their respective legal representatives; a right which both women had indicated they wanted as soon as it was offered.

There was an air of quiet confidence in the incident room, as Carmichael and his team gathered together for their first update of the day.

Carmichael took a sip of coffee.

"I've just received Dr Stock's report on the substance used to sedate Gavin Michelson and Martin Swift before they were killed," Carmichael announced. "It's a morphine-based compound that appears to have baffled the good doctor, hence it taking him so long to get back to us. According to Stock, he's never come across it before and he can't quite work out the precise make-up of this sedative."

"I bet that will have frustrated the hell out of him," remarked Watson with a broad grin. "We all know how particular Dr Stock is."

Carmichael rolled his eyes as if to endorse Watson's remark.

"However," Carmichael continued, "Stock may not be

sure what it is but he's one hundred percent certain that the drug used was exactly the same in both cases."

"So, we can be certain that whoever killed Gavin Michelson also killed Martin Swift," remarked Cooper.

"Exactly, Paul," replied Carmichael, "and, unless I'm very much mistaken, their names are Carmen Martinez and Harriett Hall."

His three colleagues nodded their heads in agreement.

"Why don't you start, Rachel?" Carmichael asked, his eyes directed at the young DC. "What have you discovered so far today?"

Rachel looked a little uneasy. "I've nothing much to report," she replied. "I've got the CCTV footage from numerous cameras on the evening Gavin Michelson was murdered, but so far I've not been able to find any evidence of Harriett and Carmen leaving Southport in that distinctive white Mercedes she drives. Mind you, I've only just started to look, I'll probably need at least the rest of the morning before I've been through all of it."

Carmichael, happy with Rachel's response, nodded. "Just keep ploughing through them," he replied. "If you need any additional help, ask the Duty Sergeant to let you borrow someone from his team. But make sure you get all the tapes viewed as quickly as possible and, the minute you find anything, let me know."

Rachel smiled and nodded to indicate she fully understood her instructions.

"What about you, Marc?" Carmichael enquired. "How did the arrest go with Carmen?"

"It went fine," replied Watson with a nonchalant shrug of his shoulders. "Carmen didn't resist in any way, she didn't even protest that much. But she wasn't very responsive when I tried to talk with her."

Carmichael smiled. "That's fine," he replied calmly.

"We'll see what she has to say for herself when we interview her later."

"But, you were right, though," continued Watson, "I've got Carmen's passport and she isn't Spanish."

As he spoke, Watson pulled out a small maroon passport with the words 'Comunidad Andina, Republica Del Ecuador' emblazoned on the front in gold lettering above a symbol of what looked like a vulture, open-winged, above a harbour scene, with a boat in the foreground and a mountain rising in the distance.

"Ecuador," remarked Rachel, her pitch raised higher than normal.

"What was it that made you think she wasn't from Spain?" Watson enquired, the tone in his voice suggesting he was hugely impressed with his boss's deductive powers.

Carmichael smiled broadly. "I'd like to say it was my in-depth knowledge of Spanish dialects," he replied, "but it was simply something that Janet Sutherland said yesterday when I met her briefly here. She called Carmen a Latino. To be honest, at the time it didn't register, I thought she was being insulting. However, with Carmen and Harriett firmly in the frame, Janet's throw-away remark got me thinking."

Rachel had a puzzled look on her face, indicating she wasn't yet on Carmichael's wavelength.

"What do you mean, sir?" she enquired.

Carmichael gave out a wry smile. "When I started to recall Janet's Latino comment," he continued, "I couldn't help thinking maybe there was a link between Carmen Martinez and one of Gavin Michelson's cocoa-producing, farm co-operatives, many of which are in Latin American countries."

"Like Ecuador," Rachel remarked, the penny having now well and truly dropped.

Carmichael smiled again, but this time a broader grin.

"Precisely," he replied, "but, of course, up until just now I had no idea it may have been Ecuador."

"So, I guess the next step will be to see if Carmen has any connection with one of Gavin Michelson's co-operatives in Ecuador," remarked Rachel.

"Which is exactly what I'm hoping to establish this morning," interjected Cooper.

"Yes," interceded Carmichael. "Last night, I asked Paul to go to The World of Chocolate first thing today and get as much information as he could on their Latin American co-operatives. How did you get on?"

Cooper looked over at his colleagues. "I spent an hour or so with Janet Sutherland and Jean-Paul Mercier going through their records on the data base," he announced. "Of course, I had no way of knowing the exact country to focus on, but as instructed, I focussed on the Spanish-speaking ones."

"That's good," interjected Watson. "How many were there?"

Cooper looked down at his notes.

"There are two plantations in Peru, one in the Dominican Republic and…"

Before Cooper had a chance to continue, Carmichael cut him dead.

"Paul," he said firmly, "how many in Ecuador? That's all we need to know."

Cooper looked a little surprised at his boss's impatient rebuke, but wasn't ruffled in any way.

"No co-operatives," he replied. "But they do own outright a five-hundred-hectare plantation in the south west of the country called *Guayas Los Rios*. According to Jean-Paul, it produces some of the premium Arriba beans in South America, and, in his view, Arriba beans are the finest beans in the world."

"But it's totally owned by the company?" Carmichael asked.

"Yes," confirmed Cooper.

"And how long have they owned the plantation?" Carmichael enquired.

Cooper shook his head. "I'm not sure," he replied, "but I can check that out very easily. Janet Sutherland sent me over the files on an email, so I'll take a look as soon as we've finished here."

Carmichael nodded. "Good," he remarked, his tone now much more calm and controlled. "But I'll say the same to you as I did to Rachel. The minute you find anything, let me know."

"Absolutely," confirmed Cooper.

"Right, Marc," continued Carmichael, his eyes fixed upon his sergeant. "While these two are doing more digging, you and I need to start interviewing our two suspects."

Watson nodded. "Which do you want to talk to first?" he enquired.

Carmichael weighed up the two options. "Let's start with Harriett Hall," he remarked.

Chapter 67

The atmosphere in Interview Room 1 when Carmichael commenced the formal interview with Harriett Hall was highly charged.

The playful gestures, the relaxed, welcoming body language and those warm smiles that had passed between the pair during their previous meetings, had evaporated completely; replaced by serious faces, icy stares, and a palpable air of hostility.

"I'd like to start by asking you to confirm your movements on the evenings of Saturday, thirteenth of August; Monday, fifteenth of August; and Tuesday, sixteenth of August," Carmichael enquired, his eyes firmly fixed on Harriett Hall.

"As I've already told you," replied Harriett angrily, "on the evening Kendal was murdered, I was with Gavin. I arrived at about eight thirty and left just before twelve. And on the evening Gavin died, I was at home until about eleven. I then went to Harri's Bar, locked up, and helped Carmen out with the cleaning job she was just starting. I was with her until about two thirty in the morning, then I went home again."

"What about the evening of Tuesday, sixteenth of August?" Carmichael asked.

Harriett paused for a few seconds before responding, those intelligent, deep-blue eyes that had captivated Carmichael at their previous meetings, now glaring back at him with contempt.

"That afternoon, I travelled down to Birmingham," Harriett replied. "One of our suppliers was having a launch evening for a new range of their beers and they'd asked me to attend."

"And at what time did you get back?" Carmichael enquired.

"Oh, I didn't," replied Harriett, her voice triumphant and with a smug smile on her face. "I stayed overnight at a hotel in Edgbaston called the Norfolk. I'm sure they'll be able to verify this if you care to check with them."

Not for the first time during this case, Carmichael's heart sank. Surely, he couldn't have it wrong again, he thought.

After exchanging a fleeting glance with Watson, who looked equally surprised, Carmichael continued.

"Of course, we'll need to check that out," he replied, trying hard to disguise his disappointment.

Harriett's conceited expression remained on her face. She knew she'd knocked the wind out of Carmichael's sails and seemed to be thoroughly enjoying her victory.

"So, it would appear that my client has a strong alibi for all three evenings when these terrible murders took place," remarked Harriett's brief. "Which begs the question why she's been arrested for these murders?"

* * * *

Rachel Dalton had followed Carmichael's suggestion about getting help to view the CCTV footage. With the support of WPC Twamley, the pair scoured over the tapes to try and find any sight of Harriett Hall and Carmen Martinez making their way over from Southport to Barton Bridge in the early hours of Tuesday morning.

"I'm up to two in the morning on my tapes," remarked WPC Twamley. "There's absolutely no sign of any car even resembling Harriett's white Mercedes."

Rachel looked briefly away from the bank of screens in front of her.

"Keep looking," she remarked. "It's got to be here."

* * * *

Twenty meters down the corridor, Cooper was enjoying far greater success.

After having only looked at the documentation for a few minutes, he discovered that Michelson's Ecuadorian plantation, *Guayas Los Rios,* had been previously owned by a wealthy family called... Cooper smiled as he read the name Martinez.

"Gotcha!" he exclaimed excitedly, before continuing to pour over the information on his laptop screen.

* * * *

Although Harriett's pronouncement about being in Birmingham on the evening Swift had been killed had considerably disarmed Carmichael, he was determined to continue the interview. They'd have to check out her story, and if it did hold water, it would certainly mean their hypothesis that Carmen and Harriett were in this together was flawed. However, Harriett's alibi for Tuesday evening wasn't substantiated and, until it was, Carmichael was going for her with all guns blazing.

"Tell me about your shared passion for the night sky?" he remarked. "You and Kendal were both keen on stargazing."

Harriett shrugged her shoulders. "Yes," she replied, "it's true. What of it?"

Carmichael smiled, an intimidating smile, a deliberately constructed smile that he hoped would suggest to Harriett that he knew a little more than he really did.

"Well," he continued, "for a good while we couldn't work out why Kendal would be rushing out to the beach, seemingly on his own. But then I spoke to that interesting man at KADAS, Harold Parker. Do you know what he told me, Harriett?"

Harriett's eyes widened. "Do tell me, Inspector," she replied sarcastically. "Harold can talk for England, but sadly few people listen for very long."

"Oh," replied Carmichael, "Mr Parker was very interesting. He told me all about Vega, the brightest star in the constellation Lyra the Harp. I'm reliably informed that on Saturday, thirteenth of August, the night Kendal was killed, it was clearly visible with the naked eye and I think Kendal went down to the beach so that he could view Vega. But you know that don't you, Harriett?"

Harriett shrugged her shoulders. "What makes you think that?" she retorted dismissively.

"Because you called him twice that evening when you were at Gavin's house," replied Carmichael.

A puzzled expression came over Harriett's face. "I made no such calls," she replied indignantly.

Carmichael smiled again. "Oh, but you did," he continued, "once at eleven thirty-eight and then again at eleven fifty-four."

"You can check my mobile records, if you like," remarked Harriett. "You'll find no records of any calls to Kendal."

"We have," replied Carmichael, "and you're right; there were no records of calls made to Kendal using your mobile. But, of course, the calls you made weren't made on your mobile and they weren't made to Kendal's mobile. You made the calls using Gavin's landline and they were made to Carmen's mobile number."

"This is ridiculous," announced Harriett loudly. "I'd like to see you prove that claim."

Carmichael eased himself back into his chair.

"You and Carmen somehow swapped Kendal's mobile for Carmen's," he continued. "My guess is that Carmen hid Kendal's mobile before he left for the Steampunk venue. And when he realised he couldn't find it, she kindly offered him hers as a temporary loan while it was missing. A clever plan you both concocted to ensure that the calls you planned to make could not be traced back to you. So, you see, Harriett, I'm certain that the mobile Kendal had that night was Carmen's and I'm equally certain that the person who rang Kendal on two occasions that night from Gavin's house was you."

Chapter 68

Rachel Dalton and WPC Twamley continued to pour over the CCTV footage from in and around Southport on the evening Gavin Michelson was murdered, but the distinctive white Mercedes V-Class MPV was nowhere to be seen.

"What time are you up to?" Rachel enquired.

"Three twenty-two," replied WPC Twamley.

"I'm at three thirty-five and there's nothing here, either," remarked Rachel before placing her hands behind her head and puffing out her cheeks, Carmichael-style.

"We're not going to find anything," continued Rachel. "We need to go on at least for another hour, but I'm convinced we won't see Harriett's car."

* * * *

Having decided to initiate a break in proceedings, Carmichael and Watson walked up to the main incident room, where they found Cooper still scrutinising the documents he'd been sent electronically from The World of Chocolate on one screen while, on a second, looking at information he'd found on *Google*.

"How's it going, Paul?" Carmichael enquired.

"Brilliantly," replied Cooper. "It's definitely Carmen."

It was unlike Cooper to be so definitive, a fact that

prompted Carmichael and Watson to exchange a quick sideways glance before gathering around their excited colleague.

"Tell us more," remarked Watson.

"Well," replied the enthusiastic Cooper, "*Guayas Los Rios* was once owned by a family called Martinez. It became a co-operative for The World of Chocolate nine years ago and then, two years later it became fully owned by The World of Chocolate. I'm not sure how that came about yet, but I'm checking."

"That's very interesting," replied Carmichael, "but we need more."

"I agree," conceded Cooper, "but what's the chance of a cleaner from Ecuador working at the Michelson's house in Barton Bridge having the same surname as the previous owners of Gavin's company's only Ecuadorian plantation? Miniscule I'd imagine."

"Do you have anything more?" Carmichael enquired.

Cooper nodded. "I've an article from the local paper up here on the screen," he added. "It's in Spanish, so I'll need it translating, but I'm assuming the word *suicidio* means suicide, which if that's right, I think this is probably saying that the previous owner, Dominik Martinez took his own life about nine months ago."

Carmichael looked at the picture of the tanned and wrinkled face of a middle-aged man looking wearily at the camera. "This could well be a relative of Carmen's, her father maybe. And, if that's the case, we appear to have her motive," he remarked with a look of victory etched across his face.

* * * *

"You keep looking," Rachel said, instructing WPC Twamley to scour the CCTV footage. "I'm going to find

Carmichael and give him a quick status report, not that there's much to tell him."

WPC Twamley turned her head, smiled, nodded, then looked back at the screen.

* * * *

"So, how's the interview with Harriett Hall going?" Cooper enquired.

"She's not admitting anything," replied Carmichael, "and there's an added complication in that she says she was away on the night Swift was killed."

Carmichael had only just finished his sentence when Rachel Dalton appeared at the door.

"How are you faring?" Carmichael enquired.

Rachel shook her head. "We've not found anything on the footage yet," she said. "To be honest, I'm not sure we will, either. We've already almost got to four o'clock and there's absolutely no sign of Harriett's car."

"Really," he replied despondently. "That's not what I was expecting to hear."

"What's our plan?" Watson enquired.

Carmichael thought for a few seconds before replying.

"You need to go and check out Harriett's alleged movements for the evening Swift was killed," Carmichael replied.

"She maintains she was in Birmingham that evening and stayed overnight," Watson remarked, his comment an update aimed at Cooper and Dalton.

Rachel Dalton let out a loud sigh. "With us not finding any sign of her car on the night Gavin Michelson died and now this revelation," she commented, "doesn't that suggest we may have this wrong?"

Carmichael looked back at Rachel, his face stern and

his eyes intense. "Keep searching through those images, Rachel," he replied. "I'm still convinced these two are our killers. So, they must be there somewhere. And while you're doing that and Marc's checking out Harriett's new alibi, Paul and I will go and have a chat to our friend from Ecuador."

Chapter 69

Carmichael waited patiently as Cooper turned on the recording equipment in Interview Room 2 and completed the formalities of announcing the date, time, and details of all those present.

As soon as he'd finished, Carmichael, eyes fixed on Carmen, started the interview.

"According to your network provider," he announced in a calm, clear voice, "you took two calls from Gavin Michelson's land line on the evening that Kendal died. Do you remember receiving these calls?"

Carmen screwed up her face as if she was trying to recall them.

"That would be on Saturday evening," she replied, confirming that she understood exactly when Carmichael was suggesting she had been contacted.

"Yes," replied Carmichael, again his tone calm and unconfrontational. "At eleven thirty-eight and then again at eleven fifty-four, to be precise."

Carmen's expression changed, as if she suddenly remembered.

"Yes, Mr Michelson did call me," she replied. "On the first call, he just wanted to let me know that he was not going to have time to clear away the mess he'd made in the kitchen that evening and apologised that I'd have to sort it out in the morning."

It was now Carmichael's turn to look puzzled.

"And what about the second call?" Carmichael enquired.

"That was as Miss Hall was about to leave," replied Carmen. "He wanted to know where I'd put her jacket. She took it off when she arrived and I'd put it in his study as all the hangers on the coat stand in the hall were full."

Carmichael wasn't in the slightest bit convinced by Carmen's version of events.

"Are you trying to tell us that he called you twice, one of the calls being at almost midnight, for such mundane reasons?" he remarked. "Also, was Gavin in the habit of calling you on your mobile when he knew you were in the house?"

Carmen shrugged her shoulders. "All I can say is that is what happened," she replied.

Carmichael shook his head gently from side to side. He remained sceptical about Carmen's lame explanation and wanted her to know it.

After pausing for a few seconds, Carmichael pulled out Carmen Martinez's passport from the folder in front of him and placed it carefully, face-up, a few inches away from her.

"What is an Ecuadorian citizen doing in Barton Bridge?" he enquired, his eyes fixed firmly on the woman sat across from him.

The sides of Carmen's mouth dropped and her shoulders hunched upwards.

"I'm here to work and to earn money," she replied indifferently.

Carmichael frowned. "Why England? Why Barton Bridge?" he enquired, the puzzlement palpable in his tone of voice. "We're over five thousand miles from your home and I can't imagine it's easy for an Ecuadorian citizen to get a visa to the UK. What was it that really made you choose to come to work for the Michelsons?"

Carmen remained impassive.

"I wanted to come here as I'd been told that the money was good and the English people were so nice," she responded.

Carmichael smiled. "Now I know that's not completely true," he remarked. "I think you came here specifically to work for the Michelsons for a reason."

Carmen remained impassive and said nothing.

"Tell me about *Guayas Los Rios*, Carmen?" Carmichael asked.

Almost immediately Carmen's expression changed. She suddenly looked uneasy and by the way she was now shuffling in her seat, Carmichael could sense she was uncomfortable.

"Why don't you show her the article?" Carmichael continued, his instruction aimed at Cooper, his eyes remaining firmly fixed on Carmen.

Cooper slowly removed the photocopy of the newspaper cutting he'd found earlier.

"It's in Spanish, so I'll need it translating," admitted Carmichael, "but, from what I can gather, it's an article about the previous owner of *Guayas Los Rios*, a man called Dominik Martinez. Did you know Dominik Martinez?"

Carmen took hold of the article and stared at the words and the picture of the forlorn looking man.

"He was my father," she replied, her voice trembling as she spoke and her eyes becoming watery.

Carmichael allowed Carmen a few more seconds before continuing with his questioning.

"We know he took his own life about nine months ago," he continued, his tone sympathetic. "Not long before you arrived in the UK."

Carmen looked up from the cutting, her angry, moistened, brown eyes looking directly at Carmichael, but said nothing.

"I think that your father's death and your arrival here are

connected," Carmichael remarked, his voice still controlled and compassionate. "I think you came here specifically to kill Gavin and Kendal, didn't you?"

"That's ridiculous," replied Carmen as she dabbed her eyes with the back of her hand. "The Michelsons were my father's friends. Why would I want to kill them?"

"So, why did you come here so soon after your father's death?" Carmichael enquired.

Carmen's solicitor grabbed a couple of paper handkerchiefs from the box on the table and handed them to his client, who smiled politely at him before proceeding to wipe the tears from her eyes.

Again, Carmichael allowed her a few seconds before continuing.

"What made you come here, Carmen?" he asked her.

Carmen pushed the newspaper article back towards Cooper and leant back in her chair.

"I don't want to talk anymore," she replied, before turning her head to face her brief, who gave her a reassuring, approving nod of his head.

For a split second, Carmichael toyed with the thought of continuing with his questioning regardless of Carmen's decision to remain silent. However, he quickly rejected that idea in favour of a break in proceedings, to allow Carmen to compose herself, talk with her legal advisor and reconsider her situation now she knew they were aware of who she was and where she'd come from.

* * * *

Watson leaned back in his chair with a sense of frustration and trepidation. The news he was going to have to break to Carmichael was not good. Harriett's alibi for the evening Martin Swift had been murdered was watertight. Her supplier verified that she had attended their launch in Birmingham that evening. They confirmed the event had started at 8pm and that Harriett had been one of the first to arrive. To make matters worse, the Norfolk Hotel in Edgbaston, corroborated her version of events too, the Manager claiming she had checked in at 6:35pm that evening and had not checked out until 8:25am the following morning.

Unless both Harriett's supplier and the hotel Manager were lying, there was absolutely no way Harriett could have been the person that arrived at Swift's house when he had to abandon the voice mail message on Carmichael's phone to answer the door. In short, Harriett was not Swift's murderer.

Watson had little time to work out how he was going to tactfully communicate his findings as, within a few seconds, Carmichael, followed closely behind by Cooper, entered the incident room.

Watson had no need to worry. Within an instant of seeing his colleague's face, Carmichael realised that Harriett's version of events on that evening had been supported.

"Is it that definite?" he enquired of his Sergeant.

Watson nodded. "I'm afraid so," he replied. "The supplier and the hotel, both back her up. There's not the remotest chance of her being Swift's killer."

Carmichael walked over to the window and stood, despondently looking out across the car park.

As he stared intently out of the window, Rachel Dalton appeared at the door. "We've been through the tapes," she announced disconsolately. "There's no sign of Harriett Hall's car on any of the footage."

Carmichael turned back to face his colleagues and shook his head. "What the hell is going on?" he remarked, a rhetorical question that went unanswered.

Chapter 70

In complete contrast to his drive in to work that morning, Carmichael's mood as he made his way home was a mixture of frustration, confusion, and deep melancholy.

Having established that neither Harriett nor Carmen could have killed Martin Swift and in the absence of any CCTV footage to contradict the stories of the pair for the evening Gavin Michelson was murdered, Carmichael had had no choice other than to let the two women go.

As soon as he walked in through the front door, Penny could see that her husband wasn't happy. And, as she'd done countless times before, she decided to leave him in his silent world of contemplation until he elected to emerge out of his bubble and start to share his burdens with her.

He'd been home for three hours before he finally brought up the case.

Dinner long over and alone with his wife in the kitchen, Carmichael took a swig of his favourite red wine before opening up.

"I'm really struggling on this case," he confessed. "I would have wagered a month's salary that I had it all worked out this morning, but I was wrong."

Penny listened intently for the next twenty minutes as her husband relayed to her the events of the day and the extent of his frustrations.

"So, are you now totally discounting Harriett and Carmen from any of the murders?" she enquired.

Carmichael shook his head gently and stared down at his now half-empty glass of Pinotage.

"My gut tells me they're involved. Well, at least the first two murders are down to them," he replied. "But, apart from the coincidence of Carmen's mobile receiving calls at about the same time Kendal was alleged to have been on a mobile, and the fact that we now know Carmen's family once owned the cocoa plantation in Ecuador that now belongs to The World of Chocolate, we've got nothing tangible on either of them. There's no way we'd get beyond the first ten minutes in court with just those facts."

"Are you completely sure the third murder was definitely not carried out by either of them?" Penny asked.

"A hundred per cent," replied Carmichael.

Penny poured more Pinotage into Carmichael's glass.

"Then, as far as I can see, there's only one of three alternatives," she remarked assuredly.

Carmichael looked up at his wife, one eyebrow raised.

"Which are?" he asked.

"Well, firstly the unpalatable thought that none of the murders are the work of any of the people you've listed as suspects," replied Penny.

That thought had already crossed Carmichael's mind.

"Then there's of course the possibility that the two women you interviewed today aren't the murderers," Penny continued. "And Carmen's family connection with The World of Chocolate has no bearing whatsoever on the murders."

"And the third scenario?" Carmichael enquired, as he took a large gulp of wine from his now full glass.

Penny puffed out her cheeks and opened her eyes wide.

"That you're not looking for two killers," she announced. "There's actually a team of three or maybe even four involved."

Chapter 71

Saturday 20th August

Neither Janet Sutherland nor Jean-Paul Mercier had been particularly impressed when they'd each received a call late on Friday evening summoning them to The World of Chocolate at 8:30am on Saturday morning.

The same could equally be said of Cooper, Watson, and Rachel Dalton, all of whom had been expecting to have the weekend off rather than to be given fresh assignments by Carmichael for Saturday morning.

Rachel in particular was hugely disappointed, given that Carmichael's 11:30pm call had scuppered her day trip to the Lake District, which she and Matthew Stock had arranged.

Carmichael was already outside the factory gate when Watson arrived.

"Have you been here long?" Watson enquired as he clambered in through the passenger door of Carmichael's trademark black BMW.

"Long enough," replied Carmichael obtusely.

"Is there something wrong with your mobile, sir?" Watson enquired. "I tried to call you on the way over but I couldn't get through."

Carmichael pulled his mobile from his pocket.

"Bugger," he remarked angrily. "It's out of battery. I must have forgotten to put it on charge last night."

Watson smiled. "Not to worry," he said, "I've got my charger in the car. It should be the same as yours as we've similar mobiles. You can put it on charge when we get inside."

"Thanks, Marc," replied Carmichael. "I don't often do that."

"What makes you think there's more than just Carmen and Harriett involved?" Watson asked, trying hard to move the conversation on. "Maybe we've just got the wrong two people."

Carmichael stared forward through the windscreen.

"No," he replied firmly, "Harriett and Carmen are involved, they just didn't kill Swift and, as I'm sure Rachel will find out at some stage this morning, they did leave Harri's Bar on the night Gavin was killed, but maybe not in Harriett's car."

Watson wasn't totally convinced his boss had it sussed, but was not about to argue or play 'devil's advocate'.

"So how do you want to play it once we get in?" he enquired.

Carmichael didn't need to consider his response; he'd thought that through already.

"I want you to get hold of Janet Sutherland and go through all their records relating to that plantation in Ecuador," Carmichael replied. "Check out anything and everything that's been recorded, as far back as you can go. Press releases, PR photographs, correspondence, the lot. I want to see if we can link any of our other suspects to the plantation."

Watson nodded.

"And," continued Carmichael, "if Janet can get access to check the personnel records again, I want to know if any of our other suspects have any links to The World of Chocolate.

Carmen and Harriett would have needed the assistance of at least one person who knew how to make chocolate, I want to know who helped them."

Watson nodded again.

"But what if Janet is that other person?" Watson asked.

Carmichael shook his head. "No, I'm convinced she's not involved," he replied assuredly. "Her skype call alibis are water tight. Also, Gavin's murder was meticulously planned, so it doesn't make sense that she'd have sex with him and leave her DNA, if she was involved. She's smart enough to know we'd find it. No, I'm certain Janet is in the clear."

"I can't fault your logic," remarked Watson.

"What's more," Carmichael added, "Janet's fluent in Spanish, so any articles you find produced in Ecuador will be meat and drink to her."

"And what will you be doing, sir?" Watson enquired.

"I'm going to have a good chat with your friend Jean-Paul Mercier," replied Carmichael. "I feel I need to know more about this company, and I suspect he's the guy that can educate me."

* * * *

Without WPC Twamley to help her, Rachel Dalton sat down in the same chair that she'd spent the best part of the previous day in and switched on the bank of screens in front of her once more. Only this time she was no longer looking for the distinctive white car belonging to Harriett Hall, her goal was much more arduous; to try and identify any vehicle that could have been transporting Carmen and Harriett away from Southport in the direction of The World of Chocolate's factory in Barton Bank.

With a large mug of coffee at her side, Rachel took a deep

breath and commenced her search. She was in no doubt that it was going to be a long morning.

* * * *

Cooper's task, on the face of it, was far more straight forward. However, as he soon discovered, obtaining details of visa applications on a Saturday morning was neither a quick nor straight-forward assignment.

* * * *

Within twenty seconds of meeting with him, Carmichael concluded that there could not possibly be a more perfect Gallic stereotype than Jean-Paul Mercier.

With his dark hair and an almost comical enunciation, the head chocolatier at The World of Chocolate, in Carmichael's eyes, was as complete a caricature of anything French or Belgian that he'd ever seen.

"I am not 'appy you bring me 'ere," was Jean-Paul's opening remark in an accent that was so pronounced Carmichael had to work hard to avoid laughing. "Why we could not do this yesterday or on Monday, I do not know."

As he spoke, the tall, thin Belgian flailed his arms about like some angry eccentric scientist.

"I'm so sorry we had to disturb you today," replied Carmichael, his response calm and sincere, supported by a friendly smile. "However, I'm convinced that with your help we may be able to identify who murdered Gavin Michelson and secure a conviction."

Jean-Paul's puzzled expression suggested he found that difficult to believe. "What is it I can do to 'elp?" he enquired, his shoulders hunched up and his arms outstretched with his palms facing upwards.

* * * *

With Janet Sutherland's assistance, Watson had managed to locate a large number of dusty, sun-bleached folders that contained press cuttings relating to The World of Chocolate going back over twenty years.

Fortunately for Watson, the cuttings looked in almost perfect chronological order, so it was easy for him to discard some very early pieces and start from around the period when they believed Gavin Michelson had first started a relationship with the plantation in Ecuador.

Sat with his press-ganged associate, Watson started to slowly turn the pages and study the articles.

"What exactly are we looking for?" Janet enquired.

"Anything to do with *Guayas Los Rios,*" replied Watson, who didn't want to divulge too much to his newly acquired assistant.

* * * *

Rachel Dalton had only been looking at the CCTV footage for twenty minutes before she saw something. Quickly stopping the tape, she zoomed in to try and read the number plate.

"Bingo," she muttered to herself as she could clearly see the licence plate and it matched perfectly the number plate she had on her list belonging to one of their suspects.

She was just about to call Carmichael when her mobile started to ring. Picking it up, she saw the name Matthew Stock emblazoned on the screen.

A smile appeared on her face as she took the call.

"Hi," she said. "Are you missing me already?"

"Of course," replied Matthew, without any hesitation. "So much so that I was wondering if you wanted a coffee at some stage this morning. I'm assuming Carmichael allows his workers a coffee break every so often."

Rachel laughed. "Yes," she replied, "that could work, but it may have to wait a while as I think I've just found something of major importance to the case, so I need to talk with him."

"Well," continued Matthew, "I'll just wait here then."

"Where are you?" Rachel asked.

"I'm in the car park at the back of the station," announced Matthew.

Rachel shook her head in disbelief. "I'll call Carmichael then I'll come down," she replied.

Carmichael, didn't see Rachel's call coming through. His mobile was still on charge in one of the meeting rooms while he was on the factory floor listening to Jean-Paul give him a detailed explanation on how quality chocolate was made.

Having left a voice message, Rachel grabbed her bag and headed for the exit and her sneaky coffee break with the handsome Matthew Stock.

Chapter 72

After seven separate telephone calls and more than an hour hanging on lines and being passed from person to person, Cooper finally received the email he'd been asking for, a copy of Carmen Martinez's visa application; and it made interesting reading. He dialled Carmichael's number and waited.

After several rings, his call was directed to Carmichael's voice mail.

"Morning, sir," he began, "it's Cooper here. I've located Carmen's visa and it's clear she's entered the country illegally. Her application was based on what's known as a tier 2 application and has been sponsored by Logan-Lane Labs, the pharmaceutical company on the outskirts of Moulton Bank, where Gabby Johns works. According to the application, Carmen's a qualified chemist and had a post with the company. Do you want me to get over and pick Carmen up again?"

Having left the message, Cooper walked over to the printer to retrieve the printed copy of the visa application, before returning to his desk.

* * * *

Matthew Stock's bright red Ford Fiesta sped out of the car park and down Kirkwood High Street.

"Where do you fancy stopping for coffee?" he enquired,

his seemingly perfect teeth, in Rachel's eyes, gleaming as he spoke.

Rachel thought for a few moments.

"Why don't you head over to Linbold," she replied.

"Linbold," exclaimed Matthew who briefly glanced over at his passenger, with a perplexed expression on his face. "That's a bit far to go for a coffee break."

Rachel smiled. "There's someone I want to talk to over there, so we can kill two birds with one stone."

Happy in the knowledge that he was going to be able to spend even longer in Rachel's company, Matthew, his eyes fixed firmly on the road in front of him, gave a tiny nod with his head.

"Linbold it is," he replied.

* * * *

"What's this?" Watson remarked, pointing to a faded article in Spanish with a large black and white group photograph of around ten people.

Janet Sutherland stopped what she was doing and peered over his shoulder.

"It appears to be relating to one of Gavin's early visits to *Guayas Los Rios.*" Janet remarked. "It's talking about the wonderful relationship between the local Martinez family and The World of Chocolate, who had recently invested over a hundred and fifty thousand dollars into the plantation."

Watson squinted hard to try and see if he could pick out any of the people in the photograph. In the centre, shaking hands, were Gavin Michelson and what looked like a much happier-looking Dominik Martinez, who seemed far younger than he'd appeared in the article Cooper had found the day before.

However, it was the sight of four much more familiar faces that were of far greater interest to Watson.

Hurriedly, Watson grabbed the cutting before rushing over to the door and out to find Carmichael.

* * * *

After listening for over fifteen minutes to Jean-Paul Mercier's continuing monologue regarding chocolate manufacturing, Carmichael's attention span had been exceeded by a considerable margin. *The next time he pauses, even by a split second,* he thought, *I'm going to ask him about the suspects and whether they'd ever worked at the factory.*

Fortunately for Carmichael, his prayers were answered when Watson, clutching a newspaper cutting and with Janet Sutherland in tow, came bounding across the gleamingly-clean, grey-painted, factory floor.

"I think we've found the link," Watson shouted excitedly when he'd almost reached where Carmichael and Jean-Paul were standing.

Carmichael had rarely, if ever, seen his sergeant so eager. So, he figured, the link he was referring to must have been important.

Before Carmichael had a chance to say anything, Watson had reached them and opened the article to show his boss.

"It's a piece from a newspaper in Ecuador from about the time The World of Chocolate started to take part-ownership," announced Watson, who was slightly out of breath. "Look at the photo!"

Without any argument or need for further clarity, Carmichael did as he had been requested.

"Look it's Michelson with Carmen's father," announced Watson enthusiastically. "They're shaking hands after The

World of Chocolate has invested a hundred and fifty thousand dollars in the plantation."

"Right," replied Carmichael rather disappointedly, "but we know that. It should be no surprise that Gavin would have gone over when The World of Chocolate first invested in the plantation, so what's the big deal?"

Watson grinned from ear-to-ear; he loved it when he knew something his boss didn't, and this was one of those rare occasions.

"But look at the others in the photo," Watson added.

Carmichael peered intently at the other faces.

"Bloody hell," he remarked, before making eye contact with Watson. "They're all there."

Watson nodded.

"Yes, Gavin, Kendal, Martin Swift, Harriett Hall, and a very young-looking Carmen Martinez," continued Watson, his excitement almost impossible for him to contain.

Carmichael nodded. "Yes, I can see," he replied. "And look who else is there…"

Watson narrowed his eyes and peered at where Carmichael was pointing.

"It's Gabby Johns," announced Carmichael.

"Now there was a truly gifted chocolatier," remarked Jean-Paul Mercier. "If she'd have stuck it out here, she could have been as fine a chocolatier as I, by now."

Carmichael swiftly turned his head to face the Belgian. "Gabby Johns worked here?"

Jean-Paul shrugged his shoulders, as only a Gallic person could do.

"Mais oui," he replied. "She was here for almost six months. It was many years ago, but she was a rare talent. I do not know why, but she decided to leave us and go to some pharmaceutical laboratory. I never could understand that."

Had either Carmichael or Watson bothered to look up

from the faded newspaper article, they would have noticed the bemused, almost disgusted expression on Jean-Paul Mercier's face, which he wore to compliment his words.

"Actually," interrupted Janet Sutherland. "Now I think about it, I'm sure I saw that woman the other night. It was after I left Mr Michelson on Monday evening. I'd swear she was sat at the wheel of a car parked-up just outside the factory gates."

Carmichael and Watson exchanged a sideways glance.

"Why didn't you mention this before?" Carmichael asked her, his voice raised and sounding irritated.

Janet Sutherland's cheeks started to turn pink.

"I'm sorry," she replied. "I've only just remembered. Do you think it's important?"

Chapter 73

Matthew Stock's red fiesta arrived outside Gabby Johns's house, on the outskirts of the pretty Lancashire village of Linbold, at just after 10:15am.

Other than that initial meeting at Harri's Bar on the previous Sunday, and very briefly when she'd provided DNA samples, Rachel hadn't spent much time in Gabby's company, so other than the image portrayed by Carmichael and the others at various team briefings, Rachel didn't know what to expect.

"I'll be ten minutes," said Rachel as she undid her seat belt.

"Hang on," replied Matthew, "I'm coming with you. You've just told me that this woman's a possible murderer. You can't go in there on your own."

Rachel rolled her eyes skyward. "You've been watching too much TV," she replied, her mild rebuke couched in a tone which suggested to Matthew that he was worrying needlessly. "I'm just going to ask her a few questions."

"Shouldn't you wait to get some back-up?" asked Matthew, "or at the minimum try and talk to Carmichael before you go in?"

Rachel puffed out her cheeks, then smiled and shook her head gently from side to side. It was a while since anyone had expressed that sort of genuine concern about her, and she liked the feeling, although she wasn't about to let Matthew know.

Rachel removed her mobile from her trouser pocket and called Carmichael.

Once more her call was diverted to voice mail.

"Hello, sir," she said in a clear voice. "It's Rachel again. I just thought I'd let you know that I've gone over to Gabby Johns's house. I'm just about to go in and talk with her now. I'll let you know how it goes."

Rachel ended the call, smiled warmly at Matthew, placed the mobile back in her pocket and clambered out of the car.

"Be careful," remarked Matthew, before Rachel had had a chance to close the door.

Despite her outwardly blasé demeanour, Matthew felt very uneasy about Rachel's decision. He was sure police procedure dictated that officers should go in twos in such circumstances, but nevertheless for some reason he still allowed her to go.

"I will," replied Rachel. "Don't worry, this is what we do every day."

Rachel shut the car door and sauntered up the crunchy, gravel pathway, past the green saloon car, that she'd spied on the CCTV earlier that morning, then up to Gabby Johns's large, wooden front door.

* * * *

Had Carmichael not forgotten to charge his mobile, or had he not taken those few extra minutes with Watson explaining his latest theory, having just identified Gabby Johns in the press cutting, Carmichael would have taken not only Cooper's call but also either one or both of Rachel's. But he had forgotten to charge his mobile and he had lingered with Watson, enlightening his sergeant on his view that Gabby Johns was not only their third killer, but quite possibly the main driver behind the three murders.

As a result, by the time he checked the three messages on his mobile, Rachel was already inside Gabby Johns's house. As he listened to Rachel's last message, Carmichael became very worried.

"What on earth is she doing?" he bellowed.

Watson, who had not heard the message, looked on, Carmichael's clear anxiousness instantly making him feel uneasy, too.

"Come on, Marc," continued Carmichael briskly, "we have to get over to Linbold without delay. Rachel has gone to see Gabby Johns on her own."

"What!" exclaimed Watson. "Why has she done that? She knows the procedure."

Carmichael shook his head. "God knows," he replied. "Let's just hope when we get there Rachel's in a good enough shape to receive the rollicking she deserves."

As Watson announced to his wife later that evening, he knew Carmichael was genuinely concerned, as in all the years he'd worked with him, he'd never seen Carmichael run as swiftly as he had when they made their way to his car.

* * * *

Gabby Johns seemed genuinely shocked when she opened her door and saw Rachel Dalton standing alone on her doorstep; and Rachel's reassuring smile did nothing to defuse her uneasiness.

"I was passing and wanted to just clarify a few things," Rachel remarked. "Can I come in?"

Gabby, dressed in a tight-fitting pair of ripped jeans and a very loose-fitting sweatshirt opened the door wide.

"Be my guest," she replied. "Go through to the lounge."

Rachel did as she was requested and, once inside, sat herself down in a large, comfortable-looking armchair.

"I'm sorry to bother you on a Saturday morning," Rachel said, "it's just there's something I wanted to ask you regarding your statement about the evening Gavin Michelson died."

Gabby went to sit down on the sofa, which was positioned directly opposite her guest. However, before she managed to sit herself down, she suddenly sprang to her feet.

"Actually," she said, her voice calm and controlled, "I was just about to make myself a coffee. Would you like one?"

Rachel smiled. "I can't stay too long," she remarked, "but a coffee would be nice. White, but no sugar, please."

Gabby smiled and walked through towards the kitchen.

"What exactly do you need me to clarify?" Gabby shouted down the hallway.

"Just the timings again of when you eventually got home on Monday evening," Rachel shouted back down the hallway.

Before Gabby had a chance to say anything more, she heard the sound of a mobile ringing from down the corridor. It wasn't her ringtone, so she knew it must have been Rachel Dalton's phone.

Quietly, Gabby tiptoed back towards the open door that led to the lounge, but she didn't enter.

"Hi, sir," she heard Rachel say in a hushed tone, as she put the mobile to her ear. Then after a slight pause, she heard Rachel Dalton whisper, "It was her car in Southport in the early hours of Tuesday morning. There's no question about that."

After another brief pause, Gabby then heard Rachel, in a hushed voice, inform the caller that she would *get out as soon as possible* and that *she knew what she was doing*.

Gabby's facial expression changed as soon as she heard

those words. She didn't need to listen anymore, and she knew instantly what she had to do.

* * * *

"I cannot understand what she was thinking," Carmichael yelled at Watson, as soon as his brief call with Rachel Dalton had ended. "Why on earth would she put herself at such risk without back-up."

"I'll call the station and get the nearest police car over there now," replied Watson, who quickly dialled the station number.

"I reckon we'll be another fifteen minutes at least," remarked Carmichael. "I hope that's not too late."

* * * *

Within a couple of minutes of Rachel finishing the call with Carmichael, Gabby Johns returned to the room, but carrying only one mug of coffee, which she held out towards Rachel with her left hand, her other hand remaining behind her back.

Rachel did wonder why Gabby had only brought one mug of coffee, but smiled gently and, still seated, took hold of the mug with both of her hands.

As soon as Gabby had released the mug, her right hand shot out from behind her back.

In a split second, the syringe she had been concealing came crashing down with force into Rachel's thigh, with its contents released into the DC's unsuspecting body.

Rachel propelled the mug away from her and lunged forward at Gabby, but whatever had been injected into her was already taking hold. Almost immediately, she could feel a numbness in her leg spreading rapidly into her stomach, then her arms and, within what seemed like no time at all, Rachel could not move and, still partially conscious, she felt herself falling.

By the time Rachel hit the floor, the same compound that Gabby had used on Gavin Michelson and Martin Swift had done its job; and Rachel was totally poleaxed, lying helpless on the lounge carpet.

Chapter 74

With its siren blazing and the blue lights concealed behind the radiator grill flashing furiously, Carmichael's black BMW sped along the country lanes en route to Linbold.

"I reckon we're less than five minutes away" remarked Carmichael. "Any news from the station about other officers getting there?"

Watson shook his head. "Cooper's on his way and there's also at least two other cars trying to get there," he replied, "but, as far as I know, none have arrived yet."

* * * *

Matthew Stock looked at his watch. Rachel had been inside for over twenty minutes, and the anxiety he'd had about her going in alone had escalated to a real fear.

He knew that she'd be less than impressed if he barged in on her interview only to find her safe and well and simply engaged in an extended discussion, but he decided he'd have to risk the potential fall-out from that scenario.

The truth was he was sure all was not well and he couldn't continue to just sit outside when something sinister could be happening behind the seeming normality of Gabby Johns's front door.

Without any further hesitation, Matthew jumped out of

the car and ran up the gravel path. He didn't bother with the doorbell, choosing instead to thump loudly on the front door.

He had no way of seeing Gabby Johns slip out of her back door and walk slowly down the side of her house.

When Matthew's loud thumping received no answer, he decided to barge then kick the door down.

To his surprise, the door frame splintered with the third heavy kick and the door flew inwards.

Seizing on her chance to escape, Gabby activated the door to her car and quickly jumped into the driving seat. Locking the door behind her, she then turned on the engine and pushed the leaver into drive.

Matthew hadn't gone more than two or three paces into the house when he realised that someone was making their escape. Turning back, he ran out of the house only to see Gabby's car, wheels spinning on the gravel, shoot down the drive.

Without bothering to look if the roads were free, and with Matthew running after her, Gabby turned left out of her drive.

There was only a second or two between her exiting the drive and the car colliding with Cooper's old beaten-up Volvo, which he was in the process of manoeuvring across the road to park-up at the entrance to Gabby's drive.

The sudden impact was loud and decisive, leaving both cars immobile.

With no obvious signs of injury, Cooper clambered out of the car and managed to reach Gabby Johns's car door at about the same time as Matthew Stock.

"Who are you?" Cooper enquired.

"I'm Matt Stock," he replied, "I drove Rachel here."

"So, where's Rachel now?" Cooper asked.

"She's still inside the house," said Matthew.

Cooper pulled at the driver's door on Gabby's car, but it was still locked.

"You go and see how Rachel is," he instructed Matthew, "I'll sort her out."

Matthew nodded, and proceeded to run back towards the house.

* * * *

When Carmichael arrived, there were already two police cars on the scene, with uniformed officers attempting to break the glass in the side window on the passenger side of Gabby Johns's car. Although she was still very dazed, Gabby was conscious and, apart from a nasty cut to her head, which was bleeding heavily, she didn't seem to be too badly hurt.

As soon as the first police car had arrived on the scene, Cooper had left them to extract Gabby Johns from her car and detain her, and he'd joined Matthew Stock inside the house, where Rachel remained motionless on the floor.

"There's an ambulance on its way," Cooper advised Carmichael and Watson as soon as they appeared in the room. "It looks like she's been injected with something."

As he spoke, Cooper pointed at Rachel's thigh, where a large patch of blood indicated where the needle had hit its mark.

"Is she breathing?" Carmichael enquired.

"Yes," interjected Matthew Stock, who had been cradling Rachel's head for the past five minutes.

"Who are you?" Carmichael asked.

"I'm Matthew," he replied. "I work in forensics."

"So how did you get here so quickly?" Carmichael enquired. "I'm surprised Stock's team have even been called."

"He maintains he's Stock's nephew," interjected Cooper, "and he informs me that he drove Rachel here."

Carmichael's expression suggested he was still none the wiser.

"So, what the hell were you doing when Rachel was being attacked?" Watson asked, his angry eyes directed at the sheepishly-looking young man.

"We can sort all that out later," shouted Carmichael. "Our immediate concern is to find out what that lunatic out there has injected into Rachel and how much she's been given."

Cooper took this as his cue to leave them to it, go outside and get some answers from Gabby Johns.

* * * *

The next thirty minutes were chaotic, with paramedics trying hard to ensure that Rachel's condition was stabilised, followed by two ambulances arriving; the first to ferry Rachel to Southport Royal hospital, followed shortly by a second which took Gabby Johns and two uniformed officers to Kirkwood minor injuries, so she could be checked out by a doctor.

Once the ambulances had gone and Carmichael, Cooper and Watson were left with only a couple of SOCOs and one uniformed PC for company, Carmichael pulled his sergeants to one side.

"What was it that Gabby Johns maintained she'd injected into Rachel?" he asked.

"A formula she is working on at the lab," replied Cooper. "She reckoned it was based mainly on a substance called Xylazine, but with some added elements. She says she injected about forty-five milligrams of the stuff into her, which the doctors reckon will keep her out cold for a good few hours, but shouldn't be fatal."

Carmichael shook his head. "I can't understand what she was thinking," he remarked. "The rawest recruit knows that you don't put yourself in danger like that without backup. This is so out of character for her."

Watson sniggered. "I suspect she was trying to impress that nephew of Stock's," he said cynically. "Trying to demonstrate to her new boyfriend what a tough cookie she is."

Carmichael shook his head again. "What a bloody idiot she is, more like," he remarked.

Cooper sighed. "At least she'll be OK," he observed dryly. "Unlike my poor car. I'm going to have to get a new wing for the old girl."

Watson laughed. "I'd just cut my losses, if I were you," he replied. "If you take my advice, scrap it and get yourself something from the twenty-first century."

For the first time in hours, Carmichael allowed himself a small smile.

"Come on, you two," he said. "We've got a couple of ladies that need re-arresting and, assuming Gabby Johns is given the all clear and discharged, we've got a long afternoon of interviewing ahead of us. I want this whole case wrapped up before any of us go home tonight."

Chapter 75

Carmichael despatched his two sergeants to arrest Harriett Hall and Carmen Martinez.

With Rachel still at the hospital, he spent the next couple of hours behind the closed door in his office, alone with his thoughts.

Carmichael played through the three slayings, over and over in his head, until he was certain that he knew what had taken place and how the three women had managed to so cleverly carry out the murders. He thought long and hard about their motives, too; and how it was that it had taken him and his team so long to the solve the conundrum.

By 2:30pm, Cooper and Watson had succeeded in bringing Harriett Hall and Carmen Martinez back to Kirkwood Police Station. Cooper had apprehended Carmen Martinez, her bags all packed, just minutes before her taxi was due to arrive to transport her to Manchester Airport. He discovered she'd booked a one-way flight with Turkish Airlines, to Quito in Ecuador, via Istanbul in Turkey and Bogota in Columbia.

The two detained women had been assigned to interview rooms 1 and 2; and, with Gabby Johns having been checked-out and discharged by the doctors, she completed the trio, sitting quietly in Interview Room 3.

"How do you want to handle the interviews?" Cooper enquired.

Without hesitation, and with total assurance that he now knew the facts, Carmichael looked directly at his two trusted officers.

"I think we should all interview them together," he replied, his face indicating complete confidence in his ability to finally bring closure on the case.

"I'll lead, of course," he continued. "And to keep everything neat and in chronological order, let's start with Carmen Martinez. After all, it was she who was the first to carry out a murder."

* * * *

Once again, Carmen had the company of her legal advisor, Mr Humphreys; a pale, sickly-looking man in his early forties, who sat next to her just as he'd done the day before.

Flanked on either side by his two sergeants, Carmichael started the interview.

"I understand we were fortunate to have caught you," he remarked. "I hear you were just about to head back to Ecuador."

Carmen Martinez looked back at Carmichael, her expression sombre and her small dark eyes transfixed on her inquisitor.

"I have no reason to be here anymore," she replied, "so I have decided to go home."

Carmichael raised his eyebrows, then nodded. "I can imagine," he replied, "with the three men you wanted dead now gone, and with us closing in on you, I can fully understand why you'd want to get away. And it's fortunate for us that my sergeant managed to apprehend you, as I suspect it would have been a long and arduous task to get you extradited from Ecuador, even with such serious charges against you."

Carmen seemed indifferent to Carmichael's comments. "As I told you yesterday," she replied calmly, "I have nothing more to say to you."

Carmichael smiled. "You don't need to, Carmen," he said. "You can save your talking for your trial, as far as I'm concerned."

Carmichael paused to see if his comments would cause a change in Carmen Martinez's position. When it was clear it didn't, Carmichael continued.

"First of all," he remarked, "I'd like to advise you that we have your two partners in crime in custody, too. And, for the benefit of your legal counsel, I can confirm that these two people are Harriett Hall and Gabby Johns. Gabby Johns, for your information, having been arrested after sedating one of my officers with a drug that appears to be the same drug used to sedate both Gavin Michelson and Martin Swift."

Carmen's legal representative scribbled the two names down on the note pad in front of him, but said nothing.

"We also have two new pieces of information," continued Carmichael, "which I'm convinced will confirm to the jury, when you come to trial, the significant part you played in these murders."

Carmen looked totally disinterested in what Carmichael was saying and to emphasise her stance, sat back in her chair and folded her arms tightly over her chest.

Carmichael didn't care, he was unmoved by Carmen's attitude and was quite happy to tell her what they knew, as he was sure of the part she'd played in the murders.

"Don't you want to know what additional evidence we now have?" he teased.

Carmen remained impassive.

"Well," Carmichael remarked, "firstly, we have this

article and a photograph taken several years ago, back in Ecuador."

As he spoke, Carmichael motioned to Watson, who obliged by pushing across the table the article he'd located at The World of Chocolate that morning.

Carmen didn't touch the newspaper cutting, but her eyes moved downwards so she could read it and look at the faded photograph.

"Happier times," remarked Carmichael, with a hint of cruel pleasure in his voice as he delivered his words.

"There's you, your father, Gavin Michelson, Kendal Michelson and Martin Swift in the photograph," continued Carmichael. "Can you see?"

Again, Carmen said nothing.

"But the key thing is the presence of Harriett Hall and Gabby Johns in the photo, too," Carmichael added. "So, we have the three unfortunate victims and their three killers."

"This proves nothing," replied Carmen, her arms still folded and her fiery eyes shooting daggers in Carmichael's direction.

"I disagree," replied Carmichael calmly. "This demonstrates the relationship that existed between you and your cohorts. It also confirms the link between you three and your three victims and it will provide the court with an understanding of why it was that these three innocent men were killed. Well, at least your motive in becoming involved."

Carmen shook her head, but said nothing.

Carmichael paused for a few seconds before signalling to Watson to pull the newspaper article back from the table, which his sergeant duly did.

"Now let me tell you what I believe happened on the evening of Saturday13th August," Carmichael remarked.

Arms still folded, Carmen puffed out her cheeks and

rolled her eyes to the heavens; gestures that Carmichael saw, but ignored completely.

"At around eight fifteen, you were picked up by Gabby Johns, I suspect from a location quite near to Gavin's house, but far enough away that Gavin would not notice," Carmichael said. "He was already pre-occupied with his meeting with Harriett, and he believed you were upstairs on your evening off, so I can imagine it would have been very easy for you to have slipped out unseen."

Again, Carmichael paused to see if his words made any impact on Carmen, but again she remained seemingly unmoved by his observations.

Unperturbed, Carmichael continued.

"Anyway," he continued, "it was important that Gabby was able to arrive at the China Garden before the others. They were due to meet at nine and she knew that Martin Swift was collecting Carly and Kendal from the Fairfax Hotel, so I suspect she and you arrived at the restaurant at about eight forty-five. Is that correct?"

Carmen didn't answer.

"Anyway, whatever time it was, we know that Gabby arrived first," continued Carmichael. "Carly confirmed this to us. So, having arrived, you then got out of the car, walked down onto the beach, and made your way to the place where the three of you had decided you would kill Kendal. The rest was then straight forward. You'd wait patiently on the beach until he emerged down the steps. I suspect he was a little surprised to see you alone, but my guess is that, from one of those calls Harriett made to him on your mobile, he was fully expecting someone to join him. Was it you alone? Or was it both Harriett and you? Maybe it was both of you and you just made an excuse for Harriett, saying she was parking the car. Anyway, whatever was said, and whoever he expected to meet down on the beach that night, the fact that you arrived wasn't a shock to him. So much so, that he was oblivious to your movements when you ran him through so cruelly. He was far too preoccupied lying on his back, looking up at the stars. Isn't that what happened, Carmen?"

Carmen shook her head. "This is nonsense," she replied. "Complete nonsense."

Carmichael smiled. "Oh, no, Carmen," he said. "This is what happened."

Once again, Carmen rolled her eyes upwards and sighed deeply.

"And it was your mobile Kendal had that night, wasn't it?" Carmichael enquired, although his question was more of a statement of fact than an invitation for Carmen to answer.

"That did throw us for a long time," Carmichael conceded. "That was a very clever ploy of you all to try and prevent us from tracing that call. Did you just hide his mobile from him before he left? Then, when he couldn't find it, offer him yours to use for a few days? That's what I expect you did."

Carmichael once again paused for a few seconds before continuing.

"However, pretending to find his mobile later in the house was probably not your best move, Carmen," he added. "In hindsight, you probably should have just jettisoned it somewhere. I think that was a mistake."

For the first time, Carmichael's comment almost sparked a reaction from Carmen, who although remaining silent, did show a slight sign of annoyance at Carmichael's deliberate criticism.

"All that was then left to do was for you to get yourself home," continued Carmichael. "I suspect that was something that Harriett helped you with. My guess is that after she left Gavin's house at midnight, she drove to the China Garden carpark, or maybe another pre-arranged rendezvous point, picked you up, then drove you home. It would have had to have been Harriett who collected you afterwards as you all knew Gabby's car would be under observation, so you couldn't risk being seen getting a lift with her."

Carmen shook her head. "This is rubbish," she remarked dismissively. "I was in my room all night when Kendal Michelson was killed, I was working through the night cleaning at Harri's Bar when Gavin Michelson was killed and I was with your Sergeant at the time when everyone thinks Martin Swift was killed. You cannot show any evidence that I was involved in any of those murders."

Carmichael smiled. "That's where you're wrong, Carmen," he replied calmly. "The second new piece of evidence I mentioned before is the discovery of a very clear image of you, Harriett, and Gabby, in Gabby's car, making your way from Southport to Barton Bridge on the night Gavin was murdered. So, you see, Carmen, we do have proof you lied and we do have proof you were in this together."

Carmichael could see in Carmen's eyes that she was now becoming very worried.

"I think it's going to be a very long time before you ever see Ecuador again," Carmichael remarked. "My suggestion to you is that you start to think seriously about the position you're in. Remaining silent won't do you any favours when you come to being sentenced. Your best bet is to co-operate fully. If you do, you never know, it might help you when the judge comes to pass sentence."

Having achieved all he wanted, Carmichael stood up and left the interview room, followed close behind by Cooper and Watson.

Chapter 76

"You seemed very assured about the events you outlined to Carmen in there, sir." Watson remarked as the three officers made their way from Interview Room 1 to Interview Room 2. "Are you really as confident about them as you sounded?"

Carmichael hesitated as he reached the door of the interview room, turning his head by 90 degrees, so he could make eye contact with his unconvinced sergeant.

"It may not be one hundred percent accurate," he confessed with a wry smile, "but I'm sure it's close enough. Carmen now knows enough to understand she's not getting away with it; and I think, by the time we've finished with Harriett Hall, she'll be under no illusions either"

Watson nodded. "Let's get on with it then," he said.

* * * *

The three officers sat down facing Harriett Hall and her legal counsel.

"As I've just mentioned to your associate, Carmen Martinez," Carmichael remarked, "I'd like you to know that we have your two partners in crime in custody, too. And, for the benefit of your legal counsel, I can confirm that these two people are Carmen Martinez and Gabby Johns. And, to save us all time, I want you to be aware that Gabby Johns has this morning been arrested after sedating one of my officers with a drug which appears to be the same drug used to sedate both Gavin Michelson and Martin Swift."

The expression on Harriett Hall's face suggested she was surprised by this news.

"We also have two new pieces of information," continued Carmichael, "which, as I've just told Carmen, will, in my opinion, confirm to any rational thinking jury, the significant part you played in these murders."

"You are being quite presumptuous that this will come to trial," suggested Harriett's brief.

Carmichael had, for many years, regarded the legal aid councils that accompanied suspects during their interviews as little more than necessary irritants, and he treated Harriett's brief accordingly.

"You may change your tune in a few minutes time," he replied with scathing disregard for him.

As with the previous interview, Carmichael motioned to Watson, who dutifully responded by pushing across the table the newspaper article.

"We have this article, including a photograph, taken several years ago in Ecuador," Carmichael announced. "Do you recognise anyone in the picture?"

In contrast to Carmen, Harriett took hold of the newspaper cutting and peered at the faded photograph intently.

She smiled. "I remember it being taken," she replied. "It was when I was still with Gavin, and Kendal and Gabby were still together. We all went to the plantation in Ecuador. Gavin was completing some deal he had out there and we took the opportunity to have a bit of a holiday at the same time."

"Happy times," remarked Carmichael.

Harriett nodded. "As a matter of fact, they were," she replied, before placing the cutting back on the table. "But I don't see what this has to do with anything."

Carmichael smiled again. A smug smile, a smile of self-satisfied certainty and one designed to make Harriett feel uneasy.

"As I advised Carmen earlier," he replied, "this article demonstrates quite clearly that a relationship existed between you and your accomplices. It confirms the link between you three and your victims and it will provide the court with an understanding of why it was that these three innocent men were killed."

"I find that a bit hard to swallow," replied Harriett cynically, "but do go on, Inspector. I'm eager to see your second piece of evidence."

Carmichael nodded.

"The second new piece of evidence is the discovery of a very clear image of you and Carmen in Gabby's car making your way from Southport to Barton Bridge on the night Gavin was murdered. That's the night you both maintained Carmen was doing her first night as a cleaner. The image is clear and demonstrates not only that you lied to us in your previous statements, but also that the three of you were in league regarding the three murders."

Harriett looked shocked by this latest revelation. "I'd like to see that footage," she said.

"And you will," replied Carmichael, "just as soon as I'm ready to show it to you."

"In that case, I'm not sure what you're expecting me to say," remarked Harriett brusquely.

Carmichael smiled again, he was enjoying this interview.

"You went to great pains to make us think that you and Gabby were not friends." He remarked. "You even insinuated that, in your view, she was a prime suspect for Kendal and

Gavin's murders. That was a very clever ploy and, I must say, it did throw me."

Harriett shrugged her shoulders. "I can't recall ever saying anything of the sort," she replied. "I think my exact words were that I give her a wide berth. That's not the same thing at all, however, given that you seem to continually get things wrong, at least you're consistent."

Carmichael eased himself back into his chair.

"Do you want to, at last, tell us the truth about the murders and your involvement?" he enquired. "Or do you want me to tell you what we now believe happened?"

Although Harriett was clearly looking anxious and uncomfortable, there was no way she was going to admit anything. "I've nothing more to tell you, Inspector," she replied, "but please do enlighten us with your current theory."

Carmichael smiled. "We talked at length yesterday about the circumstances of Kendal's death," he replied, "so I don't intend to go over that again. And we checked out your movements on the evening Martin Swift was killed, and it was as you'd told us yesterday, so I've no great need to discuss that with you either. However, let me tell you what we think happened on Monday evening, the night Gavin Michelson was murdered."

"I'm all ears," replied Harriett mockingly.

Carmichael's smile disappeared, just as the warmth he'd felt when he first met her only five days earlier melted away. He suddenly found Harriett Hall arrogant and irritating and he was determined to wipe that smug smile from her face.

"On Monday evening," he announced in a clear, calm voice, "just as you and your two partners in crime had so meticulously planned, Gabby Johns arrived at The World of Chocolate after work, as she'd agreed with Gavin Michelson.

"This meeting was not a chance meeting, it was pre-arranged by the pair. Gavin believed it was the continuation

362

of their reignited romance, Gabby of course, who no doubt played the part of Gavin's secret lover, had other things on her mind. We know this as Gavin had told the night watchman he didn't need to turn in, an action he took when he didn't want his evening liaisons to be discovered."

"If they were seeing each other again," Harriett interrupted, "that was news to me."

Carmichael's eyes widened to signify his scepticism at Harriett's claim. "But," he continued, "Gabby's real intent that evening was to heavily sedate Gavin, start the factory machinery to get the vats up and running, then go home. You'd all carefully planned this. She deliberately visited the Chinese take-away near her home, to give herself an alibi. However, once Gabby had that alibi sorted, she drove over to Southport to collect you and Carmen. Then the three of you drove over to The World of Chocolate in Barton Bridge where you completed the murder. Still sedated, you stripped poor Gavin, tied him to the chair and drowned him in the vat of chocolate."

Carmichael paused and looked deep into Harriett's eyes.

"How am I doing so far?" he enquired.

Harriett shook her head slowly from side to side, but said nothing.

"It must have taken the three of you a good couple of hours to carry out that ever-so-theatrical murder," Carmichael continued. "According to Jean-Paul Mercier, once out of the vat, it would take a few hours for the chocolate to set properly, even in the cold room. Then you had to bring him out and place him for all to see when they came to work. He wasn't to be spared that humiliation, even after death."

Carmichael looked directly into Harriett Hall's eyes, but was not surprised when she said nothing.

"I suppose," continued Carmichael, "with the three of you working together, given Carmen's skills as a cleaner and

Gabby's knowledge of chocolate production, it was probably quite straight forward for you all, and you did have plenty of time."

Carmichael again paused for a few seconds.

"Then, after you'd finished," Carmichael remarked, "Gabby took you and Carmen back to Harri's Bar, then she went home. I suspect you and Carmen both quickly did the tidying, then Carmen caught her early-morning train home. There's no CCTV footage at all of your car that evening, so my guess is that you stayed at the bar with her."

Carmichael smiled. "Now, tell me, how am I doing?"

Carmichael didn't need Harriett to answer as his question was entirely rhetorical and he could tell by the expression on her face that he was doing very well indeed.

Chapter 77

It was just before 4pm, when Watson, Cooper and Carmichael entered Interview Room 3 and sat down across the table from Gabby Johns and her appointed solicitor, a lady called Fay Charlton. Carmichael knew her well and, as legal representatives went, in his eyes, she was as good as they came.

Carmichael looked over to his left, where Cooper was stationed.

"Can you please confirm to Ms Johns and Ms Charlton, the charges?" he asked.

"The charges against you are as follows," Cooper announced, peering down at his notes. "You are charged with the murder of Gavin Michelson and with the murder of Martin Swift. In addition, you are charged with the attempted murder of DC Rachel Dalton and you are also charged with aiding and abetting in the murder of Kendal Michelson."

Carmichael took a deep breath through his nostrils.

"Do you have any comment to make about these charges?" he enquired.

With an unnerving smirk, Gabby Johns fixed her glare on Carmichael.

"They all deserved it," she replied without a hint of remorse. "Those three excuses of men were devoid of any morals and, to be quite candid with you, Inspector, I'm pleased they're dead."

In the many years he'd been in the job, Carmichael had encountered suspects who admitted their crimes in the early stages of being interviewed, so, to some extent, Gabby's admission should not have come as a major surprise. However, it did, as Carmichael had fully expected Gabby Johns to adopt the total denial or silence stance, in keeping with her cohorts.

Carmichael could see that Ms Charlton was as shocked about Gabby's admission of guilt as anyone in the room and, to prevent her from attempting to restrain her client's willing openness, Carmichael quickly probed for even more ammunition he could use to bolster the case against the three women.

"So, you don't deny any of the charges?" he asked.

Ignoring the look of panic and consternation on her solicitor's face, Gabby took no time to consider her response before replying. "I think your claim about your colleague is a bit over the top," she remarked. "That injection was never going to kill her. She'll be a bit woozy for a day or so, but there will be no lasting harm. So, I'd argue about that charge, but I'm not going to deny my part in the deaths of the other three. Why should I? I was doing the world a favour."

"It might be a good time for me to have a private talk with my client," announced Fay Charlton, her startled eyes aimed in Gabby's direction.

"That's up to your client," replied Carmichael, his response aimed at the brief, but his eyes also remaining firmly on Gabby Johns.

"There's no need," said Gabby Johns with not a trace of concern in her voice. "To be honest, I'm relieved it's all out in the open. I don't regret a single thing I've done."

"What about the others?" Carmichael asked. "What about your two accomplices?"

Gabby Johns expression changed slightly.

"Who are you talking about?" she enquired.

Carmichael smiled.

"We have Carmen Martinez and Harriett Hall in custody," he replied. "We know this was a carefully-planned and well-executed series of murders and we know all three of you were involved."

Gabby Johns thought for a few seconds.

"I do feel sorry for Carmen," she remarked. "Harriett and I, well, we're fair game, I suppose, as our motivation was revenge in my case and money in hers. But Carmen's involvement was more honourable."

"And what was that?" Carmichael enquired.

"Justice for her father and family," replied Gabby. "Gavin and Martin cheated the Martinez family out of their plantation and caused her father to commit suicide. So, her involvement was for justice, some would say a crime of passion."

In truth, he doubted the court would moderate the sentences handed down based on their motivation, but he wasn't about to tell Gabby that.

"So, tell me what your role was in these murders?" he asked.

Gabby looked back at him with complete incredulity.

"I planned it all," she replied proudly. "Harriett and Carmen were just foot soldiers directed by me. They were more than willing to take active parts, but it was I who took the lead."

Having spoken to the other two women, Carmichael had no doubt they would let Gabby take this dubious honour once her claim became common knowledge to them, whether it was true or not.

"Really?" Carmichael asked. "In that case, why don't you tell us everything?"

Chapter 78

It was 8pm by the time Carmichael, Watson and Cooper concluded their interviews and called it a day. Having listened to Gabby Johns explain, in great detail, how she, Carmen and Harriett had planned and carried out the murders, Carmichael and his team had made sure the charges against the three women had been correctly recorded and all the necessary steps required by law had been executed to the letter.

Safe in the knowledge that the case had come to a successful conclusion and confident that not even the most inexperienced prosecutor, faced with the most liberal of juries, could fail to win a conviction against the three killers, Carmichael had suggested they should have a quick drink in his local pub, the Railway Tavern in Moulton Bank, to celebrate their triumph.

The pub was packed to the rafters when the three men arrived and located themselves at the end of the bar.

"You've got to hand it to them," remarked Cooper, "they planned the murders meticulously."

Carmichael nodded. "Yes," he replied, "and to be honest, had it not been for there being two people who saw Kendal on his mobile on the night he died, and had we not discovered that Carmen was from Ecuador, then they might have got away with it."

Cooper nodded. "You may be right," he concurred before taking a sip of the soft drink he had in front of him. Being the only one of the three who didn't live in Moulton Bank, Cooper had to drive home and was therefore unable to join the others in something a bit stronger.

"I'm annoyed with myself for not realising that Kendal had gone down to the beach to watch the rare sight of Vega with the naked eye," continued Cooper. "J.C. Palmer had told me he'd been watching a live programme about it when Kendal was murdered. That was his alibi for Saturday evening. I should have twigged that would be the reason Kendal was on the beach on his back, as soon as I found out about his obsession with night sky."

"It wasn't just you," Carmichael remarked with a slight shake of his head. "We all missed that one. God knows how as he had a huge planetarium installed in his house, which is not exactly a tiny clue."

The three officers took another sip of their respective drinks before Watson changed the subject.

"But what I can't understand is what possessed Gabby to turn on them," he remarked. "I can understand Harriett's motive, to acquire the total ownership of Harri's Bar, and I can understand Carmen being driven by the fact that Gavin Michelson and Martin Swift, in her eyes, jointly swindled her family out of their farm and that then prompted her father to commit suicide. But, other than being dumped by Kendal Michelson after she'd been with his father, I can't see what her motivation was."

Carmichael shook his head. "It's like this, Marc," he replied, pulling a copy of the happy, smiling photograph of the group in Ecuador from his pocket and laying it on the bar. "Back then, for Gabby, all was ideal. She was dating Kendal, they had gone on an exotic holiday to Ecuador and life could not have been better. Little did she know at that time that Gavin and Swift were already plotting to acquire the plantation by cleverly wording the agreement in a way that meant they could take full control should the Martinez family not fulfil the supply of cocoa beans that The World of Chocolate required, something I suspect the pair knew was almost impossible."

"I get that," replied Watson, "but don't those sorts of things happen in business?"

Carmichael nodded. "True," he remarked, "but for Gabby it was the deceit that she found so hard to accept. That coupled with Kendal having so many affairs during their relationship, then dumping her as soon as she strayed."

"Well, it was with his father," replied Watson, his eyes wide open to suggest some sympathy with Kendal's decision to ditch Gabby. "I think that's completely understandable."

"That may be the case," continued Carmichael, "but, you have to see it from her perspective. I think it was that event that cemented Gavin, Kendal and Swift, in her mind, as being the immoral individuals she was so animated about this afternoon."

"She's barking mad," remarked Watson, before taking a swig of beer from his glass.

"Maybe so," agreed Cooper, "but still clever enough to plan these murders, solicit the help of Carmen and Harriett, falsify Carmen's visa entry application so she could get here, and lead us on a merry dance for the last week."

"You're not wrong," added Carmichael. "She was even prepared to rekindle her relationship with Gavin Michelson to help Carmen secure the job with him and Kendal."

"I suspect she would have hated doing that," remarked Cooper, "but I guess she knew Gavin wouldn't say no. After all, she would have known only too well that pretty young women were clearly one of Gavin's passions."

"If it helped her to achieve her ultimate goal of killing

Gavin, Kendal and Swift," Carmichael added, "then I suspect she was prepared to do anything."

"For me, it was that Chinese meal she bought the night Gavin was killed that was the cleverest move," remarked Cooper. "That convinced me she couldn't have been involved in Gavin's death."

Carmichael nodded. "Me too, if I'm honest," he concurred. "And, in a way, that was a smart move, but in hindsight we should have questioned why she didn't have it delivered, as she normally did from that restaurant. If we had, we'd then almost certainly have deduced that she had to collect it, rather than have it delivered, to save time and enable her to get over to Southport to pick up Harriett and Carmen."

The three officers paused once more while they took advantage of the drinks resting on the bar in front of them.

"Did you believe Mad Gabby when she said her motive was revenge?" Watson enquired, once he'd swallowed a large gulp of beer.

Carmichael stared in front of him for a few seconds before answering.

"You know," he said, "I believe almost everything she told us today, but I'm not convinced her motive was just revenge. I think it was a combination of her unrequited love for Kendal, money and revenge."

Cooper nodded. "I agree," he added. "I don't think she ever stopped loving Kendal and, let's face it, she stood to gain a considerable amount from the deaths of Kendal and Swift after that ridiculous agreement the four of them came up with regarding their wills."

"Wow," remarked Watson, "it's just occurred to me Carly Wolf stands to inherit quite a bit from all this."

Carmichael rolled his eyes. "Yes," he replied, "She'll be a very rich young woman now."

The conversation stopped for a few seconds while the

three officers each continued to ponder the case they'd just resolved.

"Talking of pretty women," remarked Watson, "isn't that extremely good-looking young lady over there with your son?"

Carmichael span around to spy his son, Robbie, in deep conversation with an attractive young woman who seemed familiar to him, although he couldn't place where he'd seen her.

His curiosity getting the better of him, he placed his beer glass on the bar and made a beeline over to where his son was sitting.

Cooper remained at the bar, but Watson, never one to let the opportunity of meeting a pretty face pass him by, followed a few steps behind his boss.

"Robbie," said Carmichael, as he arrived at their small table. "You don't often come in here."

As he spoke, Carmichael smiled across at the young woman, who he still couldn't place.

Robbie looked up at his father, clearly surprised.

"Hi Dad," he said, while at the same time getting to his feet. "It was just a convenient place to go. Marie-Claire's only got a few hours off so we couldn't go into town"

At the mention of the name Marie-Claire, Carmichael suddenly realised where he'd seen the young woman before.

Carmichael smiled at Marie-Claire, who returned the greeting. "Nice to meet you," he remarked. "I'll leave you two alone and get back to my colleagues."

"Ok, Dad," replied his son. "I'll see you later."

Carmichael smiled over at Marie-Claire once more, before turning away.

"The new girlfriend's quite a stunner," remarked Watson as they made their way back to the bar. "Looking at how well they seem to be getting on, I expect you'll be seeing a lot more of that pretty young thing."

"You'd be surprised to learn just how much I've seen of her already," remarked Carmichael, not bothering to make eye contact with Watson, who looked suitably mystified by his boss's reply.

Chapter 79

Sunday 21st August

"Now try not to be too scathing with her," Penny remarked, as she and her husband made their way down the corridor of Southport Royal to visit Rachel Dalton.

Carmichael shook his head in exasperation. He'd refused point blank to carry the large bunch of flowers that Penny had picked that morning from their garden and, despite knowing the presence of Penny, who had always got on so well with Rachel, would certainly dampen down the execution of the rollicking she was due, there was no way Rachel was getting off scot-free. She'd acted foolishly and he was not about to pull his punches in letting her know so.

The pair entered the small, private room to find Rachel propped-up in bed reading a magazine.

"If Watson were here, he'd tell you that you were malingering," Carmichael remarked as soon as Rachel caught sight of them.

"He came here earlier and that's pretty much what he said," Rachel replied with a warm smile. "His language was a bit less polite, but he reckons I'm milking it."

"Nonsense," remarked Penny, who miraculously managed to give Rachel a hug and the flowers in one movement.

"These are beautiful," Rachel remarked as she took a sniff of the brightly coloured arrangement. "What are they?"

"They're from our garden, I'm afraid," Penny confessed. "I didn't have time to go to the florists, what with Steve only telling me at eleven o'clock last night that you were in here."

As she spoke, Penny shot a disapproving glance in her husband's direction.

"They're mainly verbascum and snap dragons," Penny continued. "I put some carnations in as well, for their nice scent."

Rachel smiled. "To be honest," she said, "Marc's not far wrong. I do feel a bit of a fraud in here. The drug wore off by about six o'clock last night, but they wouldn't let me go home. They wanted to keep me in for observation. Apart from a sore leg where she stabbed me with that needle, I'm fine."

"You're damn lucky," interjected Carmichael. "What on earth possessed you to go into Gabby's house alone yesterday? You'd established she was involved in at least one murder, so you should have waited for back up."

Rachel looked suitably embarrassed.

"I've no excuse," she admitted, "it was very stupid of me. I don't know why I did it."

Carmichael shrugged his shoulders.

"Really," he remarked, his tone suggesting he wasn't having any of it. "Maybe you were trying to impress Stock's nephew."

"Oh, Steve didn't mention you had a new man in your life," remarked Penny, trying her hardest to move the conversation on. "What's his name?"

"Well," replied Rachel nervously, "he's called Matthew. I'm not sure you could say he was in my life yet, but I admit his presence there yesterday may have clouded my judgement."

"Clouded your judgement," repeated Carmichael irately. "I'd say your judgement went straight out the window."

Rachel's pained expression suggested she was feeling very remorseful for her actions.

"Anyway," Penny remarked, "Rachel's doing fine and those three murdering women are all in custody, so shouldn't you two be congratulating each other?"

"Yes, well done, sir," remarked Rachel. "Marc said that Gabby Johns told you everything and once the other two knew that she'd confessed, they started to be more co-operative."

Carmichael refused to crack a smile, but chose to curb any further admonishment of his young DC. There would be time for that when they were next together in the Police Station, without any unwanted intrusion from his wife.

Instead he just nodded. "We got there in the end," he replied. "All three ladies will be going down for many, many years, in my view."

Rachel suddenly frowned. "Marc was a bit vague on a few things, though," she remarked. "I may have been confused, but I didn't understand how the three women teamed up. After all, Carmen was in Ecuador and I thought Harriett and Gabby didn't get on."

Carmichael smiled. "That line they spun about not liking each other was an act, to throw us off track. Don't get me wrong, I don't think they were bosom pals, but I also don't think there was any animosity between them. I'm pretty sure Gabby and Carly don't have a great deal of time for each other, but I think the Gabby-Harriett relationship was always fine. However, they knew that we'd never be able to pin the murders on just one of them, as they both had alibis for Kendal's murder. By making us believe they were enemies they were deliberately trying to prevent us from linking them together, should we start to think the killings were being carried out by more than one person."

"I get it now," Rachel said, her face serious. "That's really cunning, but also rather clever."

Carmichael nodded. "Extremely cunning," he replied. "And, as for Carmen, it appears that Gabby and she built a strong relationship when Gabby was in Ecuador, which they maintained in pursuing years. It was the news of Dominik Martinez's suicide that appears to be the catalyst for Gabby to solicit Carmen's assistance with the murders and with her knowing that Harriett was desperate to attain full ownership of Harri's Bar, I think getting her involved was quite easy."

"What about the inheritance from those wills?" Rachel enquired. "Do you think that was a factor in all this?"

Carmichael paused for a few seconds before answering.

"It must have been a real bonus for Gabby, when it was mooted that she, Kendal, Carly and Martin Swift should change their wills in favour of the other three," he remarked, "especially when she realised that Martin Swift was actually going to do it. But I don't think that was the main motivation as far as Gabby was concerned. Harriett definitely did it for financial gain, Carmen for revenge, but Gabby's motivation was based on a cocktail of reasons."

"Money, revenge for their treatment of Carmen's father, and revenge for the way she felt she'd been treated by Kendal and Gavin, I suppose," Penny added. "I'm not condoning it, but in a way, I can understand that."

Carmichael raised his eyebrows. "It looks like I may have to watch my step, Rachel," he remarked.

Rachel smiled. "So, the three words on your scrap of paper were correct," she remarked. "Your intuition was right."

"What's that?" Penny enquired.

Carmichael shrugged his shoulders almost dismissively. "I was thinking about motives the other day and wrote 'passion, revenge and money' down as potential motives. I didn't expect them all to be right."

Penny frowned. "Outside of passion, money and revenge, there can't be many other motives for murder," she remarked glibly, much to her husband's surprise.

"So, it was Gabby who killed Swift?" Rachel enquired, quickly trying to move the conversation on.

"Yes," replied Carmichael. "She did that alone. He was always on their list to be murdered, but they brought his death forward after Gavin's death. Before he tried to call me, he'd made an error in calling Harriett. He told her he suspected that Carmen was involved, taking her revenge on the people who she blamed for her family losing their plantation. He guessed that he might be next and in that call with Harriett, he asked her to come over. But Harriett was, of course, already in Birmingham at her supplier event, so she called Gabby, who quickly rushed around to Swift's house and killed him before he could share his theory with us."

"And she arrived just as Martin Swift was calling you," Rachel added.

Carmichael nodded. "It was just his bad luck that I was on the phone to Marc when he called me, otherwise we may have prevented him from being murdered."

Rachel shook her head, as if to acknowledge the tragic consequence of that short call.

"What about that mistakenly-sent text from Harriett on Kendal's mobile on the evening he was killed," enquired Rachel. "Was that some sort of message from Harriett to Carmen?"

Carmichael's eyes widened. "I'm impressed you remembered that tiny detail, Rachel," he remarked. "That injection hasn't dulled your thinking one iota." By the expression on her face, Carmichael's compliment clearly delighted Rachel.

"That's exactly what it was," continued Carmichael, "a coded, prearranged message from Harriett to Carmen. She knew that by the time she sent the message, Carmen would have Kendal's mobile and would have lent Kendal hers. It was her way of letting Carmen know that their heinous plan for Kendal was still on track and that Gabby would be collecting her, as agreed, in twenty minutes' time at their prearranged meeting point, just down the road from Gavin's house."

"To take her to the China Garden," Rachel added, "where Carmen would then make her way down the beach."

"Yes, that's correct" replied Carmichael, who continued to be impressed by the young DC's rapid grasp of the facts. "Gabby made sure she arrived early, before Kendal, Carly and Martin Swift. Carmen got out of the car and made pretty much the same journey I made the other evening, before we all met at the China Garden."

"And what about the theatrical way the men were murdered," Rachel then enquired. "What was that all about?"

Carmichael shook his head.

"Apparently, that was all Gabby's idea." Carmichael replied. "All intended to demonstrate the victim's cravings, their faults, and their vices. Well, at least as Gabby's warped mind viewed them. Kendal dying by his own Steampunk sword while staring at the stars, Gavin naked and cocooned in chocolate, and Martin Swift being choked by his own money. I think Gabby found the drama of their ends in keeping with how she saw their lives."

Penny shuddered as she heard the details being relayed by her husband.

"In short that woman, Gabby Johns, is seriously unhinged," she remarked.

"No question about it," agreed Carmichael. "As Marc has already said, she's barking mad, but you have to hand it to her, the planning and execution of these murders was very impressive!"

"I'm not sure she deserves any compliments," replied Penny. "That woman is evil."

"I'd not even try to argue with you on that point," conceded Carmichael, his hands raised as if in mock surrender.

As he was speaking, an industrious-looking, rotund nurse entered the room.

"Doctor says you can be discharged," she remarked with business-like abruptness.

"Well," announced Carmichael, taking this as an instruction for them to leave, "we'll go then and let you get yourself ready to depart, too."

Penny smiled and bent down to hug Rachel.

"Thank you for coming," Rachel said with a smile. "And thank you for the lovely flowers."

Penny hugged Rachel tightly.

"You're very welcome, my dear," she replied. "I'm just so relieved that you're OK."

Then, as her mouth got closer to Rachel's ear, she whispered, "It got me out of going to church, too. So, thanks for that."

As they parted from their friendly embrace, both women smiled. A knowing smile, which Carmichael missed completely.

"Will you need a lift home?" Penny asked. "We could drop you off."

Rachel shook her head. "Thanks, but no," she replied, "Matthew said he'd take me home."

Lips firmly closed, Carmichael looked over at his DC.

"I'll see you in the office in the morning," he remarked. "Don't be late."

Carmichael then turned and left the room, followed closely by Penny, shaking her head at her husband's apparent lack of suitable concern.

Chapter 80

"You weren't very sympathetic with poor Rachel in there," remarked Penny as the two of them walked, arms linked, down the corridor of the hospital.

"That's because I'm not very sympathetic," replied Carmichael. "She cocked-up, she knows it, and to be honest she's damn lucky she's still alive. She should be reprimanded for being such a plonker, but I suspect Rachel will get away without any serious repercussions, other than Marc Watson teasing her mercilessly for months about it."

Penny grabbed Carmichael's arm tighter and pulled herself closer. "I'm sure she can cope with that," she replied. "I like Rachel. She's far nicer than that Lucy Clark who was in your team before, don't you think?"

It had been some time since Carmichael had thought about Lucy Clark, but the mention of her name by Penny made him feel uncomfortable.

"Rachel's a good officer," he agreed, "I reckon she's destined for bigger things if she keeps it up. And I think she'll learn from the experience of yesterday. I sincerely hope so."

As they wandered on down the corridor, Carmichael noticed the figure of Carly Wolf coming towards them in her royal blue tunic.

Carly was almost upon them when she spotted Carmichael.

Somehow, she seemed different, less brash, less conceited.

"Morning, Inspector," she said, "what brings you back here?"

Carmichael smiled. "We're here to see DC Dalton," he replied. "She was admitted yesterday after an altercation with your friend, Gabby Johns."

Carly shook her head. "Gabby Johns is no friend of mine," she remarked. "I've heard what she, Harriett and that bloody cleaner did. They're monsters, all of them."

"Even your Aunty?" Carmichael asked.

"Yes," replied Carly without hesitation. "Especially her. She killed them just so she could own her precious bar, what sort of person does that?"

Carmichael nodded. "As I think I told you last Sunday, when we first met, there's nothing glamorous about murder and, in my experience, when you do understand their reasons for killing, their acts seem even more sickening."

Carly managed a slight smile.

"Well, I've already told her that I'm not looking after the bar while she's in prison," Carly continued. "She'll have to ask some other mug. As soon as those wills are sorted out, and the money from Kendal and Martin's estates comes rolling in, I'm packing this job in and I'm off."

Carmichael nodded. "Where will you go?" he asked.

Carly shrugged her shoulders. "I'm not sure," she replied, "but it will be as far from here as I can get."

"Good luck, wherever you go," Carmichael remarked genuinely.

Carly smiled again, this time a broader, friendlier smile.

"Thanks, Inspector," she replied, before heading away.

The Carmichaels both watched as the young nurse disappeared down the corridor and around the corner.

"She's a pretty thing," remarked Penny. "Is she the *marmite girl* you talked about?"

"Yes," he replied with a faint smile and nod of the head.

"But she's now a much wealthier and, it would appear, a much more mature young woman than the one I told you about last week."

Penny held her husband's arm tightly once more as they turned and started to continue their walk down the corridor.

"Talking of pretty young things," she remarked, "Robbie's invited his new girlfriend over for dinner this evening. I don't know anything about her, but he seems keen and he tells me she's lovely."

Carmichael puffed out his cheeks.

"We might need to have a little chat about that before she arrives," Carmichael replied. "Let's go and get a coffee somewhere."